A Box Of Bones

A NOVEL

With my sincere
Appreciation for
Your Support.
Enjoy

Chris Monack

2004

A Box Of Bones

To my mom, Diane.

I
Wednesday afternoon, August 13th

"Come on, you guys. I'm not paying you by the hour to screw off. I've got to get this house ready to show in two days, so pick up the pace."

Eric Champs, self-proclaimed real estate ace, stood hands on hips and scowling over his hired help. Over the last five days the four-man crew had painted the twelve-hundred-square-foot house inside and out, replaced the linoleum flooring in two bathrooms and the kitchen, and hauled away an assortment of old wood, cardboard boxes, and rusted metal that had accumulated along the side yards. All that was left, aside from a few last-minute touch-ups, was the removal of the old carpet so the installers of the new carpet could start first thing the following morning.

Champs had used two of the four men on other jobs, but this house was a quick pick up by his real estate company and the only way he could have it ready to show was to hire a couple more men. As time was tight, searching for competent laborers meant more time. And for Eric Champs, time was money. He asked his two regulars to bring a couple of strong backs to the job, but soon regretted that decision.

The first day's work was good. The men had prepped the entire outside of the house for painting and started on the interior. Champs thought there was no way they couldn't finish dressing up the place by the weekend. But the next day the foursome showed up late and hung over and barely finished spraying the walls, which meant the trim and eaves would have to wait until the following day. They showed up late again—hung over again—and proceeded to engage in a routine of work followed by some clowning around that eventually turned into clowning around followed by some work. As each successive day got worse, Champs found himself spending more and more of his time supervising and rescheduling and, to his dismay, staying late into the evening actually doing some physical labor to keep on track for the coming Saturday's open house.

"Jesus, Jeff, watch the walls, huh? I don't need a patch-and-paint at this stage."

"Sorry, Mr. Champs."

Sorry, Mr. Champs. He'd had been hearing that all week, annoying as much as for the number of times he heard it as for their mispronunciation of his name with a hard "ch" instead of the traditional French "sh". The apology usually followed with a chorus of childish snickering, at times intoxicated but more often just plain insolent. Champs couldn't understand why. He thought he was paying them well, and paying them daily with cash. He had never had a problem with Carl or his younger partner, Gabe. He used to give them a list of things to do and come back in a few days to find them done. But now with their friends alongside them, they had turned into irresponsible kids needing constant watching. Champs attributed most of the problem in allowing Carl and Gabe to convince him to hire their friends, Jeff and the other guy they kept referring to as "C". Jeff seemed to take Champs' demands and criticism in stride, just a grin and a nod or that smart-assed, grating "Sorry, Mr. *Ch*amps". C, on the other hand, apparently didn't take direction well and openly challenged the realtor's authority.

"You wanna paint this for me?" C groused one red-eyed

morning. "I'll gladly step off the ladder and hand you the brush."

And so it went for Eric Champs. *You wanna paint this? You wanna swing this hammer? You wanna have to replace this window?* What Champs wanted to do he couldn't. C had a good six inches and fifty pounds on him and a brusque demeanor that could have been all for show but was convincing enough that Champs didn't want to risk a trip to the hospital to validate it. So Champs kept his distance and told C what to do through Carl or Gabe. The work got done, albeit slowly, and it looked like Champs was going to make his deadline after all. His urgency in stepping up the pace at this point was more for ridding himself of Jeff and C, and to an extent Carl and Gabe, than having the house ready for potential buyers.

"That's the last of the carpet and padding, Mr. Champs," Carl reported. "And we took up all the old tack strips. Just gotta sweep up all the crud."

"That's okay, Carl. I'll take care of that." Champs pulled out his wallet and handed Carl a thin stack of twenties. "This should cover the day. I'll need you and Gabe back tomorrow afternoon to touch up the walls. There's bound to be some marks after they put the new rug in."

"You got it, Mr. Champs. We'll come around two or so."

"Good. Just you and Gabe, though," Champs called to Carl as he turned to walk away. Then as a point of emphasis he added, "I'll only be paying for you and Gabe."

Carl grinned and nodded and then turned and left. Champs blew out a deep sigh, relieved that the house would be done on time as much as he was relieved that he would no longer need concern himself with Jeff and, in particular, C.

Through a narrow part in the drapes hanging across the window of the front room, Champs watched Carl walk over to the driver's side of Jeff's pickup where Carl peeled off several of the twenties and handed the remainder to Jeff. A dispute ensued with Carl and C exchanging what appeared to be a few angry words. Carl's hands came up as he gestured a what-do-you-want-me-to-do surrender before he retreated to Gabe's pickup. C leaned around Jeff and shot an angry glare toward the house. Reflexively, Champs pulled back from the window. Though fully concealed behind the heavy curtains, Champs felt at the moment like someone had drawn the drapes fully open leaving him exposed to C's hostility. Champs moved forward again, cautiously confident C couldn't see him through the slit, and watched as the two vehicles pulled away from the curb and disappeared down the street. Champs closed his eyes and sighed relief yet again. When he opened them, he reached out to slide the left drape wide and surveyed the neighborhood through the glass. Before he left tonight his sign would be posted out front and, not long after that, another sale by Eric Champs will have been completed.

"Can't see anything getting in the way now," Champs told his reflection in the window. "Now that our problems are gone."

"Asshole short-changed us." C slapped the money down on the seat of Jeff's pickup and crossed his arms angrily. "All that fuckin' money we probably saved him. Cheap asshole."

"Come on, C. That's not the fairest amount of cash, but, hey, no taxes. We were lucky to even get the work."

C waved Jeff off and stared out his window as Jeff pulled away from the house. "We could'a got some jobs."

"What? And take a chance on getting caught? This whole town's hot. And even if we took a job, where're we gonna fence the stuff? A few things here and there—and not nothing big or fancy—ain't worth the risk trying."

"Yeah?" C snapped back. He slapped his hand over the money. "Was this worth all the bullshit that realtor-guy gave us?"

Jeff shook his head. "No. And if ever the chance comes up where we can maybe do a little shopping at his house, I say fine. But what I'm saying for right now is let it go. Don't fuck over Carl and Gabe 'cause you got a bone to pick with the dude. All right?"

C returned to staring out the window in silence.

"All *right?*"

"Yeah, okay. Whatever."

Moments after relenting to Jeff's demand, C's anger turned to an unexpected chuckle. Jeff watched his friend straighten out in the seat and fish something out from his pocket.

"Whatcha got?"

Pressed between his thumb and forefinger, C held up a ring. "Something I picked up back at the house. Maybe it'll make up the difference on the pay that guy stiffed us."

"Shit, C. I swear to God, if you ripped that guy off—"

"Relax. I found it in that shed we tore down. Remember that box that the bottom busted out of?"

Jeff thought back to earlier that morning when Champs told them he wanted all the stuff in the shed dumped along with the rusting hulk. He and C spent an hour hauling loads of debris from the shed to Jeff's pickup and were down to the last few boxes, one of which broke loose when C lifted it, dropping the contents at C's feet at the same instant Champs walked in on one of his anal spot checks of their progress. When Champs saw the pile of spilled clothes he naturally accused him and C of clowning around and not taking their jobs seriously, which, in truth, they didn't. And Jeff once again found himself placating Champs with apologies and assurances that it wouldn't happen again, which in truth Jeff knew would happen for no other reason than he knew C enjoyed how acutely it antagonized the man.

"When I was picking up the clothes and stuffing them back into the box," C recounted while inspecting his prize, "I heard this metal clinking noise along the floor. I didn't think nothing of it at first, thought maybe a quarter dropped out of my pants. When I got all the stuff picked up and slid the box away from the wall, I saw this."

C held the ring in front of Jeff's face. It was a thick gold band with a large, deep red rectangular stone centered between two narrow rectangular diamonds. Jeff's jaw dropped. The pickup began drifting to the side of the road as Jeff's attention locked on the ring. C barked a quick warning and Jeff, without overreacting like his friend, calmly pulled the vehicle to a complete stop at the curb.

"Lemme see that thing." Jeff whistled, impressed. Not only was the ring something to look at, it was something to hold. "Damn, that's a heavy piece. And expensive, I'll bet. You swear it was in that junk pile?"

C nodded.

"What a score," Jeff laughed in amazement. "No one'll ever believe this was just sitting on the floor behind a box in some beat up shed."

"Yeah, well, no one's gonna know. Know what I mean?"

"Who am I gonna tell? As if I would. You know me better'n that."

"Yeah. Anyway, I figure since irresponsible people don't deserve to own such nice things, we should look after it."

"You figured that, huh?" Jeff said it with raised eyebrows, then narrowed them accusingly. "You were gonna tell me about this, weren't you?"

"Hey, fuck you! Have I ever held out on you before?"

Jeff's face sagged to guilt and he handed the ring back to C as a gesture of trust. "No, man. I'm sorry. I didn't ... I mean, that's a lot of money sitting there. I wouldn't fault you for thinking about it."

"Good, 'cause I did think it. I just wouldn't *do* it." C slid the ring onto his index finger and spun it with his thumb. "This is probably worth something. I just hope we can get some of the cash out of it."

"We still owe McEwan, you know."

Jeff's reminder brought a wincing frown to C's face. They had taken a small advance from the loan shark to pay off a gambling debt and now found themselves short of both money and time in repaying their *new* debt, which was growing daily and was the reason they took the job at the house to begin with, hoping a little scratch would defer a big, aggressive itch. C took off the ring and slipped it back into his pocket.

"Shit. I don't want to give him this. It's gotta be worth three times what we owe him. McEwan doesn't strike me as the kind to make change."

"I guess. So, what do we do? We need to come up with some cash by the end of next week."

"We could take it to Rey," C suggested. "If he can't figure out what to do with it, I'm sure he knows somebody who does. Maybe we can get a little of the proceeds up front."

"Great," Jeff sighed. Having spent most of his life balancing stealing against borrowing, he couldn't help seeing it as another debt. "Do we tell Carl and Gabe about any of this?"

C returned to staring out the window. It didn't take him long to decide who was in and who wasn't. "We don't tell nobody jack shit."

Jeff and C were at Rey Piña's antique shop within an hour. Piña was preparing to close for the day and had his key in the front door lock when Jeff and C arrived and hinted at a lucrative business opportunity. After sternly admonishing them about wasting his time, Piña welcomed them inside, locked the door as he intended, and motioned them to follow him to the rear of the shop.

Rey Piña was a short, stocky Hispanic man with thinning black hair combed back over his round skull and a pencil-thin mustache trimmed perfectly over his upper lip. The middle child of seven, Rey was born into a family of migratory farm workers fortunate enough to have permanently settled in the northern Sacramento valley town of Williams when his father became foreman of a large ranch. Rey roamed the fields planting, irrigating, and picking crops from nearly the time he was able to walk and despised the harsh, sun-baked, skin-blistering life that his father thanked God for every Sunday. Rey's education was what he learned in the fields from the men and women he toiled alongside. The most valuable thing he learned was that if he didn't find a way out of the dirt soon, he would be destined to live a life of sweat-soaked clothes and aching muscles and days that would last longer than the sunlight did.

Rey made his break one day when a coworker told him he had broken into a warehouse and took a box of truck parts. The problem for the thief, beside his lack of English, was not knowing what to do with the parts now that he had them. Rey told the man he knew a guy in the neighboring town of Colusa who would buy the parts at a discount. The man, excited at Rey's news, gave the box to Rey and told him to make the best deal he could and keep ten percent for himself. That became the first of many transactions Rey brokered for fellow workers. Eventually, Rey earned enough money to leave the ranch and strike out on his own. He made a modest amount of money as a middleman for stolen property, but never became adept at appropriating goods himself. Rey bounced from town to town with a number of stops in jail on theft charges before, under the threat of a prison sentence, he recognized he was a much better businessman than he was a thief. He took his earnings and set up a quasi-legitimate antique/pawn shop in what was then the small, out of the way town of Santa Ramona.

Piña's shop became almost as well known over the years to collectors for it's assortment of furniture and art as it was to the police for the accumulation of stolen items recovered from within its walls. Rey, as the owner of the shop, had been charged and released numerous times for possession of stolen property. Yet he never spent a night in jail because of it due to his self-proclaimed ignorance.

"How em I soo-posed to know when someone's geeving me hot chit?" he'd declare to the police through his deliberately slow, Spanish-infused English.

Piña's attorney was similarly skilled in this defense practice by translating a more acceptable version of his client's query—"How's my client supposed to know when someone's giving him illegally obtained merchandise?"—to the courts.

Piña wasn't much on wanting explanations or histories of merchandise on the premise that the less he knew, the less he could tell and the less he could be held liable for. Now the three of them, Jeff, C, and Piña, hovered over the table where the ring sat nestled in the center of a soft black cloth. Piña had spent the better part of half an hour looking at, measuring and weighing it. Jeff and C remained silent as not to disrupt Piña's intense examination, from which the shop owner broke for fleeting seconds as he scratched out notes of his assessment. His flicking release of his pencil onto the notepad signaled completion. He leaned back in his chair slowly nodding his approval.

"So, what do you think?" C asked.

"I theenk you have a peece of money there."

"How much?"

Piña scratched his head and smoothed over a few loose strands of hair. "More than I can pay. Plos, you have a couple of problems."

"Problems?" Jeff echoed.

"Jes. First of all, een order for me to pay you what eets worth, I have to sell eet myself. That takes time and co-nections."

"Shit, Rey. I'll wait," C said. "Just give me a little up front and you'll be good for the rest."

"The other theeng, eets marked."

"Marked?" Jeff repeated.

"What are you, a focking parakeet? Look on thee band." Piña picked up the ring and held it up to Jeff's face. "See? There's a name etched there."

"Couldn't that be the designer or something?"

Piña shook his head. "A designer might put hees mark or a production code on a peece, but not a full seegnature. So thee band eesn't worth chit, my friend, unless you melt eet down and recast eet. I don't have thee kind of time to find someone to do eet. Too much effort for thee return. Eets cheaper to sell eet outright. Wheech brings me to my second point.

"Thee best way you can make money off thees ees to sell thee stones. These stones are good quality, so you'll get a good price. Again, eet'll take some time for me to find a buyer."

"How much are we talking about, Rey?"

Piña shrugged. "I got to pull thee stones out and get them appraised. Then I have to find a buyer. Whoever buys them will cut them, so that will factor eento thee cost." He shrugged again. "I can geeve you four hondred now and we can settle after we sell."

"Four," C scoffed. "One of them fucking diamonds is easily *ten times* that by itself."

"Chure. And good luck trying to find a buyer, you ungrateful motherfocker!" Piña snapped back. "And eef you do, try not getting screwed over, okay? I'm trying to do you a favor!"

"Hey, hey, come on you guys. Let's not blow a good thing here." Jeff turned to C. "We don't have the contacts Rey has, so we'd be stupid to do this on our own." Then to Piña, "You've been square with us before. We do good business for each other. I know you won't fuck us over."

C backed down and nodded. "Sorry, Rey. I guess I got a little greedy."

"Greedy ees good. Eet makes money," Piña said with a grin. "But trosting thee right people will make you some *more* money, my friend. A *lot* more money."

Piña wrapped the ring in the black cloth and took it to an old wooden file cabinet. He unlocked the drawer, put the cloth inside and peeled four one hundred dollar bills from a slim stack. He folded the remaining five or six bill in half and tucked them in his pocket, relocked the drawer, and handed the payoff to C.

"You guys come see me een a few days. Let's say Mahnday. I should have some money or an offer. Eether way, you'll like what I have to say."

The payoff would never happen for Jeff and C. The following day, Detective Henry Lepsky and Detective Gary "Turk" Turkell, along with five Santa Ramona police officers, walked into Rey Piña's shop and executed a search warrant for stolen property. Piña's had been under surveillance for nearly a month and video from a camera set up inside a florist's shop across the street confirmed at least three instances when known burglars entered Piña's with stolen items and left without them. Witnesses later identified the men as having been seen in areas where break-ins had occurred. So armed with the court order and a list of missing items, Lepsky and Turk began their scavenger hunt. When it was over, twenty-five of forty listed items had been recovered, and Rey Piña was in handcuffs in the back seat of a patrol car.

"I hate to do this to you, Rey," Lepsky admitted. "You know how it goes."

"Eets okay, Meester Henry," Piña replied with a wry smile. "I don't blame you. Eets part of thee bad side of my beesness. I know there are some bad people out there, and I take eet on faith that what they bring me they leegally own. I just hope you catch them and return thee property to thee rightful owners."

"That's right upstanding of you, Rey," Lepsky replied, equally melodramatic. "You got a big heart."

"Jos trying to be a good ceetizen, Meester Henry. Jos trying to help out where I can."

2
Thursday morning, August 14th

Lepsky and Turk deposited Piña into a police holding cell so he could make his call to his equally kind-hearted attorney. The officers figured they had roughly five hours before Piña made bond and was released, so they concentrated on completing the detailing of the confiscated evidence in case they needed to talk to Piña before he got out. The last item they inspected was a wooden file cabinet with three locked compartments.

"Shit," Lepsky cussed as he yanked on the top drawer's handle. "And what'll you bet Rey's got the key."

"And what'll you bet it got booked into his property and he won't give it up," Turk said. "I don't want to bust it open, and I certainly don't want to have to get another warrant."

As Lepsky and Turk bemoaned their predicament, Detective Floyd King and his longtime friend and partner, Detective Marty Doenacker entered the evidence room. They were in the process of depositing their own recovered property from a separate theft case and, having heard Rey Piña had been arrested again, were also curious as to what was recovered in the latest haul.

"Nice cabinet," Floyd commented.

Floyd stepped closer to check out the file cabinet. As he did, Lepsky noticed a distinctive limp.

"Your leg bothering you again, Floyd?"

It was a question Floyd had heard regularly for over a year since being shot while rescuing his daughter from a fugitive armed robber who used Floyd's daughter as bait to lure him into near death in his own home. While Floyd had fully recovered from the leg injury and returned to duty a few months earlier, there was always curiosity when Floyd groaned, winced, or, in this case, stepped awkwardly.

"Nah. Marty clipped me with the car door. Got a nasty charlie horse on the thigh."

"At least the car wasn't moving," Marty said in his defense. "And I got your good leg this time. So, we hear you guys cleaned out Piña's. *Again.* Find anything good?"

"Little over half the list," Turk said proudly. "Henry thinks there might be some small stuff in the cabinet, but the drawers are locked tight."

"I'll open it."

Marty stepped forward but was stopped by Lepsky. "You'll do no such thing."

"Come on, Henry. Marty's a good lock picker. He'll pop that sucker open before you know it."

"Bullshit, Floyd. I've seen what this ox can do to drawers ... and tables and doors. And legs," Lepsky added, gesturing toward Floyd's. "And besides, it's tampering. And if there is anything inside, Rey will claim we got it illegally."

"Can Rey say for certain it was locked?"

"Jesus, Floyd. I thought you better than—"

"It's open," Marty announced.

While Lepsky was distracted debating with Floyd, Marty stepped behind them and picked the lock. Turk saw him do it, but said nothing and seemed rather impressed at Marty's deftness and speed. Lepsky heard the drawer slide and spun around and glared at Marty.

"I think it was just stuck," Marty assessed unconvincingly.

"Stuck my ass!" Lepsky barked. "Why'd you let him do it, Turk?"

"I didn't see him do shit except pull the drawer open."

"Bullshit! It was locked!"

"I don't know, Henry. It didn't take but a little tug to pop it loose," Marty proclaimed innocently while teasing the drawer in and out of the cabinet.

"Goddamn you, Doenacker!"

"Henry, take it easy."

Lepsky spun back around at Floyd and glared. "Don't tell me to take it easy! Your partner's messing with my case. How would you like it if Lomas came down and started messing with *your* stuff?" Lepsky attempted to make his point with Floyd by using Floyd's chief departmental adversary, fellow detective Mark Lomas, with whom Floyd had maintained a long-running feud, as a comparison.

"Well, no, I can't say as I'd take that very well. But to my advantage, Lomas is an idiot. All I'd have to do is disguise my evidence."

"Yeah, disguise it as evidence," Marty cracked, "and hide it in the evidence room. "He'd never find it. Oh, look. Another drawer opened."

Lepsky spun around again and looked even more sour than before.

"Henry, I think it's the humidity outside that made the drawers stick," Floyd said.

"You know what? To hell with all of you! I'll have no part of this, you hear? I'm outta here!" Lepsky turned on his heels and took three steps, stopped, and glared back at Turk. "If you want to stay here and play bullshit games with those two clowns, be my guest. You're responsible if anything turns up missing."

Lepsky took another fives steps toward the door and looked back at the sudden burst of snickering behind him, and also at the third drawer that was gaping open at the bottom of the cabinet. A series of unintelligible curses followed Henry Lepsky out of the room.

"You okay with this, Turk? I mean, I'll lock'em up if you're not. I only did the other two to fry Henry a little."

"Nah. It's cool. It's not like we're gonna nail a big case here. It's Rey, for crissakes. And I think Henry's just pissed 'cause he knows we're spitting into the wind on this. But you *can* lock'er back up, right Marty?"

"Well, yeah. I mean, I never had to *un*pick a lock. I think you just go backwards."

"Jesus," Turk sighed. "Floyd?"

"He can do it," Floyd said with a smile. "So, let's take a look."

The bottom drawer, being already open, was searched first. It was a quick search as there was nothing inside except a few empty hanging files dangling on their guide rails. The middle drawer was just as empty, leading all three men to suspect the top drawer would likely hold nothing of value. But when Turk pulled it open, the detectives were pleasantly surprised.

"Jack-paaaht," Marty sang.

Turk unfolded his list of stolen property and spread it out on a table. Floyd began removing items from the drawer and handed them to Marty, who handed them to Turk, who checked the items against the list. Two items — a gold pocket watch and a silver chain with a small silver cross with alternating diamonds and emeralds set within the perpendiculars — raised the total number of recovered items to twenty-seven. The remaining items, along with fourteen hundred dollars in cash, were unlisted and unremarkable in terms of notable value or owner identification.

"That it?" Turk asked after noting the latest item handed to him on a separate sheet of paper.

"One more thing," Floyd said. He reached toward the back of the drawer and removed a black handkerchief. Floyd immediately noticed an unexpected weight to the cloth. "There's something inside it, too."

"Careful. Could be snot," Marty warned.

Floyd set the cloth on the table and pulled the corners apart exposing a man's gold ring. All three men stood motionless, staring hypnotically as the room light glowed off the gold band and illuminated the red and clear stones set into it. Turk broke his gaze and ran his finger down the property list.

"No ring on the list." Turk cast his eyes back on the ring and sighed a whistle. "That is one beautiful piece of jewelry. Must have cost a chunk of cash, too."

"No shit," Marty agreed. He bent over to get a closer look and saw the smoothness of the light on the inside of the band broken. "Except for the scratch it's almost perfect."

Floyd took a closer look, moving his head to play the light across the inside of the band until he could see the flaw. When he found it, he moved closer. His brow furrowed as he tightened his focus, then he reached out and picked it up.

"Hey, we haven't checked it for prints yet," Turk protested.

"You won't find any," Floyd replied through the band, which he pinched between his thumb and forefinger and held up to his face. "Rey's no idiot. He'd have cleaned it well. This is no scratch, Marty. It's a signature."

"A what? Can you read it?"

"It's kind of tough. Looks like ... E ... E—D—I ... S—O—N. Edison."

"Thomas Edison?"

"Edison looks like the first name." Floyd peered harder at the script scrawled on the gold. "Last name starts with either an 'F' or a 'T' ... like Tarm-something or Farm-something."

"Edison sounds familiar," Turk said. "It's a name I've heard before. I just can't place it."

"I know," Floyd concurred. "Not recently, but still familiar."

"Edison? Edison Farms? Was there ever an Edison Farms in Santa Ramona?" Marty asked.

"It's not a farm, Marty. There's more to the name. You were close in calling it a scratch, though. Whoever this is has one shitty signature."

"Henry's been around a while. Maybe he'd know."

"I don't think asking Henry for anything is a good idea right now, Turk," Marty said. "Especially if it has to do with something coming out of this cabinet."

"We could ask Bern," Floyd suggested. "He's kind of a who's-who man."

"It would be safe to assume that the owner of an expensive ring like this would be a who of who's," Marty said. "But how do you explain finding the ring to the lieutenant?"

"Specifically, how do you explain finding it in a locked drawer inside the evidence room, Floyd?" Turk asked.

"Who says I have to say anything about the ring? I'll just ask him if he knows a guy named Edison, that the name came up and I was curious."

"I don't know, Floyd," Marty said in a warning tone. "When it comes to shit like this, Bern's got you dialed in. He's gonna know something's up besides your curiosity."

Floyd put the ring back onto the black cloth and wrapped it up. "I'm going to hang on to this for a while, Turk."

"Are you nuts? Henry'll kill me if he finds out I let you walk out of here with that."

"Why? It's not on your list. Henry doesn't know it even exists. And we all know it doesn't belong to Rey." Floyd slipped the bindle into the pocket of his sport coat. "If it turns out to be nothing, I'll turn it in as lost property. If we find out whose finger it belongs on, we can return it as found property."

༕

Floyd, Marty, and Turk entered the detectives' squad room, Turk doing so cautiously in case his partner was still angry. The twelve-officer squad of detectives had remained virtually unchanged in the last five years. Turk was the newest member, having been promoted two years earlier. Henry Lepsky had the longest tenure as a detective at fourteen years, half of his twenty-eight total years in law enforcement. Floyd, Marty, and Mark Lomas were second at twelve years. Brenda Garibaldi, with whom Floyd had recently rekindled a romantic flame that flickered off and on over the last few years, had put in eight. The remaining six detectives had put in between eight and five.

Floyd and Marty, partners since their academy days, were as close off duty as they were on. Marty had been Floyd's best man for his failed first marriage, and would have been his best man a second time had Floyd's engagement not been called off. And they were Godparents to each other's kids: Marty to Floyd's twenty-two-year-old daughter, Shelby, and Floyd to Marty's two boys and little girl. As close as they were, the two men were also about as opposite a pair as one could find.

Floyd, still a handsome man in his mid-forties, maintained a rather athletic build on his solid, six-foot frame. Though the years only gradually took their toll on him in much of his appearance, time had not been as gracious to Floyd's head of dark brown hair, still thick but now noticeably weathered with an increased infusion of gray strands. He had a strong face, gently contoured rather than sharply chisled, and a pair of hazel eyes, alert and critical in their softly wrinkled frames.

Marty, in contrast, was stocky and thick with a flattened crew cut of red hair. He had an impish side that was punctuated by a gargoyle grin owing from an upper lip that didn't quite reach the lower causing a perpetual display of front teeth. When he smiled, the corners of his mouth curled devilishly and pushed his bulbous cheeks high until his eyes compressed to a squint. Marty was also strong. Very strong. His latest head-shaking feat of strength occurred during a raid on a suspected drug dealer when, as a part of the entry team, Marty kicked the door open with one impressive thrust of his leg. Afterward, when officers went to secure the house, it was discovered that Marty had actually kicked the wrong side of the door and broke it off the frame at the hinges.

Marty's strength was complimented by Floyd's sharp mind. Not that either lacked the abilities of the other, but Marty excelled physically while Floyd demonstrated a greater proficiency at reading into people and situations. As a hobby, Floyd kept a drawer full of unsolved cases that he occasionally dipped into from time to time. He had solved six of the cases, with one nearly ending his life the year before. That case, the Mark Feldman case, culminated in the arrest of a robbery suspect and the solution to a double-homicide years earlier. It would have been enough for most to give up their career after having been nearly shot to death. Not for Floyd King. Floyd lived for being a detective, so much so that it ruined every relationship he ever had with the exceptions being those with Shelby, Marty, and Brenda. His ex-wife, Lynn, despised what she described as his obsession with his work. His former fiancée, Laura, never got the chance to hate Floyd's world as Lynn did, though she did get an opportunity to redefine her future needs with taste of what living with Floyd could be like with him being a stalker's target.

Floyd's professional standing took quite a beating over the years, as well, as he forged a reputation as the man most likely to close a case with a reprimand rather than a commendation. Stubborn and openly critical, Floyd focused more on the outcome of the case rather than the impact of the publicity it could generate—good or bad—toward the department or himself. He was as skilled at rationalizing abstract concepts as he was at analyzing the elements of a crime. Floyd King didn't only digest crime scenes visually, he listened to them and felt them as if they were a living entity, another witness. Based on ability alone, his name would be the first on the list for assignment to a difficult case. Unfortunately, the powers making the choice usually skipped down the list as there was a general reluctance to parade Floyd King as the model representative of the department. Strong-willed and determined, though some would counter bull-headed and arrogant, Floyd regularly tested the tolerance limits of his supervisors and peers. Sometimes simply by entering a room.

The room most frequently targeted by Floyd belonged to Lieutenant James Bern, the squad's commander. He'd been in charge of the Santa Ramona detectives as long as Floyd could remember, long before Floyd got promoted into the unit. Short and stocky, bald, and with virtually no neck, he was what people described as a fire plug, though with his protruding jaw a bulldog seemed more appropriate. Bern's success as a supervisor was in the balance he struck between maintaining control of his troops and allowing them certain liberties in the creative aspects of doing their jobs. Although Floyd pushed the limits of both on a regular basis, Bern had a great deal of respect for him. Still ...

Floyd knocked on the lieutenant's door and let himself in before the lieutenant could lift his head from the report on his desk. Bern stood when Floyd entered and, without a word, walked around his desk to the office door. He pulled it open, looked at the nameplate affixed to the outside, and nodded. He closed the door and returned his desk, stood behind his chair and took pause to study the wall from which hung numerous photos of himself with dignitaries and family members and meritorious plaques and certificates inscribed with his name. He sat and took another moment before addressing Floyd to spin the nameplate centered at the front of the desk around so he could read that, too.

"You know, Floyd. With my name and face plastered all over the room, I don't see how you can continually confuse my office as being yours."

"I don't have an office."

"Ahhh!" Bern sang, thrusting his index finger toward the ceiling. "You don't have an office. And yet knowing this, you still treat this little room as your personal annex, feeling free to come and go without regard for my personal privacy."

"I knocked," Floyd said as he sat on Bern's small sofa, naturally, without asking permission.

"Knocked like you were a SWAT member on a tactical entry."

"I was trained well. You got a minute?"

"Great, something else of mine you want." As he spoke, Bern opened the center drawer in his desk and fished around for a cigar, which he never smoked but regularly used as a prop to mask his self-consciousness about his jaw. "Well, if I have a free minute there's no doubt in my mind you'll use it eventually. May as well be now."

"I came across a name today and I know I've heard it somewhere. I just can't place it."

Bern wedged the rolled tobacco between his molars. "What's the name?"

"Edison Farm-something?"

"Farnsworth?" Bern suggested with hardly a thought.

Floyd thought about the extended scribble on the ring and shrugged. "Could be."

"If it's Farnsworth, then it's Edson, not Edison. And if it's Edson Farnsworth, he hasn't been seen for something like ten years."

Floyd snapped his fingers. "That's right. Now I remember. He's that property developer that dropped off the face of the earth."

"Well, I don't think it was that dramatic. As far as anyone could tell he simply bailed out of a bad marriage."

"Believe me, boss, there's no simple bail out of a bad marriage."

"Yeah, well ... how come you're interested? How'd his name get to you?"

Floyd shrugged innocently. "Just happened."

"Riiight. You know what happens, Floyd? Shit happens, and you're full of it."

Floyd laughed.

"Seriously. What do you know about Farnsworth?"

"Nothing, L.T." Treading the line of honesty, and having

nothing more than the ring at this point, Floyd crossed his heart. "Swear to God. Beyond him disappearing, I don't know a thing. Is there a report or something on him? I mean, it's for sure he just up and left?"

"No report with us. If one exists, it's a Sacramento case."

"Sac? I thought he lived here in Santa Ramona."

"He lived here, but I think he and his business partner had an office in the city. His partner was the one who initiated the report when he found out Farnsworth took off. Dipped into the company till before he split. Ripped him off pretty good, too, if I recall. Farnsworth's wife never filed a missing person report, so we had nothing to investigate. Even if she had we'd have probably turned it over to Sacramento."

"Interesting. So he never came back to town?"

"Nope. A Sac parking officer found his car a week or so later downtown by the bus terminal. I don't know what they did with it."

"Just like that. Dumped the business, the car, and the wife and split."

"Apparently." Bern shifted the cigar to the other side of his mouth, breaking his suspicious grin. "I can get you a copy of the report ... if you want one."

Floyd sensed Bern's playfulness and grinned back. "Why would I want a copy of the report?"

"To follow up on whatever it is picking at your brain." Bern held up a silencing hand before Floyd attempted denial. "You don't have to tell me, Floyd. I probably won't get the straight story until someone calls and complains about you sticking your nose where it doesn't belong. And anyway, if I want to know that badly all I have to do is step out that door and sweat it out of Doenacker."

"In this case, Marty doesn't know any more than I do."

Bern pulled the cigar from his mouth so it wouldn't interfere with his all-knowing smirk and pointed the damp, chewed end at his detective. "The difference between what Doenacker *does* know and what you tell me he *doesn't* know is always more than what *you* tell me up front."

Floyd bowed his head, smiling, and conceded the lieutenant's point. He reached into his pocket and removed the black cloth.

"This turned up today." Floyd unwrapped the cloth and exposed the ring. Bern, who had resumed gnawing on his cigar, plucked it from his mouth to prevent it from freefalling to his desk as his jaw slackened, mirroring the reaction that was no different than his, Marty's, or Turk's. "Yeah. Nice. And on the inside of the band is what looks like a signature, which, thanks to your incredible memory, seems to be Edson Farnsworth's."

"I'll be damned. And this just turned up?"

"Yup."

"Where?"

"Uh ... you don't want to know yet."

"Floyd ..."

"Fine. You know that raid on Piña's shop today? It sort of fell out of a cabinet."

"Really? Just fell out? What do you suppose the odds are on something like that happening," Bern replied with flighty sarcasm. "And to you, of all people." Bern wrapped the cloth over the ring to keep it from distracting him from Floyd. "This being Henry's and Turk's case, explain how you happened to get a hold of it."

"It wasn't on their list of stolen property, so Marty and I volunteered to track down the owner and see if it had been stolen."

"And if I talk to Henry he'll corroborate that story?" Bern threw up a hand and interjected quickly, "Forget it. It's enough for me to keep you and Lomas from playing dueling banjos on each other's nerves.

"This could be nothing, Floyd," Bern continued. "A guy walks away from his life, leaves everything he owns, so why not the ring, too? Maybe he's driving down the road, sees the ring on his finger and gives it a toss out the window." Bern gestured with a quick flip of the hand into the air. "Some guy comes walking along the road, looks down and finds it."

"Ten years later," Floyd reminded.

"History's full of endless searches and accidental discoveries."

"So you think I'd be better off not bothering with the effort."

"I don't want the effort bothering *me*. Or the chief. Some of your investigative feats have turned into administrative nightmares."

"What can I say?"

"Say this accidental discovery won't turn into an endless search that will interfere with your assigned duties." Bern shoved the cloth-wrapped ring toward Floyd. "That's condition one. Condition two is that if at any point this opens Sacramento's case you back off. The D.A. is still cheesed about not getting the heads-up on that Feldman fiasco."

Although it had been over a year since Floyd's encounter with Mark Feldman, the man who stalked him, kidnapped Shelby, and eventually shot Floyd in the leg, old wounds—physical, mental and professional—were not a distant memory. It was the capture of Feldman that exposed the sordid truth about Feldman's family, in particular how his mother, Jessie Bellington, was connected to the double homicide of her sister and brother-in-law in Sacramento, concluding a bizarre tabloid-esque love triangle complicated by an undocumented surrogate birth and multiple blackmail schemes. The district attorney's office and Sacramento P.D., though credited with convicting Jessie Bellington of the murders, harbored resentment toward Floyd and Santa Ramona for not including them earlier in Floyd's investigation and forcing them into the unwanted public relations position of crediting a Santa Ramona detective for solving a case they couldn't.

"In fact," Bern continued, "Why don't you save us all the impending grief and stay out of Sacramento altogether?"

"Does that include my off time?" Floyd asked. "That could have a serious impact on my social life."

"If the alternative is the chief's boot seriously impacting my ass, then yes. I tend to give you a lot of leash as it is, Floyd. You don't need to stretch it to the limit all the time, okay?"

"I'll try to restrict myself to in-house affairs, sir." Floyd gathered up the cloth and stuffed it back into his pocket. He got up and turned to leave, but stopped and turned back to Bern. "What do you believe?"

"Huh?"

"About what happened to Farnsworth. Do you think he's still kicking around somewhere?"

"I don't see why not. You hear stories every now and then about someone taking a walk to the store for a pack of smokes and nobody hears a word about them for thirty years, if ever."

"I guess. Thanks, boss."

As Floyd left Bern's office he sensed a lack of conviction in the lieutenant's voice, a hint of doubt. Floyd patted the pocket containing the ring. He was curious how a man so thorough in planning his own disappearance could act so impulsively by recklessly casting off a highly identifiable item. Assuming he did. And if he didn't, Floyd wondered, who took it from him? And why? And what else was taken? A life? All the questions began streaming into Floyd's mind, but one in particular he knew he could get answered without too much work.

"How'd it go?" Brenda asked Floyd when he emerged from Bern's office. She had joined Marty at his desk and received an abridged version of the ring's recovery as Floyd pitched his case to the lieutenant.

Floyd told them Bern identified the owner, but seemed skeptical on any effort in finding him. "Nonetheless, he gave me the usual doubt and conditions, but didn't say no."

Marty clapped his hands approvingly. "Sweet. Where do we start?"

"You guys start by getting me anything you can on Edson Farnsworth." Floyd spelled the first name. "It's a likely an embezzlement case, but we won't have any report because it originated out of Sac. Bern said he'd try to get a copy of it. The wife never filed anything here. You'll have to go back a ways, like nine or ten years." Floyd looked at his watch. "Can you guys hang over a little tonight?"

Marty shook his head. "Wife's going to open house at the kids' school. I got the either/or from her this morning. Either I come straight home or she comes and gets me."

"I had dinner plans, but I think those are shot now."

Floyd grimaced at Brenda's subtle reminder that her dinner plans were also his. They had gone out a few times since Floyd's recovery, and missed out a few times due to work. This evening had been one of those that had been put off three consecutive times, twice by Floyd, and the latest attempt was now earmarked for a fourth. Marty, an outspoken Floyd/Brenda booster, came to Floyd's rescue.

"Why don't I give what I get to Brenda? You guys can sift through it tonight and fill me in tomorrow."

"No," Floyd countered. "We can wait until morning. I just wasn't thinking."

"Yeah, you were," Marty cracked. "Just not about the right stuff."

"Look, it's no big deal," Brenda said. "We're going to end up talking about it at dinner, anyway. Let's bring whatever we have along instead of wishing we had."

"You're sure?"

Brenda grunted a sigh and rolled her eyes as she walked away. "I'll see you tonight, Floyd."

After Brenda left the squad room, Marty stepped to Floyd's side and tossed his beefy arm over his friend's shoulder. "Let me offer you some advice about dealing with women: Shut up and nod your head."

Floyd extracted himself from Marty's playful wrap and headed for the door. "Find me something to work with."

"Where are you off to?" Marty asked.

"I'm going to have a little chat with Rey Piña and find out where the ring came from."

3
Thursday afternoon, August 14th

Rey Piña and his attorney were sitting inside an interview room engaged in casual conversation when Floyd entered. Their faces marked opposite feelings—Piña's bright and grinning; the attorney's dark and distrustful—at Floyd's unannounced appearance.

"Keeng! My friend! How are you?" Piña stood and extended his hand welcomingly, as if Floyd were a guest in his home. "You remember my lawyer, Sy-mon Vasquez?"

Simon Vasquez was a taller, thinner version of Piña, with a similarly thin mustache and similarly thinning hair. Vasquez had a constant squint as if any light seemed to irritate his eyes, making him look as if he was suffering a constant source of strain. Floyd had never seen anything close to a smile cross Vasquez's lips, and he wasn't even sure if the man ever let a friendly word pass through them. When Floyd shook Vasquez's hand he felt like he was gripping a piece of gel-filled rubber.

"Come. Seet. Eet's been a while since we've crossed paths." Piña turned to Vasquez. "Sy-mon, please, get up and let our guest have a chair." Then back to Floyd, "You want some coffee?" Then immediately back to Vasquez, "Sy-mon, go get another cup of coffee."

Vasquez held a tight expression at being ordered around like a servant, but he nonetheless complied though not before issuing a stern admonishment to Floyd regarding questioning while he was out of the room and politely requesting to his client that he refrain from engaging in any conversations with the officer until he returned.

"Pain een thee ass," Piña mumbled as Vasquez closed the interview room door. "But he keeps me out of jail. For what I pay heem, he can ron a few errands. So, how are you? I heard you got a boo-let en thee leg."

"Just a little nick. Been good, otherwise. And you?"

"Some days are better than others," Piña said, motioning to his current surroundings. "Some day all of you will have better theengs to do than spy on me and my friends."

"Some day you'll realize your friends are mostly an assortment of thieves who will always be watched. It's all about the company you keep, Rey."

"And what company am I keeping now, Keeng?"

"I was wondering if you could help me out."

"I theenk Sy-mon would advise me not to."

"But Simon isn't here."

"Here or not, Sy-mon ees my attorney. I may not respect all of hees advice, bot I do respect thee money I pay for eet." Piña's seriousness lightened. "Maybe you and I could work out a compromise?"

Floyd laughed. "Simon will get you out of here faster than any deal I could put together. Besides, this isn't about today's raid. Something else."

Piña opened his palms invitingly. "That's deeferent. I'm always willing to help thee poleece, and especially my poleece friends."

"Your social responsibility is touching, Rey."

Floyd, hoping for some sign of instant recognition, never took his eyes from Piña as he produced the black cloth from his pocket. He set it on the fake wood-grained Formica tabletop and pulled his hand back. "Ever seen that before?"

"A black hanky? Who hasn't? I didn't know you were a mageecian, Keeng," Piña snickered. "You gonna pull a bird or something out of that, or make eet change colors, perhaps?"

Floyd opened the cloth and exposed the ring. When Piña's jovial tone died, it registered the familiarity Floyd looked for as a signal he should press on.

"We found it inside one of the cabinets taken from your shop," Floyd told him. "In a drawer with papers belonging to you."

"You broke eento my cabinet?"

"It was unlocked."

"Bull." Piña rocked his head back and forth. "I'm disappointed een you, Keeng. I didn't theenk you'd stoop to breaking thee law. I treat you like a friend and—? You're right about watching thee company I keep."

"Look, Rey. You're not on the hook for this. It wasn't listed as one of the missing items, and it's not on anyone's hot sheet of stolen goods. Let's just call it found property for now. But there could be some trouble in it for you if you don't help me out."

Piña processed the tone of Floyd's admonishment as he cautiously measured the detective's sincerity. Floyd read the wariness in Piña's narrowed eyes.

"Rey, you know me better than that. I don't play those kinds of games."

Piña nodded. "Okay. But there's nothing I can tell you about that reeng."

The interview room door opened and Simon Vasquez walked in. He froze at the door as he looked upon his client and the detective and the ring centered between them. Vasquez snapped from his moment of shock when, inattentive to the cup tilting in his hand, a steaming splash of coffee rolled down the backs of his fingers. Biting through anger and pain, he set the coffee cup on the table before he ended up dropping it on the floor and hurriedly shuffled to Piña's side.

"I *knew* it! I told you, Rey. I told you they were up to something." Vasquez thrust an accusing finger at Floyd and shook it. "I warned you about talking to my client! You have violated his rights!"

"Sy-mon," Piña called calmly.

"You can be assured this will not go unreported to your chief!"

"Sy-mon," Piña called again, a bit sterner and, to his frustration, on deaf ears.

"This is an outrage of the—"

"For crying focking out loud, Sy-mon!" Piña barked. "Chut thee fock up!"

Vasquez's jaw hung open as Piña's scolding choked the anger at the attorney's throat. As quickly as Piña's temper flared, it fizzled. Piña settled back into his staid character and with a subtle nod of his head issued a sitting command to his attorney.

"Eet's all right, Sy-mon," Piña calmly explained. "I believe Keeng was jos about to offer some help een our benefit." Then to Floyd, "Go ahead, Keeng. You were going to tell me about some trouble?"

"Rey, Mr. Vasquez, this ring belongs or belonged to a man who hasn't been seen for around ten years. There's never been any indication that his disappearance involved any criminal activity, but the ring turning up after all this time certainly raises some questions."

"Suspicious questions, no doubt," Vasquez said. "But why? It is just as conceivable that this man sold the ring or gave it away. Perhaps the person who had it decided to part with it. Perhaps it was lost and finally recovered. There are so many possibilities, Detective King, that it would be narrow-minded to focus primarily on my client, and just as irresponsible to look solely at the worst-case scenario."

"Except my job revolves around worst-case scenarios, counselor. If it is nothing, great. If it turns out to be something, Rey's going to be first in line as the thermometer for the hot seat."

"But I told you, Keeng. I don't know anything about thees reeng."

"I have no doubt you don't know the *history* of the ring, Rey. But you know where you got it. You know who gave it to you."

"Rey, I don't like this. It's so out of the ordinary, and," turning to Floyd, "it wouldn't surprise me to find out how little authorization there is to conduct this interview."

"There's nothing to authorize, Mr. Vasquez. We're just having a friendly conversation over coffee. One I hope doesn't turn into a question-and-answer session over a tape recorder."

"So, Keeng, you jos want me to tell you how I got thee reeng? Jos like that?"

"That's all I want."

"Say, hypothetically, I don't tell you."

"Say we find out on our own. Are you confident that no one will roll over on you to cut a deal and save his or her own ass? At the very least the D.A. will come after you for obstructing. So, who do you want to work with? Me or them?"

Vasquez leaned closer to Piña and lowered his voice. "Rey, Detective King is making a good point. My success in keeping you out of jail has always predicated itself on you maintaining a low profile. You can work on damage control to your reputation among your associates, Rey, but if your name hits the papers you won't be able to sell sight to a blind man."

"Yes, Sy-mon. Keeng's point ees good." Piña rose and paced across the room, then back to the table. "You're a very smart man, Keeng. And because you respect me enough to approach me like a man, I'll help you.

"There were two of them. One ees a skeenny white-boy named Jeff. The other ees a rough-looking guy that calls himself 'C', like thee letter. I don't know their last names, and I don't know where they hang out. I've dealt weeth them a handful of times over thee years, but I don't usually handle their merchandise when they come een."

"Why?"

"Because I don't deal een stereo equipment and cell phones and mountain bikes and breek-a-brac. I'm more of a referral service for them."

"So how was the ring different?" Floyd asked.

Piña grinned. "I'm a smart man, too, Keeng."

"Surely smart enough to recognize how hot a marked piece can be."

"Chure. I saw thee signature. But it's in thee gold, Keeng, and thee gold ..." Piña waved his hand in disregard. "Thee *stones* are thee money."

Floyd looked at the ring and the light refracting against the cloth. "Break'em loose and re-cut the big one, reset them or resell them. But you don't do that."

"No. But I know people who do. And when they're done, I get a leettle and I pass on a leettle."

"And these two guys, Jeff and C, are expecting a little."

Piña nodded. "I told them to check een weeth me next Mahnday."

"No chance they'll be late? Maybe show up Tuesday or call a meeting somewhere else?"

Piña laughed. "Not a chance. Those two sonsofbeetches don't trost me, Keeng. They'll be there Mahnday, for chure."

"If I happened to be in the neighborhood shopping next week ...?"

Piña reclined in his chair and smiled, stretching his thin mustache thinner across his upper lip. "What kind of merchant discourages customers from entering his beesness?"

Floyd reached out and shook Piña's hand. He picked up the ring and cloth, then got up to leave. "I'll see you in a few of days, Rey. And I'll do what I can to preserve your upstanding reputation."

"I won't hold my breath for thee plaque from thee Better Beesness Bureau, but I'll appreciate whatever you do for me, Keeng."

A few hours after talking with Rey Piña, Floyd pulled into the parking lot of Anson's, a popular, moderately-priced restaurant that had a history in Santa Ramona almost as long as Santa Ramona had a history. The bar and one-third of the kitchen were the only sections of the original building left relatively unchanged as Gary Anson, the third-generation owner, enlarged and remodeled the main dining area like his father and grandfather did when control of the place fell into their hands. It was just another sign of progress. As the town grew and the attitudes and incomes of her residents grew, so did Anson's. Even with increased competition, business was steady during the week and generated thirty to forty-minute waits on weekends.

Floyd checked in with the hostess and she led him to a

booth at the far end of the dining room. He was about ten minutes late having decided at the last second to detour home to take a quick shower and put on a clean shirt and unwrinkled slacks. He felt a twinge of regret for making her wait, but Floyd knew Brenda would appreciate him taking the extra time to be less pungent over being more punctual. When he saw Brenda seated in the booth he was grateful he took the time. She had changed from her working wardrobe of slacks and jeans into an olive-green, knee-length pleated skirt that showed off her toned and tanned calves. The Mediterranean bronze of her arms and broad shoulders were done justice, as well, with a khaki V-neck tank that cut tastefully to the top of her cleavage. She had also released her dark brown hair, normally tied up on duty, to its full length at just above her shoulder blades. As magnetic as her appearance was and with her being alone in a bar and restaurant crowded with men, Floyd was almost surprised she was sitting alone.

"Sorry I'm late," Floyd said as he slid along the opposite bench in the booth. "I ran by the house to clean up a little."

The waitress stopped at their table long enough to drop a coaster and a beer in front of Floyd, and offer an approving smile to Brenda.

"I told her to just bring it when you got here."

"Thanks." Floyd hoisted his glass to Brenda. "What shall we drink to?"

Brenda lifted her half-empty glass and clinked Floyd's. "World peace."

"And that we don't become alcoholics drinking to it," Floyd added before tipping the glass to his mouth. "You look great."

Brenda blushed and bit her lip trying to restrain her

smile. In the last year she had grown increasingly fond of Floyd, finding and building a deeper connection with him now than she tried in the past when they were both on the ends of damaged relationships and caught each other's fall. When she realized two failed relationships later that she never gave herself a true chance with him, he was already engaged and weeks away from his second trip down the aisle. The subsequent twisted turn of events that interrupted that trip opened the window of opportunity for her, and she was determined to make an effort to see if fate was teasing her or telling her something.

Drinks and dinner were pleasantly mixed with light, non-job conversation. Floyd covered the latest comings and goings with his daughter and her job as a physical therapist, as well as her budding romance with an assistant athletic trainer at Sacramento State. Brenda talked about her family and her indecision about buying a new car. A little politics and world events, some desert and coffee, and then it was on to the topic of the day.

"Marty and I found out as much as we could about Farnsworth that was readily available. I started with the news files from the date Sac P.D. initiated their investigation on behalf of his business partner." Brenda took a photocopy of a news write-up and handed it across the table. "The first part has the general P.R. quotes downplaying any speculation about what happened, which, naturally, is followed by speculation as to what happened. The middle highlights his personal and professional history, and the end covers his marital and professional problems."

Floyd nodded over another sip of beer. "Bern hinted Farnsworth's leaving was in part because his marriage was failing. How bad was his business?"

"Didn't seem bad at all. He had completed one housing development and six business complexes. Did a bunch of remodels." Brenda handed Floyd another paper. "According to people in the construction trade Farnsworth seemed to get along with his partner, but there was occasional conflict and friction with a couple of contractors, primarily with Jay Whiting."

"Whiting? Hell, pick a fight you can win," Floyd said facetiously.

Jay Whiting, a long-time construction mogul in the state whose influence was a particularly strong force all around the Sacramento Valley, was known as the king of the phase-built, planned residential community in the real estate industry. He was also hard-headed, devious, and corrupt according to those in the construction trade who found themselves shunted to less lucrative projects as a result of their inability to secure the permits and financing that Whiting bought like lottery tickets. Allegedly, as no one ever had the proof or the money or the political support to challenge Whiting's operation. Farnsworth and Vossen, like most, settled for the scraps they were thrown.

"No kidding," Brenda agreed. "That's why Farnsworth's company stopped home construction after their first residential build. They couldn't secure the land they wanted, and the banks weren't too hot on them for some reason."

"Whiting's influence."

"That's the word. They didn't have the same trouble with commercial property, though. As long as it didn't conflict with Whiting's plans."

"Now this guy, Len Vossen, his partner. What's the story on him?"

"Architect. Farnsworth's background was in financial

management and accounting. He handled the dollars; Vossen handled the designs. They had their share of debates about which way to take the company. But despite any strains in the relationship, business seemed strong."

"So why did Farnsworth bolt?"

"The eternal mystery. When Farnsworth took off Vossen took a financial beating. Apparently Farnsworth had the ability to move money without Vossen's co-signature. One Friday afternoon they were solvent, and by the time the banks opened the following Monday morning, the company's history. Story is that Vossen didn't find out until Tuesday. A majority of the company assets were reserved for land purchases with payments due on what they already owned. What was left Farnsworth took. There wasn't enough money for Vossen to continue on. He scrambled to reconsolidate his debts but ultimately filed for bankruptcy to battle the stream of lawsuits against the company."

"And Farnsworth's wife?"

"Said she was out of town. Didn't know where he was, wasn't looking, and didn't care."

"Nice. Where is Vossen now?"

Brenda shrugged. "Shouldn't be hard to find out."

"What else?"

"A lot of social climbing. Charities. Balls. Fundraiser here, fundraiser there." Brenda flipped through a stack of papers. "Farnsworth had family money and connections. He definitely wasn't trying to fit in where he didn't belong."

"Except in the residential development game." Floyd turned to another article, one about the discovery of Farnsworth's car and scanned it. "So his car sits downtown for a few days, a parking control officer runs it as a possible stolen or abandoned. The registration comes back clean."

"The next article touches on the police search, which is pretty limited," Brenda continued. "The car gets impounded and—I'm supposing here—searched for any evidence of assault or kidnapping. No leads, blah, blah, blah. The news articles get smaller and deeper into the paper as the weeks progress."

"What we really need to know we won't find out until we get the copy of the police report. I'd like to see Mrs. Farnsworth's and Vossen's statements, and how many other people the police interviewed, all of which I'm sure are lacking."

"And the investigators' summary that led them to conclude old Edson just tossed his life aside and walked away." Brenda watched Floyd's eyes drift in thought. "What?"

"That ring," Floyd answered. "Let's say Farnsworth pulls a Copperfield and makes himself vanish. Assume he eliminates all traces of his life—his wallet, I.D., credit cards, library card, the whole nine yards. He owns a ring that has his name etched on the band, so it'd follow that he'd get rid of that, too."

"Okay. And someone comes along and—" Brenda stopped when Floyd shook his head.

"Why would he go to all the trouble of vanishing yet leave such a highly identifiable marker behind? Two big rivers, God-knows how many sloughs and irrigation canals, and he's going to flick it aside like a cigarette butt? No way. Farnsworth had every move dialed in. He didn't throw the ring away carelessly. He didn't toss it out the window of his car, like Bern suggested. No one stumbled across it picking through a dumpster looking for bottles to cash in. The ring was clean, Bren. There wasn't a mark on it. And based on what Piña told me about the two guys who gave him the ring, they aren't roadside scavengers. They're backdoor lock pickers. They found it because somebody else had it."

"Did Piña offer any names when you talked to him?"

"Yeah. A guy named Jeff and a guy named C. Rey couldn't tell me where to find them, but all we have to do is wait. He's expecting them back next Monday to collect their part of the payoff."

"Great. That'll give us some time to set up on Rey's shop and pick them off when they go in. Hopefully they'll cooperate and explain where or from whom they got it."

The waitress stopped at the table and checked with the couple to see if she could get them anything else. Floyd and Brenda politely declined and the waitress set their meal check on the table, which Floyd pulled in front of him.

"You still think there's more to Farnsworth's disappearance, don't you?" Brenda asked.

"I don't see why we shouldn't find out as much about the man as we can," Floyd told her. "I'd like to be prepared in case there's more. It won't end with Jeff and this C person, I know that."

Floyd fingered several bills from his wallet and pinned them along with the check beneath a salt shaker. He and Brenda left their booth and snaked around the tables in the open dining room to the exit, trading an atmosphere of situated chaos inside Anson's for the swarm of bodies that had massed around the restaurant's front patio door straining to hear the hostess's soft voice above the din of conversation and laughter as she called the name of the next party over the speaker system. Floyd took Brenda's hand and led her through the mob, sidestepping and excusing a path into the parking lot. Even as the crowd thinned, Floyd left his hand in Brenda's and continued across the lot to her car.

Reluctantly, Brenda freed her hand to retrieve her car keys from her purse. After opening her car door she slipped her hand back into Floyd's and leaned into him, kissing him lightly on the cheek. "Thanks for tonight. I had a good time."

"You didn't mind the little bit of work we brought?"

"That's part of hanging out with you, Floyd. That, and putting up with Marty."

Floyd laughed. He knew the mutually professed tolerance between his partners veiled their true respect for each other. As much as one picked on the other, they as often watched the other's back and promoted their best interests. Even tonight, as Floyd called Marty on the drive to the restaurant to ask a favor, he spoke with Marty's wife, who was as surprised to hear about her school meeting as Floyd was to find out there wasn't one. He decided to accept his friend's pre-planned absence from dinner as intended, and didn't give up the deception to Brenda, which was to the benefit of all three of them.

Floyd opened Brenda's car door but blocked her immediate entry by dipping his shoulder between her and the open driver's seat. He casually leaned forward and pressed his lips against hers. It was quick, almost as quick as her peck on his cheek, but to Brenda it was perfect. Floyd pulled back and watched Brenda slide her legs into the car. When she was in and buckled, Floyd closed the door. Brenda started the engine and rolled down the window and beckoned Floyd with a lusty smirk behind a crooked finger. As Floyd leaned forward she met him with a slightly more sensual kiss.

"Drive safe," Floyd said, pulling clear of the car. "I'll see you in the morning."

"Bright and early," Brenda replied.

Brenda put the car in gear and pulled out to the lot exit, peeking back in her mirrors at Floyd until she lost him among the other cars. A mix of relief and happiness washed over her and she smiled. She recalled how she felt the first time she and Floyd kissed, back when their lives were spiraling into separate abysses and they reached out in desperation hoping the other's fall was shorter and less painful. But their time together was merely a distraction for each other's woes, an additional burden neither was prepared to shoulder. Instead, they only succeeded in falling deeper and farther apart. The connection Brenda felt now seemed stronger. It seemed right. There were no frayed nerves to mend, no crushed confidences to rebuild, no need to exchange reassurance that the failures they suffered were not their own doing. Slates were clean and the emotional bloodletting staunched. For Brenda, tonight was a new beginning with an old friend and she was determined to make it work. Not because she needed it to work. Because she wanted it to.

4
Friday midday, August 15th

Floyd and Marty returned to the squad room after a morning testifying in court on a forgery case that took an unexpected turn. The suspect in the case was a small, bi-spectacled, grandfatherly man who neglected to report his wife's death and continued depositing her Social Security checks while keeping her body preserved in a garage freezer. The police were called when the bank manager suspected a problem after finding one of her checks endorsed with his name.

"It was completely accidental," the manager told Floyd and Marty during their initial visit to the bank. "The deposit envelope with their checks got mixed in with the cash deposits when we serviced the ATM."

The manager went on to explain how after the envelopes are collected from the machine, they are sorted between cash deposits and check deposits, with the cash deposits being entered into customer accounts at the bank and the check deposits being sent to a clearinghouse for processing.

"When we opened Mr. and Mrs. Craig's envelope and saw the checks instead of cash, we figured we'd do the right thing and just make the deposit. That's when we noticed Mrs. Craig's check was signed by Mr. Craig. I thought maybe they inadvertently signed each others check, but when I looked at Mr. Craig's check, I saw he endorsed that one, too."

"That doesn't sound like a big deal to fix," Marty commented.

"It shouldn't have been. I called him at home to advise him of the error. I assumed it was just an oversight, so I offered to hold the check until Mrs. Craig could come in and make the correction. He told me his wife was ill and traveling to the bank would be too much of a strain on her. He said he would pick it up himself, have her sign it, and then he would bring it back."

"I'm sorry, sir, but I don't see where a crime has been committed here," Floyd said. "It sounds like a little clerical thing that needs to be sorted out. Unless there's more to it than that."

"I think there is," the manager said with deep concern. "I just had a peculiar feeling when I spoke with him, like he was being evasive, like he was going out of his way not to make his wife available. When I offered to drive the check to his home, for instance, he became unsettled and irritated. I tried to explain I was just trying to be helpful, just trying to save him the extra trip. He accused me of meddling in his affairs, of spying on him. He really wasn't making any sense. Then Mr. Craig told me to tear up the check, that he would call Social Security and have them issue a new one. I tried to explain that none of this was necessary, that the bank would make it as convenient as possible for Mrs. Craig."

"And he still refused your help?"

"In a manner of speaking. He, uh, said that if he couldn't pick up the check, that I could, um, make my own deposit, if you know what I mean."

Marty cracked a broad smile. "I do, indeed. Couple'a weeks ago I had a crook tell me where I could put his inch-thick criminal history. He wasn't so smart when I held it up to his face, ripped it in half, and offered to share it with him."

"Uh, yes, I, uh, I suppose one would rethink their position under such circumstances," the manager agreed, uncomfortably shifting in his seat. His voice returned to its previously dour tone. "Officers, I've been the bank manager here for six years. Up until seven months ago, Mr. Craig always made his deposits in person with Mrs. Craig at his side. He suddenly starts making his deposits through the machine. Same trip to the same bank branch. I checked. I don't recall having seen Mrs. Craig once in that time. These checks are all they have to live on, and their account balance can't support them for the time it will take to have a new check issued. I don't want to start any problems. I'm just very concerned."

"Well, sir, we can appreciate that. I think what you've attempted to do seems genuine and sincere. But as I told you, you haven't provided us with any evidence of a crime, just evidence of a mistake." Floyd turned to his partner. "What do you think?"

"People do goofy things with their money all the time. I saw a guy light a cigar with a hundred-dollar bill. Go to Vegas and you'll see rooms packed with people gambling one last shot against their retirement." Marty shrugged and turned to the manager. "Guy wants to toss away a perfectly good, government-backed check ..."

"If it's the money you're concerned about, that's between you, the Craigs, and Social Security," Floyd added.

"I understand. But it's not the money issue. I'm more worried about Mrs. Craig," the manager said. "If she is ill like her husband told me, I feel her welfare may be at issue if they become short of funds. After all, this is half their income."

"We could do a drive-by," Marty suggested to Floyd. Then to the manager, "But if Mr. Craig is as ticked off as you say he is, you'll likely hear about it."

"As long as Mrs. Craig is reasonably well, I have no problem accepting any complaint that follows from her husband," the manager proclaimed as he passed the Craigs' address to the detectives.

D. Lawrence Craig and his wife, Amelia, lived on Regent Street in an older section of Santa Ramona. It was a neighborhood of thirty-year-old homes being nibbled at or eaten whole by contractors whose clients sought partial or wholesale modifications. Every home that was sold, it seemed, went through an upgrading transformation. Of the twenty houses on Regent Street, only six owners could claim to have had added nothing more than a new coat of paint since their home's original construction. The Craigs lived in one such house.

Mr. Craig was collecting his mail from the box near the curb in front of his home when Floyd and Marty pulled up. Craig paid the two men no mind. Three houses around him were undergoing minor renovations and two were up for sale, so he was used to seeing a regular coming and going of appraisers and inspectors and workmen. Even when the men walked toward his house, it wasn't out of the ordinary. Realtors appeared on Regent Street weekly, and most of them made a courtesy call to the Craigs in the off chance the elderly couple might want to sell or, as Craig believed, to keep a death watch on the old folks. Craig was halfway up the walk to his front door before he peeked over his shoulder to see if he was alone. He wasn't. Floyd and Marty had just made the turn toward the house from the sidewalk.

"You gentlemen go on, now," Craig said sternly. "I have

no interest in selling anything or buying anything. There's plenty other houses in the neighborhood you can work on."

"We're not here to sell you anything, Mr. Craig," Floyd told him. "We'd just like a minute of your time."

"We're with the police."

When Marty identified himself and Floyd, Craig's obstinacy melted to retreat. He took a stumbling step toward the front porch steps, latching onto the handrail to maintain his balance.

"Are you all right, sir?" Floyd asked.

"I'm, I'm fine." Craig straightened himself and tried to mask his embarrassment with a dignified air. "I'm just fine. And I didn't call any police, so you best be on your way."

"We'll be gone shortly, Mr. Craig."

"Sir, we came to speak with Mrs. Craig." Marty said.

"Is she here?" Floyd asked.

"She's, uh, no, she's not here. She went out of town. Up north. To Washington. To, uh, Spokane. To visit her sister."

Marty shot Floyd a sidelong glance, catching Floyd doing the same in return. Craig's eyes bounced nervously from one man to the other, trying to read the telepathic message the detectives were sending between themselves. Craig was unknowingly sending his own, and with years of exposure to the most subtle lies by more accomplished liars, Floyd and Marty were too astute to be easily taken down a deceptive path.

"How long has she been gone?" Floyd asked.

"A week."

"Will she be back any time soon?"

"Uh, no. Her sister's sick and, uh, we didn't make any definite plans, so ..."

"Mr. Craig, we just came from the bank." The old man's body jerked with a start when Marty spoke. "The bank manager told us about the checks you deposited two days ago."

"The bank manager expressed some concern about your wife," Floyd continued.

"My—?"

"She's not in Spokane, is she, Mr. Craig." Marty challenged mildly.

"I—"

"Is she home, sir?" Floyd asked again.

"She, uh, she's—"

Craig slowly sat himself on the steps, letting the day's mail slip from his hand to the ground. His eyes glazed over as he stared across the street, across the town, across his life.

"Marty, go call for an ambulance. And we may need a couple of patrol units to stand by."

While Marty jogged back to the car, Floyd knelt down in front of Craig, now leaning his head against the rail struts but still holding a distant gaze. Craig's pulse was a bit more rapid than Floyd was comfortable feeling, but it was strong and except for the apparent state of shock, Craig didn't appear to be on the verge of dropping dead on the spot. Even Marty's assurance that the medics were on the way didn't curb Floyd's silent willing of a quicker response.

The ambulance arrived within minutes and raced Craig to the hospital. Floyd and Marty searched the rooms of the Craigs' house but found neither trace of Amelia Craig nor any indication that she had left on the trip to Spokane. The house impressed Floyd for its cleanliness, for its inviting warmth. It was a stark contrast to the eeriness that crept down Floyd's neck upon entering the musty, lifeless garage.

As soon as Floyd spotted the chest freezer sitting off in the corner, he knew.

As it turned out, Floyd's and Marty's testifying, along with that of the bank manager, were performances solely for the record. The case against D. Lawrence Craig was hardly a case at all. Mrs. Craig died of natural causes, so there was no criminal liability on Mr. Craig's part. As for the forged signatures on the Social Security checks, the judge ordered reimbursement of the funds. Because of Craig's age and deteriorating health, the judge waived any jail time but maintained a probationary period of three years "as a matter of course".

"Hey, Floyd," Turk called from across the squad room when he and Marty stepped inside. "Bern wanted to see you when you got in."

Floyd blew a mild curse as Marty peeled away to his desk. The ring had been burning a hole in his pocket throughout the court appearance and he was hoping to feed his curiosity after the judge dropped the gavel for adjournment. Floyd walked to the lieutenant's door and knocked, pushing it open and stepping through, as was his custom. He got three paces into the office before noticing a man and woman sitting on Bern's office sofa. Floyd hit the brakes and excused himself.

"I was told you wanted to see me, Lieutenant. I'll come back when you're finished."

As Floyd retreated from the office, Bern called him back inside. "This meeting wouldn't be complete without you." Bern stood and motioned toward his two guests. "This is Detective Keller," he said, pointing to the woman, "and Detective Tiner. They work for Sac P.D."

As the two visitors stood to exchange handshakes, Floyd saw the badges hanging around their necks by plastic straps. Floyd guessed them both to be close to his age, but sensed that Keller either had time on Tiner in the department or at least had seniority over him in their unit she exuded a confidence and maturity, a command presence, that indicated she was in charge.

Keller was tall and slender with short, strawberry-blonde hair and strikingly attractive green-brown eyes. She took Floyd's hand first in a strong though unchallenging grip and continued the less-formal introductions.

"Grace. And this is Curtis."

Tiner reached across his partner to shake Floyd's hand. "Curt," he clarified.

Bern motioned for everyone to sit. Keller and Tiner returned to the sofa. Floyd took one of the chairs in front of Bern's desk and cocked it so he could face the Sacramento cops and his boss, who remained standing behind his desk. Bern picked up a thin folder and handed it to Floyd.

"There's your report on Farnsworth."

"Thanks," Floyd said. He opened the folder and found a five-page report that didn't look very impressive in either quality or quantity. "You guys didn't have to drive it all the way out here," he said to Keller and Tiner.

"And we shouldn't have," Keller replied matter-of-factly. "But we were told to give you a copy, so ..."

"I'm going to assume there's more to the personal delivery than interdepartmental courtesy."

"There must be, because that courtesy hasn't been established yet." Keller's tone was sharp, but not maliciously cutting. "I'd have no doubt that our having to come out here has less to do with an information exchange than it does with you being connected to another one of our unsolved cases."

Keller's comment stung Floyd. He looked at Bern for a reaction, but all he got was a wry grin wrapped around his cigar.

"My understanding was this case was closed not long after Mr. Farnsworth disappeared," Floyd countered.

"The case was filed as inactive. But since there may be new information available, it's active again. And it's been assigned to us. As such, we'd appreciate it if, in the spirit of interdepartmental courtesy, you'd enlighten us as to what's put you on Farnsworth's trail."

"Lieutenant?"

"You really want my 'cooperation' speech, Floyd?"

Floyd responded to Bern's offer by removing the black cloth containing the ring from his pocket and handing it to Keller. Keller unfolded the cloth and, with Tiner peering over her shoulder, gazed wide-eyed upon the ring.

"That was found in an antique shop here in town," Floyd explained. "The owner is a middleman who connects less reputable sellers and buyers. He said two men dropped it off on him a couple of days ago. If you look inside the band you'll see Edson Farnsworth's signature."

"That's a beauty," an awestruck Tiner said. "Do you know what it's worth?"

"I didn't have it formally appraised, but I'd guess somewhere in the neighborhood of ten thousand."

"Do you know who these two men are?" Keller asked.

"We don't have a positive I.D. yet," Floyd told her, intentionally withholding the information Piña told him. "We have a description and the possibility they'll return to the shop sometime next week to collect the rest of their payment."

Keller wrapped the cloth over the ring but made no attempt to hand it back to Floyd. Seeing this, Floyd extended his hand, but Keller simply looked at it.

"We'll hold on to the ring, if you don't mind. Since our case is active, anything associated with it belongs to us."

Floyd left his hand out. "We'll turn it over to you when *our* investigation is complete."

"*Your* investigation? Detective King, this is a Sacramento case. Naturally we're grateful for whatever assistance you can give, but—"

"I'm not investigating your case for you, Detective Keller. I'm investigating a property crime, and that ring is my evidence. I only asked for your department's cooperation for some background on the owner. As yet there has been no substantiated information that connects that ring to Farnsworth's disappearance. If and when that information comes to bear, I'll return the favor and drive to your office to give you whatever turns up. In the meantime ..."

Floyd pushed his hand closer to Keller. Keller, though, was not one to be intimidated. But she could be ordered. As much as Bern was enjoying seeing Floyd meet his match in stubbornness, he knew which side he had to take and did so with the proper decorum.

"I understand your desire to take the ring as part of your case, Detective Keller. But Floyd has a point in that the ring is part of a Santa Ramona investigation. The ring may hold some significance to you, but it won't make a dramatic impact on your case. It most certainly will for us. I'll make sure that Floyd keeps his probe within our jurisdiction. We'll also maintain a line of communication so your concerns are addressed. When we're done," Bern turned to Floyd, "when *I* say we're done," then back to Keller, "anything we have is yours or will be shared," then to Floyd once more, "without conflict."

"That sounds reasonable," Keller replied. She handed

the cloth to Floyd, who, Keller noted, put it back in his pocket only after giving it a squeeze to ensure he felt the hard shape of the ring inside. "If it's all the same, sir, we'd still like to get some background on what Detective King is working on."

"I don't see a problem with that, do you, Floyd?"

"I'd be a fool if I did," he told Bern, then to Keller, "I was planning on getting some lunch. If you and Curt come along I can charge it to the chief's expense account instead of mine."

"Fair enough," Keller replied. "At least we're guaranteed to receive something for our trip out here."

Bern thanked Keller and Tiner for stopping in and asked that they pass along his appreciation to his counterpart in their office. Floyd led the pair into the squad room, momentarily excusing himself while he locked the ring in his desk, then returned and led them to Brenda's desk.

"Grace Keller. Curt Tiner. This is Brenda Garibaldi."

Handshakes and smiles were exchanged courteously, except for Tiner who developed an immediate attraction to Brenda and held his handshake, smile, and eye to her with more than casual interest. Brenda took note of the all-too-familiar target acquisition response and put a mental restriction on any continued or future interaction with him.

"Where's Marty?"

"Right here." Marty walked into the squad room as Floyd spoke.

"Marty Doenacker. Keller and Tiner out of Sac."

"Nice to meet you," Marty greeted. "Are you here on business or just passing through?"

"Business. It seems we have a mutual interest in Edson Farnsworth," Keller said.

"Ahhh. Floyd spies."

"Marty," Floyd warned.

"Just kidding. Although I must admit you do have a knack for drawing ants to a picnic. No offense to our guests," he said to Keller and Tiner. "We gonna eat?" he asked Floyd.

"Loredo's," Floyd said, naming the trendy, slightly expensive restaurant. Marty winced but Floyd eased his partner's financial pain by telling him, "It's on the boss."

"Man's a freakin' saint. Let's go."

The Sacramento duo followed the Santa Ramona trio the four miles to the restaurant. Similar conversations took place in each car. Floyd replayed the exchange in Bern's office for Marty and Brenda before outlining his desire for a limit on how included Keller and Tiner would be and how much information would be shared.

"We're talking about Farnsworth and the ring and nothing else," Floyd instructed. "Piña or details about the two guys, Jeff and C, aren't up for discussion."

Keller recognized she and her partner would have little leverage to position themselves strongly or create a fair field of play. She had heard about Floyd, mostly by reputation, and her introduction to him in Bern's office did nothing to dispel the rumors that defined the man. Keller knew that outside Bern's office, Floyd would not fall to coercion and intimidation. She suggested to Tiner that they sit back and wait and let the opportunity knock.

"The objective here is not to push, to be cooperative," Keller told Tiner. "We weaken his position by making him look like the hostile opposition. We turn his so-called case into ours, then we make him eat it."

"Why, Grace? The two cases aren't even related. They're just trying to do a job, same as us."

Keller turned and glared at Tiner. "Don't be a fool, Curtis. The chief is still fuming over the Feldman homicides. We looked like idiots while King and Santa Ramona reaped all the glory and the press. We're here to make sure it doesn't happen again, and I'll be damned if I walk up to the brass with my tail tucked between my legs. Nobody gives a shit if we find Farnsworth, but they'll remember anyone who gets burned by Floyd King's fire. I plan on lighting my own torch with it before I hose him off."

Keller pulled the car into the parking lot and slid it into a spot a few spaces away from Floyd. "If you don't have the stomach for this, say so now."

Curt Tiner knew better. He worked hard to get promoted into the detective bureau and didn't relish picking up a jacket as a bad partner. Even worse, though, was the prospect of being sent back to patrol, where Keller would have more control over his reassignment than he would.

"If you say it's good, Grace, I'll be okay with it."

"It's good," Keller beamed. "I didn't get where I'm at by letting guys like King kick me around. I can play his game. You just watch and learn."

The hostess at Loredo's led the five detectives through the dining room to a booth that had a chair placed at the open end to accommodate the extra diner. Brenda remained close to Floyd and Marty since getting out of the car as she felt the continued assessment of Tiner's eyes. As they reached the table, Floyd slid into the booth. He assumed either Marty or Brenda would take a seat next to him. Instead, Keller stepped forward and, to Floyd's surprise, dropped next to him. Marty offered the bench to Tiner, who deferred to Brenda. Brenda, sensing a trap much like the one Keller pulled on Floyd, excused herself to the restroom, giving Marty and Tiner the open side of the booth. When she returned Marty made an attempt to get up, but Brenda stared him back and took the open chair. Marty smiled and gave Brenda a surreptitious wink signaling he was aware of Tiner's interest as well as his intent to make her suffer for it.

"Having not had the chance to read the report," Floyd began, "but skimming the pages before we left I noticed only two people were interviewed by the investigating officers."

"That's right," Keller replied. "Farnsworth's wife, Collette, and his business partner, Len Vossen."

"No neighbors, no friends? And yet the investigators concluded rather confidently that Farnsworth disappeared by design."

"They made their conclusion based on the lack of evidence to the contrary. The techs went over the car bumper-to-bumper and found nothing out of the ordinary. His fingerprints. Her fingerprints. No indication of a wipe down. No signs of a struggle, not even a scratch on the car's leather seats."

"And the statement given by Mrs. Farnsworth appears to support her husband leaving on his own accord," Tiner added. "She wasn't secretive about the marital problems, though she stopped short of making them public. She said she told her husband that any time he wanted to leave he could go ahead and go, that she'd only take issue if he tried to put her on the street."

"Mrs. Farnsworth made out okay," Keller said. "She got a custom home and retained several investments that should keep her well off until she dies. Her attorney did well to protect her from claims due to the collapse of the business."

"What about Vossen?" Brenda asked Keller.

"Vossen apparently didn't really know what was going on until he called the bank to make a withdrawal and found out there wasn't any money. The investigators only asked Vossen questions pertaining to the missing man as it related to the missing money."

"It doesn't seem like there was a whole lot of effort put into finding any witnesses or doing any intensive probing of the two they had."

"But at the time no one was looking," Keller reminded Floyd. "Did Edson Farnsworth have enemies? Sure. Land development and construction are cutthroat businesses worth hundreds of thousands of dollars. Sometimes millions. But, and remember the case was based on this alone, there was no reason, no evidentiary indication that Farnsworth did anything other than steal some money and leave home."

"Sounds like some things were skipped out of convenience."

Floyd's mild criticism of her department's report was meant to bait Keller, a jab intended to draw a reaction from her, hopefully an over-reaction, and give him a feel for an opening to exploit.

"Sounds like we're talking outside of your jurisdiction."

Keller's repsonse was a perfect block intended to put Floyd on notice that she wouldn't back down as much as to see how he'd react to a challenge. Floyd reacted as if he saw it coming, half-grinned, and casually sidestepped it.

"We should probably order," he said, signaling for the waitress.

The meal was pleasant enough, though the conversation was lacking substance. Floyd and Keller continued a subtle cat-and-mouse game by alluding to and avoiding the subject of Edson Farnsworth. Tiner paid more attention to Brenda than his food with his frequent queries into her background—where she'd grown up, how she got into law enforcement, what she does with her free time. Brenda, while polite, found answering the questions annoying, diverting her attention from her concern of the moment: the attractive woman sitting next to Floyd. Marty, the odd-man-out, remained uncharacteristically quiet throughout the meal.

After Floyd signed off the lunch check, the group exited toward the restaurant lobby. As soon as they stepped outside, Keller's hip emitted a series of muted beeps from under her jacket. She reached inside, withdrew her pager, and silenced it. Keller's face furrowed into annoyed lines as she exchanged the pager for her cell phone. She excused herself and drifted away from the group as she made her call.

Tiner fell back but Keller ushered him on. He joined Marty a few yards from where Floyd and Brenda were waiting. "Can I ask you something?"

"Shoot."

"I was wondering about Brenda, you know, about if she's taken."

Marty's cheeks swelled below his eyes, stretching the corners of his mouth apart in the unmistakably devilish Doenacker grin.

"I mean, she's a good-looking gal," Tiner went on. "And I didn't see a ring—not that that means anything 'cause I know a lot of women cops who are married or engaged but don't wear jewelry. That's why I asked. I don't want to make an ass of myself asking her out if she's already spoken for, you know?"

"Yeah, it pays to have a little foresight in these sorts of

pursuits, hedge your bet a little to take the edge off the gamble. Good heads-up on your part, Curtis. No sense wasting time chasing your tail for some tail."

"Curt," Tiner corrected for what he figured was the millionth time in his life.

"Brenda's not married, so—"

Marty turned and looked over at Brenda, who was standing next to Floyd. They weren't touching or looking at each other in any longing fashion. They were just standing there like they would stand over a crime scene or over each other's desk or over mundane conversation. So many times their lives had shattered and been put back together only to shatter again. Every time, Marty was there fitting pieces and gluing, watching his friends rebound emotionally like over-inflated rubber balls exaggerating their spring while testing the strength of the skin that keeps them from bursting. Instead of seeing either of them on the brink of another disastrous relationship, Marty saw the two of them in the process of strengthening a foundation that was once weak and abandoned.

Marty knew Brenda had no interest in Tiner, had watched her avoid his looks and harmless chitchat throughout lunch. At any other time in his life, Marty would have relished the opportunity to send the hopeful detective Brenda's way to irritate her with a Tiner-like rash that would take weeks to go away. At any other time in his life, Marty likely would have encouraged Tiner to test fate knowing its predestined doom. Not today.

Marty turned back to Tiner, ready to discourage his advance. But the lustful teenage glimmer in the Sacramento detective's eyes instead stimulated a need within Marty to protect. "Look, I don't normally get involved in Brenda's personal life—well, I do, but only to the extent that I try to annoy the crap out of her. Anyway, I think you ought to pass on this one."

"Pass? Why? You said she's not married."

"She's not. I just don't think it's a good idea. She's sorting out some things in her life and—"

"And maybe I can help her," Tiner cut in, grinning. "No reason not to offer a hand."

"What, besides the obvious fact she doesn't like you?" Marty pointed out.

"She doesn't know me. She'll see a different Curt Tiner away from work."

"But you won't see a different Brenda. Do me a favor, huh? Don't ask her out."

"Do *you* a favor?" Tiner scoffed. "I'm thinking about doing *me* a favor. Do you always tell people who she can and can't see?"

"Never have," Marty replied.

"Don't start."

Marty flashed his palms in surrender as he moved to join Floyd and Brenda. "Just know when to say when."

"Sorry about that," Keller said, returning to the foursome. Then to Tiner, "We have to go. The captain's called a briefing for a pre-op review on that vice sting being set up this weekend."

"I thought that meeting was for tomorrow morning?" a confused Tiner replied.

Keller's eyes tightened slightly exposing a reaction she hoped the Santa Ramona detectives didn't pick up on. "I thought so, too. He must have changed it so he wouldn't have to come to work on a Saturday." Keller turned to Floyd, her eyes now soft and friendly. "We didn't get a chance to discuss the ring and the information you've gathered so far."

"We can get together another time and do that," Floyd said.

"Great. How about tonight? Seeing as how you sprang for lunch, I'll even things up and throw in a dinner." Noticing Floyd's hesitation she added, "In the spirit of cooperation, and all."

Facing the option of Lieutenant Bern's cooperation speech should word get back of a one-sided exchange, Floyd accepted. "I suppose. Guys?"

"Can't," Marty said. "Ladies' night out. I got the kids."

Floyd, recalling Marty's last dinner excuse, gave his friend a skeptical look.

"For real this time," Marty whispered to Floyd.

"I'm covering for Henry for a few hours tonight," Brenda said.

The dejection in Brenda's voice and posture was a direct contrast to the elated rise in Keller's. The Sacramento detective lightly clapped her hands together and smiled widely at Floyd, adding a few flirtatious bats of the eyes that drew a sneer from Brenda. Keller wrote her address on the back of her business card and handed it to Floyd.

"My number's on the front. The apartments are in a gated complex. Just buzz the intercom at the entrance when you get there and I'll let you in."

"About seven sound good?"

"Perfect. We should get going. I'll see you tonight, Floyd."

"I don't trust her," Brenda said as soon as Keller and Tiner were out of earshot. "Keller's up to something, Floyd. There's more going on here than a courtesy call between agencies. This case isn't even a case, so why is she so interested?"

"Maybe she's not interested in the case," Marty said.

With Keller and Tiner no longer present, his earlier compassion for his friends' mutual well-being reverted to the routine needling he found acceptable among partners. "Maybe she's interested in Floyd."

"Nobody asked your opinion, Doenacker," she snapped bitterly.

"You're both right," Floyd said. "Keller's up to something, and it has nothing to do with the case." Before Marty could bellow out an "Ah, ha!" and jab another pin prick of jealousy into Brenda's skin, he added, "And I doubt it has anything to do with me. At least on a intimate level."

It set Brenda's mind at ease hearing Floyd downplay Keller's interest in him, but she still had reservations about him meeting with the woman. "So cancel tonight. You've got nothing to gain. They certainly don't know any more than what's in the report."

"And if they do, they ain't giving it up to you, Floyd," Marty said.

"But if I don't go, then we look like we're holding out. We look like the bad guys, like we're keeping secrets. One little complaint like that and Bern gives the ring back to Henry and Turk, or worse, turns it over to Keller and Tiner."

Across the lot Tiner bemoaned his and Keller's own procedural shortcomings. He fell into the passenger seat of their car and blew a sigh of dejection through his frustrated lips. "That kind of sucked that we get called back before getting a chance to find out more about that ring."

Keller smiled from behind the steering wheel. "Or before you got a chance to make your move on that detective."

Tiner blushed through his denial before making a half-hearted attempt at changing the subject. "Something big must have happened for the captain to call a meeting so close to an op kicking off."

"Nothing happened," Keller told him from behind her mischievous grin. "I paged myself as we walked out of the restaurant."

"Paged yourself? Why?"

"Change of venue. I want to get King out of his comfy little town and away from his friends."

"That was expecting a lot, don't you think? What if he refused to meet? And what if his partners were free to join him?"

Keller shook her head. "I already knew Garibaldi was committed. I heard her agree to take that shift from another detective while we were waiting for that lieutenant to see us. The other one, Doorknocker—"

"Doenacker," Tiner corrected.

"Whatever. He's the only one I took a chance on. King had to show for two reasons. First, he doesn't trust us. He may think we know more than we're telling, that maybe there's more than what's in the case file. Or he may think we're fishing and he wants to know why. Second, he was told to play fair. We gave him something, and we expect something in return. If he backs off, he'll look like he's trying to hijack another one of our cases. In light of his past trespasses, he'll be afraid that won't sit well with our commander or his."

"Okay, so you got him over a barrel as far as meeting us. But you can't force him to talk, and I'm willing to bet whatever he does tell you won't be worth jack shit to us."

"As long as it isn't a lie. And he's not meeting with us, he's meeting with me."

"What?" Tiner's brow creased as he became clearly

annoyed at his surprise exclusion. "Come on Grace. I know you didn't ask to have me for a partner when Sid transferred out, but while I'm here, I'd like to be involved in things more than you've been allowing."

"Relax, Curtis," Keller said in a mothering tone. "This isn't personal. I've got a special project for you."

"I'm guessing Piña's bond got posted," Marty said from the back seat of the sedan. He leaned between the headrests and pointed out the windshield at Rey Piña and Simon Vasquez, who were waiting for the traffic signal to change so they could cross to a public parking lot near police headquarters.

Floyd checked his mirrors and timed a quick lane change ahead of traffic, barely beating the red signal as he turned into the lot ahead of the pair. The unintentional scratching of the sedan's tires on loose gravel as he turned caused Piña and Vasquez to quickly stop and look around for the reckless driver. Piña broke into a smile when he recognized Floyd while Vasquez's face seemed to pinch tighter. Piña changed direction and headed toward the sedan, waving a salute as he neared the detectives.

"Keeng! Ha-ha! You scared thee chit out of me and Sy-mon."

"No problem getting released, I see."

"Nah. Sy-mon's got thee whole process down to an art." Piña laughed. "Eef we get any faster at eet, my release will be processed before my booking."

"Just as long as we don't test that before Monday," Floyd admonished. "Think you can lay low over the weekend?"

Piña winked. "Eet just so happens I'm going to my seester's house een Lodi for a family get-together. I'll be back Sahnday night. Should I call you when I return?"

"No, Rey, that won't be necessary. I trust you to be at the shop come Monday morning."

"Knowing that you'll be there weeth or weethout me, my friend, your trost shall be honored. Good-bye, Keeng."

5
Friday evening, August 15th

Grace Keller's apartment was located in a moderate-sized complex between North Sacramento and Charmichael. Following the directions he roughed out from a copy of The Thomas Guide he kept under his front seat, Floyd snaked his way into town and parked in front of Grace Keller's apartment complex at ten minutes of seven. He stopped at the entrance and checked Keller's apartment number on the complex directory. He pressed the call button. Without any recognition of who stood at the gate, the electronic lock buzzed and snapped sharply. Floyd pushed through and, after getting his bearings, began walking the flagstone path checking for a reasonably close set of numbers. He stopped once and backtracked, then stopped again as the numbers he was following made a dramatic jump in sequence. Turning back yet again, he found himself in front of the manager's apartment. Floyd poised his knuckles to rap on the door but a voice from behind stopped him.

"Don't feel bad. You're not the first to wander lost through here."

Floyd turned to face Keller. "And yet knowing the possibility, I wasn't forewarned."

"My bad," Keller said through a sheepish grin. "Perhaps I overestimated those superior detective skills I've heard so much about."

Keller linked her arm into Floyd's and walked him toward her apartment.

"Skill is achieved through the practice of overcoming obstacles to attain goals. I don't consider myself lost toward failure as much as in the process of finding my way toward success."

"Positive affirmation. The mental road to success. Although one could make a case that it's also a loser's way to skirt around the inevitable loss rather than admit to an inability to succeed."

"Charming *and* insightful," Floyd lauded. "You must have been top of your class in detective school."

"Charming got me in the door," Keller bragged. "Insightful kept me in the room."

They reached Keller's apartment door and she stopped and faced Floyd. Suddenly the soft, inviting green speckles he first saw in her bi-colored eyes faded into the muted brown surrounding them. "It's knowing who to step on that keeps the climb to the top going."

Almost as if on a dimmer switch, the emerald flecks returned and her mouth broke wide, exposing near-perfect white teeth framed by the bright red of her lipstick. The chameleon had changed and Floyd found himself once more struck by her alluring presence. At the same time, his attraction became guarded, tempered by caution. Keller unlocked her apartment door and pushed it open invitingly. Floyd held fast. Keller noted this and she chuckled lightly.

"I just need to get my purse."

Keller returned and locked the door behind her. She took Floyd's arm again and escorted him to the complex carport and a brand new silver Lexus. The car's alarm chirped twice as Keller disabled it and simultaneously unlocked the doors. Floyd's wariness of Keller didn't prevent him from being a courteous gentleman. He opened Keller's door for her before walking around to the passenger side.

Floyd saw Keller's driving as a dead-on reflection of her personality. She carefully maneuvered the car through the confines of the complex, but wasn't so spiritless when she got it onto the open street where she could display power and control.

"Nice car," Floyd complimented, admiring all of the car's interior features. "I bet a few eyebrows were raised the first time you drove it to work."

"More than a few," Keller said. "And a couple of red flags. Internal Affairs. How can a detective afford such an elegant car on such a meager salary, you know?"

"Did you tell them if they saved their lunch money they could buy one, too?"

Keller laughed. "That's good. I wish I'd have thought of that. It would have been wasted on our boys, though. They had their humor administratively removed when they got their jobs. Along with their common sense."

"Nah. Lack of common sense is an application prerequisite."

Keller laughed again. "Don't ever put in for I.A., Floyd. Humor suits you too well. Anyway, the car was a gift of sorts."

"One hell of an admirer."

"Hardly. My ex-husband got a reduction in alimony after losing his job. He was an executive for DNAnalysis."

"The privately-contracted forensic DNA lab? The one that got the ass-whipping by the SEC?"

Keller nodded. "He wasn't in the securities fraud loop, but he lost his position and a substantial investment. The judge took pity on the poor bastard. About three months ago I found out he got a new job, another executive position, and took his unreported signing bonus shopping. Needless to say, my attorney took less pity on him than the judge. I got his new car as part of a settlement to keep him out of court."

"Well done."

Keller nodded her thanks. "I understand you were married once before, weren't you? Did you get hammered in the divorce?"

"At first. She moved off to Colorado, took our daughter with her, and I had to come up with half of what my life was worth to pay her off. But in the end I came out ahead. I got my daughter back."

"A complete pay-off? No alimony?" Keller shook her head when Floyd smiled and nodded. "You got off lucky. She could have attached herself to you like a leech."

"I made the right concessions, didn't fight the assault against my dignity. She remarried a year later, so I'm off the hook financially."

"What about emotionally?"

"I don't like failure or leaving things open ended so, yeah, it still bothers me a little. I saw it coming so it's not like we just woke up one day and said it's over. I think by the time we both realized our problems we were already too far apart to fix things. We both gave up. I used to wonder if it could have turned out differently, but ... we'll never know. You?"

"I knew. Not many missed signals when you walk into a room where your spouse is having an orgasm and you're not giving it to him. It shook me up at the time, but I got over it." Keller smiled and squeezed the steering wheel. "Any lingering ill feelings now are remedied with a nice drive around the city."

Keller pulled off the main street and into a commercial district containing a number of shops, restaurants, and bars. She guided the car down a side street and pulled into a parking lot.

"I take it we aren't picking up your partner. Will he be meeting us inside the restaurant?" Floyd asked as Keller deftly guided the car into an empty space.

"Curtis won't be joining us," Keller said. "Some work suddenly came up that we felt would best be taken care of before tomorrow."

Floyd saw through Keller's misdirection but allowed it to pass, offering a sympathetic "As things tend to do" in lieu of a sagacious "How convenient".

With her father out for the evening and her boyfriend on the road with Sacramento State's football team, Shelby King dropped onto the sofa in front of the television for a quiet night of pizza and Antonio Banderas on DVD. When Floyd called her from work to tell her of his dinner plans, she couldn't have been more encouraging in the face of an empty house and an extended, undisturbed hot soak in the bathtub. She felt completely relaxed in her favorite loose sweats and thick cotton socks. Her dark blond hair that spent most of the day strangled behind her head in a ponytail hung damp and loose over the towel draping her shoulders. She reached for the remote with one hand and one of her father's beers with the other and took a quick, appetite-wetting sip as she aimed the remote at the television. As soon as she pressed the power button, the doorbell rang. Shelby emitted a low, disgusted groan at the door but didn't think twice about not getting up to answer it. She muted the audio and waited quietly for her unwanted visitor to leave. She thought sufficient time had passed in silence, but as soon as she pointed the remote and returned the sound to the TV, the ring returned, as well.

Shelby gave the controller a traitorous scowl, shut off the TV and DVD player, and got up. With catlike stealth she padded down the entry toward the door, not wanting the sound of her approaching footsteps to encourage the unsolicited visitor's loitering. Stopping short of the door, Shelby stretched her neck until her eye could see through the door's peephole. She pulled back, emitting a sigh mixed of pleasure and dismay.

"Hi, Brenda," Shelby warmly greeted as she pulled the door open invitingly.

Brenda saw the towel around Shelby's neck and her damp hair and her face fell apologetic. "I'm sorry, Shel. I hope I didn't get you out of the shower."

"You didn't. I decided to give my scalp a break and air dry. Come in. Have you eaten? I've got plenty here."

"No thanks. I got a quick bite earlier." As she stepped into the front room from the entry, Brenda saw the pizza and beer and open DVD case on the coffee table. She pivoted off a halted step and turned back to the front door just as Shelby closed it. "Geez, honey. I am interrupting, aren't I? I should have called first."

"Don't be silly, Brenda. Door's always open for you and Uncle Marty."

Brenda couldn't help flashing a disjointed smile hearing Shelby refer to Marty as "uncle". Shelby had been calling him that for as long as Brenda had known her and, according to Floyd, since the girl first learned to speak.

"You sure I can't get you a plate?"

"I'm fine."

"At least have a beer with me." Shelby returned from the kitchen with an opened bottle and handed it to Brenda as she joined her on the sofa. "They're dad's. I'm trying to get him to cut back, keep his waist trim. He doesn't listen too well so I've resorted to drinking them for him."

Brenda accepted the bottle and gave it a slight hoist. "To Plan B," she toasted.

"So, what's up?" Shelby asked after an extended moment of silence. Though she suspected Brenda's visit had something to do with her father's dinner with the woman detective from Sacramento, she didn't want to make Brenda uneasy by pressing the issue.

"Not much. I was in the area and thought I'd stop by. I haven't really seen much of you lately. I was just wondering how you're doing, how things at work and things with Ken were going. You know, catch up with you."

Though Floyd hadn't made a big production of it, Shelby was aware of the increased interest between Brenda and him. Shelby always liked Brenda and was disappointed when the "little fling" she and her father had didn't amount to much more than that. There always existed a strong attraction between them, but it was tempered by a fear of each one hurting the other. Brenda and her father hadn't enjoyed much success in maintaining relationships with others, and neither one seemed anxious to test their professional partnership and personal friendship with another futile commitment. A big change in both of them and between both of them, though, came after her father was shot.

Shelby saw how deeply shaken Brenda became at her father's close brush with death. She heard Brenda's muted cries in the hospital corridor outside his room in intensive care and her constant reassurance to her father that she would be there for them. Brenda never broke from her steadfast vigil in the waiting rooms and lobbies as Floyd was moved from wing to wing and finally home as his condition progressed. Her father seemed stronger for that, knowing Brenda was watching over him, that the responsibilities for the daughter he was unable to look after were being met with as much care and attention as he would have provided. While at home, not a day passed that Floyd didn't ask about Brenda, and every single inquiry met with a short note or card or a phone call in lieu of her presence.

"Everything's going well," Shelby told her. There was another too-long pause, and Shelby could see Brenda's growing distraction and discomfort. "Is there anything you want to talk about, Brenda?"

"Huh? No. Not really." Brenda blew at herself a little disbelieving snort. "I didn't need to come here. I just ... I should go."

Brenda started to get up but Shelby slid across the sofa and stopped her with a hand to Brenda's forearm.

"It's okay, Brenda. I want you to stay."

Brenda sat back down. Her eyes got misty as she fought to hold back the cry she felt coming. She sucked in a deep breath and held it for a second. "Shit," she exhaled. Then she laughed.

"It bothers you that he went out tonight, doesn't it?" Shelby asked.

"Yeah. I guess it does," Brenda admitted. "And I know it shouldn't."

"Yes, it should," Shelby countered. "And it should bother you when he goes out with Uncle Marty. Or with me. Or when he stays late at work. It should bother you any time he's not around, Brenda, because you care about him."

"I do. And it's getting to the point where I feel a commitment needs to be made." Brenda swallowed hard. "I'm afraid, kiddo. With your dad there's more for me to lose than just 'us'. There's work, being around you ..."

"So there're no guarantees. I learned that when dad

and mom split up. It was reinforced when dad almost died on the floor at the other end of this sofa. The three of us went through hell not long ago. I saw what it did to you, Brenda, and I saw what you did for us. You already made that commitment to him then. And to me. But mostly to yourself."

Brenda leaned into Shelby and gave her a hug. "You're a wise kid, Miss King. Wise like your old man. I wish you could tell me it's right."

"Like Uncle Marty says, if it ain't right, then it's gotta be left. But if it's left because you're afraid to face it, then you'll never know if it could'a been right."

Brenda fell back into the chair and rolled her eyes. "God help me," she groaned to herself, amused. "I'm getting advice from a woman almost half my age quoting the warped mentality of a man I can barely stand."

"And following it," Shelby gloated.

"Somebody send the devil an overcoat. I think Hell's starting to get a little chilly."

"You haven't told me about East Pines. I would think that would be the highlight of your career."

Keller raised the subject as the busboy finished clearing their table and the waiter poured their coffee. It was a continuation of the conversation that dominated their meal as she and Floyd volleyed war stories back and forth. She had had, as Floyd discovered, a rather distinguished resume of case closings, but her accomplishments, while earning her high marks among her peers in the state's capital city, were hardly as media worthy as some of Floyd's. Keller found it strange that Floyd would intentionally skirt the topic.

"Yeah, a lot of people would say that mess in East Pines, catching Sylvan Fitch and all, was big. But there was a close, personal loss I had to deal with, as well as some other life changes I was going through. My highlight ...?"

Floyd took a sip of coffee and paused, letting the cup hover in front of his mouth. He stared into the steam rising in front of him as if looking mystically into the hazy past as he described one of his first cases which involved finding a missing eleven-year-old boy.

The boy's mother went to pick him up after school. She was late and he wasn't there. Floyd arrived and checked with the teacher and the office. The mother made call after unsuccessful call to anyone who knew him. She was such a wreck that Floyd had to drive her home. The whole way she kept asking him to slow down. She had to see every inch of the way home so she knew she didn't miss anything, miss overlooking her son. It was late afternoon and while it was still bright out, the sun hung noticeably low in the sky. "He doesn't like the dark", she told Floyd probably a dozen times. The woman's husband pulled up to the house just as they did. He'd been driving around the city, too, checking out the parks and neighborhoods. Floyd didn't have to speak to him to realize his mind wasn't in much better condition than hers. Floyd recalled the unnatural look about him. Haunted.

"I found out later that his own brother got kidnapped walking home from school," Floyd explained. "He never saw him again."

"Wow. I imagine all sorts of things went through his head when his wife called."

Floyd recalled the feeling of his own helplessness standing at the door as the parents ran through the house, room to room, checking closets, checking the backyard, desperately calling out for the kid. The mother came back into the kitchen, half-stepping in one direction, then another, her face blanked in confusion. The house she never thought twice about moving freely around suddenly enclosed upon her, became a maze she couldn't solve. She was lost, but not just lost in the house.

"Lost in her own mind," was how Floyd described her to Keller. "She finally dropped to the floor in the kitchen and started crying. It was an exhausted cry. The kind of cry that's all you got left after you think you've done everything but know you haven't, and yet you can't think of anything else to do. It really tore at my gut to stand there because that's all *I* could do. I couldn't cry for them, and it's senseless to try to reassure them that everything's going to be okay."

"Like the old band-aid on the severed leg," Keller said. She'd had her share of emotional victims, usually as the woman cop called to a domestic dispute to sit with the beaten wife. That was the stereotyped part of her profession she dismissed without hesitation. "You know, I asked for a career highlight, so I expect there's a happy ending to all of this."

"About thirty minutes after they tore the house apart the boy comes romping in like any other day, except any other day he wouldn't find a cop in the kitchen standing over his huddled, sobbing parents. Turns out he had a planned hospital visit with a friend of his for one of their community service projects for their scout troop. Mom and dad just forgot. The phone started ringing off the hook not long after the boy came home. The mother of the boy's friend got their frantic message and felt so bad that she drove to their house to apologize in person. She said she wasn't allowed to have her cell phone on inside the hospital and was so used to not turning it off that she forgot to turn it back on."

"And this is a blue-ribbon career story, why? All in all, you basically didn't do anything."

"You're right. I didn't." Floyd grinned and let his comment stand, much to Keller's annoyance.

"If you and I were partners, I'd have to believe we'd be at each other's throats a lot. You'd make me think too much."

"That afternoon I learned you can't have life to the point all the time," Floyd told her. "All the theories and statistics and profiles, procedures and practices and preparedness ... The only thing that's for sure in our line of work, and as my lieutenant religiously reminds me, is that shit's gonna happen."

"How profound," Keller said drolly. "Speaking of shit, let's get down to business and talk about the Farnsworth shit."

"You mean the ring."

Keller's eyes narrowed and her tone shifted to mildly accusing. "You know what I mean."

"What do you want me to tell you?" Floyd asked, shrugging innocently. "That we uncovered information that Edson Farnsworth is alive and well and living a secret life calling bingo numbers in an Indian casino? Or that he's dead and some fisherman hooked his ring-clad severed hand somewhere along the American River and tried hocking the jewel? I can't."

"But what you do know—what *I* suspect you know— you're withholding. I've done my homework, Floyd. And I've talked to people. You do a soft-shoe to get close to other peoples' investigations, but won't hesitate to put on the boot when they get close to yours."

"Sounds like you've been talking to Mark Lomas."

"Among others, though he probably had the least amount of praise for you."

Floyd chuckled. "President of my fan club, he's not."

"So now you're dancing around me. I want to know why."

"I'm not dancing around you, Grace. I'm not even dancing *with* you." Floyd took a sip of coffee. It had become cold and bitter and he slid it aside in favor of the inch of melted ice in his water glass.

"That's because I don't dance, Detective," Keller remarked.

"You *can't* dance, Detective," Floyd shot back. "That's why you have to resort to sophomoric tricks like paging yourself."

Floyd watched Keller's eyes dart away from his as his comment hit the mark and stuck. Floyd didn't intend for their get-together to turn into a joust, but he certainly didn't intend on letting Grace Keller continue to play the innocent, above-board, just-doing-my-job cop.

"I've got nothing to gain by hiding anything from you," Floyd continued. "The fact of the matter is we found a ring and now we're trying to find the owner. It's only coincidence that links our department's case to your department's case. I'm not looking for brownie points. I just want to complete an investigation. If my case happens to grind against yours, too bad."

Keller's eyes locked back on Floyd's. Like the stone of a mood ring, their luster once again faded to a muddied hue, cold and unappealing. She flagged down the waiter and asked for the dinner check. He returned with her credit card and the final bill, which she signed with hardly a glance at the total. She pulled her keys from her purse and rose from her seat.

"Dinner's over. Let's go."

The knock at the door was the last thing she wanted to deal with tonight. Collette Farnsworth had spent the entire evening at the organizational center of Sacramento's annual Festival of Fine Arts, the chairperson with the chair no one wanted to occupy. With a financial standing straddling the borderline between upper- and middle-class, this was the type of self-sacrifice she was forced to make to maintain acceptance in the higher echelon of a society that was once her right. She blamed her husband for the deterioration of status that changed her into the upper-class equivalent of a street-corner day worker relegated to an assortment of odd jobs others deemed beneath them.

So went another night of pimping business owners and entrepreneurs to needy causes. For that, she was awarded nothing more than a token place among those she once dominated, a place where she could get her picture in the society pages and reaffirm, at least to herself, that she belonged. It was a place where she once looked down on the poor pretenders that held those chairs for her, those wannabes who made that unconscionable justification that their time could compensate for their small portfolios. Now it was her turn to look up from below. Collette took solace in knowing some of those women offering her nothing more than a courteous, tight-lipped and toothless smile in passing would eventually fall from grace. She cursed every one of them as much for their arrogance as for the fact that their fall would land on her and bump her down another rung or maybe off the ladder entirely to complete her aristocratic demise.

Another knock. A harder one. The hard rap of a

hand that knew she was home, one that demanded to be answered. She approached the large, oak double doors, crossing a tall pane of frosted glass through which she could see the shaded outline of a single human form under the porch light. She released the deadbolt but kept the security chain attached, opening the door to the chain's length.

"Can I help you?"

"Yes ma'am. Are you Collette Farnsworth?"

The man's question wasn't really one. He could have just as easily said "You are Collette Farnsworth" in the same knowing tone and not altered the intent. There was an ominously familiar ring in his presentation, too, similar to an encounter she had years earlier. Farnsworth closed the door slightly and unhooked the chain. When she reopened the door, the man was, as she expected, displaying a police badge.

"Yes. I'm Collette Farnsworth. I'm guessing you'd like to talk to me."

Grace Keller pulled her Lexus into the carport behind her apartment and parked. Floyd got out and walked around to her door, but unlike when they left the complex and when they arrived at and left the restaurant, Keller didn't allow Floyd the opportunity to assist her with the car door. He simply waited until she extracted herself from the vehicle and followed her to her apartment door. The silent walk was a continuation of their drive. With nothing having been said between them since leaving the restaurant, it was as if Keller signed off the dinner tab and signed off on Floyd at the same time.

Floyd waited as Keller unlocked her door. There was no

thought as to staying, only thought about what to say in concluding the evening. Floyd had been wary of Keller from the moment he met her in Bern's office, and distrustful of her since spying her reflection in door window at Loredo's as she made the phone call to herself. There was more to her reaction tonight than getting a hand caught in a cookie jar. The whole Farnsworth business appeared to strike a nerve in Grace Keller. It was tinged with an anger that went beyond any obsession Floyd ever surrendered to, even the emotional drive that smoldered when they found young Bill Anders in East Pines. It was personal, determined and laced with venom.

Toward me? Floyd wondered.

The apartment door swung open and Keller turned to Floyd. The stalemate on who would speak first could have continued indefinitely, but it was clear to Floyd he would have to concede the last round to her. She bought him dinner, so he owed her at least thanks for that.

"If anything comes up, I'll call and let you know." Floyd thought that adding a no-hard-feelings gesture of cooperation would placate her ire. It didn't.

"And if anything comes up on our end," she echoed icily, "I'll let you know."

Keller stepped toward the opened doorway, but her temper got the best of her. She spun on her heels and pointed a cautioning finger at Floyd.

"I'm watching you, King. Just so you know, just so you don't forget there are more people affected by what you do than just Floyd King."

"You mean people like Edson Farnsworth's wife and the partner he ruined." Floyd knew Keller's warning was aimed specifically at him, an attempt at intimidation or, at the very least, a boundary being set. It was a misstep on Keller's part allowing Floyd to maintain the noble high road. "Because, naturally, we should all be working toward what's best for them. Don't you think so?"

"You know what I mean."

"Do I? And if I need it spelled out more clearly?"

Keller shook her head and entered her apartment. "I'm sure you'll figure it out yourself, Detective."

6
Saturday morning, August 16th

"Good morning, sunshine."

The early greeting was courtesy of Marty, who had seated himself at Floyd's kitchen table, a cup of coffee in one hand, a slice of buttered toast in the other, and a copy of the Sacramento Bee spread out before him. The detectives had decided to introduce themselves to Collette Farnsworth as their first order of business this day, a day that started earlier than Floyd anticipated. Wearing only a T-shirt and boxers, Floyd ignored Marty and shuffled across the linoleum to the coffee pot. He poured himself a cup and returned to the dining area, taking a seat opposite his friend.

"You couldn't put on a robe?"

Floyd looked at Marty sleepy-eyed over the smoldering rim of his mug. "You don't like my morning attire, don't break into my house."

"I was thinking more for your daughter's benefit than mine. Hell, I've seen you bare-assed naked. And more than once."

"Where is my daughter, anyway?"

"Headed out to the university to have breakfast with Ken. She's going to try and get some sideline passes for me and the boys for the game against UC Davis."

Floyd sat back, yawned, and stretched his legs. "I knew there was a reason why you continue to hang around with me."

"Nothing wrong with abusing one's friendships." Marty

took another slice of toast and slid the plate to Floyd. "Have a piece. I made it for you."

"Liar. You *left* some for me."

"How was dinner last night?"

"The food was good. The service was so-so. The company turned out to be a little less than pleasant in the end."

"Awww," Marty pouted. "No goodnight kiss?"

"I got admonished."

"I take it our colleague from down the road still thinks we're holding out. What did you tell her?"

"That our case revolves around finding the owner of the ring and nothing more. She didn't buy it. She seemed rather doubtful of our intent."

"God, and she just met you, too," Marty laughed through a mouthful of toast.

"What's that supposed to mean?"

Marty choked down the bread as his face lit up and stretched cartoonishly wide. "Floyd, you're like an eighteen-year-old girl walking around in a blouse with an extra button undone who pretends to not know why everyone is looking at her. You draw attention to yourself, which isn't necessarily bad until you start shooing people away. *That* tends to draw even more attention."

"Great. Now I'm the equivalent of a high school tease. All I did was ask for a little report for some background information."

"From a police agency that ended up publicly embarrassed not too long ago by a local detective—you—who solved a case they should have solved, a case they didn't even know you were looking at until *after* the fact. The nerve of them being suspicious."

"That's why I had Bern call ahead this time, so they'd

know I was poking around. I didn't expect to incite damn cries of conspiracy throughout Sacramento."

"Hell, if I were their chief I'd make you wear a GPS device every time you crossed inside the city limit. And let's not forget one other thing. You don't trust Keller, either."

"More so now than before. She's taking this whole matter personally." Floyd shot up a hand before Marty could open his mouth. "Don't give me any of that crap about how she's just determined like me."

"I was going to say obsessed like you, but go ahead."

"I mean personally like if Edson Farnsworth is found her reputation is going to take a severe hit."

"I don't see how. She wasn't involved in the original investigation."

"Maybe there's a promotion on the line. She admits she squashed some toes on her way to the bureau. Clearing old cases can go a little ways in healing wounds."

"Or maybe someone gave her a no-winner to put her in check. I mean, think about it. If Edson Farnsworth doesn't happen to pop up somewhere, she can't lay claim to keeping you at bay. If for some reason he does, she's screwed because of you. I'd take it personally, too."

"But we're not looking for Edson Farnsworth," Floyd reiterated with as serious a face as he could hold. "We're tracking down thieves who stole a ring for the possibility of returning it to its rightful owner, whomever that is."

Marty stretched forward and pulled the plate of toast toward himself, then got up from the table with it before Floyd could take a piece.

"What are you doing?"

"I'm putting the food away," Marty called back from the

kitchen, "because the plate of bullshit you're dishing out will be enough to get us both through the day."

Collette Farnsworth's custom home was situated just below the crest of a small rise on the eastern end of town. It was a located in an enclave of ten 1950's ranch-style houses all set on well-maintained half-acre lots shaded by oaks and sycamores, and not one worth less than a few million dollars. Driving along the street one could see the obvious attention put into design as each home retained a secluded appearance while each manicured yard melted seamlessly into the next to create a sense of neighborhood. It was a rural oasis buffered from nearby Santa Ramona by a few rolling hills and quieted by the large trees whose branches reached out to block the audible discharge of the nearby town.

Floyd and Marty parked on the street and walked along the semi-circular driveway. As they approached the front door and took their familiar positions aside each other on the trellised veranda, Marty raised the back of his hand to Floyd's shoulder in light restraint.

"Can I lead this time?"

"What?"

"For years we've been coming up to doors and businesses and whatnot, and you always knock or lead in, and then you introduce us as Detective King and Detective Doenacker. Makes me feel like ... well, not second class, 'cause I know you'd never treat me like that."

"I've never thought of you as anything less than an equal partner," Floyd acknowledged.

"For which I'm grateful. But sometimes it's like 'Hi, I'm Mr. King and this is my wife'."

"You don't find me attractive?"

"Cut it out. I'm being serious here."

"Sorry."

"I'd just like to drive the horses once in a while, that's all."

Floyd extended his hand toward the door and took a step back. "I'll ride in the coach."

Marty nodded his appreciation and leaned in to knock on the door. He gave it four strong raps and fell back alongside Floyd, though keeping his shoulder in front of Floyd's as a measure of dominance.

"And I do."

"You do what?" Floyd asked.

"Find you attractive." Marty bit his lip and winked. "Of course it would never work out."

"I'll take your word on that," Floyd sighed thankfully.

The large oak door pulled back and Collette Farnsworth stepped into the open door frame with a cordless telephone receiver pressed to her ear and a tall glass filled with ice and a clear liquid in her free hand. She was a wiry woman, tall and thin. Her presence reeked of money through the Lilly Pulitzer floral dress, Versace shoes, and assorted golden ornaments decorating her ears, neck, fingers, and wrists. Her carefully tended, highlight-tipped brown hair framed a narrow face with skin pulled tighter than a drumhead. She held up her reedy index finger from the glass as Marty began to speak. In response, Marty held up his badge. Farnsworth surrendered her eyes skyward and shook her head. She excused herself from her caller, promising a return call shortly, strongly emphasizing 'shortly' as she leveled her eyes at Marty.

"Mrs. Collette Farnsworth? I'm Detective Doenacker and this is Detective King. We'd like to speak with you, if you don't mind."

"Not again," she groaned in dismay.

"Not again?" Marty echoed. "Have we met somewhere before, ma'am?"

"Not us. The other officer."

Marty looked at Floyd, who responded with a puzzled shrug.

"No, not him, either. The man who stopped by last night."

The three stood on the doorstep silently staring at one another until Farnsworth threw up her full hands. It was clear to the detectives this woman had a recent encounter with the police and was confusing that visit with their visit.

"You have no idea what I'm talking about, do you?" she asked.

Marty fell back a step, his shoulder now behind Floyd's, and surrendered his position of authority to his partner. "Take the reins, dear," he whispered.

"You'll have to excuse our confusion, Mrs. Farnsworth," Floyd apologized. "We don't know anything about an officer coming out to meet with you."

"Well, one was here, all right. And judging by how quickly he got to my door after I arrived home, I'd say he was camped out waiting for me." Though both encounters were equally unexpected and annoying to her, Farnsworth's irritated tone took a directional shift from the Santa Ramona detectives to the officer who appeared at her door the previous night. "He said his name was Tiner."

"Young guy? Dark hair, with a trim build?" Floyd asked.

"Young is a relative term, but yes, I'd say that's him," she confirmed. "Don't you officers keep track of who's doing what down there at headquarters?"

"Detective Tiner doesn't work for Santa Ramona,"

Floyd explained. "He's with the Sacramento Police. What did he want?"

"Probably the same as you two. He wanted to know about Edson."

"Your husband," said Marty in a for-the-record clarification.

"*Ex*-husband," she rasped with contempt.

Floyd continued. "What specifically was the officer's interest in your ... in Mr. Farnsworth?"

"He wanted to know if I'd seen him recently."

"And?"

Farnsworth's chin lifted as she sneered, "And I told him the only reason I'd have to see Edson would be to identify his body in a morgue."

"Mrs. Farnsworth, could we step inside and speak? We need to get a couple of things clarified, in particular Detective Tiner's visit."

Collette Farnsworth sighed, blowing her alcohol-tainted breath at the detectives. She reluctantly stepped aside and motioned Floyd and Marty into the large entry. The interior carried the rustic theme of the exterior with oak hardwood floors and earthy-toned colors mixed in the walls and furniture fabrics. Farnsworth led the detectives into the front room and offered them seats on one end of the curved sectional sofa arcing around a burl coffee table. She sat at the opposite end and presented her edited version of what she suspected they wanted to hear based on what Tiner attempted to cull from her.

"Edson's been gone for ten years. The termination of our marriage was settled quite some time before he left. Any bank lawsuits that tried extorting me as a means of compensation have long been dismissed. I don't understand the sudden interest in him." Farnsworth paused to take a drink. "So, what then? You find his body or something."

Floyd found Farnsworth's comment was amusing in its indifference. He produced the ring from his pocket and showed it to Farnsworth. She expressed what was becoming the standard reaction by dropping her jaw, but hers was more of genuine surprise than awe. And it was sobering. Farnsworth set her drink on a small glass end table then took the ring from Floyd.

"Or something," Floyd said.

"I'll be damned, if I'm not already."

"You recognize the ring," Floyd observed.

Farnsworth nodded as she stared at the jewel. "It's Edson's, all right. He bought it twenty-odd years ago. I think this is the first time I've ever seen it off his finger." She looked up at Floyd and Marty with an inquisitive smirk. "Or maybe it was still on when it was found?" To the lack of a response by either man she said of the ring, "I guess he made a complete and clean break when he decided to leave."

"According to what I read, your statement at the time, you told him to leave."

"I told him he *could* leave. Just as long as he didn't screw me over." Farnsworth waved her hand around majestically at the array of high-end furniture and art in the room. "As you can see, he didn't."

"Was a divorce pending at the time he disappeared?" Marty asked.

Farnsworth laughed. "You say 'disappeared' like an alien craft came down a plucked him off a street corner. He planned his trip, Detective. He packed. He took sixty-five thousand dollars in cash out of our wall safe. He left, plain and simple."

"Sixty-five thousand?" Marty repeated.

"Yeah, well, he got to it before I did," she muttered, expressing dismay, clearly disappointed in herself.

"But no threat of a divorce settlement?"

"Hell, no. Edson wouldn't have dared. He knows I would have bled him dry if he filed any papers on me. That's why I made the deal with him."

"What deal?" Floyd asked.

"Any time he wanted out, he could pack and go. As long as he left a roof over my head and money to live off. *Sufficient* money. I do have standards to maintain. The only other stipulation I placed on him was that if he left, he could never come back. Ever."

"And if he did?"

"He'd wish he hadn't."

Floyd's eyebrows pulled up, his interest peaked. "That sounds like a threat."

Farnsworth laughed so hard she coughed. "Hell, yes, it was!"

"It's not the kind of threat to be taken lightly with a man missing, ma'am," Marty said.

"That's not the kind of threat to be taken lightly, ma'am," she mocked. "Goddamn right it isn't. Edson knew he couldn't come back. But not because of me. I had nothing to lose, only more to gain. Edson was a marked man because of the other people he screwed over."

"You mean Len Vossen."

"For one. Len Vossen got the gold-plated shaft. He was left holding the bag for all of the company's debts. If Len hadn't sold his soul to get the banks off his back he'd have been out on his ass. He once told me that if he ever saw Edson again he'd gut him like a fish. You want to talk to an angry man, go see Vossen."

"We might, if things turn in that direction," Floyd said.

"Another man you might want to look up is Peter Lindell."

"Who's that?"

"He was a friend of Edson's who was the lead contractor on damn-near every project the company planned. He was all ready to go with a strip mall renovation in town before Edson pulled out. All the equipment and workers he lined up ... That was a fairly substantial contract to lose. I heard Peter was fit to be tied and went gunning for Edson."

"Did anyone else besides Vossen and Lindell take substantial hits?"

Farnsworth cocked her head in thought, then shrugged. "I'm not sure. I tried to stay out of it as much as I could. I didn't want to end up in court with attorneys and collection agencies thinking I had anything to do with Edson's business. Without a doubt, though, Vossen would know. At least about the people Edson hurt financially."

Floyd noted the drop in Farnsworth's tone in her last comment.

"Was Mr. Farnsworth seeing someone?"

"You mean was he cheating on me? Most likely. Edson had an ego to go along with his money. I couldn't tell you with whom or how often. It seems Edson had a knack for secrecy. We were already sleeping in separate rooms a good while before I suspected he had someone else, and by then I didn't care."

"I see." Floyd saw that Collette Farnsworth was being up front about her belief her husband was fooling around on her, though he doubted she didn't know with whom. He decided not to press the issue. For now.

"I don't," Farnsworth replied. "You haven't told me why the sudden interest in Edson. And don't give me that line about following up the case for administrative purposes. I didn't believe that Sacramento detective when he said it."

"Our interest in Edson has nothing to do with the

Sacramento case, Mrs. Farnsworth," Floyd said. "It's about the ring."

"What about it? Edson tossed a perfectly good life away. Why not the ring, as well?"

"It's not so much the connection between the ring and Edson that has our attention. It's more about the men who tried to sell it. There have been a number of burglaries throughout the county lately, a trend that has grown over the last few years along with the residential growth in places such as Santa Ramona. The two seem to go hand in hand. With the large number of folks who commute out of town, we've felt the increase. The men we're really interested in are those two because they might lead us to solve other break-ins and establish a link to other dealers of stolen goods. That they had Mr. Farnsworth's ring is only part of it. We want to know where they got. Since we haven't caught them yet, we can't trace the ring back from them. We thought we'd take a shot at tracing it forward from Mr. Farnsworth, or in lieu of him, through you."

"Like I said, I haven't seen Edson since he left, and the last time I saw him he had the ring on his finger where it's always been, so no one stole it from me."

"Is there anyone he may have given the ring to? A friend?" Marty asked.

"Edson didn't have friends. At least none he'd give anything of value to."

"What about—?"

"The other woman?" Farnsworth broke in, reading into Marty's thought. "Edson wasn't a giver, gentlemen. He wasn't a sentimentalist, either. No tokens to leave behind for good times sake. Nothing to remember him by."

As it was clear Collette Farnsworth didn't have any information about the ring or her husband that would make additional questions fruitful, Floyd changed the subject to the recently discovered second reason for their visit.

"About the encounter you had yesterday evening. You gave me the impression Detective Tiner was also interested in your ex-husband."

"That he was."

Farnsworth told Floyd that Tiner said he had been assigned to clean up a few old cases, and Edson's was one of them. Collette admitted she became intrigued when Tiner told her he might have uncovered evidence that Edson had been sighted back in town. Collette, though, maintained that any report on the return of Edson was unconfirmed unless she saw him with her own eyes.

"I told him the same as I'll tell you two: Edson would be a fool to show his face anywhere on this side of the Sierras, maybe even the Rockies, and not for sure safely west of the Mississippi."

"Did Detective Tiner say what evidence he had?" Floyd asked.

"No. And he sure as hell didn't tell me about that ring."

"I'd say not, judging by your reaction when you saw it."

"By the way, what's going to happen to it?"

"Assuming we don't find Mr. Farnsworth?"

Farnsworth choked out a cackling laugh and her tightly stretched cheeks strained around a smile that should have torn at the corners of her mouth. Without saying a word she set the odds low that the ring would ever land on her ex-husband's finger again.

"Once we've completed our investigation it will be turned over to our property room and held until a formal claim is filed. Assuming no one has a stronger claim to ownership than you, they'll arrange for its release."

"The only person who'd have a stronger claim than me would be Edson himself, but he'd have to show up." With a victorious smirk, she added, "I'll have my attorney prepare the necessary papers in the morning."

Floyd left his business card with Collette Farnsworth and asked that she call him, discreetly, if she received any other unsolicited police visits, especially by Tiner or Keller, in the future. He also asked that she keep the matter of her ex-husband's ring between them, explaining that it would expedite its release if there weren't additional claims to sort through. Floyd added as an incentive, "You also never know what creditors might crawl out of the woodwork if they find out Mr. Farnsworth still has more assets to pick from."

Drink in hand, Collette Farnsworth saw the two men to the door. There were no wishes of good luck or thanks exchanged, and good-bye took the form of Farnsworth's rather halfhearted "Let me know what you hear" to which Floyd gave an equally indifferent nod of the head. Out at the curb, Floyd leaned back against the front quarter of the sedan and stared at the house. Marty stood propped inside the opened passenger door, resting an arm on the car's roof and an arm on the top of the doorframe.

"Well?" Marty asked.

"Well, what? Keller got over on us. I should have suspected something when Tiner didn't show up at the restaurant."

"Not like any of us figured they'd pull a cheap diversion like that."

Floyd brought up the subject of Keller's self-page at Loredo's, in which Marty found a degree of humor. Not Floyd. He was angry enough with himself for not anticipating Keller pulling a follow-up routine and wondered if Tiner had made it as far as talking to Len Vossen. Or further. Perhaps far enough to scare off Piña's two thieves, in which case he might as well leave the ring with Collette Farnsworth right then and there.

"What do you make of Mrs. Farnsworth?" Marty asked.

"I'd say it's a safe bet Edson won't be coming home soon."

Floyd pulled himself from the fender and walked around the front of the car to his door. He dropped behind the wheel and started the engine as Marty joined him on the passenger side.

"Let's go back to the squad room," Floyd said. "I need to make a phone call."

❧

Grace Keller detoured on her way to work that morning. It seemed a long time since she cut her way into the foothills north of Sacramento, surely since spring when the hills were lush from the late winter rains, she thought. The pastures had since turned dry and thin, with only splashes of faded green brushed into the pale brown grasses. By late afternoon dust devils would kick up in patches of dirt cleared of any vegetation courtesy of the small herds of grazing livestock still maintained by the few remaining ranchers.

She took a frontage road leading to a narrower dirt road that ended at a locked vehicle gate. She knew the gate well. It was a portal to a special place for her, taking her back to a magical land in a little girl's mind. Her father brought her here to walk, to talk, to listen and be listened to. It was a place where she felt closest to her mother, whom she lost at such a young age. A place where she watched the burdens of her father, a career police officer and single parent, melt away like a spring thaw. A place where his smile came naturally, where his stride became light and youthful. It was a sanctuary where the weight of the world came off his shoulders, making room for a little girl upon them. When she grew bigger, he'd release his hold on humanity and fill his hands with hers. And when he became too weak to go with her, she'd bring back a piece of their escape to share with him—a piece of dirt to rub between his fingers or fresh blades of grass to break and inhale.

Keller got out of her car and lifted herself over the gate. She walked along one of the two ancient dirt ruts cut into the dry grass that led toward and beyond a large, solitary oak. About three-quarters of the way to the tree, she stopped and stared at the earthy parallel tracks that continued to a distant rise and narrowed to what seemed a single point before falling below the small hill's crest. Her father never took her that far, and she never ventured there herself.

"Where do the tracks end, daddy?" the little girl asked one day.

"They don't," her father replied with a spirited twinkle in his eye. "They go on forever. They'll go wherever your imagination wants them to go."

Today, like every day, Grace Keller imagined they could take her back to him. And like every day Keller bowed to reality and veered away from the tracks, walking instead through the knee-high grass toward the oak.

It was their tree. For years her father had her believe that the spirit of her mother lived in that tree. "That's why it's so dignified and strong, just like your mother", she recalled him telling her. She stopped under the oak and took a seat on a large granite boulder, her princess throne when she was a child. She closed her eyes and let the soft, morning breeze caress her face. The ground sloped gradually downward from the oak's graying trunk to a pond that would all but disappear in a few months. She sat and listened to the world as it should have been, the way it must have been once a long, long time ago. Peaceful. Quiet. It always amazed her how loud silence could be and at the same time how insulating. How calming.

"Don't stop coming here, Grace." Her father made her promise this on one of his last trips to the tree. "Don't let those tracks end. I need you to do this for me, and for yourself."

Her father's heart attack came without warning. That was the first of two major setbacks in his health. The second was the pneumonia he contracted during his recovery. All the while, between trips to doctors and specialists, he found time to come to the oak. Demanded it, actually.

"Are you ready to go home, daddy?" Keller would ask her father as they left the hopsital after he'd been run through a battery of medical tests.

"Sure, Grace. But let's make a stop first, okay?"

Keller often balked at his requests. Her father had been under a microscope, been poked and prodded, for the better part of the day and he looked drained as he labored to her car. She assured the doctor her father would rest, but her assurances didn't take into account her father's stubbornness.

"The doctor said I need some peace and quiet," he countered, smiling deviously. "I can't think of a better place to get both."

It wasn't long before it became increasingly difficult for him to walk. The opening she secretly cut into the fence to make it easy for him to access the trail was now of no service since he couldn't make the hike to it. Keller regretted not being able to carry him the way he carried her those many years ago. Now, with him gone, she had to carry herself. And while she disliked the thought of being alone on her rock, under their tree without him, she continued making regular visits as she promised, at first for him, then for herself.

After he was cremated, Keller took her father's ashes and buried him there. It had been five years since he passed and Keller made the trek as often as she could to sit on her throne, near her father, under the protection of the outstretched arms of her mother's spirit. She had followed him as a child, then followed him as an adult, picking up the burdens he carried for so long and putting them on her shoulders, bringing them here to discard them where they would do no harm. And in the warmth of the morning, she sat and listened as the intense silence swallowed the clamor of the world. It was a world she couldn't keep at bay forever, though.

As Grace Keller made her return trip to Sacramento, the chaotic drone of humanity steadily grew as she emerged from the buffer of the foothills. Pushing her car through the increasing traffic into the core of the city, she felt tightness creeping up her back, into her neck, and down the backs of her arms. The hard exterior that melted as she sat on the shaded rock in the pasture began curing into the tough shell that protected her and defined her character. She would never be mistaken for her father and his warm and gregarious demeanor and easy temperament. By the time she reached the halls of the police department, Grace Keller's emotions had, once again, chilled to the world.

"Grace, you had a phone call this morning."

"Really, Curtis? I don't get but maybe twenty or thirty a day," she said as she passed him with hardly any notice.

"It was from Floyd King."

Keller stopped in mid-stride. "What did he want?"

"To talk to you. I presume it has to do with last night."

"More likely to discuss what you were up rather than our choice of entrées," she said smugly. "My guess is that he met with Collette Farnsworth today and didn't like finding out he was second in line. What did you tell him?"

"Nothing. But he didn't bring the subject up, nor did he want to talk to me. Are you going to call him back?"

"What the hell for? We have as much right to talk with Farnsworth as he does as long as we don't interfere with his case and he doesn't interfere with ours. Until either of us crosses that line, there shouldn't be anything to talk about."

"Why the heck are we even bothering with Edson Farnsworth in the first place? The case was closed years ago and—"

Keller shot an evil, silencing glare at Tiner. "First and foremost, it was assigned to us. That's all you need to know."

"That's all?" Tiner unwisely pushed in front of Keller, blocking her path. "What else is going on here, Grace? This can't be solely about us babysitting King out of fear of him turning up a man who's been non-existent for a decade. What other reasons are you not telling me about?"

"Any other reasons I have are none of your business," Keller snapped. "And if you can't be a good soldier and follow while I lead, then I'll handle this alone."

Floyd made two more attempts to reach Keller. The

Sacramento desk officer maintained that Keller was out of the office on an assignment and had left instructions not to be disturbed until she cleared her surveillance. Floyd recalled her talking about an operation being planned by the Sac detectives for the weekend, and originally dismissed it as more deception on her part owing to the fake call and her open mistrust of him with regard to the missing Farnsworth. The desk officer Floyd spoke to as much as confirmed something was going down somewhere in the city, though he remained, as expected, tight-lipped about it. Floyd simply left another message he knew would go unanswered and let the matter alone. Tomorrow would be his one day off and he and Shelby had a father-daughter lunch planned, something he looked forward to and wasn't about to ruin thinking about Grace Keller and her motives behind warming up to him one minute and icing him off the next. He also had plans to make with Marty and Brenda for Monday morning at Piña's shop.

Floyd locked up his desk and walked out to his car. Away from the police department, the world became a different place for Floyd, more so over the last year. He never clung deeply to life-altering experiences, but his priorities changed since the shooting—some would say dramatically, though Floyd would argue that they were simple adjustments to growing old. The biggest change for Floyd was in being able to disconnect from the job when he wasn't there.

Floyd's history was driven by work. His reputation was built by a dogged commitment to being the best detective on Santa Ramona's force. There wasn't a time, day or night, when his passion waned. He could never seem to find the off switch. Toward the end of his marriage, he never looked.

Part of what drove him was Lynn's fault, he reasoned. As his ex-wife turned her attention to raising Shelby, she shunned Floyd's needs. Floyd, in turn, occupied himself with work, developing a consuming passion that led him to Santa Ramona's detective bureau where his talent and tenacity brought him the success but not the satisfaction he pursued. Floyd continually raised the bar at work, pushing himself to higher rewards both personally and professionally. But Floyd neglected to attain balance, so as the bar rose at work, it fell at home. Shelby knew no difference. She grew up with a father who gave his free time to her. It was different for Lynn, however. As Shelby matured and sought independence, the daughter's ambitions created voids in the mother's life. Unfortunately for Lynn, she had no outside release, no distraction. And she didn't have Floyd, who had become so committed to his job that he neglected his commitment to her. They fell farther apart and their misery compounded, creating a rift between husband and wife expanded by the emptiness of one and deepened by the emptiness of the other.

They tried reconciliation, first for themselves, then for their daughter. The first trip to a counselor concluded with the summation that Floyd and Lynn needed to rebuild their life by building bridges to cross the existing river of separation. But those new bridges of communication and compassion were built atop rotting pilings of resentment and anger and suffering and, unable to support the tremendous weight of Floyd's and Lynn's heavy hearts, they buckled, eventually bringing the bridges to rest below the murky depths of tedium and apathy. In the end, they resigned to having lives situated on opposite banks. Eventually, Lynn left to forge crossings over other rivers.

Though the effects beyond his failed marriage and,

more recently, a failed second engagement made him reevaluate his future, it took seeing Shelby standing bound and gagged with a gun pointed at the back of her head to shake Floyd to the core of his soul and make him understand his world and his life were not just his own. He fought through the searing pain of a bullet ripping a hole in his leg to save his daughter, and fought through the light-headed sensation of life pouring out of him to save himself. When it was over, Floyd came to realize how the world he was continuing to create for himself had the potential to destroy others. And it had to stop with him first.

When Ken stopped by the following morning to see Shelby, Floyd felt a strong urge to invite him on along for lunch instead of running him off. In return for her father's gracious inclusion, Shelby made a quick call to Brenda, who was more than happy to change her plans for an afternoon with the Kings. Floyd bit back his impatience with Shelby as she wrung the humor dry out of double dating with her father as she prepared the sandwiches for the decided-upon picnic. Ken wisely cowered from the desire to laugh with his girlfriend at the expense of her father's respect for him.

After lunch, the younger couple took a walk while the older couple stayed behind to relax, prompting another volley of witticisms from Shelby. Once more, Ken showed considerable restraint and walked away, pulling his giddy girlfriend along by the arm. Before getting comfortable, Floyd cleared the remains of their meal, topped off his and Brenda's plastic cups with wine, then settled back on the blanket. Brenda settled at his side and kissed his cheek.

"This was nice. Thanks for bringing me along."

"You're more than welcome."

"They make a cute couple," Brenda said of Shelby and Ken.

"Not as cute as us," Floyd said, patting Brenda on the hand.

"Yeah, the cute old folks lazing on the blanket."

"I prefer to think of it as conserving energy for more important things."

"Oooo," Brenda cooed seductively. "Such as?"

"Big day tomorrow at Piña's."

"You ass."

Floyd laughed as he blocked Brenda's backhand swat with his forearm.

"What's our plan?"

"Nothing too complicated," Floyd told her. "I figure we hit the shop first thing in the morning and post up inside until our two guests arrive. I can't imagine they'll wait too long to show up if they're as greedy as Rey made them out to be. That means we won't have to wait long, either."

7
Monday morning, August 18th

After unlocking the front doors and flipping the "Closed" side of his business' sign to "Open", Rey Piña went to the rear of his shop and unlocked the alley door. As soon as the lock clicked and released, Floyd, Marty, and Brenda paraded through the door into the rear office.

Piña led his guests through the back room to the front and took what was his customary seat behind a sales counter as if it was just another business day. Floyd and Brenda stood among the rows of free-standing clutter comprised of end tables, lamps, a stack of picture frames propped on end—everything from an armoire to a ceramic zebra—trying their best to look like shoppers and trying their best not to appear disappointed at the selection. Marty took a position inside the rear doorway leading to Piña's office where, judging by Piña's initial objections, the owner's "other beesness" was conducted.

"Eef you see anytheeng you like, I'll geeve you a good discount," Piña told Brenda, who was looking with mild disgust at a candleholder cast in the shape of a naked, sexually embraced couple. "Be careful, though," he teased, noting her nauseated expression. "Thee discount doesn't apply eef you break eet."

"I'd have to touch it to break it," she replied sourly over her shoulder. "That ain't happening, Rey."

Piña laughed. "Weemen, huh, Keeng. You'd theenk they'd be a little more open to thee more classical, romantic peeces."

"This is a piece, all right," Brenda observed.

Not to be excluded, Marty's voice boomed from the back room. "I've always thought that Brenda was rather hesitant to get in touch with her warm, feminine side."

"I'll get in touch up the side of your head, freak!" Brenda barked back, then to Floyd, "If this thing is still here at Christmas, I'm buying it and sending it to his wife."

Piña laughed and shook his head. "You let them carry lo-ded gahns?"

Another two hours passed without a customer. Piña remained behind the counter reading the newspaper for a second time. Marty found a stack of National Geographic magazines from the mid-seventies and was reliving parts of world history that sneaked past him in school when he wasn't paying attention. Floyd and Brenda sat off in the corner out of sight of the front doors and occupied their time with a game of checkers Brenda found stuffed inside a cabinet. Near the half hour, the radio handset at Floyd's side crackled to life.

"Floyd, Turk here." As a favor to Floyd, and without Bern's permission, Turk took advantage of Henry Lepsky's sick day and set up an observation position across the street from Piña's shop in order to give the detectives inside a heads-up call on any potential Jeffs or Cs.

"Go ahead, Turk."

"I've got a tan Plymouth with two guys inside that passed by Rey's for the third time in the last fifteen minutes."

"Hang on a sec," Floyd radioed Turk, then turning to Piña, who lowered his paper and was listening, "Any idea what either guy drives?"

"Not a clue. My guess ees that they don't drive thee same theeng very often."

Floyd turned back to the radio. "Turk, if you can get a plate, call it in to dispatch and have them run it."

"Already got it. I'll phone it in in a minute. The car turned up a side street. I can get in my car and follow if you like."

"Go ahead and get in your car, but sit tight in case they run. We'll never make our car from in here."

"Copy, copy."

"Rey, you don't let folks in the back, do you?"

"Nah. Thee back door ees for me," Piña said with a wink. "They'll come een thee front."

"Here. Put these on." Floyd slid a pair of handcuffs across the counter to Piña and he obliged Floyd by ratcheting them loosely around his wrists.

"Floyd, Turk."

"Go ahead."

"The two guys are on foot and coming back around the corner. One guy's tall and beefy. The other one's a pup, a young white kid."

Floyd looked over to Piña. Piña heard the descriptions over the radio and nodded.

"Sounds like our guys," Floyd affirmed over the radio. "As long as we've got them on foot, see if you can find their car. If you can block it where it's parked, do that and hike on back to us."

"Got it."

"Shall we go shopping, dear?" Floyd asked Brenda.

The couple walked over to a roll top desk and began inspecting it. Floyd kept his back to the door so Brenda could keep her eyes on it over his shoulder without appearing to be doing so intentionally. She rested her hand atop his and gave it a gentle squeeze signaling Jeff's and C's entrance into the shop. Jeff and C exchanged glances upon seeing the man and woman hovering over the desk. Jeff apparently deemed the pair harmless and continued walking to the rear counter to meet with Piña. C hesitated, giving Floyd and Brenda another quick assessment before following his partner.

As soon as Floyd picked up the men in his periphery, he nudged Brenda with his elbow and the detectives fell in behind the pair. C was a few strides behind Jeff, who was halfway to the counter. When C cranked is head back and saw Floyd and Brenda on their heels, his instincts kicked in and he shouldered past Jeff, making a beeline to the doorway leading into the back room and the rear exit.

"Cops," C whispered to Jeff as he brushed by.

It took an extra second or two for the word to register in Jeff's brain, an extra second he shouldn't have wasted. Jeff turned full around and found himself face-to-face with the two detectives. His head snapped from one shoulder to the other and back as he looked for a quick escape within the corral of Piña's merchandise. Finding no avenue before him, Jeff pivoted sharply in the narrow aisle to follow C. As he got the rest of his body turned, Floyd grabbed Jeff's shirt at the shoulder and jerked him back.

"Just stay put and keep your hands where we can see them."

Floyd's command was stern but calm, and Jeff, stumbling to a stop, suspended his half-hearted flight. C, on the other hand, didn't heed Floyd's order to freeze and continued toward the back room. C took a final glance over his shoulder into the shop as he stepped through the doorway and right into Marty, who, responding to his partner's ignored command, simultaneously moved into the doorway to block C's escape. C bounced off the detective's wide frame and, startled by the unexpected bump of Marty's chest, took a reflexive step backward.

"Say 'Excuse me'," Marty told him.

C was a head taller than Marty and, though not as wide, cut an imposing figure standing in the doorframe. He looked down his nose and puffed his chest.

"Fuck you," C replied defiantly as he cocked his arm to throw a clenched fist at Marty's head.

Marty didn't bat an eye as C threw the punch. To C's astonishment, Marty reached forward and caught C's fist in his own massive hand and clamped around it, fingers over knuckles and thumb over thumb. The corners of Marty's mouth curled up toward his cheeks, pushing up his eyes into devilishly narrowed slits. He compressed C's curled fingers into themselves, flattening the ball of knuckles. C's index and pinkie fingers popped out of his fist as if spring loaded but the remaining three digits stayed pinned into his palm by his thumb. Marty continued to apply pressure until the pain registered on C's face. Then he squeezed just a little more and C dropped to one knee.

"Ahhgh! Jesus!" C yelled. "You're breaking my fucking hand, man!"

"No, I'm not ... yet."

"I can't believe this!" Jeff snapped at Piña. "You set us up!"

"I deedn't set you up, you peece of chit!" Piña countered angrily, raising his cuffed hands above the counter.

Turk pushed through the alley doors and stepped carefully around the clog of Marty and C at the interior doorway. He leaned his face closer to the knot of the two men's thick fingers and winced at the controlling grip Marty had applied to C's hand.

"Oooo," he moaned sympathetically to the kneeling suspect. "That looks like it hurts." Then to Floyd, "I found their car and blocked it, but looking around here I'd guess no one'll be running off any time soon."

"Turk, take Mr. Piña out and put him in your car. Marty, Brenda, and I want to have a talk with these two fellas."

Turk waved Piña to come forward and led him out of the shop. Floyd pointed to the chair Piña had occupied and Jeff obediently sat on it. Turning to Marty, who still maintained a tight grip on C's hand, Floyd nodded for his partner to release his captive.

Marty dropped to a knee and met C's pain-pinched, watering eyes. "You gonna behave if I let you up?"

C nodded. Marty eased his grip and raised C to his feet. With his free hand, Marty patted down C's shirt, waistband, and pockets for any weapons. Only when he was satisfied with the search did he release C's hand completely. C held his hand up. The only two fingers he could move were the two outside ones that avoided Marty's crush.

"Shit, man, I can't straighten my fingers out!"

"Hell, I can fix that," Marty offered a bit too willingly. "Stick out your hand."

C yanked his temporarily crippled hand tightly to his chest and massaged it with his other. "Get the fuck away from me!"

"Relax, you baby. They'll feel better in a few hours. If not," Marty raised his hand and extended his own index and pinkie, "move to Texas and become a Longhorns booster."

"What's going on?" Jeff asked Floyd. "We didn't do anything for you to be messing with us."

"We just want to talk."

"You ever thought about asking?" C grumbled, still rubbing his knuckles.

"Before or after you hit me?"

C turned to Marty. "All right, man. My mistake. Still no cause for breaking my hand."

"We'd like some information," Floyd told them. "You two cooperate and we'll save a trip to jail."

Jeff's brow furrowed. "Jail? For what?"

Floyd answered by taking Edson Farnsworth's ring from his pocket and placing it on the counter. "You recognize this?"

Jeff dropped his head and sighed.

"This ring turned up in some property confiscated here last week. It's our understanding you and your friend found it and are looking for a buyer."

"Shit, I was right. Rey rolled over and told you we'd be back today, huh?"

"Rey was a tough fight, but when I tell you what I told him I think you'll cooperate in the same manner." Floyd went on explaining the history behind the ring, playing up the circumstances of Edson Farnsworth's disappearance as mysteriously as possible. He also spelled out the inevitable consequences for those found in possession of it under the wrong circumstances. "Based on what we know, it isn't very likely Mr. Farnsworth gave up the ring voluntarily. So, just like it was for Rey, it would be in your best interest to tell us what you know about where you picked it up."

Jeff looked at C. C shook him off.

"They got nothing," C told Jeff, then defiantly to Floyd, "You got a ring. So what?"

"We've got someone who says you brought it here."

"Who? Rey?" C scoffed. "I'll bet *his* word goes a long way in court, huh?"

"It only has to go far enough to get you in front of a judge, at which point it's only a matter of us asking to get a permission slip to violate your fourth amendment rights," Marty replied. "After that, it's all about sorting what you have from what you own. Or what you can *prove* you own."

Jeff spun toward C. "Dude, I don't want to do jail for some bullshit charge."

"Shut up!" C snapped. "Don't you see? They ain't got shit else they'd have us cuffed up in a holding tank right now."

"It ain't the shit they don't have that worries me. It's the shit they can make out of whatever it is they *do* have."

"Jeff's got a point," Brenda told C.

"We are a creative group," Marty crowed proudly.

"The ring is gone, regardless of how we play it."

"Jeff's right, C," Floyd said. "The ring means nothing now. It's a hot potato. From us to Rey to you to ..."

"If you really want to sit tight on this, I'm with you," Jeff said. "But, goddamn, C, think about all the bullshit we're gonna have to go through."

"I'll bet you don't have receipts for your TV or VCR," Marty mumbled in C's ear.

"Fuck," C sighed. "All right. We'll tell you what you want to know. But right up front, so there's no games later, I want your word you won't pull any backdoor shit on us."

"You don't trust us?" Marty asked, disappointed.

"Them," C pointed at Floyd and Brenda while looking back at Marty, "maybe. You? Your word ain't shit."

"Aw, that's just your hand talking."

"We were working for a guy cleaning up a house he was selling," Jeff said.

"This guy have a name?"

"Eric Champs." Jeff pronounced the last name properly with the French "sh" instead of the hard "ch" that irritated Champs so much. "He's a realtor."

"I've heard of him," said Brenda. "He made a ton of money over in the Bay Area counties in the mid-eighties and parlayed that into another ton around Tracy before coming up here. When the tech industry stalled, he stalled. From what I've read, he's just hanging out in the Sac area until the next boom, not that he needs one any time soon. I understand his bank account is pretty solid."

"That's because he's a cheap bastard," C snarled.

Jeff continued. "A friend of mine who does regular work for Champs asked if we could give them a hand on a job. I guess Champs was in a hurry to get the place fixed up to show, like it was a last-minute deal."

"What was the job?" Floyd asked.

"Paint. Pick up shit. Haul shit away."

"And how did you find the ring?"

Jeff turned from Floyd to C. C rolled his eyes.

"I found it," C reluctantly admitted. "It was on the floor of an old shed we tore down."

"And you found it? Just like that?"

"Just like that," he told the astonished detective. "Picked up a box and there it was."

"More or less." Jeff interrupted to clarify C's rather simple explanation. "There were a bunch of boxes and one C picked up broke out from the bottom. I remember him cussing about having to pick shit up. It must have fallen out of that one."

"What was inside the box?" Brenda asked.

C shrugged. "Clothes."

"Men's clothes or women's?" Floyd asked.

"The one that broke open looked like men's stuff, but nowadays who can tell? The other boxes had different stuff in them."

"You looked?"

"Nah," C said. "Most of the boxes were marked."

"Except for the one that broke," Jeff added. "Didn't have nothing on the outside."

"Did Champs know what was in them?"

"Probably not at the time," Jeff said. "He told us to take all the boxes out of the shed and toss them. I asked him about the clothes thinking he may want to give them to a church or something. He told us he didn't care what was in them, that he was paying us to haul it away. So that's what we did."

"Bullshit," C interrupted. "He said he wasn't into doing charity work and didn't have time to sort trash for the Salvation Army, and that if we wanted to we could pick through it all at our place because he didn't care which dump we took it to."

"Where is this house?" Floyd asked.

"I don't remember the address."

"Me, either," Jeff said. "It was down on Mill Creek Road. Like five or six houses on the right."

"Maybe look for the one with Eric Champs' frickin' 'For Sale' sign stuck in the lawn, detectives."

Finding his smug comment mildly amusing, C chuckled to himself. His humorous moment didn't last long. From behind, Marty's hand wind milled swiftly past C's ear and smacked open-handed on the countertop with a heavy, meaty slap that made C jump sideways. Marty picked up his hand and turned the palm upward to his face then shifted his gaze through his fingers at C.

"Missed."

"I think it's time for a road trip," Floyd announced.

"So we're cool then? Me and C? We can go?"

"Not quite. After you show us where the house is, and after you tell us the names of your friends who work for Champs."

"Aw, man, don't," Jeff moaned. "We're telling you the truth. You don't need to get the others involved. They don't even know about the ring."

"Fine. But I still want to know who they are so I can feel better about who you are. Think of them as character references."

"Or lack thereof," Brenda chipped in.

"Shit. We're gonna have to roll up out of town."

"That's another thing. You guys will stay close to home until we say you're clean. It will upset me to have to go looking for you."

The five exited through the rear door and crowded into the sedan parked in the alley. Marty drove with Jeff at his side to direct him; Floyd sat in back between Brenda and C. Marty pulled onto the main street and passed the side street where Turk sat in his car waiting with Piña. As soon as Turk saw the fivesome drive away, he turned to Piña and thumbed him out the car door.

"Okay, Rey. I guess the show's over."

"For now I suppose, Meester Turk. I no doubt will be seeing you and Meester Henry soon. Probably when you guys come to return my theengs."

Turk and Piña shared a laugh as Turk started the engine.

"Right, Rey. See you in court."

Marty knew the way to Mill Creek Road, so the inside of the sedan remained silent as they cruised along Ramona Road, the main thoroughfare in Santa Ramona, until they reached the point where it bisected Mill Creek. Marty slowed on approach. "Left or right?"

"Left," Jeff told him.

Marty waited for the oncoming traffic to clear and swung the sedan onto Mill Creek. He rolled the car to a stop at the curb and looked over at Jeff.

"It's about five houses down on the right, where the sign's posted." Jeff pointed through the windshield as if the others could follow his aim. "It's kind of tan colored."

Marty guided the car down the street and stopped in front of the tan house with the blue and white "For Sale" sign bearing the flamboyant script of Eric Champs' signature, phone number, and a "By Appointment Only" designation that served as an expression of Champs' arrogance, intended to affix a more exclusive character to himself than to the property. At the bottom of the sign in quotations was Champs' trademark line, "Whatever it takes!"

"Nice place," Brenda commented.

"All looks," C told them. "Lots of cosmetic work. There's some hidden dry rot. Plumbing's not in the best shape. He's probably asking about thirty-, maybe forty-thousand over what it's worth."

"And knowing Champs, he'll probably get it," Jeff added.

"We're not in the market to buy," Floyd reminded them, "just to look. Come on."

Jeff and C led the detectives to the side gate. The pull cord to the gate latch was missing, but C was tall enough to reach over and trip the latch by hand. He gave the gate a nudge and its hinges creaked softly as it swung back to the side of the house. Single file, with C leading and Marty bringing up the rear, the entourage followed the concrete walk to the back of the house. When the yard opened wide C stopped and let the others join him on the patio.

"Looks like nothing's changed since we left it," C told Floyd.

The concrete patio extended fifteen feet from the back of the house. From there, another twenty feet or so, was a lawn in splotched shades of green where newly-seeded blades of grass, thin and pale, mixed with the darker, thick-bladed established patches. Along the fenced perimeter were a variety of flowering plants and low shrubs. Floyd saw there were only two spaces in the yard that didn't support any growth. In the right rear corner was a large square of bare soil. To the left of that lay a smaller, less symmetrical patch of recently turned earth with two dreary-looking shrubs spaced a few feet apart.

"The shed was over there." C pointed to the large void. "In the back corner."

Floyd walked to the site and checked the ground. He tried gouging his toe into the dirt but left only a surface scratch. It was flat and hard soil where the heavy structure obviously sat for a long period of time. Something else, something he felt inside drew him toward a smaller patch of dirt a few feet to his side. Floyd bent over and picked at one of the two withering plants at his feet. Its leaves, like its adjacent twin, were a mottled brown, nothing like the fresh green of the flourishing shrubbery further away. He broke a thin twig with little effort, and the slight snap caused several leaves to jump free and drop to the ground. The dirt at the base of the plants seemed well watered, but the surrounding soil appeared harsh, with more rocks and clods than nutrient-rich loam. Floyd also noted wood slivers and flecks of blue mixed plastic with the soil.

"What was here?" Floyd asked to neither man in particular.

"Weeds," C told him. "A small pile of old wood, like fence planks and end-rotted two-bys and a couple of four-by posts. It was covered with one of those cheap blue plastic tarps. Fucking thing disintegrated when I picked it up. That's the blue stuff you see."

"You turn the dirt, too?"

"Nah. Somebody else must'a done it. Probably Champs. He kept bitching about those being the third set of plants he set down that wouldn't grow and goddamn if he'd plant another set."

"Tell me about the shed."

C shrugged. "It was a shed. A cheap metal one about the size of the square there."

"We cleaned it out, then tore the thing down," Jeff explained.

"And you found the ring inside?" Floyd asked Jeff.

"I did," C said. "There were like six or seven boxes. Like we told you before, the bottom of one broke open and some stuff came out before I caught the flap. I heard the ring hit the floor when I started picking the stuff up."

"And you didn't find any other trinkets with the ring?" Brenda asked.

"No, ma'am."

"It'd be nice to know what else was inside those boxes," Marty said.

"Yeah," Floyd agreed. "Finding some more of Farnsworth's things would be nice." He turned to Jeff and C. "And you guys have no idea who the owners are? You never saw anyone else but Champs here?"

"Just Champs and the two guys who work regular for him," C said.

"And the inside of the place was empty when we got here," Jeff said. "No furniture. No refrigerator. No toilet paper."

"Can either of you think of anything else inside the shed that may have been odd or out of place?"

"It was all crap, as far as I know," C told Floyd. "I mean, hell, the ring itself was way out of place. If I'd have found something more out of place than that, I'd have had Rey working on that, too."

"One thing I find hard to believe," Brenda said, "is that

after finding the ring you didn't pick through the rest of the boxes. What stopped you?"

"Champs," C said. "That micro-managing asshole. Nothing but nagging. Always watching over the shoulder. Believe me, if Champs hadn't been crawling up our butts every five minutes—"

"It started getting late by the time we finished," Jeff said. "I didn't want all that shit sitting in the back of Carl's and Gabe's truck if we missed getting to the dump with them before it closed. And Champs gave them the dump fee. If we waited, we'd have been out that money for maybe nothing."

"Who are Carl and Gabe?" Floyd asked, smiling at Jeff's faux pas.

Jeff cringed in embarrassment at letting slip the names he tried to keep away from the detectives. "Ah, man! Don't. They didn't have nothing to do with this. They don't even know about the ring."

"We helped you guys out," C added. "We're not hiding anything from you."

"Except the names of the other two fellas who were here with you," Marty pointed out.

"Carl's a buddy of mine," Jeff confessed. "He and his friend, Gabe, do a lot of prep work for Champs. Champs was under the gun to get the house ready to show this past weekend, so Carl asked me if I wanted to pick up a few extra bucks. He said I could bring someone along."

"So these guys know Champs pretty well?"

Jeff and C nodded.

"All right. I'll make you guys a deal. Stay close to home—and I mean a place that has a working phone you'll answer—and I'll keep Carl and Gabe off the record. If it comes to having to have them swear you were with them here, I'll tell them Champs gave them up." Floyd's conscientious tone turned warning. "But if either of you disappear or make it hard for us to find you, your heads better be on a swivel. You saw how easy it was to snatch you up this time."

"I guess we got no choice." Jeff wrote a phone number on the back of one of Floyd's business cards. "That's my sister's place. I'm sort of house-sitting there while she and her husband are on vacation. I'll be there for two more weeks."

"If we need you beyond that you'll update me, right?" Floyd asked, implying Jeff would do so. Jeff said he would. "And what about you?" he asked C.

"I'm renting space in the garage. I got no phone."

"He only sleeps there," Jeff interjected. "You'll be able to get him with me most of the time."

"Okay, but most of the time's not good enough." Then, to Jeff, "You've got the phone so you'll be responsible for whatever isn't covered under 'most of the time'. If I call you, you bring him."

Jeff dropped his head and rocked it side to side a couple of times, turning it to reluctant nods as he lifted it.

Floyd thumbed the pair to the gate. "Okay, guys. Take off."

"What? We have to walk?"

"We have some things to discuss that don't concern either of you," Floyd told them.

Marty and Brenda parted to let the disgruntled pair pass. C walked by Marty and gave him a sidelong glance through a watch-your-back sneer that invited a future encounter. Marty read the expression and responded by raising his hand to C's forearm, halting him.

"Thanks for your cooperation," Marty told him in a

manner clearly reminding C of their backroom encounter and how C's cooperation was attained while subtly cautioning C against following through on his desires.

C said nothing and looked down at the large hand resting on his arm. Marty held it for an extra second, then released and let C join Jeff at the side yard gate. As soon as Jeff and C disappeared, he and Brenda walked to the rear of the yard.

"What do you think?" Brenda asked. "Are they being honest?"

"They've got nothing to gain by not being straight with us," Floyd said. "And one thing C said made sense. If they took more than the ring, Piña'd have told me. I don't think Rey would want to be holding anything linking him to those two if Farnsworth turns up dead."

"So the question now is how the ring got here."

"Well, that's *a* question, Marty. An easier one to answer is what connection Farnsworth had to this house. We can place the ring here, but that doesn't mean Farnsworth himself was here. The next logical step is to find out who the owner is and see if they have some association with Farnsworth."

"You mean the ring," Marty reminded his partner. "It's about the ring."

"Finding the owner is no big deal, Floyd. Convincing Bern to let you run out to Sacramento to pull property records ...? You know he's going to make an issue about you digging into Farnsworth's disappearance, which means he'll make an issue about you back-dooring the Sac detectives again."

"Brenda's right," Marty said, adding, "And if Keller and Tiner find out you were poking around without telling them, you know they're going to make some noise. You don't want Bern hearing about it between chiefs."

"I don't plan on either happening. Come on."

Floyd led his partners to the front of the house, stopping near the "For Sale" sign. He pulled out his cell phone and dialed the white numbers painted boldly under Eric Champs' name. He waited through five rings before Champs picked up.

"*This is Eric Champs—*"

"Mr. Champs, this—"

Floyd, not immediately recognizing the mechanical drone in Eric Champs' voice, was interrupted by the continuation of Champs' recorded message bragging to all callers he was currently away from his office "selling another quality home" and asking potential buyers and sellers to leave their name and number on his voice mail.

"*I check it every hour, on the hour, so you can be assured I'll get back to you for all of your property needs.*"

Floyd left his name and cell number, purposely omitting the fact that he was a cop, which he found to be a general hindrance when it came to having phone messages returned. He checked his watch: Ten minutes to two. There was no objection from Marty or Brenda to hanging out until the top of the hour for a return call, but by two-fifteen there had been no such callback and the discouraged trio decided to return to their squad room. No sooner had Marty turned the ignition key, Floyd's cell phone chirped to life.

"Floyd King."

"Mr. King. Eric Champs returning your call. How are you today, sir?"

Eric Champs' voice was loud and excited. It was an over-enthused, clichéd, genuinely-happy-to-serve-you tone worthy of any car sales lot or carnival game. Floyd pictured a man with slicked back hair and capped teeth beaming through a practiced smile stretched across sunlamp-tanned skin, whose highly-greased personality was as flamboyant and as bold as the name rolling across his sign. Floyd wanted to hang up on the spot.

"I'm well, thank you."

"Great, *great!*" the over-enthused agent roared. "I have some fantastic properties listed right now, and in a very broad range of styles. I can also connect you with some of the best financial institutions and insurance carriers. Anything you need in the way of services. All the way to the close of escrow. Whatever it takes!"

"I'm really not in the market for buying right—"

Without missing a beat, the opportunistic realtor immediately shifted from buyer agent to seller agent. "I can also get you the best selling price in the county. And the homes I list don't stay on the market long. I have appraisers and inspectors at the ready, and a repair crew on call. Whatever it takes!"

"Well, Mr. Champs, I'll certainly keep you in mind if the need for a realtor comes along. My reason for calling has to do with a property you have listed on Mill Creek Road."

"That's a fine home, sir. Just got it ready to show last Saturday. And I have a few offers pending as we speak."

"That's good, but like I said, I'm not calling about making an offer, Mr. Champs. I'm a detective with the Santa Ramona Police. I had a specific question regarding the seller of the property. My partners and I are conducting an investigation that—"

"A police detective?" A long silence followed as Champs tried to make sense of Floyd's unexpected inquiry, which he clearly couldn't when he told Floyd, "If your business is with the seller, I don't understand why you'd be calling me."

"We thought you might be able to help by telling us who currently owns the home and how to reach them."

Floyd's request had the same result as driving a tire over a sharp object. He knew he blew it, didn't know how much further he'd be able to go, but suspected he'd have to pull over soon and repair the damage. Like that tire, Champs' effervescent salesmanship deflated and he became of little use.

"I'm sorry, sir," Champs responded indignantly, "but client names are held in confidence, and I adhere to that confidence strictly. I'm sure you have the resources to obtain the name. It's actually a very simple process for anyone. I'm rather offended you would have the nerve to consider me a shortcut rather than pursuing more legitimate avenues. No, sir. I can't help you."

"Can't help, or won't."

"Whichever. I don't even know that you *are* a cop. Could be you're another realtor looking to cheat a deal through my client. I'll save you the trouble, Mr. King—I mean, *Detective*. I know all the tricks of the trade, and I've mastered a few, myself. I'm not like one of those housewives trying to earn an extra buck playing real estate agent between school plays and dinner or around the kids' soccer games on the weekend."

"I assure you, Mr. Champs, I—"

"I don't know you, sir, so your assurances mean nothing to me. Now, I have a schedule to tend to, so unless you have any *real estate* business to offer, I'll say good-bye."

"If you give me a couple of minutes to explain, Mr. Champs—"

"Good-bye."

There was an abrupt click in Floyd's ear. Floyd lowered the phone and shut it off before clipping it onto his belt.

"That didn't sound productive," Marty said.

"It wasn't."

"So, what do we do now?"

"We don't really have a choice. I'll have to talk to Bern and explain what we've got. Hopefully I can sell him on it. I've sold him on a lot less in the past."

"And don't think he doesn't know that every time you walk in the door," Marty said as a reminder.

"Unless someone has another suggestion."

"You know, I may have a friend down in the county recorder's office. I haven't talked to her for three years or so. We're not the closest friends, but—" Brenda shrugged. "I don't know if she's still there or not, or if she even help, but it's a shot."

❧

Brenda called the county recorder's office when she got back to the squad room and was happy to find out her friend, Lisa, was still working there. They were close for a time as Lisa's husband was a buddy of Brenda's first husband. While Brenda's marriage didn't last, her friendship with Lisa, though having waned over the last few years, continued. Brenda gladly waited the ten minutes on hold until Lisa was free to take her call.

"Brenda!" Lisa squealed with excitement. "My gosh, it's been so long. How are you?"

"I'm fine, Lisa. Busy, but doing well. How about you?"

"Oh, plugging along, I guess. I'm getting a little more free time now that the girls are becoming increasingly self-sufficient."

Brenda shook the images of Lisa's two girls from the recesses of her memory. They were vague images, though, as Brenda realized from her own personal experience how much three years of change girls can go through, physically and emotionally, into their mid-teens.

"I think you mean independent. But I recall that Kristen and Karla were always like that, like their mom. Have three women in the house been too much for Ben?"

"He's made adjustments," Lisa said laughing. "Of course, I don't know if it's as much tolerance as from practice turning a deaf ear to me. So, what's up, Brenda?"

"Well, I feel kind of awkward calling and asking for a favor, having turned into a stranger over the years."

"Nonsense, honey. I don't measure my friendships by time. And favors? I seem to remember someone who would never say no to my last minute plea for a babysitter. Just ask."

"I was wondering if you could look something up for me. A property record."

"That shouldn't be too difficult. Can I ask why?"

Brenda hesitated. She felt guilty enough calling Lisa in the first place, and now any relief she sensed by the openhearted reception her friend gave her suddenly transformed to pangs of shame for not reciprocating that openness.

"It's job related, but kind of sensitive. Mostly for us. The house may be connected to a man's disappearance, and right now it's up for sale."

"Is the owner a suspect then?" Lisa asked more out of curiosity than of prying.

"No. At least not that we're aware. But then, we don't know who the owner is."

"Give me the address." Lisa wrote down the Mill Creek Road address Brenda recited to her. "I'm not getting involved in something I'll get called on later."

"Not that I can see. But all the same, let's keep this between us."

"Do you want me to call you back?"

"How about I come into the city tomorrow and buy you lunch? It'll give us a chance to catch up. You can give me the information then."

"Sure. That'd be great. I'll sneak out a little early so meet me outside the lobby at, oh, eleven-thirty."

"Eleven-thirty, then. I'll see you there."

After hanging up, Brenda crossed the squad room to Floyd's desk. Floyd closed the file he was reading and rested it against his chest.

"Looks like we caught a break. My friend still works in the recorder's office. I'm meeting her tomorrow."

"Great. Hopefully we'll catch another break if she turns up a name we can use."

"Interesting reading?" Brenda asked, pointing to the file.

"The report on Farnsworth," Floyd told her. "I'm trying to understand why the investigator stopped. He talked to Collette and Vossen and that's it. There's a forensic report on the car that's all negative. Then a summary by another investigator that concludes Farnsworth made a few bank transactions, then took hat in hand and hit the road on a never-ending vacation. Doesn't make sense."

"Maybe it did at the time. Can you tell me there was never a time when you were still with Lynn that you didn't want to just pick up and go?" Brenda regretted the question seeing Floyd's eyes fall and jaw set. "Sorry. I shouldn't have gone there."

"It's all right," Floyd told her. During those difficult days with his ex-wife, it never once crossed his mind to abandon his family, or, more so, Shelby. Now, looking back, Floyd considered if things would have been different had he not faced the obligation of being a parent while suffering as a husband. There was no doubt in his mind the end result would have been the same. "You did it to make a point, and your point is well taken. I guess some people have the guts to do it."

"And some have the guts not to," Brenda added in praise.

Floyd pushed the report away to the center of his desk. He closed his eyes and stretched the tightness from his arms and shoulders. When he opened them, he saw the faint smirk on Brenda's mouth. He smiled at her. She smiled back.

"What?"

"What?" Brenda echoed innocently.

"You have something else on your mind."

"I do." A few seconds passed while Brenda swallowed the girlish giddiness rising in her throat. "I was hoping we could talk."

"We are talking."

"About work. I want to talk about us."

Floyd's smile turned into a broad grin. "What about us?"

Brenda could tell Floyd was intentionally feeding off her discomfort, and she caught herself between wanting to laugh and wanting to reach over the desk and hit Floyd on the head. "Don't be a jerk. This is serious."

"Yes, it is. What are you doing for dinner?"

"Can of soup."

"Enough for two?"

"Split that and a sandwich ... I don't see why not."

"Let me go home and clean up," Floyd told her. "I'll be over around seven."

꒜

At seven o'clock sharp, Floyd knocked on Brenda's door. A yell came from deep inside the house.

"If that's you, Floyd, come on in."

Floyd opened the door and Brenda delivered the second half of her invitation.

"If you're not Floyd and you come in, I'll shoot you."

"What if I'm Floyd, but not the right Floyd," Floyd called down the hallway.

Brenda emerged from the kitchen. She was wearing blue jeans and a white cotton T-shirt. She was barefoot and her hair was damp. "You're the right Floyd," she said, turning back into the kitchen.

"Good thing," he called down to her.

"Sorry I'm running late. My mom called and wanted to talk my ear off about my cousin. I think. Or maybe it was … hell, I can't remember. Some relative. I stopped paying attention after the first five minutes."

Floyd walked into the kitchen to the stove where Brenda was stirring a small pot of soup. He reached around her and stuck a finger in the simmering broth. Brenda raised her elbow up to deflect his reach but too late to keep him out. Floyd quickly pulled the finger to his mouth and tasted the soup.

"It's minestrone. How's it taste?" Brenda asked.

Floyd replied by gently turning her face toward his and kissing her softly. She could taste the tomatoey broth on his lips and tongue and could think of no better way to sample either the man or the meal.

"Well, that settles it for me. That's the best damn soup I've ever made," she said.

"What's for desert?" Floyd asked.

Brenda turned off the burner and slid the pot to the side. She turned fully around and leaned into Floyd, taking both of his hands in hers. They kissed again, slowly at first, then with increasing passion. The kissing broke off into an embrace as they pulled one another tight. Floyd could feel the cool dampness of Brenda's hair through his shirt. He lowered his head, kissed her brow, and rested his cheek against her forehead. Brenda rolled her neck back until their lips met again.

"Is this part of what you wanted to talk about?" Floyd asked.

"Part," Brenda answered. "Should we go discuss the other part?"

Floyd nodded and Brenda led him out of the kitchen and down the hallway to her room.

8

Tuesday morning, August 19th

It took Brenda longer to find a parking space than she expected. She inadvertently got turned by traffic and, caught in the maze of downtown Sacramento's one-way streets ended up traveling in the opposite direction on Seventh Street when she wanted to be on Eighth Street. With her police I.D. she could have easily parked anywhere without fear of a ticket or towing, including the jury parking lot directly across the street from Lisa's office. But in keeping with Floyd's low-key approach to anything related to Santa Ramona being in Sacramento, she opted for a more civilian showing and took to the search for public parking. The extra driving turned fortuitous as she found a space on the street not quite three blocks away. It was posted for two hours, which was more than she figured she'd need. Brenda checked her watch, cursed at her tardiness, and anxiously stepped up her pace in an effort to catch the seconds that already passed her.

Brenda spotted Lisa waiting at the base of the steps outside the white stucco box of the county office building. Lisa, who was a good half-dozen years older than Brenda, hadn't changed noticeably since the last time Brenda saw her. Her hair was lighter, though from the distance Brenda couldn't tell if it had been highlighted or began graying, and it wasn't knotted into one of the ever-changing patterns of braids Brenda recalled her friend styling. Lisa looked to have trimmed a bit of weight, though she still carried some plumpness on her short frame. None of the physical changes seemed to have affected her personality. When Lisa spotted her approaching from half a block away, Brenda could see the woman's face light up. Lisa threw her hand up and waved it like an excited third grader seeking the teacher's attention.

"Oh, let me look at you!" Lisa squeaked. "You are still the prettiest thing ..." Lisa's voice trailed as she studied Brenda with a discerning squint. "So, who is he?"

"Who's who?"

Lisa pursed her lips, cocked her head and threw her balled hands to the hips on her pear-shaped frame. Brenda never told Lisa she was seeing anyone, but somehow Lisa picked up on something radiating from her that gave her secret away.

"His name is Floyd. He's a detective I work with. And before you give me the lecture on seeing someone I work with—"

"Are you happy?" Lisa cut in.

"Yes. I am."

"Then no lecture. Relationships can fail in-house or out. If you're happy and you believe it's worth the effort, I say it's no one's business but yours."

"Thanks. Where are we going?"

"There's a place a few of blocks away. The walk will do me good, work a little off the butt." Lisa gave her ample rear an exaggerated shake. "Oh, before I forget, here's the information you asked for."

Lisa handed Brenda a folded sheet of paper that Brenda tucked into her pants pocket without reading, not that Brenda had to read it as Lisa started divulging her findings as she passed it off. According to the recorded deed, a woman named Eileen Sherman owned the house on Mill Creek for the past six years.

"By herself?" Brenda asked. "No Mr. Sherman?"

"No. Just Eileen. But there's something interesting about that—at least I thought it was interesting. Since the title changed in ninety-seven, I thought it might be worth pulling the previous record in case you needed to go back further. The title was recorded under the name of Eileen Lindell since ninety-one."

"I wonder if that's a coincidence, or if both Eileens are the same Eileen."

"It's possible. The record before was under Peter and Eileen Lindell. I would have picked deeper, but I didn't know exactly what you wanted."

"No, this is great. Really. At least it gives us some background on the house."

"So, do those names mean anything?"

"Not to me. Maybe to my partners, or maybe something will come up down the road." Brenda shrugged at the information. "You never know. Sometimes a little thing that starts out as nothing turns out to be a big thing or leads to one."

"So this will be useful?" Lisa asked hopefully.

"I'm guessing it will in one way or another. In any case, it's something to work with. I owe you one."

Lisa waved her hand. "Owe, schmowe. I told you I'm not keeping book, girl."

The women stopped at a small café across from the downtown convention center. They spent three-quarters of an hour getting each other up to speed on their lives, which were as dissimilar as the women's physical appearances. Lisa never seemed anything less than comfortable in her stable, twenty year marriage to her husband, Ben, and felt as blessed now with her two daughters as the days they were born. It was the kind of life Brenda sought, one that continued to elude her but one she felt was on track with Floyd.

The relatively subdued but continuous pedestrian flow outside the café was punctuated by a noticeable surge, a signal that the lunch hour for the majority of the city and county employees was coming to an end. Lisa and Brenda waited a few minutes for the crowd to thin before rising to join them. A screech of brake-locked tires nearby caused a simultaneous turn of heads. When Lisa turned forward, her attention was drawn beyond Brenda. Her face brightened and she threw a smile over Brenda's shoulder.

"Well, Curt. Hello."

"Hi, Lisa."

Brenda turned around and was as startled to see Curt Tiner standing on the sidewalk behind her as Tiner appeared to be at seeing Brenda in front of him.

"Curt, this is—"

"Detective Garibaldi," Tiner finished. He stuck out his hand toward Brenda, who reluctantly took it. "A nice surprise. How are you?"

"Fine, thank you." As soon as Tiner released her hand she dropped it to her side and as discretely as she could wiped her palm against the outside of her pant leg.

Lisa found the coincidence surprising, though in a much more innocent nature than either detective would concede. "You two know each other, then," she said with a what-a-small-world laugh.

"Our paths crossed recently on a case," Tiner explained. "It seems we are looking for the same person."

"But for different reasons," Brenda interjected pointedly. She was not about to allow Tiner to return to his office with any suggestion that their cases were related and cause an unnecessary stir for Floyd and the department in doing so. "And the two of you?"

"Curt took a hit-and-run report for me a few years ago," said Lisa. "Now I see him in passing every now and then, and sometimes we share our lunchtime."

"So, have you and Detective King made any progress investigating the trinket?"

"Nothing to write home about."

"Or to call a friend about?"

Brenda could feel her blood simmering. It was enough for Tiner to approach the line by bringing up the ring, now he was tiptoeing ever closer to it by insinuating there was a common thread binding their cases and, even more distasteful, that there was even the slightest hint of a friendship between them. Brenda wanted badly to set the detective straight on both counts but decided to leave the matters alone. Tiner was her problem, not Lisa's, and she viewed the situation in the same light she viewed Floyd's and Marty's friendship. It was not her place to criticize Lisa's choice of friends any more than she would Floyd's, and she would tolerate the annoying presence of Tiner as she would Marty. Though given her druthers, Marty would be the lesser of the two evils.

"Too bad we're on our way out or you could have joined us," Lisa told Tiner.

"My loss. Perhaps some other time, that is if Brenda is up to coming back out our way."

Lisa glanced at her watch and frowned. "We really should head back."

Though uninvited, Tiner joined them. He explained to Lisa about having some business or another at some building or another. Brenda only paid enough attention to his words to conclude he was making something up off the top of his head that sounded like an excuse for his being downtown when he should have been somewhere else. And Brenda wished he was. Of all the people she desperately wanted to avoid running into right now, Tiner headed the list. And not just because word of her presence in town would get back to Keller.

The corner of Eighth and F Streets was the split point for the two women. Brenda could have walked Lisa to her office, but it wouldn't have mattered with respect to detaching Tiner's company as he didn't seem to be in any hurry to get wherever it was he alleged to have been going. Lisa stepped forward and gave Brenda a hug.

"You *will* call me, now. We have some more catching up to do."

"I will," Brenda promised. "Say hello to Ben and the girls for me."

"Bye, Curt."

"See you around, Lisa." Tiner turned to Brenda as Lisa walked away. "Where are you parked?"

"I'm just down the street a ways."

"I'll walk with you."

"I'm a big girl, Tiner. I think I can manage."

"You wouldn't want me to breech my oath to my civic duty? Protect and serve?"

Brenda gestured toward the concrete with and open hand. "Free sidewalk."

They walked a full block in silence before Tiner broke it. "So, was this a business lunch or purely social."

"If it was business, it would be none of yours," Brenda told him. Then, on second thought, Brenda realized she ought to give something for Tiner to take back to Keller beside suspicion. "Lisa and I have known each other for years."

"And so well, I take it, that you still have a lot of catching up to do."

"We haven't seen each other in a little while," Brenda admitted, "so yes, we have some catching up to do. Tell me you don't have friends you haven't seen in a year or so. There's nothing to be suspicious about."

"Easy, now. I'm just trying to have a pleasant little conversation here. Let's not confuse interest with intrigue."

"Let's not, or I might think you were walking me to my car to make sure I left town. Or maybe you're going to try to pick my brain about Farnsworth again."

"Guy's gotta try," Tiner said sheepishly. "I'll admit I was on thin ice back there. Right now my intentions are purely chivalrous. I'm walking you to your car as a gentleman."

"Respectable, but as I said, quite unnecessary."

"Necessary to the extent that I get a private second or two of your time. Since I was unfortunate to miss lunch with you, how about dinner?"

"That won't be possible. I'm seeing someone at the moment."

Tiner comically looked side-to-side and to the rear. "I don't see anyone other than us at the moment."

"You know what I mean."

"Are you afraid you'll succumb to my charms?"

"Succumb. That's an interesting way to put it."

Brenda stepped off the curb and between two cars, one hers. She keyed the car door and Tiner, still maintaining his gentlemanly presence, followed and reached out to open it for her. His hand brushed lightly against hers as she pulled the key from the lock. Brenda couldn't ignore the prickling of flesh across the back of her neck as she resisted the urge to recoil from his touch. Pretending the contact was nothing but incidental, she slid into the driver's seat and buckled herself, then reached for the door handle to pull it closed. Tiner, though, was leaning cross-armed over the top of the doorframe gazing down at her salaciously. Brenda gave the door a gentle pull toward her and Tiner released his crossed arms from the frame and dropped them against his chest allowing her to close the door completely. Tiner remained stationed outside her door, like a soldier waiting to be dismissed. Brenda started the engine and rolled down the window to do just that.

"Thanks for walking me to my car, Detective Tiner. I think I can find my way back home from here."

"Right. Well, think about it, okay? Dinner?"

Brenda thought about it as long as it took to put the car in gear. "Good-bye, Detective Tiner."

As Brenda's car pulled away, Tiner stepped back to the sidewalk. He watched Brenda merge into the thinning traffic. Holding his eyes on the sedan as she drove off and convinced she was doing the same to him in her rearview mirror, Tiner untwined his left arm from his right and gave a little salute. He stepped back to the curb and began the return walk to the county administration building. As he passed the recorder's office, an idea popped into his head that prompted a quick detour.

Up the steps and through the glass doors, Tiner was met by a mass of bodies lined into the narrow lobby leading to the clerks managing the vital statistics—birth and death records and such. He made a quick right through a side door to another small office that held property records. He spotted Lisa on the opposite end of the room.

"Lisa."

"Oh, Curt. Long-time, no-see," she laughed. "I still can't get over you and Brenda knowing each other. Small world."

"Well, you know, in our line of work we make connections all over the place."

"Yeah. I guess I never thought about that. Still ..."

"I need a favor, Lisa."

"I'm not fixing you up with her, if that's what you're thinking."

"No, not at all. You know I do fine on my own," he said with a wink. "No, this has to do with Brenda's trip into town, about that case we're working on."

"The one involving the owner of that house? Is there a problem? I wrote it down just like it read in the record."

Tiner was thankful Lisa volunteered the information so easily. Tiner assumed Brenda's need for the title listing for any house meant the Santa Ramona detectives located the discovery point of the ring, and that put them one step closer to Farnsworth. It was a step he wanted to be on, a step from which he could stand above his partner and for once hem and haw over allowing her a place at his side. But the reality of any partnership with Grace Keller, as Tiner was fully aware, didn't make room for two. In order to keep her from knocking him off, he'd need a bigger platform to establish his ground, his worth. Or better yet, establish a place for her one stride behind him.

"No problem with the info you got. It's ... well, it's kind of embarrassing."

"What? Did she lose the slip of paper?"

"No, not exactly. We were talking about it, the case, and Brenda showed me what she was working on—you know, her end of the investigation—and she was telling me how our ends might be connected, and then ... God, I feel so stupid."

"You're not stupid, Curt. What happened?"

"Brenda handed me the paper and like a klutz I dropped it in a puddle of muddy water. Can't even read it. Now Brenda's ticked off because she had to return to Santa

Ramona and didn't have time come back. Can you help me out here, Lisa? I mean Brenda shouldn't have to drive all the way back out here because of my clumsiness. It's my fault and I want to make it up to her."

"Wait here." Lisa disappeared into a back room and came back a few minutes later with a folded piece of paper. She handed it to Tiner but didn't let go when he took hold of it. "I can put it in a plastic baggie for you, keep it nice and dry."

"Ha, ha, ha," Tiner sang as the giggling Lisa let go of her end. He put it in the breast pocket of his shirt and gave it a secure pat. "It'll be fine right here." Tiner reached out and gave Lisa's left hand an appreciative squeeze with his right. "Thanks, Lisa. You don't know how much this means to me."

"Just don't fall into any puddles," Lisa teased as he turned to leave, eliciting an over-the-shoulder thumb's-up from the exiting detective.

Once outside, Tiner removed the slip of paper, quickly read it, and stuck it back in his pocket. "Oh, Gracie?" he said proudly to himself. "Guess what *I* found?"

What Tiner actually found upon returning to the squad room was Grace Keller wasn't in the mood for playing games, especially guessing games and especially with him. They had fallen behind in their caseload, though she had to concede very little of that was Tiner's fault. He was merely following her lead like the good little soldier he was, the obedient she expected him to be. It was Keller's own insistence in putting Floyd King ahead of their regular assignments that created the backlog, and now, instead of blaming herself for the burden, she blamed Tiner for holding her back. With her desk covered in late reports, the last thing she wanted to see was Tiner strolling into the office late with a cat-ate-the-canary grin.

"Where in the hell have *you* been?" Keller snapped harshly.

Tiner stopped short as he approached his desk, which was butted up against hers. He had rehearsed his approach, his opening, and the amount of theatrics all the way from the recorder's office. Keller's sharp tone when he neared, not at all rare and never to be unexpected, still caught him off guard and broke his stride and his spirit.

"I ... I ...," he stammered. He swallowed dry, unable to speak, unable to offer anything in his defense, as if it would matter anyway.

"I swear, it's like I need one of those kiddie leashes for you," Keller ragged on. "The next time you're going to be late coming back, call me. I'll have someone sit in for you and maybe I'll get some work done."

Tiner sensed the eyes of the other detectives on his back as he fought against wilting in front of them as the weight of Keller's belittling pulled his shoulders and head down. The conscious effort he made to hold his head high resulted in an exaggerated upward tilt of his chin, a show of false bravado that only served to punctuate his distress.

"It's only ten minutes, and I'd have been back on time if I didn't have to make an unexpected stop."

Keller had already fallen back into the report she was editing, oblivious to Tiner's presence and refusing to acknowledge his explanation. Disheartened at being ignored, Tiner dropped into the chair behind his desk and opened one of his file drawers to retrieve a case file. The scratching metal-on-metal of the drawer along its guide, a screech that usually resulted in a scowl from Keller, failed to induce any form of response, though with her brow knitted tightly as it was there would hardly be room for another angry crease.

"I ran into someone down near the county building." Tiner finally blurted.

Keller remained steadfastly glued to her report. Tiner's comment, intended to elicit interest from Keller, did not. Not even interest in prolonging the reproof she leveled upon him.

"It was one of Floyd King's partners. The woman. Garibaldi. She was having lunch with a mutual friend."

Hearing the Santa Ramona detective's name stopped Keller's hand for a brief second, a pause long enough to let Tiner know he caught her ear before she continued her notation.

"The woman is Lisa Cooper," he went on. "Lisa works for the county recorder."

"So what? A Santa Ramona detective has a friend who works for the county and decides to have lunch with her. At any given time there are, what, a few hundred cops walking the mall. I bet they all have a friend or two in government buildings, and I bet most of them eat lunch at lunchtime. Honestly, Curtis, I—"

Tiner silenced her berating when he pulled a folded slip of paper from his pocket and sailed it across his desk and onto hers. Keller opened it and read it.

"You're right, Grace. There isn't much to an out of town cop taking lunch with a county employee. But I'd say it takes on a bit more importance when the cop is a detective from Santa Ramona who works with Floyd King, and the employee works in a repository for county archives."

"Well, I'll give you credit for paying attention."

That was as close to an accolade as Tiner would ever expect to receive from Keller, and he didn't even expect *that* much. She was always cold to him. He couldn't recall at any point in their year-long partnership when they had anything remotely close to a casual conversation, let alone a polite one. Tiner didn't understand her perpetual foul mood or what he did to cause it, if he indeed was the cause. He just accepted it and resigned himself to sucking it up until the next rotation—still a painful six months away—when he would happily bid for another partner or a complete transfer.

"I think they're trying to make a connection between this Eileen Sherman and the ring," Tiner reasoned.

"You mean between Sherman and Farnsworth," Keller corrected. "I'm not buying any of that crap about King investigating the theft of the ring. If he's looking for the owner of the ring, that means he's looking for Edson Farnsworth."

"Should we go talk to this Sherman woman?"

"How do you propose we pull that off, Curtis?" she snapped condescendingly. "We have no reason to even know about her, and absolutely no connection tying her to Farnsworth."

"Ease off, Grace. I was just throwing out a suggestion."

"Yeah? Well come up with something useful. Things that aren't useful can be 'thrown out' in the trash, okay? What we need to do is catch King out of bounds without landing there ourselves." Keller picked up her phone and started tapping out a number.

"Who are you calling?"

Keller ignored Tiner and listened for her call to be answered. "Pitway," she acknowledged into the receiver when the police records clerk picked up the line. "Grace Keller. I'm doing all right. Listen, I need you to run someone for me. No warrants, just an address." Keller read the name from the paper, spelling Eileen phonetically but referring to Sherman as a common spelling. "Sorry, no birth date or approximate age ..." There was a pause and Keller rolled her eyes. "So, narrow the hits to Sac County addresses ... County's not *that* big, Pit." An impatient sigh. "No, I'll hold."

"Do you mind telling me what you're doing so I can at least follow along?"

Keller covered up the mouthpiece and told Tiner, "I'm doing what you should have done, which is turn this scrap into something we might be able to use."

Tiner had taken as much criticism and exclusion from Keller as he could stand for the moment and pushed out of his chair to leave. He cursed her under his breath as he passed her desk to leave the room, not that she would care any more or less if he expressed his thoughts out loud. He knew she wouldn't, being the heartless, inconsiderate bitch she lead people to believe she was. Tiner realized that his exit, in essense, was a compliment to her. His exit was his standing ovation applauding her evil character.

Keller, on the other hand, acted as if Tiner's departure was just another coworker passing in the hall. So what if his feelings got hurt, she told herself. She was never coddled on the job. She'd had her hands hit more than held, been chastised by supervisors and attorneys and judges. She resented all the pretty-boy types who rolled into work in their sporty toy cars to trade their manicured personal lives for ten hours of playing cops-and-robbers like they were trying out for parts in a school play instead of digging in for battle. Keller believed the job included a hardening process designed to weed out the weaklings, or, at the very least, identify those whose weak spines wouldn't protect those with the stronger backs.

"I'm still here, Pit." Keller listened and wrote down what the clerk recited to her. She studied her own writing, tracing over it with the pencil lead. "You're sure of the name? ... Don't get your shorts in a wad, Pit. I'm just double-checking. But do me one more, huh? Run the same last name with a first of Peter ... No, no D.O.B. on him, either, but same address ... Yeah, yeah, I'll hold."

Keller didn't have to wait as long for the response. "Really? Ninety-five? Okay, Pit. Thanks for your help."

Keller hung up and gave her pencil a disgusted toss to the desktop. "You sneaky sonofabitch," she said to the paper as she thought of Floyd.

Keller got up and left the office, finding Tiner exactly where she expected, sitting in the break room nursing a can of soda and his damaged pride. She pulled a chair to his table and sat. He looked up briefly and gave her a contemptuous snort.

"You done moping?"

Tiner swallowed the last of his drink and got up, leaving the empty can on the table. He was nearly to the door when Keller's voice caused him to stop in his tracks.

"Hold on, Curt."

It was the first time she'd ever called him that. After the hundreds of attempts to correct her, all the times she'd introduced him as Curtis that he had to reintroduce himself as Curt, Grace Keller, a master at getting peoples' attention, got Tiner's. Tiner couldn't help but laugh that she did or the manner in which she did it.

"What do you want?" she continued. "For me to pat you on the back and say, 'Ya' done good, kid'?"

"Maybe a little credit for doing *something*. Jesus, Grace, it's like you're incapable of saying thanks or offering a compliment. There's no pleasing you. I can't think of one time when I've done anything that you haven't found fault with."

"If I'm hard on you it's because I know you can do better. I expect you to do better. You walked into a good piece of information, but you didn't follow through and pick it apart to see what other good information you could squeeze out of it. It's called being thorough."

Keller nudged out Tiner's vacated chair with her foot and Tiner returned to it.

"You thought enough of seeing that detective with your friend to suspect something was going on. Enough to catch up to her and finagle the reason why they met. Enough to get the name of the person the detective was after." Then Keller leaned in and her tone turned critical. "But not enough to question who Eileen Sherman was, or how she may be connected to Edson Farnsworth or his stupid-ass ring."

Keller flipped the same slip of paper to Tiner that he flipped to her earlier. Under his information was the information she found through her phone call. Tiner read the bold lettering at the bottom, sighed, and shook his head.

"You know who Peter Lindell is, right?"

"The contractor who worked for Farnsworth and Vossen. So Eileen Sherman is his wife?"

"Was, it looks like. Her name was changed from Lindell to Sherman. Why she did that?" Keller shrugged. "Who cares? *Peter Lindell*, not Eileen Sherman, is the connection to Farnsworth. That detective came to town specifically to find this same information. No doubt King sent her because he didn't want to show his face around here."

"But Garibaldi didn't come for information on Lindell. Lisa Cooper told me the record she pulled was for the owner of a house. If all she gave Garibaldi was what she gave me, then they're focusing on the property."

"Something led them there."

"What about the ring?" Tiner suggested.

"Go on," Keller encouraged.

"King said the ring was found in some antique shop and they were waiting it out to catch the guys trying to sell it. Let's say they caught the guys and, however they got the ring, they got it from this house. The crooks give up and, maybe to cut a deal, tell their story. Garibaldi has a friend in records and has her run down the address for her, which is the information we both got from Cooper."

"Anything else?"

Tiner thought for a few seconds. "We don't know if King knows who Eileen Sherman was, or might have been. Or that he's made the link to Lindell."

"I'd be willing to bet it won't take much time before he does."

"Then assuming the connection is made, he'll be looking for Lindell, too. But will that be enough to cross him over that line?"

Keller grinned. "A toe or two. Enough to make an issue of it."

"How do we play this?"

"We wait. Give him a day to lock in on Lindell. Let him do the legwork. Then we take a trip to Santa Ramona and expose King's little bullshit investigation for the fraud it really is."

9
Tuesday afternoon, August 19th

Even though she was expected, Brenda knocked as a courtesy before letting herself into Floyd's house. She closed the door behind her and called down the front hall toward the clinking of dishware coming from the kitchen. When the narrow hallway opened into the expanse of the main part of the house, she saw Shelby setting a kettle on the stove.

"Hi, Brenda. Come on in."

"Is your dad around?"

"Yeah. He's out back. I'm making us some tea. You want a cup?"

"Sure, that'd be nice."

Brenda moved through the kitchen and stepped onto the back patio. Floyd was reclining in a lounge chair with the day's edition of The Bee separated in sections across his legs. It was Floyd's day off—a mid-week rarity for him—and he was doing something that up until his rehab period he seemed to have an aversion to: relaxing. Brenda felt a pang of guilt that she should come to his house with work, but it was at Floyd's insistence that she do so on her way back from her lunch date. The alternative would be Floyd waiting in the office on a day he was expected to not be there, something that would have been counter-productive in getting the man to stop and smell a few roses aside from those growing at crime scenes. Worse, she would have invited Shelby's wrath for not helping her father do so. As a compromise, Shelby agreed to allow Brenda an unofficial job-related visit.

"You look comfortable," she told him.

"I am," Floyd admitted. "Did you just get back?"

"A bit ago. I had to stop at the office to check a few things," Brenda told him while flapping a manila folder at her side. She pulled a web-backed chair from the patio table and sat next to Floyd. "I found out who owns the house."

"Anyone we know?"

"You tell me. It's a woman named Eileen Sherman. The deed was recorded in her name in ninety-seven, about four years after Farnsworth disappeared."

"Doesn't ring a bell. That's not a name we came across from either Collette Farnsworth or out of the Sac report."

"How about the name Lindell?"

Floyd sat up. "Lindell?"

Brenda nodded. "My friend took it upon herself to see who owned the house before Eileen Sherman. Turns out it was under the name Lindell. Eileen Lindell. I thought the coincidence was too good so I ran Eileen through DMV. She had her license changed from Lindell to Sherman, also in ninety-seven."

"Divorced?"

Brenda shrugged. "My friend didn't follow that line because she didn't know what we were after. But she did check the books before ninety-seven and found the house recorded under Peter and Eileen Lindell up until ninety-one."

"Here you go." Shelby, announcing her presence as she usually did when her father was talking business, came out to the patio carrying two steaming cups of tea. She set them on the table and turned to leave.

"You're not going to join us, honey?" Floyd asked.

"I don't want to interrupt if you guys need privacy."

"We'll stop," Brenda said, patting the chair next to her. "Sit."

"Okay. I'll be right back."

"Does the name Lindell mean anything?" Brenda continued.

"Marty and I came across it when we met with Collette Farnsworth," Floyd explained. "Peter Lindell was one of the main contractors Farnsworth and Vossen used. He lost huge when Farnsworth split. She threw his name out as someone who had an axe to grind against her husband. But I couldn't justify going to Lindell without making it look like we're interested in Farnsworth. What you found out changes everything. Now we can approach him as the owner of the house where Farnsworth's ring turned up."

"If you can find him," Brenda told him. "I ran Peter through DMV after I ran Eileen. His license expired in ninety-nine. Never renewed, at least not in this state. The house on Mill Creek Road, owned then by Eileen Lindell and now by Eileen Sherman, was the last known address for Peter Lindell. And I checked him as best as I could for a contractor's license on the Contractor's State License Board website on the Internet. A Peter Lindell was a licensed general contractor doing business out of Santa Ramona until nineteen-ninety-four."

"What happened in ninety-four?"

"Contractor licenses need to be renewed every two years," Brenda explained. "The CLSB listings showed Lindell's license was initially issued in eighty-six, but is expired as of ninety-four with no forwarding contact info."

Floyd digested what Brenda told him to piece together

a timeline. "So if his contractor's license expired in ninety-four, it had to have been renewed in ninety-two. His D.L. expired in ninety-nine, but those are good for four years, so that renewal took place in ninety-five."

"Kind of makes you wonder where he's been the last four years."

"Kind of," Floyd echoed. "Also kind of makes me wonder what he's been doing for the last nine."

"Not contracting, at least not *licensed* contracting." Brenda and Floyd gazed into their cups as if they were looking for tea leaves to read. The silence broke when Brenda asked Floyd what she correctly presumed was his pressing thought. "You think maybe he's involved with Farnsworth's disappearance, don't you?"

"At a minimum there's a connection between Lindell and the ring. Enough to try and track him down."

"Easier said than done, judging by the expired trail he left behind."

"That leaves Eileen Lindell. Or Sherman. Where do we find her?"

Brenda frowned. "Looks like that'll be a problem, too. Like Peter, DMV's listed address for Eileen came back to the house on Mill Creek."

"And we already know she's not living there. Jeff and C said the house was deserted. She must be staying with friends or renting a place while the house is on the market."

"Maybe a neighbor might know."

"It might not be a good idea to launch anything that could arouse outside interests. Someone might assume that looking for Sherman to find Peter Lindell is a roundabout way of looking for Farnsworth. Especially if those Sac detectives find out about it. As suspicious as that Keller seems to be, she'll be on our doorstep screaming bloody murder about us highjacking their case. We'll have a hard time explaining that to them."

"I'll give you one worse than that," Brenda added, following with a dramatic pause. "How about explaining it to Bern when he finds out about it after the fact?"

Floyd cringed theatrically.

"What about that Champs guy?" Brenda suggested. "He's got to be able to get hold of her to let her know when he gets a buyer. What if we pretend to make an offer?"

"He still wouldn't be obligated to connect us with Sherman. And at some point we'd have to give ourselves away as cops."

"What if we press him a little, make up some interfering with an investigation play?"

Floyd shook his head. "Champs won't bite. He's a player, himself. He'd probably dare us back. If Eileen Sherman is our best bet at finding Peter Lindell, we're on our own in locating her."

Shelby returned to the patio with her cup of tea and a small plate of cookies. Floyd and Brenda ended their conversation when Shelby approached, but Shelby had picked up the tail end of her father's words, which turned out to be fortunate for him.

"There's an Eileen Sherman who teaches at the city college."

Floyd and Brenda set their cups down simultaneously and turned to Shelby.

"At least she was there a couple of years ago when I took some classes. She was in the science department. Biology."

"What does she look like?"

"Oh, about my height, a little heavier. Mid-forties. Brown hair, brown eyes. Wears glasses."

Brenda looked at the physical descriptors on computer printout and nodded. "That's her."

"Well, the description *sounds* like her," Floyd corrected.

"How many Eileen Shermans can there be?" Shelby asked thinking the answer was obvious to her.

"If there are two, we need to make sure we're looking at the right one," her father answered.

"Only one way to find out," Brenda added.

Floyd looked at his watch. It was nearing four-thirty. "By the time we get to the college it'll be after five. It might be easier to track her down in the morning."

"I've got a deposition to give at ten, so you'll have to take Marty," Brenda said, adding with a smirk, "You'll lose a little in your low-profile approach, but academic exposure might do the goof-ball some good."

"Brenda! Uncle Marty's not a goof-ball." The impact of Shelby's chastising tone softened through her giggling. The ticky-tack character shots between Brenda and Marty were a part of the duo's relationship for as long as Shelby could recall, and she would always place herself in position to defend either one against the other. Unnecessarily, of course, as Shelby knew the adversaries held profound, if forever unsaid, respect for each other. "And he's far from stupid," she added.

"Brenda's using 'goof-ball' in an endearing way," Floyd said to his daughter.

Brenda smiled. "Yeah, sweetie. Endearing. Like when you call him 'uncle'. I know Marty's not really stupid. I meant we should encourage him to get in touch with his massive, as-yet untapped intellectual resources." Then to Floyd, "Any idea on how you're going to approach Sherman?"

"Straightforward will probably be the best. Show up

at her office or classroom." He turned to his daughter. "Wanna come?"

"*Me?*" Shelby replied dumbstruck.

"Yes, you."

Shelby's eyes slid to the side toward Brenda to see if she could gauge the seriousness of her father's offer by her. Brenda was no help as she responded to the young woman's glance with a light, clueless lift of her eyebrows.

"Come on. What's your schedule like for tomorrow?"

"Well, I was going to go for a run in the morning, and I have a some of treatments scheduled in the afternoon, but otherwise ..." Shelby stopped running down her to-do list. She was waiting for her father to cut her off with a smirk and short laugh and tell her he was just kidding. He didn't. Shelby cocked her head and bit over her lower lip. The stretch of her smile pulled the lip from between her teeth. "You're really serious?"

"Yeah. I want you to come with me. We can leave in the morning, be done in time for a nice lunch before you have to go to work."

Shelby shrugged. "Okay, I guess. I don't see how I'll be of any help."

"You know the campus. You know which classrooms she taught in. And you know what she looks like. You're three up on me. All you have to do is point me in the right direction."

Shelby went back to chewing her lip contemplating her father's rationale for asking. "I guess. I mean, sure, if it'll help."

"Certainly can't hurt." Floyd turned to Brenda. "Could you do me a favor and let the lieutenant know where I'm going?"

"Coward," she coughed through her hand. "Yeah, I'll

let him know where you *went*. We still haven't spoken to Len Vossen," she reminded him. "There's always a chance he may know someone who knows someone who knows where Lindell is. I can take care of that after the deposition."

"It would save some time. There's a file on my desk with a photograph of the ring. You can take that with you. Keep the story simple, but try to get what you can from him about Lindell without making it sound like we're looking for Farnsworth."

"Aren't we?" Brenda teased.

"No, dear. We're investigating recovered property."

"Oh, that's right," she said, smacking the palm of her hand on her forehead. "Hey, before I go there's something else I need to tell you about today."

Shelby picked up Brenda's serious tone and took it as an indication the ensuing subject was private. She got up and excused herself. "I'm going to see what we've got on hand for dinner. You can't stay, Brenda?"

"Thanks, sweetie, but I need to get home and take care of some things."

When Shelby disappeared into the house, Brenda switched to the seat next to Floyd that Shelby vacated.

"This may or may not be a big deal. When I met my friend, Lisa, downtown we ran into Curt Tiner."

"Was he alone?" Floyd asked. He tried to maintain an even tone over his concern. Brenda running into Tiner wasn't the best thing to happen, but it wasn't the worst. The worst would have been running into Keller. He was relieved when Brenda dispelled that worry.

"Keller wasn't with him, if that's what's on your mind. I never saw her, anyway. That's why I said it may not be a big deal."

"Yeah, but no doubt Tiner reported it to her. Exactly where did this happen?"

"Lisa and I just finished lunch and were getting up to leave. I heard a man greet her and when I turned around, there he was. I'm sure he hadn't been following us because he seemed just as surprised to see me as I was to see him."

"Did he ask any questions?"

"Not directly. He made a couple of innocuous references to the case. I got the feeling he was trying to bait me, but I brushed him off. I figure he got the message because he didn't pursue it."

"Then what?"

Brenda held back on telling Floyd about Tiner's other pursuits: the escort to her car, dinner invitation, and the Sacramento detective's subtle but no doubt intentional grazing of his hand against hers. She convinced herself earlier the incident, too, was no big deal and bringing it up would only turn it into one, giving the matter undue attention. The counterweight of her conscience, however, troubled her as she found herself debating the pros and cons of disclosure on the drive in and, thus, doubting the confidence she had in herself about being open to a man she cared about and trusted.

"Nothing. We all said good-bye and went our separate ways."

"How well does Tiner know your friend?"

"Lisa said they've had lunch a few times over the years, and they cross paths once in a while around the county buildings. But that's bound to happen. I didn't tell her why I needed the information, so even if she told Tiner I was investigating something, she wouldn't be able to tell him what it was. I can't see how we'd have to defend anything."

"Probably not. It'd be different if Tiner saw me there

instead of you. Nah, they'll look like fools trying to create issues over a lunch. I don't think we have anything to worry about."

Brenda stood and stretched. "I should go."

Floyd got up, hooked Brenda's arm in his and walked her through the house to the front door. Floyd grabbed the doorknob and twisted it, but Brenda set her hand on top of his and stopped him. She faced him, and with a quirky grin said, "We never did get around to talking last night."

"I thought we communicated *very* well."

Floyd added a randy leer and started laughing as the blushing red cheeks painted Brenda's face. Brenda rolled her eyes and knocked his shoulder with hers.

"Floyd, you know what I mean. I want to sit down with you and have an *intellectual* discussion about us."

"All right. This coming weekend, then. I'll hire a sitter—"

"As long as his name is Ken!" Shelby called from the kitchen.

"Don't eavesdrop!" Floyd called back.

"Don't talk so loud!" she responded.

"I'll leave the two of you to work out the child care issues," Brenda told Floyd as she turned his hand to open the door. "Talk to you tomorrow."

Floyd leaned forward and kissed Brenda on the cheek, causing a lopsided smile to the affected side. With Brenda gone Floyd returned to the kitchen where his daughter was rinsing out the used cups.

"You have my blessing," Shelby told him as he took a seat at the kitchen table.

"Your blessing for what?" Floyd asked.

"You know."

"No, I don't know," Floyd said feigning ignorance. "Perhaps you should explain."

Shelby turned off the tap and dried her wet hands on a dishtowel before wadding it up and throwing it at her father along with an evil glare, the intensity of which she softened with a puckered smirk. Her father didn't so much as flinch as the balled towel left her hand, then laughed heartily as it blew open half way to him and fluttered harmlessly to the table well short of hitting him.

"You throw like a girl," Floyd teased.

"And you think like a *man*."

10
Wednesday morning, August 20th

Marty met up with the King's at their house in time for breakfast, his second. The smell of fresh coffee and pancakes made him forget the light meal of three eggs, six slices of bacon, and three pieces of toast his wife cooked for him a little over an hour before. He dropped his stout frame into a chair across from Floyd at the kitchen table and dug into two stacks of four and three, throwing down a final, unclaimed pancake he used to sponge up the remaining syrup from his plate. Between bites, Floyd got Marty up to speed on the information Brenda uncovered about Eileen Sherman, Peter Lindell, and the house on Mill Creek Road. Floyd unsuccessfully tried to downplay the obvious connection between Lindell and Edson Farnsworth, insisting that finding Lindell was the next logical step to uncovering the truth about the ring. Floyd's sales pitch fell short of convincing his skeptical friend, who had known Floyd so long and so well he could not only read the lines and between the lines, he could read between the letters making up the words making up the lines.

Floyd, Marty, and Shelby arrived on the city college grounds late in the morning, a mistake that new students make only once as the small parking lots tended to fill quickly. Floyd spent twenty minutes snaking through the different lots listening to Marty's continuous false reports of "there's a spot" and to Shelby's told-you-so's about the limited parking on campus. Floyd finally found a parking space in the back of one of the lots about as far from the

campus as one could get. He sent Shelby to a red ticket
dispenser to retrieve a parking permit, which he tossed
on the dash. Shelby took the lead as they picked their
way through the car-crammed lot. Marty, bemoaning the
weight of the two large meals settling in his stomach,
registered his protest by pointing out various other parking
alternatives that would have eliminated their trek. Floyd
reminded his partner that things like parking in a stall
marked for service vehicles with a police parking placard,
for example, would be unethical. Marty laughed and hinted
at a number of his and Floyd's past practices that bordered
ethically questionable, if not departmentally frowned
upon, behavior.

Santa Ramona City College was a collection of nine
buildings scattered along a fold in the foothills north of
town, an annex for the community college system centered
in the greater Sacramento area. It offered a variety of science
courses suited to the medical fields, particularly in the
areas of medical assisting and physical therapy. The small
campus had been around for years as an adult education
facility before being taken over in the late eighties to
accommodate the displacement of the biological science
staff in favor of the highly profitable computer sciences
at the main campus closer to Sacramento. The staff and
administration enjoyed their isolated outpost so much
that plans to return them to the main campus for fiscal
consolidation after the tech industry meltdown was met
with turbulent resistance.

Shelby hadn't been on the campus since completing her
studies there and moving on in pursuit of her career as a
physical therapist. Though knowledgeable of the layout
of the buildings and with everything appearing for the
most part as it was when she attended, she still felt like an

outsider. She looked for signs of change, which made her look at her surroundings differently than she had when she was a student. The hazy recognition rekindled memories of the queer familiarity she felt when she returned home two years after her mother had taken her to live in Colorado following her parents' divorce. Then, like now, Shelby found herself stepping backward in time while looking forward, walking in two worlds at the same moment.

Shelby gave her father and Marty a nickel tour of the campus, pointing out the administration building, the library, and a couple of classrooms she visited regularly during her enrollment. Classes let out as the trio entered the main quad. Along with a swarm of young men and women, they found themselves zig-zagging and separating through the confluence of bodies. Eventually the chaos corrected itself as the throng thinned into several orderly processions, one of which Shelby pulled the detectives into. Near one of the two Biological Sciences buildings, they peeled away from the parade of students funneling into the classrooms and walked around to the back of the building, which was a mirror of the front. There was a door on the corner leading to an office and an alcove indented in the center with two separate doors leading to their respective halves of the interior.

"This is it," she told them.

"Where were all those other kids going?" Marty asked.

"Those are the classrooms in the front. These are the labs. Usually the professors hold lectures first, give everyone a ten-minute break, then reassemble in these rooms for experiments and demonstrations. This was where I took one of my lab classes with Ms. Sherman."

"Won't she be giving a lecture about now?" Floyd asked.

"Yeah. You want to sit in on it?" Floyd and Marty both furrowed their brows. "Didn't think so. Your best chance to meet up with her will be in here, before she starts her lab."

Floyd looked at his watch. "How long will that be?"

"Forty minutes."

"Forty minutes!" Marty exclaimed. "Good thing I ate big this morning. Although I may need a restroom at some point in time."

Shelby pointed to a small out-building between the two science wings. "The cafeteria is that large building back in the quad. There won't be much in the way of refreshments, though. It'll be closed up for another hour to get ready for lunch."

"We can just hang out here. It's not like Marty and I haven't had to sit and wait for people before."

"Would you mind if I took off for a little while?" Shelby asked. "I thought I'd drop in on a couple of teachers in some of my old classes."

"Go ahead, honey. We'll be fine. It's probably best if we took it from here without you, keep the awkwardness down to a minimum. We'll meet you in front of the library in an hour. If it takes longer than that, one of us will come get you."

As Shelby wandered off, Floyd and Marty strolled around the building, coming full circle and stopping where Shelby initially left them.

"Well, we burned two minutes off the clock on that one," Marty said to his watch, then to Floyd, "Wadda you say? Take 'er around nineteen more times?"

Floyd ignored him and walked to a window on the far corner that had a number of papers plastered to the inside of the glass. They were the grade sheets for the quarter listed by instructor and student I.D. numbers. Floyd scanned each one, then checked them a second time with more scrutiny.

"How high did you score?" Marty cracked.

"Huh?"

"What are you looking for?"

"There's no instructor named Sherman on any of these grade sheets," Floyd pointed out. "That's not encouraging."

"Maybe it's an oversight. Maybe she didn't post her grades yet," Marty reasoned. "Maybe she posted them on the other side of the building."

Floyd chewed on his partner's explanation, but didn't swallow it. He nonetheless checked the front window of the office. There were flyers posted for seminars and free clinics and course credit for volunteering to be a lab rat, but nothing identifying Eileen Sherman as an instructor. Floyd wasn't a superstitious man, but the common notion that things happen in threes crossed his mind. Farnsworth had been gone for ten years and, by all appearances, Peter Lindell ceased to exist for roughly half that time. He therefore anticipated not meeting Eileen Sherman today.

"Let's see if we can find someone who knows if she's here so we don't waste the rest of the morning chasing another ghost."

Floyd tried the doorknob to the empty office and found it locked. There were two doors set on either side of the alcove leading into their respective classrooms. The one Floyd tried was locked. Marty twisted the other and the door swung free. Communicating in silence, Marty gave a little want-to-go-in head nod, to which Floyd responded with a why-not hunch of his shoulders.

Marty stepped inside the darkened room first. A faint,

sweet odor of formaldehyde halted him, triggering an ancient image, a high school recollection of dissected frogs pinned belly up in paraffin-bottomed trays. He found a wall switch with a series of four buttons and ran his hand across them sparking an explosion of flickering, fluorescent light overhead and relieving him of the memory.

The room was larger than they expected. Eight black Formica-topped lab benches set in two rows of four took up a majority of the room's center. Each bench had chromed gas outlets jutting upward at their midpoints and built-in sinks on the ends closest to the center aisle. The counter tops were mounted atop built-in wooden floor cabinets that had a large two-door cabinet centered between rows of drawers. Along the length and width of two walls were matching black counters set atop a series of cabinet sections that, too, ran half the room's perimeter minus the intermittent three-foot spaces between sections. Above the counter along the longer wall were two shelves, one above the other, supporting an endless variety of body parts in sealed glass containers. Floyd walked along the adjacent aisle and looked over the selection with macabre interest. There were four lungs showing varying degrees of disease. Two livers floating in containers marked simply "Healthy" and "Unhealthy". Floyd saw a heart, a knot of intestines, a kidney, and half of a brain. On the shorter wall, glass-fronted cabinets were mounted that contained a number of smaller jars with what Floyd assumed were smaller body parts.

Marty's interest fell on an assortment of assembled animal skeletons. They ranged from small, like the mouse and lizard, to the cat, which was the largest of the group. The cat's bones were positioned to depict it walking. Not only the shear number of bones impressed Marty, but that so many were smaller than he expected for such a sturdy animal. Entranced by the cat, Marty ran his index finger gently along its curved spine.

Unseen by either man, the door at the front of the room had pulled back. A tall, thin man clad in a white lab coat stepped into the room and short-stepped to a stop when he saw his unexpected guests. His immediate concern focused upon the stranger with his hand dangerously close to the display.

"Please don't touch that."

The man's nasal tone was uttered like that of a parent to a curious child inspecting an electrical outlet, stern and immediate, but not offensive. Startled, Marty snapped his finger back as if the skeletal sculpture suddenly turned white-hot and he shoved his hand into his pocket.

The man continued inside and set two large books on the lectern before proceeding to the rear of the room to confront the two trespassers. He was pushing six and a half feet in height and most of his physical attributes—his ears, nose, and narrowed face—seemed stretched to accommodate it. The man's lab coat hung to just below the knees, exposing bare legs down to the brown leather sandals on his feet. He stepped in front of Marty and slid the skeleton back to the wall. When he did, a long tail of his sandy blonde hair fell along his collar.

"Sorry," Marty apologized.

"It may look sturdy, but there are a number of delicate bones that can't be fixed if they break. Can I help you gentlemen?"

Floyd and Marty showed their badges and introduced themselves.

The man displayed no sign of being impressed or concerned. "I'm Neil Dobbs."

"Nice place you have here, Mr. Dobbs," Marty praised. "Quite a collection."

"An accumulation of years."

"So you've been doing this for a while, I take it."

"Fifteen years or so. Not all of it here. I started down in Southern California and migrated. I was about to head back when the district unintentionally created this little utopia for us."

"So where would someone pick up a jar of pickled body parts?" Marty asked as he inspected a pinkish-colored lump of some sort of tissue floating inside a glass container.

"We have ... connections," Dobbs said mysteriously before breaking into a short laugh. "Actually, we have a supply outlet like any other profession. If we need a jar of eyeballs, we can order it. I also get stuff when teachers leave—retire or quit or move on—and don't want to pack a lot. I find no shame in taking handouts. Most of my things are hand-me-downs, except for my display skeletons."

"You did that?" Marty asked impressed, pointing to the cat.

"That and others. Skeletal articulation is sort of a hobby of mine. And it comes in useful when I do anatomy classes."

"Is it hard to do?"

"It takes some patience and some education. And some luck."

"What kind of luck?"

"Follow me."

Floyd and Marty followed Dobbs through the door from where the teacher first emerged and down a narrow corridor that divided the building in half. Walking in the opposite direction of the office, they came to another door that led into a utility room. Dobbs flicked on the light to illuminate three metal carts with animal skeletons in various stages of the cleaning and reconstruction process.

"Each quarter I assign a class project in which my students work in groups to assemble a full skeleton. I teach them how to clean and prepare the bones, then we put them together like jigsaw puzzles."

"No humans?"

Dobbs laughed. "Not for individual projects, but I do have a box of bones I use for lectures and exams."

"No, shit?" Marty touched the side of his meaty fist to his mouth, embarrassed at being too late to suppress the words he belched.

Dobbs reached under a counter and slid a cardboard box onto the floor. He unfolded the tucked flaps, exposing the first of several layers of chalk-white bones, each layer separated by a half-inch-thick panel of gray packing foam. He lifted one of the larger bones, a radius, and handed it toward Marty, who gave Dobbs an are-you-serious furrow of his brow.

"Go ahead," Dobbs encouraged, adding playfully, "He won't mind."

"Who won't—" Marty cut himself off as he caught on to Dobbs' humor. He took the bone and hefted it, noting it was much lighter than he expected for its size, but was generally unimpressed by it other than the fact it was a human bone.

"I would have thought you'd have come across a bone or two in your line of work," Dobbs said as he accepted the return of the bone from Marty.

"I've *seen* a bone or two," Marty replied, "but never handled them. Blood, bones, and such, that's what evidence techs are for."

Dobbs took a cotton cloth from a sealed bag and

wiped the bone before setting it back inside the box. "To keep the oils from your hand off it," he explained. Then Dobbs carried on the portion of his conversation that was interrupted by Marty's aroused curiosity.

"A teacher gave them to me a while back—a hand-me-down as they were to her. She taught biology classes, too, but they didn't fit in her lesson plan. She knew I was a bone nut. I used to lay them out once in every class. The excessive handling isn't good on them and there's too much of a chance of losing one of the smaller pieces, so I stopped. I considered once hitting up the department head once about letting me have the cadavers when the anatomy classes were finished cutting them up. That was a few years ago, before computer animation gave them virtual dissection. With computers and budget cuts it makes the need for actual bodies impractical. Anyway, critters is cheaper, as an old professor of mine once said. Around here there's an endless supply of road kill out on the highway. Possums, skunks, snakes, birds. A ferrel cat. As long as they aren't mangled too badly, we'll strip them down and put them to good use."

Dobbs folded the flaps over the top of the box, tucking under the alternating corners, and slid it back under the counter. As he did, he gave the box a quarter turn before giving it a final shove. When he turned it Floyd saw the name E. Sherman handwritten on the upper left corner.

"The teacher who gave you the bones wouldn't happen to be Eileen Sherman, would it?"

Floyd's question surprised Dobbs for its from-out-of-nowhere materialization. He cocked his head and smiled. "Yes. As a matter of fact—"

Floyd dispelled the illusion of his apparent psychic ability by pointing to the box. "The name."

Dobbs exhaled an "Oh" and shook his head to himself at failing to realize the obvious. He led the men out of the room and back to the lab. Along the way he shed his lab coat exposing the remainder of his beach-bum attire of a colorfully flowered Hawaiian shirt and khaki shorts. He offered Floyd and Marty a bench stool and leaned himself back against the counter.

"So, the police are here. Why?"

"Well, as it turns out we're looking for Eileen Sherman," Floyd told him. "We understand she teaches here."

"Taught," Dobbs corrected.

"Taught?"

"She left a few of months ago. Told the administration she was moving on to greener pastures."

"Any idea where those pastures are?"

Dobbs smiled coyly. "Maybe."

"We'd appreciate any help you can give us."

"I'm sure you would." Dobbs paused and smirked. "Any particular reason you're looking for Eileen?"

"That's confidential." Floyd, in kind, paused and smirked back. "Part of our investigation."

Dobbs propped himself onto the countertop of the closest bench and rested his clasped hands in his lap in a manner suggesting it was one of his regular lecturing positions and he was about to give one.

"Look, my dad was a cop down in Orange County, so I'm pretty familiar with the investigation game. He played it on me enough as a kid that I learned there're only two kinds of investigations. The kind where you know shit, and the kind where you don't know shit. Generally, the latter kind is when you suspect something is going on but you really don't have a clue. You're trying to make a case instead of trying to build one. That's why you came here instead of going straight to the main office. You don't have any official reason to talk to her, do you?"

"Officially? No," Floyd admitted. "But we came here instead of the office because when the police go out and start asking questions, the people they talk to don't like other people to know the police are talking to them. It's nothing cloak-and-dagger, Mr. Dobbs. It's called discretion."

"Ahhh," Dobbs smiled knowingly. Dobbs sandals slapped between the tile floor and his feet as he slid off the counter top. "Discretion goes both ways, Detectives. Eileen and I weren't that close, but, yes, we were colleagues and I'll respect her privacy as her own business. So whatever she's done—"

"Ms. Sherman hasn't done anything," Floyd told him. "We're trying to track down her ex-husband."

"Ex?" Dobbs reacted with mild surprise. "Didn't know she ever had one to get rid of."

"She never talked about her personal life?"

"Not with me."

"You never saw her with a man at, say, any school functions, parties ...?"

Dobbs wrinkled his nose. "I'm not much into the ass-kissing social scene. My impression of Eileen was she wasn't, either."

"How so?"

"She'd ask me if I went, but never asked me why I wasn't there. I figured if she went it would be the other way around." Dobbs' hypothesis elicited an agreeing nod from the two detectives. "So, what did Mr. Sherman do?"

"His last name is Lindell," Floyd said. "Sherman is her maiden name."

"Huh. Never heard her go by any name other than

Sherman in the five years I knew her. So, what did Mr. Lindell do?"

"We're not sure." Floyd told him.

Dobbs coughed a laugh and grinned ear to ear, clearly amused by Floyd's seemingly forthright admission. Floyd didn't take offense at Dobbs' reaction. He recognized how, to an outside observer, their investigation, as much as it was an investigation, appeared rather shallow taking into account the basic objective of finding a man who is not suspected of anything. He took it on faith that Dobbs, having some exposure to the trivialities of law enforcement through his father, would conclude their search had a legitimate purpose. Floyd saw no point in trying to convince the teacher of that legitimacy—that he could was questionable even to him—and continued his line of inquiry.

"How long ago did she stop teaching?" Floyd asked.

Dobbs reflected toward the ceiling and took a deep, mind-cleansing breath. "She was scheduled to teach this last quarter, I'm pretty sure. She was in and out over the first part of summer prepping for the fall. A couple of weeks before classes started she took a leave."

"Like a sabbatical?" Marty asked.

"No. Word I got was Eileen was packing it in, leaving teaching altogether. The department said she was pursuing other work. I also heard it was family care, a mother or aunt somewhere who was terminally ill. But like I said, we didn't get into each others personal stuff."

"Has anyone seen her since she left?"

"Yeah. I have myself a few times. Mostly just in passing in the admin offices. We never said much beyond hello and good-bye. Again, her business, not mine. She gave away most of what she had—books and charts and such. The rest of it is sitting in storage at the district warehouse until the end of the year. If she doesn't collect it by then, the department will sort through it and pass it around."

There was a short burst of a muted air horn followed by a commotion outside the lab that translated to the dismissal of classes. A few students stuck their heads through the doorway but retreated upon seeing the three men in conference at one of the benches. Dobbs slid off the counter top, excused himself, and went to the door. He made an announcement to the gathering of students before closing the door and returning to the bench.

"I told them to take an extra ten minutes for break," Dobbs explained upon his return.

Floyd nodded his thanks. "Mr. Dobbs, we never clarified whether or not you know where Ms. Sherman can be found."

"I don't. I saw her, oh, three days ago. She was driving into the staff lot as I was driving out. She waved; I waved."

"She was alone?"

Dobbs nodded. "This business you have with her husband. Does it have anything to do with her leaving the college?"

"Not that we're aware of. Ms. Sherman changed her name about six years ago, but our reason for finding her isn't domestic. It's to find Mr. Lindell. Whatever influence *he* may have had on her career ... like I said, we're not aware of it."

"Based on what you've told me—or haven't been able to tell me—you guys aren't aware of too much."

Floyd and Marty heard the classroom door open behind them. Dobbs shot a hard, irritated stare over their shoulders that melted into a warm smile.

"Shelby King. How the heck are—" Dobbs abruptly

stopped speaking and turned to Floyd. "Hey, by any chance are you two ...?"

Floyd nodded. "My daughter."

"Hi, Mr. Dobbs." Shelby turned to her father. "I know you said an hour, but I got bored waiting."

"She's working with you?"

"Just helping out family," Floyd said.

"I work at a physical therapy office in Sac," Shelby added. "Dad brought me along so he wouldn't get lost on campus. I see you still have Cheshire."

"Who?" Marty asked while looking around for the movement of some class pet he neglected to see when he first entered the room.

"Cheshire. The cat." Shelby pointed to the skeleton Marty fixated on when he first arrived. "Remember the cat in *Alice in Wonderland*? How it disappeared except for its smile? Well, this cat—"

"Disappeared except for its bones," Marty finished. "I gotcha, Shel."

"Speaking of disappearing ..." Floyd segued back to the topic of Eileen Sherman. "No clue at all, Mr. Dobbs?"

"I'd like to help, gentlemen." Dobbs thought for a few seconds. "The office must have a forwarding address for her mail."

Dobbs walked to the telephone hanging on the wall near the corridor door, picked up the receiver, and punched four numbers. "Donna, Neil Dobbs ... Good ... Yeah, it is. Hey, I got a bag of stuff here belonging to Eileen Sherman. Do you have a forwarding address I can—? ... Oh, really? ... Yeah, I know, but—... No exceptions, huh? Well, if you can't, you can't ... Uh-huh. Interesting ... No, you don't need to send anyone out. I'll bring it up sometime during the week ... Okay, Donna. Thanks."

"I take it that's a no from Donna," Marty said to Dobbs when he returned.

"The only thing she'd say is the address Eileen left with the office is a P.O. Box," Dobbs told them. "She didn't say where and Eileen left strict instructions not to give it out, so there's no telling which city it's in."

"There's a way," Marty countered, "but not without a lot of leg work and fighting with the post office."

"What was interesting?" Floyd asked.

"They're not mailing anything out to her. Anything with her name on it is held until she comes to pick it up. She must have been doing that the last time I saw her."

"There's no way Bern's going to let us stake the school out until she returns," Marty told Floyd. "*If* she returns. Looks like we'll have to try our luck in the office."

"Stay away from Donna," Dobbs warned. He described the office manager as fat with tight, curly hair, eyes under lids as heavy as the rest of her, and a voice that wavered somewhere between a police siren and a cat in heat.

"Oh, and Mrs. Reinhart." Shelby added, with Dobbs nodding agreement. "She won't do anything unless you have a form signed by a department head."

"Your best bet is to catch one of the student interns alone," Dobbs added. "But it's not likely they'll be able to get what you need on their own."

Their best bet, Floyd concluded, was having someone simply tell them where Eileen Sherman was, but that appeared to be just as long of a shot. Floyd wasn't any more disappointed with Neil Dobbs than he was with the realtor, Eric Champs. But where Champs obviously had a means of contacting Sherman, it was clear Dobbs didn't know where she was, a point that was reinforced for Floyd when Dobbs made the phone call to the administration building. But one area of concern for Floyd, similar to that with Champs, was whether or not Dobbs would tell Sherman they were looking for her upon their next encounter.

II
Wednesday morning, August 20th

At the height of California's end of the millennium construction boom, Farnsworth & Vossen, Inc. had three offices, a full-time staff of twenty, and a Rolodex filled with subcontractors and industry contacts. Even as their business reorganized and streamlined from residential to commercial real estate, they still maintained their Sacramento and Santa Ramona offices and shifted their residual staff to other duties. Their company wasn't making the hundreds of thousands of dollars that big builders like Jay Whiting was pulling in hand over fist, but there was substantial business elsewhere in Santa Ramona and the surrounding areas to take a sizable bite of the construction pie. Their profits were modest and they had enough contracts lined up to carry them from one year to the next. From a business standpoint, they were strong, which made Edson Farnsworth's financial bleeding of the company all the more bewildering.

"We were stable. We had solid relationships with several banks. We had contracts that would have kept us in the black for a decade," a still-shocked Vossen told a business columnist for the Sacramento Bee during one of his last public interviews on the subject of Edson Farnsworth's betrayal. "I don't know why he did this to us. I had no idea anything like this was coming. It's hard to believe it's all … it's all gone."

Gone. In the blink of an eye. A man wakes up one morning to learn his company's accounts were virtually empty and his partner was nowhere to be found.

Just like that, a highly visible figure like Edson Farnsworth disappeared. Just like that, Len Vossen was dragged by his wallet through a minefield of bankers, lawyers, and creditors. Just like that, Len Vossen's comfortable and secure world sat on the edge of a sliding cliff, its stability reinforced by his own resilient character and his refusal to simply roll over and submit to defeat. He tried convincing others what he had convinced himself, that once this period of adjustment, as he called it, passed he would return to the heyday when any piece of empty land held for him the prospect of riches limited only to building codes and zoning restrictions. His vow turned out to be as hollow as the encouragement he received.

Vossen's business now comprised of architectural consultations, structural retrofits, and small scale remodeling jobs. He closed the higher-rent Sacramento office and relocated his spacious Santa Ramona suite to a two-room corner niche inside a rather obscure office park. The work was enough to keep him solvent, but only just. He loved the stimulation of the creative process, and working made him feel as if he hadn't surrendered completely to failure. It was hard enough those first few weeks driving through Santa Ramona by the shops and homes that began as concepts on paper by his hand and his imagination. Or to walk the hallway of his home, past the study he couldn't step into without seeing the books and tools used to express his creative mind. Vossen stood tall and bore the brunt of the responsibility for Edson's crimes—Vossen termed what Farnsworth did to be criminal and portrayed himself as much a victim as anyone—and though he never deserved fault for what happened, he was the only one upon which others could lay blame. He would accept the financial responsibility, but the mess began and ended with

Edson Farnsworth. It was only too bad for Len Vossen that the blame didn't disappear when his partner did.

The phone call Vossen received from the police detective was just another reminder that distance, whether as physical as another place or conceptual as time, would make no difference. The scars were not as severe as those, say, of a burn victim, but they were scars none-the-less. There would always be the same lingering question: "How could I have let it happen?" The answer never changed, but repetition created the illusion for Vossen that time had shortened the tale, compressed it much like layers of soil laying beneath years of accumulated deposits—or perhaps more appropriately, like the layers of trash in a landfill— where what once took a shovel blade to cut through many years now took only a scoop of a teaspoon.

Brenda entered the reception area through the metal-framed glass door with the script-style "V", Vossen's company logo, stenciled in black, centered at eye level. She saw the man leaning over a desk gazing at an appointment book. "Mr. Vossen?"

"Detective Garibaldi, right?" Vossen pulled himself away from the desk and approached, shook Brenda's hand and invited her into his office.

He led her around the vacant receptionist's desk and into his office, which was nothing like what it once was. The rich mahogany woods of his former desk and cabinetry had since been replaced with oak laminated pieces most likely repossessed from some Internet company that, like so many others, existed long enough to milk a handful of naïve individuals out of their retirement accounts with promises of wealth in the form of stock certificates that may well have been copied at Kinkos for all the value they truly held. The office was spacious, or would have been if not for the large table in the middle of the room where blueprints and building code manuals and various drafting tools lay scattered about. Taking up space off in a corner was another table about half the size of the first that had an assortment of computer hardware and software covering nearly every available inch. The flat screen of the monitor flashed a slide show of buildings, some familiar—she recognized the small building where her dentist's Santa Ramona office was—and some not, but all Brenda assumed to be designs or renovations of Vossen's.

"You have to excuse the mess here. I've been working on a remodeling project for some offices in downtown Sacramento. It's not like designing a complex from scratch, but it keeps my hands in the business, keeps my contacts current in the event something more creative comes along. With the economy grinding along the way it is, however, I may find myself diving into more ventures like this."

Brenda detected a dispassionate tone in Vossen's voice that contrasted his attempt to infuse a sense of pride in his work. She learned enough about the man to know he held first-rate status in the construction trade before the sub-flooring collapsed beneath him. The fall damaged more than just his business. Although Vossen wasn't culpable for the fallout of Edson Farnsworth's actions, he was Edson's partner and remained the only visible reminder of that catastrophe. As optimistic as he could be, or pretended to be, Brenda knew the banks and the construction trade viewed Vossen as a high risk. She sensed Vossen knew this, too, and even after ten years was still coming to grips with the reality that he had been relegated to second string in the construction field.

"That's one thing we can't say about our line of work," Brenda said. "There's never a shortage of people willing to go to jail, good times or bad."

"No, I suppose not," Vossen agreed.

"Mr. Vossen, I hope this isn't too awkward for you. Reliving rough periods in life are never easy, and I promise we won't stray into any areas you find upsetting."

"There's nothing we can't discuss, Detective Garibaldi. I've come to accept that what happened will never really go away. Every day I walk into this office is a reminder of what Edson did. Fortunately, or maybe ironically, every day I walk into this office reminds me that he didn't defeat me."

"That's an admirable attitude, sir, considering the extent of your losses," Brenda said. "At least those I read about. I'm sure there are personal losses none of us will ever know of."

"There were a few," Vossen agreed. "I'll certainly never give the level of trust I placed in Edson to another person, nor do I ever expect the same in return. And I'm stronger for what happened, though I admit that strength has come from a cynicism I never had before."

"That which does not kill us ...," Brenda recalled the opening to Nietzsche's famous quote. She lived through enough personal turmoil growing up to go along with the day-to-day negativity inherent to law enforcement to understand Vossen's transformation.

"I suppose we should get down to the business of why I came to see you. I imagine you're a little curious why Mr. Farnsworth's name has taken our interest."

"I assume he's resurfaced in one manner or another. Though knowing Edson as well as I did—" Vossen abruptly stopped and chuckled to himself. "I'm sorry. I kind of contradicted myself saying I knew him well when obviously I didn't. What I meant to say is that what I know of Edson *now* would lead me to believe that in whatever capacity he's returned it isn't likely to be positive."

"Is that because of the number of enemies Farnsworth left behind?"

"That's a misconception, Detective. Edson left behind a lot of angry people, but time and money—what money was left—placated them. People who did business with us don't hate Edson as much as they pity me. I can honestly say Edson doesn't have but a few true enemies."

"And you are one of them?" Brenda asked.

"Yes, ma'am," Vossen replied bluntly. "I am. I said years ago that I would relish the opportunity to have a hand in ruining *him*, in watching *him* suffer."

"In seeing him dead?" Brenda added.

"My dear detective, Edson *has* died."

The comment brought an immediate rush to Brenda. *A spontaneous declaration*, she thought. She fumbled excitedly in her mind to sort out what steps she needed to take to preserve the integrity of Vossen's voluntary confession. Brenda cursed herself for not having a pocket recorder with her and fought back the urge of curiosity to press for further details. She reached for her folded leather badge holder in which she kept a few Miranda warning cards behind her laminated photo I.D., knowing it was the right thing to do and the only thing at this point she could do. Then, like a fisherman whose fight against a taught line produces a flush of anguish as the line snaps, Brenda lost her phantom catch when Vossen edited his admission.

"Not completely, mind you." Vossen held his hands out. "Look around. These are the remains of Edson Farnsworth. Possibly the only remains we'll ever see."

Vossen moved around from the front of his desk to behind it and sat. He extended a hand toward the chair before him as an invitation to Brenda to join him. "It appears I've strayed a bit. I'm sorry. I'm sure your business today didn't include my woeful history."

"In a roundabout way it does. You and Mr. Farnsworth regularly used a contractor named Peter Lindell, correct?"

"That's right. Peter was the lead contractor on several of our projects."

"Is he still around? Have you used him on any recent jobs?"

"Peter? My gosh, I don't think I've seen or heard from him almost as long as Edson's been gone. As soon as I learned about the money and couldn't locate Edson, I called Peter to find out if he knew where he was. He went ballistic when I explained my concerns."

"Yes, we understand his business took a substantial hit."

Vossen laughed lightly. "*I* took a substantial hit, Detective. Peter? He was lucky to walk away in shoes. Some of my losses were insured. That money, along with the other remaining assets I was able to unload, was enough to appease the creditors or at least buy me some time while I refinanced the few holdings I had left. Peter had nothing to fall back on, and I was in no position to bail him out.

"On top of our company's legal and financial problems, Peter also had other obligations beyond his dealings with Edson and me. Basically, he overextended himself. When our business fell it took away a lot of capital he expected to use on other projects. Without our money, his other plans fell through. Money he had already committed couldn't be recovered, and money he needed to finish jobs in progress never came."

Brenda opened the large envelope containing an enlarged photo of the Farnsworth ring, which she extracted and handed to Vossen. Vossen centered it between his eyes and stared at the jeweled band. Though only a photograph, the two diamonds winked at him from the sides of the glowing ruby. In his mind, the image of Edson Farnsworth's face superimposed itself over the ring and the diamonds winked at him again through his ex-partner's transparent eyes.

"That was found among some items of stolen property recovered a few days ago," Brenda explained. "We're in the process of backtracking to find the person who last touched it after it came off Mr. Farnsworth's hand. Part of that process is learning as much as we can about Mr. Farnsworth's past to help establish a connection between him and anyone connected to the ring's theft."

"Okay, but I don't see what I can provide you outside of identifying the ring as Edson's. Other than that, I'm surprised to see it off his hand."

"That seems to be the consistent response. You'll concur he never removed it?"

Vossen shook his head. "That ring was as much a part of his body as any other physical feature. I've seen him tease it halfway up his knuckle with his thumb and pinkie, but I can't recall seeing him without it on."

Without taking his eyes from the photo, Vossen rose from his desk and moved behind his chair to the window. Vossen appeared lost for a moment, almost fixated on the ring. He held it up to the sunlight and uttered a barely audible, enlightened "Hmmm".

"I never knew Edson had his signature etched into the damn thing," came Vossen's revelation. "But then, how would I?"

Vossen handed the photo back to Brenda and retook his seat.

"Would you know of anyone Mr. Farnsworth would have given the ring to?"

"Detective, I'm shocked you didn't show me a picture

of the ring with Edson's finger still stuck inside. But the ring can't be the reason you came to see me. Surely Collette could have identified it as Edson's."

"The photo was only a part of my visit, along with the background info I was looking for."

"And part of that background info was to locate Peter, correct?"

"We'd like to speak with him."

"About the ring, no doubt. I often wondered if he'd ever been successful in his quest to track down Edson. I hope this isn't an indication of that success."

"Would you know where I could find Mr. Lindell now?"

Without hesitation, Vossen shook his head and said apathetically, "Nor do I care. I tried phoning him the day after I first called to tell him about the missing money. His wife said he packed and left to find Edson. After that ..." Vossen shrugged. "I realize my attitude might seem somewhat indifferent, but I simply had no relationship with the man. Never did. Peter was Edson's friend, though why anyone who was treated the way Edson treated people would want to maintain any relationship with him is beyond me."

Brenda screwed her face and Vossen, reading her mind, laughed, clearly amused at the contradiction the detective saw between Vossen's opinion and the long relationship he himself had with Farnsworth.

"Why did I remain associated with Edson, right? Edson and I were business partners. We were cordial to each other, but almost every interaction we had outside of the office was related to our business. The charities and social functions ... all of that was business."

"Keeping contacts."

"Precisely. Our relationship was built on our individual

needs. Edson was good at technical application in design, but he lacked a certain ... imagination or creativity. Or maybe it was emotion. That's where I excelled. I was good at designs. I fell short in managing the money aspects of the business, and Edson was good at finances. Very good, as it turned out."

"And Lindell was good at building."

"He was adequate," Vossen conceded half-heartedly. He went on to tell Brenda about a few instances where he had to confront Lindell regarding deficiencies reported in some of their projects. There were also complaints about scheduling conflicts that delayed jobs and change orders in design plans Lindell alleged to have never received. Farnsworth would assure him these were all relatively minor problems, problems he would take care of.

"Edson kept us apart, which at the time I thought was Edson just being a good businessman by keeping everyone happy. In hindsight I realize Edson didn't want me raising red flags that would, in turn, create issues with Peter. Edson never openly sided with Peter, but I'm sure he gave Peter the impression he did."

"That didn't bother you?"

Vossen shrugged. "Why should it? Business was good. Despite the occasional shoddy work, Peter was keeping to the bottom line. Or so I thought. That's where some of the money Edson skimmed came from. Peter would need, say, ten thousand and Edson would bill for twelve or so. On paper he'd make up some expense and hold back the extra charge. I later found out in some cases that change orders weren't being followed because Peter never got them. Edson would charge for the cost of the change, but if the change wasn't something highly noticeable, say an upgraded lighting fixture, then as long as no one complained ..."

"That's how he made all the money?"

"Nooo. That was a drop in the bucket for him compared to the money he drained from our accounts."

"But a light fixture? I mean, how much are we talking?"

"Multiply a light fixture times a building, a building by another building. We're also talking cutting corners on any aspect of the building, not just lights. That's where Edson's knowledge of architecture benefited him. And there were more than a few instances where *he* wrote the damn changes without the client even knowing and pocketed the difference."

"That doesn't say a whole lot about the business sense of your clients."

"What sense? We were making money by the barrelful—*all of us!* This was a time when people bought anything that had a dot-com following it. We were all playing with others peoples' money. We were *all* reckless and ignorant. Do you think for one minute that if a company contracting us was scratching to save pennies that Edson could have pulled off what he did?"

Brenda thought about what Vossen just said and about the times they were living in, or had been. Now, it became a regular occurrence to pick up the paper and read about another company declaring bankruptcy or some CEO or CFO being indicted for some manner of fraud. The nineties was an age of white-collar crime sanctioned by the SEC, when corporations large and small seemed to print their own money in the form of ownership shares and stock options. The turn of the century became more than a turn of the page in everyone's account ledgers, and black ink turned red and the red bled like an open wound. Brenda saw her own department retirement fund take a hit from all the corporate free spending, and she herself had been negligent in keeping track of those loose purse strings handed to those she entrusted to manage her assets. Brenda could hardly fault Vossen for failing to do the same.

"Mr. Vossen, you intimated that Farnsworth treated Lindell poorly. Why did Lindell continue to do business with him?"

"Part of it was their friendship. They'd known each other for a number of years before Edson and I joined up. Part of it was the fact that our business was good, so his business was good. There was also their mutual dislike of Jay Whiting."

Vossen explained that Lindell subcontracted for Whiting before the builder hit his jackpot in the Sacramento area, primarily in Santa Ramona. The same competency questions Vossen experienced with Lindell were apparently less tolerable in Whiting's camp.

"When Edson came back to town to get his business going, there was his old friend Peter Lindell barely making ends meet. Edson took him aboard and gave him a job here and there. Then Edson and I formed our business and we started to battle against Whiting. We didn't fare well and were kind of forced out of the housing game. Knowing Peter's history with Whiting, Edson played Peter up to be his ally and made him the lead contractor on most of our jobs."

"That hardly sounds abusive to me. A man needed work and a friend gave him some."

"Edson never did anything for anybody that didn't have a return on it," Vossen stated flatly. "He worked Peter Lindell hard. Sometimes Peter would have so much on his plate he'd forget what he ate last."

"And the added confusion only enhanced Farnsworth's ability to slip in phony design changes or kick some money back to himself."

"Exactly."

"So what Lindell saw as dedication from a friend was actually—"

"All part of the big plan," Vossen finished. "To the extent that Edson even included Peter and his wife on vacations as a bonus."

"Outside of the trips, how often did you, the Farnsworths, and the Lindells see each other as a group?"

"Not too often. Edson and I, well, we had a different social schedule." Vossen cast his eyes to the floor in embarrassment. "That sounds pretty snooty, like we were above him, but ... We all took the occasional trip together, sort of a reward for a good year's work. The last one was in ninety or ninety-one."

"Where did you go?"

"Tahoe, mostly. It was a compromise. Edson and I could go just about anywhere we wanted, but Edson didn't want Peter or Eileen to feel like they had to mortgage their home to keep up. I think the biggest trip we took was once to British Columbia."

"What was Lindell's reaction when he heard the news about Edson's disappearance?" Brenda asked, bringing the subject back to finding Lindell.

"Like mine and everyone else's, I suppose. Stunned. Confused. Eventually angry."

"But not angry enough for you to kill him."

"Threats were made," Vossen admitted, then chuckled, "I believe I even told Collette I'd slice Edson gizzard-to-gullet if I saw him again." He shrugged. "I guess when you get to a point when reality sets in, you want to lash out."

"What about Mr. Lindell?" Brenda asked.

"I couldn't say. We all have our breaking points. Where Peter's point was ...?" Yielding to further speculation,

Vossen rolled his palms open before him. "Like I said, I haven't seen him in years. He could just as easily have come to grips with the situation, like I did, and continued on with life as thrown himself from a bridge."

Brenda wasn't convinced Vossen really believed he had come to grips with his own situation, though his current demeanor was hardly the picture of a man despondent enough to cast himself head first from any of the bridges spanning the Sacramento or American Rivers. More like he was in perpetual denial, believing that his silver-plated life was merely tarnished and in need of a good buffing when in truth it was corroded beyond anyone's desire to put into practical use. Brenda likened Vossen's career to the bent spoon at the kid's table during Thanksgiving dinner—it was just as functional as any other utensil, but was out of place with the grown-ups and the good china.

Brenda stood and thanked Vossen for his time and, again, apologized for any disruption her visit might have caused. Vossen politely extended his hand and dismissed Brenda's concerns by making a water-under-the-bridge analogy. He walked her through the small lobby, then paused before opening the front door for her. He started to say something but hesitated as if maybe he thought better of opening his mouth. Experience told Brenda to delay her exit and allow Vossen's second thought to pass, adding a perk of her eyebrows to encourage the man to speak his mind. He remained silent.

"Something you want to add?" Brenda prodded.

"No," Vossen replied at first without conviction, then with a more self-assured, "No. I'm sorry if I muddied the waters for you. You came looking for answers and it seems like I only added to the questions."

"Not at all, Mr. Vossen. What you've told me will be

helpful in filling some of our existing gaps. I'm sure the rest will sort itself out as our investigation progresses."

Brenda moved through the reception area door and into the building lobby. Vossen followed her for a few steps to see her out.

"You'll never find him, Detective Garibaldi."

Vossen's blunt comment was the second time the skin on the back of Brenda's neck prickled. She remained at the door, mindful of her earlier premature reaction, and looked over her shoulder at Vossen, who met her gaze directly.

"Edson is where Edson needs to be. He always has been."

"We're not looking for Mr. Farnsworth, sir. We're looking for Mr. Lindell."

With a vacant tone Vossen said, "Peter Lindell is where Edson needs him to be, as well. In any event, I wish you good luck, Detective."

12
Wednesday midday, August 20th

"Dad, there she is," Shelby whispered excitedly. "Ms. Sherman."

Shelby discreetly pointed to a dark-haired woman fifty yards ahead of them walking toward the administration building. She was the right height but wasn't as heavy as Floyd imagined when Shelby first described her, and she wasn't wearing glasses. Her stride was a smooth but purposeful stride, not appearing at all uncomfortable or disconcerted being on the campus where she walked away from her career.

"You're sure?"

Shelby scrunched her brow. "That's why you brought me along, isn't it?"

While keeping his eyes locked on Sherman, Floyd fumbled his car keys from his pocket and tossed them to Shelby. He instructed her to get the car and drive it around to the staff lot Sherman most likely came from and wait for them.

"You want me to keep the engine running?" she quipped in a low, suspenseful tone that caused Marty to cough a laugh and drew Floyd's stony-faced glower.

"Don't look at me, Floyd. Your daughter, your genes."

"We can do without the drama, Shel. Just go get the car."

Shelby jogged across the quad, leaving Floyd and Marty behind to discuss their options. They agreed that approaching her inside the building was a bad idea as an unexpected police encounter among her peers could have the potential for embarrassing Sherman and putting her on the defensive. Based on what little they knew about her from Eric Champs, which was nothing, and Neil Dobbs, which turned out to be next to nothing, Eileen Sherman's life wasn't an open book. A close coworker like Dobbs didn't know about Sherman's former marriage to Peter Lindell, so it was more likely than not that others didn't know either. Floyd didn't see it as his or Marty's place to disclose it publicly.

"Wait by the door," Floyd told Marty. "When she comes out, fall in behind her. I'll be up near the parking lot. We'll talk to her there."

Marty did as instructed and stood near the administration entrance reading some fliers posted on a kiosk with one eye while watching the door with the other. He grew impatient after ten minutes. After fifteen he wondered if maybe he missed her or if she used another exit from the building and hoped Floyd would be ready to catch her before she drove off. Marty waited another couple of minutes then decided to go into the office to see if Sherman was still inside. As he stepped away from the kiosk, the main doors opened and Eileen Sherman walked out carrying a small box. Marty stopped and let Sherman pass and get several yards ahead before tailing her to the parking lot.

Marty saw Floyd standing off the concrete walkway that merged with the asphalt at a gently sloping curb. He reached inside his pocket for his badge and readied himself as Floyd stepped onto the path and walked toward Sherman. Marty became confused upon noticing that instead of having his focus on Sherman, Floyd was looking beyond her and at him.

Floyd continued his approach, but deviated unexpectedly from their plan by walking past their target. As soon as Floyd got one step beyond Sherman's shoulders, he shook his head signaling something had changed. Marty slowed his pace and waited for his partner's explanation.

"I've got an idea," Floyd said.

"I thought we *had* an idea."

"This one's better. We follow her home."

"It's only by a stroke of luck that we've got her right now," Marty countered. "Why would you want to risk losing her on the street?"

"I don't want to," Floyd admitted. "But let's say we try to talk to her now and she blows us off. Then what?"

"Then what-what? She could tell us to pound salt just as easily at her front door as she can at her car door."

"Not if we have a warrant."

"But we don't. And we don't even have probable cause to get one. At this point, we couldn't scrape up enough probable *bullshit* to fake it."

"We'll worry about that later. If we have to serve her, I'd like to know where to find her."

Floyd turned away from the campus and toward his car, which Shelby parked along a red-curbed fire lane. As Floyd neared he noticed the police parking placard on the dash and his daughter grinning behind the steering wheel.

"Can I take this next time I go shopping?" Shelby asked tapping her finger on the placard.

"Hop in the back," her father replied, pretending not to hear her request.

Floyd pulled both drivers' side doors open simultaneously. Shelby slid out and under her father's arm to the rear of the car. Floyd pushed the rear door closed and replaced his daughter behind the wheel. He started the engine as Marty crawled in from the passenger side. Floyd rolled the car slowly along the curb until he could see Eileen Sherman, who got into a gold Acura and backed out of her space. Floyd waited until Sherman began driving out of the lot before falling in behind her.

"What did she say?" Shelby asked from the back.

"Nothing. Your dad changed plans," Marty told her, making it sound like a regular occurrence with Floyd, as was his annoyance at it. "We're going to follow her."

"A car chase? Cool!"

Floyd immediately tempered his daughter's excitement by informing her, "It's not a car chase, Shelby."

Floyd followed the Acura off campus and through town. It soon became clear after Sherman turned onto the main highway that lead through the undeveloped fields buffering the foothills from the city that she wasn't taking residence in Santa Ramona. Sherman was heading toward Sacramento, which could have meant she had to go *through* Sac on her way north to Roseville or Citrus Heights, or south toward Elk Grove. What it actually meant, to Floyd's chagrin, was Eileen Sherman was heading toward Sacramento because she was living *in* Sacramento.

Floyd maintained a good distance between his car and Sherman's. Traffic on Folsom Road was fairly light so the increased spacing didn't hamper their tailing. Floyd kept his eyes locked on the Acura, even when Marty pointed out the approaching "Sacramento City Limit" sign and sang a sinister *Da-da-daaah* as if crossing the boundary fated the trio to an ominous doom. To Floyd it was only a sign on the side of the road marking an imaginary line in the dirt. The first true indication for Floyd that they'd crossed into Bern's forbidden zone was when the shadow from the Highway 50 overpass swept across the car.

Sherman stayed on the main road as the side streets counted down block by block from the sixties to fifties to forties. She made her first turn on Thirty-sixth Street, and a short time later pulled her car into a driveway that led to the rear of an apartment complex. Floyd drove ahead, made a U-turn, and parked on the street across from the gated entrance to the complex courtyard. He had hardly shut off the engine when Marty spotted Sherman near the gate keying open one of the small doors on the rectangular bank of mailboxes. It was confirmation for the detectives that she was staying in one of the buildings.

"What do we do first?" Shelby asked eagerly.

"What we don't do is rush. We wait for a few minutes and let her get inside her apartment."

"Okaaay." If there was a difference between approaching Sherman now and ten minutes from now, Shelby didn't get it. "Then what?"

"Then we take you home," her father replied. Shelby frowned and flopped back in the seat.

"Awww. Break the girl's heart, daddy."

"Like you'd bring your boys along?"

Marty laughed. "Are you nuts? We'd still be trying to drag them out of that lab full of bones and body parts back at the school ... Be lucky they weren't playing catch with a lung or something."

"Regardless, we're in Sacramento and I'm on restriction," Floyd explained. "Bern will blow a gasket if he finds out I came even this far. And with my daughter? We'll be better off going to Bern and letting him know what we're up to and then coming back to talk to Sherman."

"He'll tell you no."

"He only has to tell me no to keep his conscience clear. We'll work around that."

"Daddy! I'm surprised at you," Shelby scolded. "What if I snuck around behind your back after you told me not to do something?"

"Yeah, daddy. You're gonna get grounded." Marty laughed over Shelby's giggling. "Look, you're on restriction, but I'm not. The worst Bern will do is yell at me, which happens how often?"

"Daily."

"Right, so it's no big deal. If I go talk to her—"

"He'll accuse me of sending you," Floyd cut in.

"Okay, so he yells at you instead of me. I can live with that."

Marty unbuckled his seat belt and exited the car. He walked to the apartment complex entrance, soon realizing the outside of the complex was as far as he was going to go. Blocking his entry was a secured gate with an electronic lock. Marty moved to the side of the gate to the apartment directory mounted on the wall. There were two columns of nametags in pre-numbered slots. Alongside each was a red call button. Between the two columns was a square mesh screen covering a two-way speaker. Marty ran his finger down the left column, stopping it at the "E.Sherman" tag in the one-fifteen slot. He read the name in the adjacent slot in the right column, number two-fifteen, then pressed Sherman's call button.

"Hello?" the woman's voice crackled over the speaker.

Marty leaned into the speaker and notched his voice up a couple of octaves to disguise it. "Uh, yeah. I have a delivery for Mr. Binecky. Is he there?"

"You want two-fifteen," the woman replied. "This is one-fifteen."

"Sorry, ma'am. My finger must have slipped."

Marty's apology was the last thing said between them as

Sherman obviously saw no need in replying a second time. Marty retreated from the panel and moved back to the gate, frowning as he unsuccessfully twisted the knob. He was on the verge of returning to the car to when a van pulled to a stop in front of the complex and an elderly woman stepped off carrying two large bags of groceries. The bags were overloaded and she fought against the strain pulling down on her already stooped posture. She plodded up the curb toward the gate, offering Marty opportunities to be a good samaritan and to obtain access to the complex.

Certain the woman hadn't seen him, Marty gave the metal gate a quick mule-kick as the woman extracted herself from the van's narrow passage. Marty's strike caused the gate to rattle against the frame and drew the old woman's attention in his direction. Marty immediately locked eyes with the woman and pinched his face in regret.

"I'm sorry. I didn't see you coming and I let the gate close."

"That's all right, young man. I would have had to open it if you weren't here."

"But I was and ... Would you like some help, ma'am? That's the least I can do."

The woman studied Marty for a few seconds, though not as most people did. Marty's overall hulking physique tended to make people pause defensively, except, for some reason, children and old ladies, with whom Marty mysteriously gained trust against little apprehension.

"That would be very nice, young man."

She handed him her bags and fished a small ring of keys from the purse hanging from the crook of her arm. She picked through each of the keys singularly as if she was ticking them off a mental check list, pinching one between her thumb and forefinger until cognizant of which key to her life it was before letting it slide down the ring as she plucked the next. She unlocked the gate and held it open for Marty, then followed him through, letting the spring-loaded hinge pull the gate back into the iron frame with a hard clank and rattle. Marty walked a half stride behind the woman as she led him into the complex.

"I don't think I've seen you around here before," she said.

Her voice was soft, but worn with a scratch to it. There was also a subtle, unconsciously placed accent, an extra beat on the long "o" when she said "don't". It reminded Marty of his grandmother, who grew up in the northern Great Plains and could have walked right off the movie set of *Fargo* as strong as her dialect was. This woman had undoubtedly emigrated long enough ago to have only a trace of the region still stuck in her vocabulary.

"Do you have an apartment here?" she asked.

"Me? No. I was visiting my friend, Eileen. Do you know her? Apartment one-fifteen?"

"Eileen Sherman? Yes. We've crossed paths a few times. Nice young lady. Terrible thing about Mr. Sherman and all."

Mr. Sherman. "Yeah. Mr. Sherman," Marty echoed with a "tsk", trying to convey empathy with her for a man he didn't know and whose identity the old woman apparently didn't know, either. "But you know, things like that are bound to happen in life."

"I don't consider being killed by a drunken driver just a thing to happen in life," she chastened.

"Um, no, ma'am. I meant ... you know, tragedies in general. And she's held up so well. I guess time has its healing ways."

"I suppose, though I've only known her the six weeks or so she's been here. I can't imagine what it's been like for her this past year."

"Well, part of the process is breaking away from those painful reminders. Familiar places, homes ... I'm sure wherever she finally decides to settle it will be a good beginning for her."

The woman slowed her pace and cocked her head as she turned it toward Marty. "Oh? I thought her heart was set on going to Tucson. Did she change her mind?"

"Uh, yeah. I mean, no. I guess she was just being a little melancholy about uprooting, having second thoughts. Maybe I misunderstood."

"Well, whatever she decides, you be sure to support her. Even a friend from a long distance is better than no friend."

"Believe me, I'll make it part of my job to do whatever it takes to maintain contact with her." *If you only knew.*

"Good. Here we are." They stopped in front of apartment two-oh-four and Marty waited patiently as the woman picked her way along her key ring as she did at the complex gate. She opened the door and took the grocery bags from him. "Thank you for your help, young man. And remember—"

"Friend from afar," Marty said with wink and a nod.

Marty backed away from the door as the woman closed it and started across to the other half of the complex, to the one hundreds. He found apartment one-fifteen and went straight to the door and knocked. From behind the door he heard the rhythmic clack of hard heels on linoleum followed by the metallic slide of a deadbolt. The door swung back, but only as far as the security chain allowed. Sherman remained behind the door like it was a shield and peeked cautiously around it.

"Can I help you?"

"Eileen Sherman?" Marty recognized the woman whom he followed from the college office but asked her name as a matter of course.

Sherman's voice turned edgy and defensive. "I don't know who you are, and I didn't buzz you in," she told him.

"I'm Detective Doenacker, and the gate was open." *Sort of*, Marty added to himself. "I was hoping you could help me. I'm looking for Peter Lindell."

Marty thought he heard a startled suck of air from Sherman when he said the name. He definitely saw the woman's eyes flare for an instant as they locked on his. Sherman stuck her head around a little more, breaking her eyes from Marty only when he displayed his identification.

"I take it you know him."

"If you're here to find Peter then you were obviously aware I knew him *before* you came," Sherman replied, slightly miffed at what she saw as a brusque tone from the detective.

"Any idea where I can find him?"

"Why? What has he done?"

"I'm afraid I can't tell you that." It was about the only shred of honesty to cross Marty's lips since he entered the complex. He wasn't too sure if it would also be the last. "His name came up and, while the source isn't very credible, we still need to talk to him. It's really a routine matter."

"I haven't seen Peter in a number of years. He left me some time ago. We had some issues. His business failed. He walked away and never looked back."

"I'm sorry to hear that, ma'am. You don't know where he went, where he might be staying now?"

"Like I said, I haven't heard from him in years. I didn't

look for him after he left and I have no need for him now. We are legally separated. And before you ask me to contact you in the event I hear from him, I won't."

"You won't?"

"Hear from him, Detective. Anything else before you go?"

Marty wanted to ask her why the charade, why she made up the story of Lindell being killed by a drunk driver, why she walked away from her college career and dropped under the radar. Marty tried to sum it all up in one question. "Why are you selling the house in Santa Ramona?"

"It's a seller's market."

Marty smiled. "Well, no one can argue against a sound business decision. I won't trouble you again ma'am. Thank you for your time."

Sherman closed the door and Marty heard the click of the dead bolt snapping secure. He also heard the door groan with a stressing creak. He pictured Eileen Sherman pressing her back against it after locking it, supporting herself against the transitory paralysis caused by the shock that ... what? That someone knew who she was, knew her past? That the effort she put into distancing herself from that past had been too little? Perhaps that she had been found?

Marty retraced his steps and exited the complex. Before going back to the car, his curiosity got the better of him. He stopped outside the gate and looked up two-oh-four on the complex directory. Like all the other tags, it listed a first initial with the last name, H. VanGelder. Yup, Marty thought, a good old Scandinavian name.

"How'd it go?" Floyd asked as his partner slid back into the passenger seat.

"Like I expected. She was pretty vague. She said she

hasn't heard squat from Lindell in a number of years, but wouldn't say how many that number was. Said he left her and they're legally separated, but didn't use the 'D' word."

"So she wasn't very helpful," Shelby commented.

"Not in the least. Nor does she care to help. And she seemed all too sure she'd never hear from him again."

"What about the house?" Floyd asked.

"Seller's market."

"Anything else?"

"She's a liar," Marty said flatly. "The old lady I hijacked to get into the complex said Sherman told her her husband—and that would be *Mr*. Sherman, by the way—was hit by a deuce around a year ago and died. She also told me Sherman is planning to move to Arizona after the house sells. Whether *that's* true or not remains to be seen. The only thing I know for sure is Sherman moved into her apartment about a month and a half ago. The old lady confirmed that."

"So now what do you guys do?" Shelby asked.

Floyd started the car's engine and put it in gear. "We go back home and try to piece the inconsistencies together. We've got something. I just don't know what."

They had made progress in tracking down Eileen Sherman, but got no closer to their objective of finding Peter Lindell. A lot of holes existed, and for Floyd it was time to start finding fillers to patch them. That process began on the drive back to Santa Ramona. Floyd mentally retraced his steps, going as far back as the discovery of Edson Farnsworth's ring in the cabinet taken from Piña's shop and the ensuing encounter with Jeff and C that led to the house on Mill Creek Road where C claimed to have recovered it. From that point the trail became hard to follow. The connection between the house and the ring turned out to be Lindell through Sherman, his former wife who says she either hasn't seen him in years or claims he died some time in the past twelve months. Then again, thought Floyd, Neil Dobbs, who worked in the same department with her for five years at the city college, didn't know she even *had* a husband. That led Floyd to think that Sherman was hiding something.

*How about some*one? he considered as he slowed to a stop for a traffic signal. As elaborate as such a scheme appeared to be, it wasn't beyond the realm of possibility to be an impossibility. And Sherman's misdirection couldn't change the two things that were absolute certainties: Edson Farnsworth was missing, and Peter Lindell was missing.

Floyd wasn't ready to believe it was coincidental.

13
Wednesday afternoon, August 20th

After dropping Shelby off at the clinic—she had already arranged a ride home with her boyfriend—Floyd and Marty returned to the detectives' squad room and joined Brenda at her desk to begin compiling their collected data. Brenda spent twenty minutes highlighting her visit with Farnsworth's former partner, detailing Farnsworth's corrupt yet well-hidden business practices and the demeaning way in which he conducted them, along with the hidden abuses in the relationship he maintained with their lead contractor. Her summation was that Vossen claimed to have no idea where Edson Farnsworth or Peter Lindell could be found and believed the man didn't care beyond a reasonable curiosity where the former was, and not at all about the latter. And that bothered her.

"All the way back here I kept asking myself, 'How could Vossen not care?' Guy gets run through every cycle of the washer and makes out that he's thankful he's wearing a clean shirt."

"So? The spin cycle twisted his brain a bit," Marty said. "We don't know Vossen was all that sharp to begin with, giving his partner the financial autonomy that allowed him to systematically clean him out."

"Vossen didn't strike me as stupid," Brenda countered. "The way he explained it, the auditors discovered Farnsworth had been messing with the receipts through subtle changes. They told him without day-to-day review the changes would have been hard to decipher. And by Vossen's own admission he was a lousy bookkeeper."

Floyd pulled his copy of the Sacramento report from his desk and opened it to where the statements the investigating detectives received were written. He already knew what he wasn't going to find, but he made summary comments to Marty and Brenda to make a point.

"Collette Farnsworth said her husband up and left. Vossen said he had no clue what was going on until he went to the bank and learned about the withdrawals. He suspected the worst when he called Collette Farnsworth and she said she didn't know where Edson was. Then the worst was confirmed when the police found the car. We have a short investigation in which Mrs. Farnsworth and Vossen are interviewed and give basically similar statements that indicate no foul play. Lindell, however, isn't around."

Floyd ran his finger down the report and stopped on Eileen Sherman's statement.

"Sherman tells the investigators that her husband snapped. 'Peter became irate when Len called and told him what happened with the business and Edson disappearing,' she was quoted as saying. 'All of his business contracts were tied to Farnsworth & Vossen. He said without them, he was ruined. He told me he was going to meet with Len to find out exactly what happened. Peter didn't come home until the following morning. He went straight to our bedroom and packed a suitcase. When I asked him what he was planning to do, he said he was going to hunt Edson down and bring him back. The last thing I heard him say was that when they come to take the business, they could have it. All he wanted was Edson's head'." Floyd flipped the last two pages and closed the file.

"Nothing indicates any contact between Lindell and Sac P.D. after that."

"Sounds like Lindell would make a pretty good suspect," Marty concluded. "Except something doesn't quite add up, like the time between Farnsworth disappearing and Lindell going after him."

Floyd disputed Marty's logic. "We don't know exactly when Farnsworth took off. Everyone is basing that time from the Friday of the bank transactions. He could have still been in town for up to three days beyond that."

"Could it be possible that Lindell was in on the rip-off with Farnsworth? They were friends. Farnsworth could have transferred the money to his account on that Friday, split the money out of the new account with Lindell the following Monday, and Tuesday Lindell hits the road under the pretense he's going after the man who destroyed him."

Floyd was shaking his head. "You guys are forgetting what got us to this point. The ring in the shed. If you believe what Collette Farnsworth said, Edson never met a man he didn't want to take advantage of. He wasn't the sharing type." Then to Brenda, "And Vossen told you Lindell's contracts were charity work." Brenda nodded. "You could argue Lindell was in on the scam—maybe he felt he owed his friend for helping him out and turned a blind eye to some shady business practices, but I don't think you can make the assumption that Lindell was a full partner."

"Nor was he a friend," Brenda added. "If anything, Farnsworth only acted as one and Lindell was foolish enough to believe it."

"Then a cheated partner or friend," Marty proposed. "Lindell finds out Farnsworth conned him along with everyone else, kills him, and then comes home and ditches

Farnsworth's stuff in the shed. That would explain how the ring got there."

"But if what Sherman maintains is true, Lindell never came home," Brenda pointed out.

"Maybe she just never saw him," Marty countered. "He could have put the stuff in the shed and hit the road. Lindell must have known the police would be looking to talk to him. That would be enough incentive for him to go into hiding."

"Did Vossen say what he and Lindell met about?" Floyd asked Brenda.

"Vossen only said he talked to Lindell on the phone, and then tried calling him the following day. If they got together Vossen neglected to tell me." Brenda's thought process caught up to Floyd's. "Or he didn't tell me because they never met."

Floyd tapped his fingertip on the Sacramento file. "Sherman's statement clearly says Lindell told her he went to meet with Vossen. She says he didn't come home until the next day. If they never got together, where was Lindell all that time?"

Marty raised his hand. "Hiding Farnsworth's body?"

"Be serious, will you?" Brenda told him.

"I am serious. Could be how he got the ring."

"And the ring's what we need to concentrate on," Floyd reminded them. "I think once we solve the mystery of how the ring got to the Mill Creek house, it'll untie a lot of knots kinking everyone's stories. And right now a lot of those knots look like they were tied by Eileen Sherman."

Marty agreed. "She may not have known about the ring being in the shed, but it wouldn't surprise me a bit if she knew Lindell killed Farnsworth and helped cover her ex's tracks. Although if she had a hand in Farnsworth's disappearance, I don't see why she'd stick around."

"Because Lindell was never looked at as a suspect, dork," Brenda added. "Therefore she had no reason to be concerned that she would be one with him. So why run if you don't have to?"

"Why stick around if you can leave?" Marty countered.

"I ask that same question about you daily," was Brenda's snide reply.

As his partners' verbal sparring continued, deteriorating into childish bickering, Floyd picked up his phone and dialed the number for the Sacramento Police. What Brenda said to Marty made sense, that the investigation was limited because Lindell was never looked at as a suspect. In fairness to his colleagues in Sacramento, they weren't looking for conflicting statements or additional suspects because everything pointed to Farnsworth acting alone. They didn't know about the ring.

The ringing of the phone in one ear only half eliminated the incessant chirping of Marty and Brenda seeping into his head, and he silently thanked God he only had to contend with the responsibility of raising one child as opposed to having a second and putting up with similar bickering twenty-four hours a day. Floyd rapped his knuckles on his desktop when the line was answered, which brought an immediate cease fire when Marty and Brenda, thus far intently focused on one-upping the other, became aware Floyd was on the phone.

"Detective Bureau. This is Salvador."

On the assumption that identifying himself as Detective King from Santa Ramona would equate to lighting a match in a firework warehouse, Floyd opted to remain the anonymous caller.

"Hi. I'm trying to get in touch with Detective Saunders. He took a report for me a while back and I had a couple of questions I wanted to ask him."

"It *must have* been a while back, sir. Detective Saunders retired three years ago."

"Oh. Well, what about Detective Mitchell?"

"Detective Mitchell? Well, um—"

"Is he retired, as well?"

There was an uncomfortable silence followed by a light throat clearing sound.

"Sir, Detective Mitchell passed away a number of years ago. You could give me the report number, though, and I could have a detective call you back."

Floyd knew that would take time he didn't have, most likely two weeks by the time his request filtered around the bureau and was finally assigned to a detective. Then again, he would have to identify himself. While the response would be quicker, it wouldn't be welcomed.

"Well ..." Floyd blew a defeated sigh. "I really wanted to have this matter handled now. I have an out-of-state flight tomorrow. I'll be back east for a time."

"Yeah? Can I go with you?" Marty whispered playfully.

"Yeah, take him. Pleeease?" Brenda begged.

With the earpiece still at the side of his head, Floyd covered the mouthpiece with his palm and simultaneously flipped his partners off.

"Hold on a second," Salvador said.

Instead of being put on hold and hearing the expected canned symphony playing on the line, Floyd heard the clacking sound of the receiver being set on a desk. There was a muted conversation in the background, then the scrape of the phone being picked up.

"Sir? I'm going to transfer you to Detective Keller."

Floyd's pulse rose as his jaw dropped. Before he could interrupt Salvador and excuse himself from the call, Salvador said something that not only stunned Floyd but also gave him some insight into the reason why Keller may have been so defensive about the Farnsworth investigation.

"She should be able to help you since most of Detective Mitchell's cases were handed to her." Salvador chuckled, adding, "Although it's more like you could say she kind of inherited them since she's Mitchell's daughter."

If having his call transferred to Keller caught Floyd's breath, the officer's revelation knocked it out. Keller was Mitchell's daughter. While that didn't necessarily explain her character, it explained that Keller's aggressive posturing toward him wasn't in protecting Sacramento's reputation from Floyd as she alleged. She was protecting her father's.

A decision had to be made and had to be made fast. The transferred call was ringing in Floyd's ear and he sensed each one was the last before Keller answered. Floyd wasn't ready to deal with her yet. He still had some groundwork to lay before pressing on, part of which being going to Lt. Bern and giving him the run-down so his press forward was sanctioned. Keller's personal issues would have to take a back seat.

The phone rang a third time. Just as Floyd reached forward to depress the button on the phone base and cancel the call, he heard the click of it being answered in his ear. All he heard after that was the first syllable uttered from the other end, "Kel—", before his line went dead.

"What was that all about?" Brenda asked.

"Something I don't want to deal with right at the moment," Floyd answered. At least directly. Indirectly it mattered to the extent that he now knew why Keller would not go away. Unless he had some overriding jurisdiction when Lindell's path crossed Farnsworth's—and Floyd knew that was inevitable—Keller would have primary rights to everything and the personal pleasure of kicking him to the curb. Floyd needed to stake his claim now to establish those rights as his when Keller came to jump it. "But it's time to make our case."

Marty and Brenda followed Floyd to Lt. Bern's office. They were a bit less brash entering the office than Floyd, standing back until their partner made the initial contact before stealthily curling around the door frame and taking seats on the sofa against the back wall. Floyd took a seat in one of the two chairs fronting the lieutenant's desk. Bern, at his file cabinet in the corner, didn't react immediately. He sensed it was Floyd, and was mildly surprised when he finally turned and saw an additional two bodies in the room.

"We'd like to open an investigation."

Floyd's announcement was met with a neutral gaze from Bern that Marty and Brenda averted when it was cast at them over Floyd's shoulder. The lieutenant dropped behind his desk and took a cigar from the center drawer. As much as it was routine for Bern to do so for physical appearance, it had lately become as much a reflex action when he dealt with Floyd, giving him something to cushion the potentially tooth-cracking tension his detective had the propensity to generate. As a demonstration of control, Bern took his time inspecting the cigar and manicuring the end with his teeth.

"Yeah?" he replied, rolling the shaft of brown leaves between his fingers and thumb. "I'd like you and Maid Marion and Friar Tuck to close a few of the ones we already have open." Then he stuck the cigar in his mouth and pushed back in his chair. "What kind of case?"

"Missing person."

"Who?" Almost as soon as he asked, Bern immediately pitched forward over his desk, yanked the cigar from his mouth, and pointed the damp end at his detective. "So help me God, if you say Edson—"

"Peter Lindell," Floyd interrupted.

Bern shifted back into his chair and at such an angle so he could see Marty and Brenda, particularly their faces in the hope he could use them as human lie detectors and catch a tell in their expressions as Floyd spoke.

"Who's Peter Lindell," Bern asked Floyd, "and if he's missing, why haven't I heard about it?"

"Peter Lindell is, or was married to a woman named Eileen Sherman," Floyd explained. "He hasn't been seen for several years."

"And she's just now reporting it?"

Floyd scratched the back of his head. "Well, no. She still hasn't reported it."

"Why must you torture me, Floyd?" Bern moaned as he ran his hand across his bare scalp, thankful there was no hair in place for him to grip and rip. He brought it to rest grasping the back of his neck where he began lightly kneading the tightening muscles. "Run it down from the start, please?"

Floyd did as Bern asked and began at the beginning with the sting at Piña's shop and the encounter with Jeff and C that subsequently led to the vacant house on Mill Creek Road where the two known thieves originally found Farnsworth's ring. The recap of activity went well until he got to the part about tracking down Sherman at the city college, from which Floyd fortunately omitted his daughter's inclusion but *un*fortunately didn't exclude traveling to Sherman's apartment in Sacramento. Floyd watched the skin on Bern's forehead pull forward and crease over his brow as his barrel chest expanded with an angry suck of air that appeared trapped in his lungs, its inability to be released in a gale-force reprimand by his tightly clenched jaw. As soon as Floyd made the connections between Sherman and Lindell, then Lindell and the ring, Bern made the connection between Lindell and Farnsworth.

"It was hard enough finding her in the first place," Floyd said in his defense, "and we didn't know where she was heading when she left the college. I know you asked me to stay out of Sac—"

"Not asked. I *told* you to stay out of that city," Bern abruptly corrected. Then to the back of the room, "I suppose one of you was with him."

Marty slowly raised his hand next to his half-assed, guilty smile.

"Where were you?" he asked Brenda.

"I was in court all morning, sir."

Bern released his hand from his neck and transferred the massage to his temples. With the lieutenant's eyes shielded, Marty gave Brenda a nudge with his elbow and silently mocked "I was in court all morning, sir", putting extra emphasis on "sir" and mouthed little ass kisses to suggest she was sucking up. Brenda, however, sat perfectly still during Marty's performance, never taking her eyes from forward, which was where Marty's should have been. When he finished and faced front, Bern's glare was burning holes in him. Marty feared the worst until, to his relief, Bern continued with Floyd.

"When you say this Lindell person hasn't been seen in several years, you mean about ten, don't you, Floyd?"

"About."

"And he lived at that house during the time the whole Farnsworth mess took place."

"Right. Lindell was listed on the title up until ninety-one. The deed was changed under the name Eileen Lindell, and re-recorded when she changed it to Sherman in ninety-seven."

"What happened in ninety-seven?"

"Don't know."

"What did Sherman have to say about it?"

"The ring, or her husband?"

"Both."

"She said she and Lindell are legally separated and she doesn't know or care where he is."

"So there's a chance that Mr. Lindell just left." Floyd responded to the lieutenant's question with a half-hearted shrug. "And the ring?"

"She doesn't know about it," Floyd answered.

"God, you're annoying. She doesn't know about it, or she doesn't know you have it? *What* doesn't she know, Floyd?"

"We haven't told her about it."

"So she—" Bern started to speak, then suddenly had second thoughts about what he was going to say. A moment later he realized he wasn't going to come up with a better thought than his first and surrendered to his curiosity. "Let me ask you something. While the three of you were sitting around brainstorming your scenarios to explain how that ring got to that house, did it ever once come up that the owner of the house had a reasonable explanation that would have satisfied you had you simply asked?"

"No."

"I didn't think so. Why not?"

"We're running into some inconsistencies," Floyd said. "There are things that don't make sense, or won't until we find Lindell. Telling her about the ring if she doesn't know about it could open doors we don't want open just yet. If she's somehow involved, we don't want her tipping off her husband. As it stands now, everything points to Lindell, just not in a straight line."

"Everything points to Lindell, meaning what?"

Floyd couldn't hide the amusement he found in Bern's probing. He wasn't about to cave in, though, and through a sheepish smile he said, "That Lindell was the last person with the ring."

"Nice try." Bern jammed his cigar between his teeth and opened his Rolodex. He fingered through a dozen cards and then lifted his telephone receiver and started dialing. "Lt. Burrows," he said into the mouthpiece.

"You don't need to do that, Lieutenant," Floyd said painfully, recognizing the name of the Sac P.D. lieutenant Bern was calling.

Bern let Floyd know he could by rubbing his index finger back and forth across one of the gold bars decorating his uniform collar.

"Bob? Jim Bern ... Not bad. Listen, that business with the ring we discussed the other day? The one that my detective swears has nothing to do with Farnsworth? ... I can't say yes or no at this point, however his leads are posing a lot of questions that have potential crossover into your department's case."

While Bern exchanged a few uh-huhs and sures with the Sacramento lieutenant, Floyd shifted his eyes to the glass-covered Certificate of Merit hanging on the wall behind Bern. Not that the document held any significance. It was the ghostly reflections of his partners seated behind him he was interested in. Marty saw Floyd looking at him in the glass and gave a small shrug. Floyd reached behind his head to scratch and imaginary itch and returned a your-guess-is-as-good-as-mine flip of the wrist. When Bern spoke again, things appeared to be falling in the Santa Ramona detectives' favor.

"Right. I'd like to let him continue with the investigation …,"

Then things continued to fall out.

"… but I wanted some of your folks on hand … No, but we may need to talk with a couple of people on your turf and I'd feel better if you had some representation. Since you had a team already assigned to the case I thought—"

Bern came to an abrupt stop and pulled his unlit cigar from his mouth. That was followed by a long pause as he listened to his commanding counterpart. The three detectives watched curiously as their lieutenant's brow danced up and down in surprise.

"Oh, I agree."

The lieutenant agreed with too much sympathy, as far as Floyd was concerned. For a fleeting moment it crossed Floyd's mind that Lt. Burrows had made a successful pitch to Bern to take the ring and the case off his hands and deliver them to Sacramento. As Bern continued, Floyd realized there was another issue being discussed between the two leaders.

"Sounds like you and I have something in common beyond a case neither of us is aware of. Not at all. We'll get to the bottom of it. And if there's anything I can do in return … Okay, Bob."

Bern hung up the phone and informed his detectives that Lt. Burrows would be sending Detectives Keller and Tiner the following day, referring to them sarcastically as the same two detectives who didn't have permission to come here the last time.

Floyd cringed. He knew bringing the search for

Peter Lindell to Bern carried with it certain risks, first and foremost being the possibility of including Sac P.D. Secondary, but no less a concern, was the probability that Keller would be the designated representative if the former occurred.

Brenda cringed, too, though not for the same reason as Floyd. She hoped her last run-in with Tiner in the city had sent the message that she had no interest in even the slightest casual relationship with him. Having encountered a lifetime of Tiner-types throwing their best worst efforts at her, Brenda knew all too well that the Sacramento detective would see this as another opportunity to get in her pants.

"As it turns out Bob is in a similar position that I'm in. Apparently he has a detective, like I have," he directed at Floyd, "who has a partner," he directed toward the back of his office, "and they like to run roughshod all over God's green earth, much like mine do."

The trio of detectives said nothing.

"They'll be here in the morning. You'll have a nice discussion over coffee and decide how to wrap this thing up." Bern leaned over the desk and dropped his voice. "And, Floyd, I assured Bob that it *will be* wrapped up soon."

The two Sacramento detectives were on their way back to their desks having left their commander's office where he reprimanded them for their part in conducting an unauthorized investigation. All he asked Keller to do was send a copy of the Farnsworth report to Santa Ramona, and send didn't mean personally deliver and become involved, Keller found out. She also found out—and this bothered her more than the verbal counseling Burrows gave her—the lieutenant was tipped off to her freelancing by the lieutenant of the Santa Ramona detectives, who could only have learned of their unsanctioned foray from Floyd King.

"Do you think they figured out what happened to Farnsworth?" Tiner asked.

"I doubt it. My guess is King's found out something worth following up on and whatever it is it's not one-hundred percent his."

"The ring. I'll bet he found out where the ring turned up. Maybe who had it when Farnsworth vanished."

"No," Keller answered immediately, as if she read her partner's mind and knew what he was going to conclude. "If he'd gotten that far he'd be crowing like a rooster at sunrise. I think we can safely conclude the ring was traced back to that Sherman woman or her ex-husband, though."

"How so?"

"Why else would he be looking at property records? King obviously caught the thieves who tried to pawn the ring. They must have told him where they picked it up, and that 'where' is the property record he sent his partner to find."

"But Sherman lives in Santa Ramona. So why should King be concerned about us?"

"Because he needs something he can't get without us."

"So through his lieutenant he gets Burrows to put us in play, throws us a bone to keep us busy while he's off looking for whatever it is he's after."

Keller broke her quick pace and spun and had to throw up a hand to keep Tiner from walking into her. Her own interaction with Floyd had thus far been based on deception, so Tiner's suggestion didn't seem too far off the mark.

"Now you're starting to use that brain of yours," she lauded, tapping at her partner's temple and smiling approvingly. "It might just be that King formulated some obtuse connection between his case and ours, a connection that won't mean shit to us but will open a door or two for them."

"Doors that I bet aren't in Santa Ramona."

Keller nodded. "Doors that lead to places we don't want him to go."

14
Thursday morning, August 21st

The following morning at a coffee shop located near the imaginary boundary where cities of Santa Ramona and Sacramento seamlessly converged, five detectives sat around a small table each sipping at steaming coffee from recycled paper cups with the same tentative care in how they chose their words.

As with the last time they were together in a group around a table—the lunch that Marty jokingly referred to as "Pagergate"—Floyd and Keller sat next to each other, as did Marty and Tiner. Brenda remained content to sit as far from Tiner as possible with Marty as her buffer from Tiner's lecherous leering. Brenda still hadn't said anything to Floyd about Tiner's advance during their encounter in Sacramento, but she had divulged it to Marty. Not that she wanted to. It was out of necessity in exchange for Marty's promise to keep the Sacramento detective at bay. It came with a price, as she had to endure a litany of wise-ass remarks from him

"But if I'm watching him, how will I be able to keep Keller away from Floyd?" he cracked through his lip-curling smile.

"Ass," was Brenda's curt reply.

Floyd brought Keller and Tiner up to speed on the attempt to locate Peter Lindell after identifying him as the former husband of the owner of the house where Farnsworth's ring was recovered. None of this information surprised Keller. She as much as predicted that disclosure the previous afternoon. The revelation she found most telling about the sudden need for unity came as Floyd told them of their discovery of Sherman's current residence, the apartment in Sacramento. In her jurisdiction. It was one of the doors Floyd and his team needed her to open.

"We've noticed some discrepancies between the original report and the information gathered over the last couple of days," Floyd began only to be interrupted by Keller.

"I don't see how the information in the report can be criticized as lacking," she countered. "It was gathered for a completely different purpose, the disappearance of Edson Farnsworth, not his ring."

"True. But as a source of information for a follow-up—"

"You're saying the report is faulty," Keller jumped in angrily.

"I'm not saying anything of the sort." Floyd didn't want to get involved in a dispute with Keller over the Sacramento report, which was where he felt she was leading him. He could sense Keller wanted to defend her father's work. Admirable, but not necessary. He wasn't attacking Detective Mitchell.

Keller's face hardened. "But the implication is sure there."

"I'm sure the report was as thorough as it could have been at the time. There's a glaring omission, though, in that Peter Lindell was never interviewed."

"So? He was gone during the investigation, but that didn't mean the investigation had to wait. He was a victim, same as Vossen."

"And there's no reason to believe he'd have provided any different information from what was collected," Tiner added. "Based on his wife's statement, Lindell folded his business and went after the man who forced his hand."

"And never came back," Marty said.

"So what doesn't fit is how the ring got to the shed," Floyd added.

"Your assumption then is that maybe Lindell had something to do with Farnsworth's disappearance," Keller cut in. "I'm glad we finally got that out in the open, that you've been looking for Farnsworth all along."

"That's *your* assumption," Floyd corrected. "All we've been doing is tracking down the ring's history, looking for the man who possibly had it last. Nothing's changed except that our investigation into Lindell is officially a missing persons case."

"Oh, come on! Are we to believe there was a point in your 'search' you didn't expect it to ultimately end up coinciding with the Farnsworth case?" Keller challenged.

All attention was on Floyd and Keller as their eyes were locked upon each other. Floyd's desire to keep the focus on the meeting on track became hampered by Keller's deliberate attempts to derail him. Floyd held his tongue against the bitter taste of retaliation sitting in his mouth. He did not savor engaging Keller in a hostile exchange, not in public and certainly not one dictated by her. Floyd slid his chair back, stood, and calmly announced he was stepping outside for a few minutes. Then he issued his own challenge to Keller by inviting her to join him.

Floyd and Keller were the only two patrons outside the coffee shop's front doors. Still, Floyd felt the need for a greater degree of privacy than could be expected by the sporadic entry and exit of customers through the patio. He walked to the side of the building with Keller in step behind him. The windowless wall offered privacy from the audience seated inside, and the greasy stench from the Dumpster abutting the wall would handily deflect any pedestrian traffic.

"You can believe whatever you want," Floyd began, his tone forceful yet measured, not threatening. "You were told up front that if our investigation tied into yours we'd include you. Now we've reached that point and decided it would be best to call you in. Beyond that, I don't give a damn what you believe."

"How fucking noble of you," Keller said condescendingly. "Though I'd be willing to bet your lieutenant had more to do with your up-front sense of fair play."

Floyd reached into his pocket and removed the black cloth containing Edson Farnsworth's ring. He wasn't so much concerned that she'd take it—he didn't need it now, and because it was found in Santa Ramona, she couldn't use it without his department's release. Floyd merely wanted to see if she *would* take it.

"Here." Floyd handed Keller the black cloth containing Farnsworth's ring. "You want it so bad, take it."

"Aw, what's the matter, Floyd? Not having fun any more?"

"It's not about fun. I just don't need the grief." Floyd extended his hand closer to Keller, but she wouldn't take the cloth. "Go on. It's what you want."

Keller shook her head. "It's what *you* want."

"What *I* want," Floyd asserted, "is to find Peter Lindell and clarify how this ring got onto his property. What *I* want is a measure of cooperation that I'm not getting."

"What cooperation? You've gone out of your way to exclude us in every step of this investigation until now."

"That's because this investigation didn't concern your department until now."

"Your investigation concerned my department the

second you asked for the report on Farnsworth. You may have been able to con your lieutenant into buying that bullshit recovered property fable, but I know different, King. That ring stinks of Edson Farnsworth *and you know it*. You knew it as soon as it fell into the palm of your hand."

"What do you want me to say? That finding Farnsworth doesn't intrigue me? How could it not? But even if it did, I firmly believe nobody finds Farnsworth without knowing what happened to Lindell. Peter Lindell is the missing link for both of us. And whether you like it or not, Lindell is Santa Ramona's case."

"Which, given the right amount of time to allow you the ability to manipulate the facts, you will incorporate with our case on Farnsworth," Keller countered harshly.

Floyd shook his head to the sky and made a final attempt at bridging the expanse separating their points of views and egos. "Look, we can stand out here and exchange allegations and excuses all day or sit in there and not make any progress, or we can work together—"

"Work *together*!" Keller barked. "You mean I can come aboard and work for *you*, don't you, Floyd? Isn't that what cops do in Santa Ramona? Work for Floyd King? Make sure you stay on your personal agenda of picking apart everyone else's investigations and showing us dumb asses the way a case should be solved?"

"Make whatever you like out of this situation, Grace, the bottom line here is your lieutenant and my lieutenant don't want either of us operating without the other. We're in this together, or we're in the boss's office explaining why we're not. One's just as fine with me as the other."

Keller sighed heavily through her anger. She wasn't any more afraid of facing Burrows than Floyd was of facing Bern. But she'd already gotten her ass chewed for skirting her lieutenant's directives and been threatened with "grounding and chores", a Burrows-ism for the punishment of desk duty and filing, sanctions for "contempt of lieutenant". Yielding to her better sense, though, the sense that told her she'd be better off with Floyd as an ally if for no other reason than to keep tabs on him, she had no option but to side with the Santa Ramona detective's perspective and accept a spot on the team.

Shit rolled across her mind. "Shit" passed over her lips.

"All right, King. I concede in principal that putting our resources together is mutually beneficial. *But*, when we're in Sacramento, it's my show. Absent exigent circumstances, we confer before we act, and when we act—"

"Your show. And I know you'll honor that over there." Floyd thumbed over his shoulder in the direction of Santa Ramona, a motion that happened to be in line with the Dumpster.

"Oh, by all means, King." Keller snorted a laugh, amused at the joke Floyd neither saw nor got. "Let's get back inside so the others don't think we've ripped out each other's jugulars."

There were only casual glances of mild interest in their return as the supporting cast of the Great Clash had occupied themselves with other endeavors. Tiner had moved around the table and taken the seat vacated by Keller, the seat opposite Marty and next to Brenda. He made the move during Brenda's escape to the restroom, done more to relieve the growing discomfort of Tiner's proximity than that of her bladder. Even taking literally the myth of women taking an inordinate amount of time in the ladies room, she dallied beyond the point of reasonable and forced herself back to the table. Tiner passed the time picking her brain about her likes and dislikes in food, movies, and such. The pained expression on Brenda's face indicated the brain-picking had more in common with a Hitchcock bird than a mutually entertained conversation. Adding to her displeasure was the fact that Marty, with whom she had entrusted the task of preventing Tiner from annoying her, sat oblivious to her suffering, busying himself with the construction of a fleet of seven airplanes folded from paper napkins that sat limp and aerodynamically useless on their Formica tarmac.

"Keller and I are going to take a trip into town. It's time to press a few of Eileen Sherman's buttons and see how she reacts."

"What do you want us to do?" Tiner asked.

"Wait." Keller's response came like a command to a dog.

"You don't have to stay here," Floyd said. "Go back to the office. Maybe let Bern see you working on other things to take the edge off his irritability."

"The edge came off when you left his office yesterday," Marty cracked before giving one of his jets a very short and unimpressive test flight.

"I can hang out with you guys, if it's all the same."

Tiner's offer, likely encouraged by Keller beforehand as a means to keep tabs on the Santa Ramona crew, wasn't met with any enthusiasm, especially from Brenda, who came up with another suggestion.

"You know, we don't have any photos of Lindell. I'll bet Vossen has one or two. He told me the Lindells went on some of the year-end vacations set up by him and Farnsworth."

"I'm sure Eileen Sherman has a few," Keller said. "We can get one from her."

"Well, uh, those won't be group shots. You know, maybe

we can see how they interacted amongst one another, get an idea of how they—"

"Worth checking."

Floyd saved Brenda from sounding like she was begging and she rewarded him with an exhale of appreciation. It was fleeting relief, though, as Tiner happily volunteered to accompany her.

"No," she replied almost too abruptly. "Vossen's kind of quiet. I don't think the attention will go over very well. He's a resource I'd like to hang on to, not spook away."

"Spook him?"

Marty clapped a hand over Tiner's shoulder. "We'll hold down the fort, right, Curt? And I'll buy you lunch. There's a rib joint down the street we can't go to because *some* people find it dis*gus*ting to gnaw on animal bones with their fingers. Makes me wonder how our species survived this long."

Brenda caught onto Marty's ploy and feigned a sickened expression. It wasn't all show as she sickened by the fact that she loved barbeque and was being portrayed as prissy. The benefit of his intervention, she figured, outweighed the mild tarnish to her reputation. A price she paid for now that *would be* redeemed later.

"Your car or mine?" Floyd asked Keller.

"Yours. If we get hung up you can drop me off downtown." She tossed her keys to Tiner. "Don't get sauce on the steering wheel." Then back to Floyd, "Let's go."

15
Thursday midday, August 21st

Floyd pulled his car to a stop in front of Sherman's apartment complex close to where he'd stopped previously with Marty and Shelby after tailing the former teacher upon her departure from the city college. He and Keller exited their respective sides of the car and walked to the security gate. Floyd ran his finger down the panel of listed residents and stopped it on number one-fifteen.

"You're not going to buzz her, are you?" Keller asked.

"It would be the proper thing to do," Floyd answered, "but, no, I didn't plan on it. Do you think the manager will oblige us and let us in?"

Keller slid in front of Floyd and depressed the call button for the complex manager's apartment. A crusty male voice spit a static-filled blast at them through a small speaker in the center of the panel, a speaker of a size seemingly incapable of making such a large noise. Both detectives rocked back as if hit by a shock wave. Keller leaned toward the speaker, mindful of its explosive potential, and identified herself.

"How do I know you are who you say you are?" the cranky man asked.

"You could take my word for it, or you can walk out here and look at my ID."

"We could climb the fence," Floyd suggested in jest.

"I'm not climbing shit," Keller stated in all seriousness.

"Do you have a warrant?"

Keller pulled back from the speaker. "God, I hate that

question!" she snarled through gnashed teeth. "Do you have a warrant?" she echoed in a sniveling tone. "What about my free phone calls? Why don't you go catch a *real* criminal? *Jesus H. Christ!*" She grabbed the gate handle and rattled the decorative iron door against the frame in anger. "Oh, and let's not forget anything that starts with them saying 'You have no right to ...'"

Keller redirected her ire at Floyd, who was leaning back against a wall listening to her rant with a half smile tugging at the left side of his face.

"I'm glad you find this amusing, King." Keller composed herself with a deep breath and returned to the speaker to call the manager back. "No, sir. I do not have a warrant," she explained. "I don't *need* a warrant to talk to people."

There was a long silence before the speaker crackled to life again. "Who are you here to see?"

"I can't tell you that," Keller said apologetically. Her short-lived sincerity, however, only masked an attitude that exposed itself instantly through a tone of irritation. "I *can* tell you that if I *have* to find another way in, the first person I'm coming to see is *you* and not long behind me will be an army of building and fire code inspectors to—"

Keller didn't have to finish. There was a sharp buzz as the electronic lock released. Keller reached out and pushed the gate open with one hand while extending an after-you arm sweep toward Floyd with the other. Floyd stepped into the courtyard a few paces and surveyed the buildings. Keller, after giving the gate a frustration-cleansing slam that she hoped carried back through the speaker and perforated the manager's eardrum, joined Floyd at his side.

"The number system appears to be less confusing than some places I've been," Floyd noted, a light-hearted jab in reference to his wandering visit through Keller's complex.

He pointed to the right. "Apartment's over there, but I want to check the carport first."

"You go ahead. I'm going to check in with the manager." Keller smiled wickedly. "*That* would be the proper thing to do."

The detectives pondered their routes for a moment, then split up. Floyd headed for the rear of the complex while Keller picked her way down the numbered units looking for the manager's office. The parking area, as Floyd suspected, comprised of an overhang covering a series of numbered stalls that butted up to small storage cabinets mounted to the carport wall. The opening from the courtyard was almost centered to the parking area where Floyd saw a few cars, less than a dozen or so, scattered. He recognized one: Eileen Sherman's gold Acura. Floyd read the upside-down numbers painted to the concrete floor of the stalls at his immediate left, one-twenty, and right, one-nineteen, and determined they were marked in descending order going toward Sherman's car. He counted the assigned spaces to confirm the Acura was, indeed, in stall one-fifteen and turned back into the courtyard.

"Find the car?" Keller asked upon her return from the manager's office.

"Right where it's supposed to be. Did you find the manager?"

Keller simply grinned triumphantly.

They walked in silence to apartment one-fifteen. Floyd motioned to the door and gave Keller the honors. Keller knocked hard three times then, as if responding to a subconscious motivation developed in her readiness training, she took a step back and to the side. The deadbolt clicked and the door pulled back a few inches exposing half of a woman's face.

"If you're lost, the manager's apartment number—"

Keller held up her badge, silencing the woman. "I've already spoken to the manager," she said without detailing precisely what she spoke with the manager about, which had nothing to do with the business at hand. "Are you Eileen Sherman?"

"Yes."

"Good. I'm Detective Keller. This is Detective King from Santa Ramona."

Floyd spoke. "Ms. Sherman, we're looking for Peter Lindell. Have you seen him?"

"No, I—" Sherman paused gave a confused shake of her head. "There was a Sacramento police officer here just recently asking about Peter, too. What's going on?"

Keller knew no Sacramento detective other than herself or Tiner had any reason to inquire about Lindell, so it was clear Floyd had sent an advance scout. She stared hard at Floyd. "Little something you neglected to tell me?"

Floyd responded with a nonchalant bounce of his eyebrows. He could have easily matched Marty's call on Sherman with Tiner's on Collette Farnsworth, but it would have resulted in a repeat of their earlier disagreements: unresolved compromise.

"Perhaps you could let us inside, Ms. Sherman," Keller said, turning her attention to the half-hidden woman. "This may or may not take some time, but I'm sure you're going to want to sit. And I'm very sure you don't want us conducting business outside."

Sherman stepped aside, pulling the door open to allow the detectives in. The apartment was small: small kitchen, small living room, one small bedroom with a half bath located between the apartment door and her bedroom door. The interior was sparsely decorated and there were several boxes stacked against the far wall with writing indicating their contents.

Had he not known anything about Sherman until this moment Floyd would have assumed she was either moving in or moving out, that her possessions were enough to make a new start or only what basics she could manage to transport herself. But Floyd knew Eileen Sherman came from the roomy house on Mill Creek Road to this cramped apartment on the fringe of downtown Sacramento, knew that the boxed belongings and furniture before him were not representative of everything she owned. He made a mental note about storage units and the possibility that some of her husband's things were also stored there. Things that might clue them in to where he went.

Sherman led the way into the apartment and motioned Floyd and Keller to the living area and the small sofa, then sat herself in a matching recliner.

"Could you please explain to me what's going on?" Sherman asked.

"Like Detective King said, we're looking for Peter Lindell. You were married to him, correct?"

"Yes, but ... my God, that was years ago. Then he left. I haven't seen him or heard from him since. I told the other officer that."

"You also told your neighbor that your husband died last year when he got hit by a drunk driver," Floyd said. It caused Sherman to shrink in her seat. "That would indicate you saw him recently."

"I ... I said that, yes," she admitted sheepishly. "I got tired of people asking me about a Mr. Sherman, so I made up the story that he died. I found that if you tell people your husband left you it leads to a lot of questions and speculation, particularly speculation about what I did to make him leave. If I said he was dead, the reaction was less intrusive to me personally. I apologize for the deception, but it was only intended to limit the conversations about him."

"That's understandable," Keller said. She'd experienced similar questions after her divorce and on a number of occasions wished she'd simply said her ex was dead, though not as often as she wished he truly *was* dead, which often led to her fantasizing about some excruciatingly painful, tortuous means to that end.

"Interesting, though, that you'd tell an acquaintance your husband was dead but avoid the subject altogether with a colleague." Sherman's attention snapped to Floyd. "I spoke with Neil Dobbs when I went looking for you at the city college. You worked with Neil for five years and he said the subject of Peter never came up."

"We were colleagues," Sherman replied, "not intimate friends. Our conversations centered mostly on academics."

Floyd wasn't going to believe the subject was one that just never came up between the instructors. It was his opinion that Sherman more likely portrayed herself as single during the time she and Dobbs worked together. He let her explanation slide and pressed on to the reason for his and Keller's visit.

"When was the last time you saw Peter?" Floyd asked.

Sherman blew a thoughtful sigh through her nose and bit her lower lip as she turned the clock back in her mind. "It was shortly after the incident with Edson Farnsworth, when Edson stole the money from the business and left his partner. That would be April of ninety-three. Peter came home in the middle of the day, which was very unusual for him."

"Why?" Keller asked.

"He was a busy man. Edson and Len Vossen, Edson's partner, had a number of projects going on at the same time. As their main contractor, Peter had his hand in several of them. Most days he'd be out of the house by four in the morning and I wouldn't see him until seven or eight at night. If he had to travel out of the area I may not see him for two or three days."

"Doesn't make for a healthy relationship, does it?"

Sherman shrugged. "We did all right. It was hard at first, but I got used to it. Peter wanted to build enough assets to break free of his dependence on Edson and Len. He was getting close, too. Then ..."

"Then Farnsworth ripped off the business and put your husband in a bad position with the banks," Floyd finished. "How bad?"

"How bad?" Sherman echoed. "Bad enough that he abandoned everything. His own business. His life. Me. How bad is bad, Detective King?"

How bad, indeed? Floyd thought, recalling the emotional turmoil he suffered when Lynn took Shelby as she walked out on him.

"I never saw Peter so mad. Not even when Jay Whiting screwed him over."

Sherman paused and asked if either officer wanted something to drink. Floyd and Keller both declined, and Sherman resettled in the chair, uncrossing her legs and sliding sideways to tuck her right leg under her left thigh before continuing. It was a sign to Floyd that she was slightly more comfortable dealing with the police now than she appeared at first, if she had truly been uncomfortable at all. He considered that if Sherman had cause to be prepared, she would have been tipped off by Marty's visit.

"When he came home, as soon as he walked in the door, I knew something was wrong," Sherman continued. "Peter said Len called him and told him Edson had drained the company accounts before the weekend and had vanished. Len told him all of their projects would have to be put on hold while the bank went over their books. Peter met with Len, who after going over the contracts told him that even with a modest amount of luck they were doomed."

"And that affected Peter because the lost building contracts did what?" Keller asked. "Cut him out of some business?"

"That was part of it. Peter also had a lot of his own assets tied up in projects, assets that he expected to recoup as the Farnsworth & Vossen contracts paid out. Where Vossen had the ability to reorganize and make settlements on his end of the business, Peter stood to lose everything."

"So instead of facing the music, he left the concert," Floyd said.

"Peter didn't leave to avoid the responsibility, Detective King," Sherman countered sharply. "On the contrary, Peter took the responsibility of going after Edson when nobody else would. Including the police. The last thing he said to me was that he knew he didn't stand a chance in hell of saving his business, that his chance of finding Edson and wringing his neck was better."

"So Peter went after Farnsworth shortly after Farnsworth left," Floyd concluded.

"Yes."

"And he's been gone the whole time, all ten years Farnsworth has been gone?" Keller asked.

"All but the first few days head start Edson likely had, yes."

"And Peter never gave you any specific indication where

he was going to find Farnsworth?" Floyd asked. "Any indication he knew where Farnsworth may have gone or would go?"

"None."

"And never once in ten years did he call or write or stop by the house."

Sherman's brow knitted with a mix of irritation and frustration. "That's what I've been saying, Detective King. Peter's gone. I have not had any contact with him since he left. I don't know where he went."

"I'm just making sure I understand correctly, Ms. Sherman."

"Well, maybe you can help me understand correctly. It's been ten years and now the police are looking for Peter. Why? Do you suspect him of being involved in Edson's disappearance?"

Floyd and Keller exchanged a mutually intrigued glance before Keller asked, "What made you think we thought he was involved?"

"Huh? I ... Why else would you be interested in finding him if you didn't think he was?"

"Could be a number of reasons," Floyd said. "Old parking tickets ..."

Sherman looked down her nose with a blank expression, clearly not amused at Floyd's wry humor. "I could lie and tell you the other officer already told me that Edson's disappearance was *his* reason to find Peter, but I won't."

"And I could make up any number of other reasons for wanting to talk with him that have nothing to do with Mr. Farnsworth, but I won't lie, either. What we suspect and what we can prove are miles apart. Right now we're in the connect-the-dots phase, and one of the dots connects to your former husband. All we want is some information that moves us to the next dot."

"Okay. But I don't see how I can help. The other officer must have told you the same thing I'm telling you now, that I haven't seen Peter. So what do you know that brings you back to me?"

Floyd reached into his pocket and pulled out the black cloth. He handed it to Keller, who passed it to Sherman. Sherman peeled the sides away to expose the ring. Her face blanched in shock and she momentarily stopped breathing.

"That's ... that's his ring," Sherman whispered, pushing the last of the air from her lungs. Then, recovering to a normal tone, "That's Edson's ring."

"That's what we've been told," Floyd said.

"Where did you get it?" Before either detective could answer, Sherman stunned herself with her own conclusion. Her eyes grew large and her free hand came up to cover her mouth as she gasped again. "You found him. You found Edson and—Peter. Oh my God."

"We didn't find Mr. Farnsworth or your husband, Ms. Sherman," Floyd said in an attempt to calm her. "Just the ring."

Sherman stared at the ring and rubbed her thumb across the stones and mumbled numbly, "No, I suppose he's still gone. And I'm sure if Edson's body turned up it would have hit the news like the next coming of Christ. Where did you find it?"

"In Santa Ramona." Having not made up his mind about Sherman's trustworthiness, Floyd withheld the exact location as there was a chance she would tip her hand to any knowledge she had about its recovery point being her own house.

"And you think he did it, right? That's why you're here. That's why Peter never came back. He did it."

"He did what?" Keller asked.

"Killed Edson. Why else would he have left? Leaving would have been the most reasonable option, wouldn't it?"

Floyd asked, "A more appropriate question would be why would he wait four days before leaving?"

Sherman's face screwed in confusion, Keller's in curiosity as she tried to pick up his lead.

"Based on the investigation by the Sacramento police ten years ago, from the statements of Collette Farnsworth and Mr. Vossen, through the evidence they found—the recovered car and the theft of the money—Edson Farnsworth vanished four days before your husband learned about it from Vossen. There are only two possibilities."

The first one Floyd presented presumed Farnsworth was still in town or was someplace he could be found shortly after the theft. Not likely, in Floyd's opinion, as the whole scheme was too well planned when considering that for months Farnsworth was systematically bleeding the company and his customers. The final withdrawal was a wire transfer to another account, a transaction he made on a Friday, giving himself a cushion of a couple of days minimum before Vossen or anyone else found out. A couple of days that guaranteed he could possibly get out of the country and move the money again before the banks opened on the following Monday.

"There was no advantage for him to hang around, and it would have been inconsistent with amount of preparation needed to pull off such a highly calculated plan," Floyd concluded, then "The second possibility is that Farnsworth was dead before your husband left."

"And that makes it a likely scenario with the ring being found in town," Keller added as if she had been in step with Floyd all along.

"But why?" Sherman asked. "Why would Peter wait to leave? It doesn't make sense."

"Could be a number of reasons," Floyd replied. "Assuming he wasn't as prepared as Farnsworth, he would have needed time to hide the body and cover his tracks. And if he waited until someone else discovered the account theft and Farnsworth's disappearance, he could play that to his advantage by giving him an excuse to leave, himself."

"We have some other theories we're working," Keller said. "But you're right. All in all, it doesn't make sense, which is why we'd like to find Peter so he can clear it up."

"And we're sorry to have to bother you with finding him, but the only listing we had for him was your house on Mill Creek," Floyd added. "The deed is recorded in your name alone, correct?"

Sherman gave Floyd a quizzical look. "Yes."

"Why wasn't your husband listed?"

"That was Peter's decision. When Jay Whiting cast him off, we almost lost it. The house. After we recovered financially, Peter said he wanted to re-record the deed in my name and keep it completely independent of the business. That way, if something happened, the bank couldn't take it from us. He wouldn't use it as collateral on the business and wouldn't let me sign any papers related to the business."

"That's pretty trusting," Keller said. "I mean, with the house in your name he has no claim to it."

"I wouldn't have done that to Peter," Sherman replied indignantly to Keller's implication that she dangled that fact over her husband's head for control. "I'm a little offended that you would even—"

"I didn't mean anything personally, Ms. Sherman. Actually, in your case, it turned out to be fortuitous not having to deal with all the red tape involved in getting the house in your name after your husband left."

"Speaking of your name, why did you change it?" Floyd asked.

"Once I realized Peter wasn't coming back, I decided to take my maiden name again. I was looking at it as making a fresh start. That's why I'm in the process of moving."

"Six years of lag time is a bit much to make another fresh start, don't you think?" Keller asked.

"On the contrary, I think you can find new avenues in life at any time. The pieces didn't fall into place allowing me to uproot my life from Santa Ramona until recently."

"And those pieces are ...?" Floyd pressed hopefully.

"Personal, Detective."

"Do you have anything else to ask?" Floyd asked Keller.

"No." Keller gave the standard admonishment to Sherman that she stay close to home. "We may need to talk to you again."

Floyd and Keller stood and waited for Sherman to lead them to the door. Both detectives handed business cards to the woman, extended their thanks for her cooperation, and left. They didn't speak as they walked through the courtyard back to Floyd's car. Once in their seats, Keller began picking Floyd's mind.

"You think she knows something, don't you, King? I do. She flashes a convincing air of ignorance, including being surprised to see the ring."

Floyd recalled Sherman's reaction to seeing the ring and how it momentarily threw her calm rhythm off. "Just surprised to see it, or surprised to see it was found?" Floyd wondered.

"I'm willing to bet that at the very least she knew we got it from the shed," Keller began. She offered the theory that Lindell figured out something was up with the business accounts and caught up to Farnsworth *before* he left, perhaps not long after Farnsworth made the bank transfers. The two men argued, fought, and then Lindell, accidentally or intentionally, killed Farnsworth. After stripping Farnsworth's body down to the ring on his finger and dumping it, Lindell went home and hid Farnsworth's belongings in the shed.

"Maybe she saw him hide the stuff," Keller continued. "Maybe Lindell was just stupid and told his wife what really happened to Farnsworth. Following Vossen's suspicion that Farnsworth was on the run, Lindell came up with the manhunt-for-revenge story to explain his own ensuing absence and asks her to cover for him, to convince the police that Farnsworth's a thief and he's a victim."

"And Sherman goes along with this?" Floyd asked. "Instead of leaving with him and the money?"

"Sherman knows if she goes with him she'll be in it as deep as he is. She wants nothing to do with the plan, so to sweeten the deal Lindell promises to pay her off, give her a cut of whatever he took. She tells him 'All right, I'll keep my mouth shut if you go away and never come back'. Lindell goes away, all right, but Sherman never sees a nickel. She can't go back to the police and change her story because she'll have to admit to being a conspirator. She figures the house is already in her name, the police are off her back—"

"So it's a wash," Floyd concluded for her. "But you're saying there's no way the ring gets to the Mill Creek house without Lindell, and no way Lindell's plan works without Sherman knowing about it."

"Do you see any way Sherman doesn't know?" Keller asked Floyd.

"I'm sure a mildly competent attorney could come up with a few ways," Floyd replied. "Remember, the ring didn't turn up until she put the house up for sale, and it seems to me if Sherman knew the ring was in the shed she'd have gotten rid of it a long time ago."

Keller thought about Floyd's point. "Okay, then let's assume she didn't know about the ring. It's still possible Lindell killed Farnsworth, ditched his ring and other belongings in the shed, and waited a day or two before putting on the big drama about not coming home without Edson's head in a sack before vanishing, himself."

"And she bought it," Floyd added. "And Lindell never came back, and for ten years she never touches anything in the shed. Never questions where her husband went or where he could be. But she still clings to the hope her husband will return having cleansed the family name, which she has changed. Then, after another half-dozen years of keeping that light burning in the window, all the pieces finally fall together. She realizes he's never coming back."

"Don't be a jackass," Keller huffed. "Either way, something's missing."

"We have the something," Floyd said, patting his pocket. "We need the some*one*."

"So are we in agreement that Sherman probably knew her husband had a hand in Farnsworth's disappearance?"

"As much as not," Floyd answered.

Keller crossed her arms and grunted. "Like I said, you and I as partners ... It's a damn good thing for you a fence only has two sides, the way you go back and forth."

"Just keeping my options open, like my fence gates," Floyd told her. "Makes it easier to get at what's on the other side."

"And what's on the other side?"

"Whatever we don't have on this side," Floyd answered with a devilish smirk. "For sure there was a bit too much drama back there for my liking. The big money question is on how we proceed with this."

"I say we go on the belief that Sherman knows something," Keller said as Floyd started the car. "It's time for us to start closing some of those gates, King."

∽

Len Vossen wasn't expecting anyone at his office, so he was a little tentative opening his door to investigate the sounds of someone entering the reception area. He appeared as equally relieved as surprised to see Brenda standing at the reception desk with her hand hovering over the silver bell.

Vossen invited Brenda back into his office, which to Brenda looked even more cluttered than before but upon a second assessment came to realize it was the same mess rearranged. There was no apology this time as he cleared a stack of folders and binders from the chair she sat on previously. He offered it to her as he circled around his desk to his own chair.

"I didn't expect to see you again so soon," Vossen said.

"Why is it that you expected to see me again at all?" Brenda asked curiously.

"I guess being as close as I was to Edson, as involved as I was with him ..."

"Or that you were so deeply wounded by him?" Brenda's unintentionally pointed comment caused Vossen's casual smile to melt in stoic resignation. "I'm sorry, Mr. Vossen. I didn't mean—"

Vossen's hand went up. "That's okay, Detective. What

you said is just as much the truth. When I say it, it's like picking at a scab. Takes longer to heal, leaves a deeper scar." The hand that went up to stop Brenda now opened toward her. "You obviously have something you need to discuss with me."

"Yes. About Mr. Lindell."

"You're making progress in finding Peter?" came Vossen's enthusiastic query.

"Trying," came Brenda's less than enthusiastic reply. "The last time we spoke you mentioned some trips you, the Farnsworths, and the Lindells took."

"That's right. The sort-of company vacations."

"Do you happen to have any photos of those vacations?"

"Ones that happen to have Peter in them?"

Brenda nodded, then somewhat embarrassed added, "We don't know what he looks like. That makes it kind of hard to make an identification."

"I imagine so," Vossen said through a smile. A contemplative "hmm" purred in his throat as he reclined in his chair. His eyes drifted upward in their sockets and his brow furrowed in the classic thinker's expression. "That was a long time ago."

"I know, but if there's any chance you might have one or two ..."

A long minute passed before Vossen's eyes rolled back down and settled on Brenda. He got up and started across the room. "Come with me," he directed as he led Brenda to the outer office to a supply room. The room was six-by-six with boxes stacked askew to rafters. Some of the boxes were marked by years, suggesting to Brenda they contained business records. Vossen bent down and removed a box, nearly toppling a column as he did. He quickly shot a hand up and steadied the cardboard tower, keeping it upright, though as precariously as the Tower of Pisa.

"If I have any old photos they'd be in here."

Vossen set the box, marked "MISC.", on the receptionist's desk and unfolded the flaps, one of which flipped up too quickly and catapulted a cloud of dust toward his face. He pulled back, held his breath, and pinched his eyes tight to the cloud. He dispersed the dusty air with a few waves of his hand before turning back to the box. Vossen sifted through the odds and ends and removed two over-sized envelopes. He moved the box to the floor to make room on the desk and began sorting through the photographs he took from the first envelope. He peeled off the first five pictures without a word, and then handed the sixth to Brenda.

The photo was a group shot of three men standing at the railing of a redwood deck in front of an A-frame cabin. Each man was dressed in hiking shorts and long-sleeved, plaid flannel shirts. Their faces were shadowed by the brims of their ball caps and unshaven jaws. Each man smiled broadly and held a beer in a toast to the camera like a trio of intrepid explorers celebrating their return from an extended trek into the uncharted wilderness.

"That's Peter," Vossen said, pointing to the man on the right of the photo.

Brenda nodded. She recognized Vossen immediately and was somewhat positive which of the other two was Farnsworth based on the news photos from her research. Vossen's confirmation identified the man she would have picked as Peter Lindell.

"Not very clear, though," Brenda commented. "Do you have any others?"

As Brenda asked, Vossen was already thumbing through

the rest of the stack, pulling out one and then another and setting them aside.

"This was a trip to Tahoe," Vossen explained, extracting the memory. "Collette and Eileen didn't go with us on this trip. Collette had some function she was chairing. Eileen didn't want to be a housemaid for three men, so she stayed home, too. We hiked into the mountains for three days."

"Who took the picture?"

"Guy living in the cabin next to us. He went along as our guide."

Brenda took another photo Vossen selected from the series. Much clearer than the first, it showed Vossen and Lindell lounging in Adirondack chairs on the same deck and wearing the same clothes as in the first, though not, Brenda assumed, drinking the same beers. It was her first good look at Lindell, though still not the best.

Peter Lindell was not a large man but he appeared as physically fit as Brenda expected of a man who spent most of his life working in the construction industry. His skin was as dark as hers, though the lighter skin exposed by his drooping socks told her it was a byproduct of sun exposure and not inherited, as with her natural coloring. His face was gently rounded with skin that lacked the weathered, leathery texture that resulted from prolonged exposure to the valley summers. Through his genuine smile and soft eyes, Peter Lindell was likely more handsome than his scruffy appearance in the photo suggested.

"Do you have any in there that aren't so ... outdoorsy?"

"Let me check this pack."

Vossen set the first set of pictures down and started through the second. He picked through nearly half the pack before he came up with one. He told Brenda it was taken during some builders' convention, again in Tahoe, at a dinner held aboard a paddlewheel boat that cruised the lake. In the photo, Lindell was standing to the left of Farnsworth, with each man flanked by a woman. The men were clean-shaven and dressed in semi-formal attire with Farnsworth wearing a dark, three-piece pinstripe suit and Lindell in a navy sport coat and tie. The women were dressed equal to the men they stood beside, both in style and price.

"That was inside, at the bar. You recognize Edson and Peter. That's Collette, Edson's wife, and Peter's wife, Eileen. I guess you know she goes by Sherman. I took the picture. That was probably the last time we were together."

Though hardly a cover model for fashion and style, the clean-shaven and well-attired Lindell was indeed as handsome as Brenda envisioned. Brenda, having yet to see Collette Farnsworth or Eileen Sherman in person, gave the women a cursory inspection and felt reasonably confident on her assessment. Farnsworth looked like she was from money and every bit high maintenance. Sherman didn't have the expensive accessories—or surgeries, Brenda noted—and though she didn't look out of place, there was a giddy intensity in her expression suggesting her attendance at such a lavish affair was a privilege bestowed rather than owned.

"Would you mind if I took this with me? Just long enough for one of our guys to make copies."

"Keep it as long as you like. I've got no use for it. In fact ..." Vossen handed Brenda the entire pack along with the photos from the first pack. "Take them all."

Brenda stuffed the photos back into their envelopes and secured them with a rubber band Vossen pulled from the receptionist's desk drawer. She stood by as Vossen replaced the box in case the leaning tower decided to come down on top of him. Vossen got the box in and the door closed without so much as a lurch from the boxes looming over him and walked Brenda to the door.

"Do you really think Peter had something to do with Edson's disappearance?" he asked.

"We're still looking into his disappearance coinciding with Mr. Farnsworth's, if that's what you mean. If it comes to something beyond that, we'll start to consider investigating other aspects, such as motive. The tricky part is when multiple people have the same motive."

As Brenda said this, Vossen smiled.

"Touché, Detective. I understand your point, though having motive and being motivated are not one in the same."

This time, Brenda smiled. Vossen opened the door for her, but Brenda stopped short of leaving. Standing at the door, she recalled her last exit from the office and how Vossen seemed to have something on his mind that he was hesitant to say. Now it was on *her* mind, and Brenda felt compelled to bring it out.

"Mr. Vossen, the last time I was here you acted as if you wanted to tell me something, but seemed sort of reluctant to do so."

Vossen held the door while he held his eyes on Brenda. The pause was ominous and telling.

"You know, any information you have about Peter Lindell that might help us might help you, too. Not just in the recovery of your lost assets. I'm sure you have a lot of unanswered questions."

"I'll never recover what I've lost, Detective."

Vossen let the door loose and Brenda stepped back as it closed. He walked to the reception desk and sat behind it. His hands were clasped, fingers interlocked, and his chin was wedged into the crook created when he extended his thumbs back, a prop for his head as he spoke over the mass of knuckles in front of his mouth.

"Peter may have had another motive in his desire to track down Edson." Brenda took a few steps toward the desk, lured by Vossen's forthcoming openness. "Before Peter married Eileen, she and Edson were lovers."

Brenda bit down on her back teeth to keep her jaw from dropping. Nothing she had come across in her research of Edson Farnsworth connected him with Eileen Sherman. If true, then the ring wouldn't have been the only thing connecting Lindell to Farnsworth. Brenda remained silent as Vossen continued. He told Brenda that he learned about Edson and Eileen a couple of years after he and Edson took each other on as partners.

"I didn't have the greatest faith in Peter when Edson first hired him. One day I asked him why he continued contracting with Peter when there were more qualified men to choose from. Edson laughed and said he was doing it out of pity for Eileen. 'After all,' Edson told me smugly, 'she could have done so much better for herself if she'd only had a little faith in me'. I asked him what he meant by that, and he went on about how close they were before he went away, about the plans they had discussed for their future. But Eileen had just gotten settled into her teaching career and didn't want to pick up and go with Edson. She told him she'd wait while he went out to build his fortune. Edson was gone for five years. They kept in touch for a time, but long-distance romances being what they are ... It was during that time he got engaged to a banker's daughter."

"Collette," Brenda interjected. Vossen nodded.

"Edson said it was a marriage of convenience. He made some strong connections that lasted, well, up until he ran off. Eventually word got back to Eileen about Collette. I don't know the details, but not much later she met Peter and they got married. A year later, Edson came back to Santa Ramona with his wife. Shortly after that came the business."

"Did Farnsworth continue to see Eileen Sherman after he returned?"

"I believe so. And it was no secret to Collette that Edson was keeping someone on the side."

"And yet she did nothing about it."

Vossen chuckled. "One thing you have to understand about money, Detective Garibaldi, is that it is very forgiving."

"So Mrs. Farnsworth allowed her husband to cheat on her as long as it didn't affect her financially?"

"And socially."

"Surely others must have known."

"Suspected," Vossen corrected. "And as long as Edson and Collette kept their marital problems between them—"

"Neither one would be castigated among their peers," Brenda concluded, "and there would be no cause for social expulsion."

"Both would suffer if one spoke out."

"Asking for a divorce, then, would have been suicidal."

Vossen nodded. "Precisely. It was the ultimate deadlock, a Gordian knot neither one could cut without cutting themselves."

"And Mrs. Farnsworth? She suspected her husband was still seeing Sherman and yet she still went on trips knowing Sherman would be going, too?"

"Yes."

"And Mr. Lindell knew—suspected, as well?"

"I don't think he did. Peter knew of the earlier relationship, I'm certain of that. I'd be shocked to learn Peter was aware of it continuing and be so tolerant as to allow the affair to continue."

"And yet you suggest the relationship between Lindell's wife and Mr. Farnsworth added to Lindell's motive."

"*Might have*, yes, assuming Peter found out about it. Of course, this is all based on the premise that Peter had a hand in Edson's disappearance in the first place. If that bears out to be true then consideration should be given to the possibility that Peter found out about a continued affair between his wife and Edson."

"Based on our first conversation, and the statement you gave the police, your contention is Mr. Farnsworth left of his own accord."

"My long-held belief is he did. I, like everyone else—and that includes the police—based my conclusion on the information available at the time Edson left."

"And at no time did anyone see Sherman's prior relationship or suspect a continuing relationship with Farnsworth as a possible factor."

"A factor in what way?" Vossen asked, opening his palms toward Brenda. "The business accounts were tapped. Collette said Edson left her. Peter didn't go after him until I told him four days later, and he was never a suspect to begin with. There was no sign of foul play. My thought at the time was if Eileen had any influence on Edson leaving, it was that he wanted to get away from her, as well.

"If circumstances had been otherwise—if, say, Eileen ran off with Edson—I'd have probably said something. But my concerns were about myself, my business, and my future as I ran from the courthouse to the banks to cover their losses and mine. Any matters regarding with whom Edson was sharing a bed were Collette's business to disclose."

"But now it means enough that you'll make it your business, that Farnsworth's tryst with Sherman is now relevant?" Brenda challenged.

"Relevant only because it appears you have uncovered some new information that has implicated Peter criminally in some fashion," Vossen replied. "We weren't hiding anything, Detective. It's not uncommon for people to become pinned in a position in which their judgment dictated they were better off not saying something that would distract from the issue at hand."

Vossen's comment was a generalization but hit its mark in Brenda, who immediately recalled not telling Floyd about Tiner's advance on her during her trip downtown. The issue at hand, in Brenda's case, was twofold: She didn't want to distract Floyd from finding Lindell, and she didn't want to gouge ruts in the way of the progress she and Floyd were making in their relationship. Had Tiner's advance gone beyond just his unwanted flirting or, God forbid, she had taken an interest in his interest, her judgment, like Vossen's, would have directed her differently.

Brenda, not prepared to delve into the romantic interests of Sherman and Farnsworth, chose to shelve the matter for the time being. Any information she could get from Vossen would only be the same juicy gossip bandied around by those within that wealthy circle of aristocrats who likely didn't know the true details any more accurately than Vossen did. She had been successful in obtaining what she came for and saw Vossen's revelation as a bonus to pass on to Floyd, who would know better how to play the information to his advantage with respect to his previous dealing with Collette Farnsworth and his current encounter with Sherman. Brenda stood and gave the banded photos a couple of quick pats.

"I'll return these as soon as possible, and I appreciate your frankness, Mr. Vossen. If circumstances do turn out to be otherwise, I hope I can count on your continued cooperation."

Vossen rose, extended his hand and smiled warmly. "As much as I can count on finding you at my door if they do."

16
Thursday afternoon, August 21st

Floyd and Keller would have made great time on the return to Santa Ramona had they not been forced into a clog of traffic being detoured from Highway 50. Over the scanner they picked up a report of an overturned big rig south of them, which accounted for the traffic creeping along the city streets. It offered too much time for thought of too many things.

"This really bothers you, doesn't it?" Keller asked as traffic finally began thinning and picking up speed.

"What? The traffic?"

"No. Having to share."

"From a departmental standpoint, I could care less," Floyd said diplomatically before adding, "But personally, yes, it's distracting. I've developed a work pattern over the years. I know what to expect from the people I work with. Some I can count on; others I don't trust. I've also set expectations for myself, expectations I find harder to fulfill when I have ... when I have restrictions placed upon me."

"I've never been referred to as a restriction," Keller said bitterly. "I'll have that added to my résumé. So it's the restrictions, then, that make you buck the system and not the belief that no one else is capable of solving a crime?"

"I don't buck the system. Much. And I never said you weren't capable. And I never thought for one minute that your father wasn't capable."

"My—" Keller gasped, then recovering, "Why should it surprise me that you'd find out? How?"

"Accidentally. I called and asked to speak with the detectives who wrote the report you gave me. I was told one retired and the other passed away, and how you inherited the case."

"The family hand-me-down joke." Keller said it with the same familiar drone Tiner used transforming Curtis to Curt.

"How long has it been?"

"Five years. He had a heart attack, but that didn't kill him. His heart was his strength. My mom died when I was fourteen. Dad and I were all we had. That was part of the reason I took the job with Sac, to look after him. Why do you care, anyway?"

"Just curious."

"Bullshit." Keller turned and stared out her window at the slideshow of her image reflected in the series of glass panels of the storefronts lining the street. "You know this is the second time."

"Second time?"

"Yeah. You trashed one of his investigations before."

"How so?"

"My father was one of the lead investigators in the Feldman murders. The original ones when the parents were killed. I think that's why I reacted the way I did when I heard you were asking for the Farnsworth file. My dad wasn't able to defend himself from the backlash over you solving that case. I saw he wouldn't be able to again."

"I'm sorry. I'm not out to find flaws with the original investigation," Floyd said. "I wasn't there. I only go back to serve as a starting point for moving forward. It's no different than when I work my own cases and have to undo or redo things I've thought were right. The criticism's going to come, questions are going to be asked."

"It wasn't his fault, you know. He wanted the Feldman kid for the murders. That jackass of a D.A. we had back then said there wasn't enough to get a conviction, so they never filed and the piece of shit walked."

"Too bad. It would have saved us all a lot of grief down the road. Your father turned out to be right, though."

"Didn't do his legacy any good. The department was embarrassed, thanks to you, and it was an easy out to place the blame where it couldn't be disputed. My father *knew*. He just wanted a little more time. But there was a changing of the guard back then, a chain reaction of promotions was in place. Dad called it a Brass Orgy."

Floyd laughed lightly, which triggered an amused snort from Keller. It was the first impromptu display of emotion he'd seen from her as every interaction with her to this point had included pent up frustration or premeditated attempts at manipulation. It was a crack in her shell that gave Floyd a peek at the real person, not the contrived personality.

"He followed orders," she continued. "They told him to leave it be, so he left it. He was a good cop. Not arrogant and pushy."

"Like us."

Keller's smile was as much an admission as Floyd's comment. Floyd pulled his car into the police parking lot just ahead of Brenda, who had taken her time returning from Vossen's, her prayer answered of not having to spend any extra time alone with Marty or Tiner. She pulled her car into the space next to Floyd's.

"Did you get a photo of Lindell?" Floyd asked.

"A couple of decent snapshots." Brenda said, waving

the photo packets and wanting to add *and a little something extra*, but restraining herself until she had more privacy. She wasn't sure what Floyd had disclosed to Keller—knowing Floyd she was pretty sure it wasn't more than what Floyd confirmed Keller already knew—and she wanted him to make the call on how new bulletins would be announced.

Inside the squad room, Marty and Tiner, having finished clearing the plastic containers from their rib and chicken feast, slouched in chairs as if their weighted frames had been dropped into them from above. For Marty, a hearty eater, it was merely a break between meals. Tiner, on the other hand, looked exhausted with his eyes half open and arms resting across his midsection. As taxing as the effort was for them, they rose from their chairs and joined their arriving partners to get the lowdown on Floyd's and Keller's questioning of Sherman and get a look at the face of the man they were looking for as provided by Brenda. When all was said and done, Floyd opened the floor for comments and Keller stepped forward.

"Have any of you considered possible motives for why Lindell may have killed Farnsworth?"

Suspicion returned; the crack sealed. Keller's question, asked in an off-hand manner, was undoubtedly meant as a casual prompt to get one of the Santa Ramona detectives to slip and admit their focus, and therefore their investigation, had shifted from the recovery of Farnsworth's ring to the man, himself. Floyd had done this at Sherman's apartment when he offered his two suppositions. But it was in response to Sherman's query and based on the information in the Sac reports. Keller wanted something a little more self-initiated. Floyd disappointed her as he bit back his amusement at her attempt and with deliberate ease denied entertaining any thoughts of placing Lindell anywhere beyond the shed that once sat in the back of the Mill Creek house.

"We hadn't considered much in that arena because, frankly, our concern has been finding Peter Lindell, not determining if he was involved in Farnsworth's disappearance." Floyd saw a squint of skepticism in Keller's eyes along with an awareness that she knew he was onto her gambit. And Floyd felt as long as she opened the door, he'd be a gentleman and hold it open for everyone. "But if you're initiating a forum on the subject, we'll be more than happy to throw out our best guesses."

Keller fumed behind her mask of innocent curiosity. Floyd called her bluff, and now she had to show her hand or fold it. In turning her cards she would show she had the confidence to stay in the game and not let Floyd's arrogance to dictate what she was dealt and how much she bet. To fold, on the other hand, would be tantamount to surrender, an option Keller wouldn't consider in the face of her opponent.

"I was just wondering as to whether or not, while tracing the possession of the ring, anyone came across any indication that Lindell went after Farnsworth to split the money rather than split his skull."

"Like they were partners?" Marty asked.

"Will the difference change things enough to get our case reopened, Grace?" Tiner asked.

"It will change Peter Lindell from a victim of a theft to a suspect in a theft," Keller said. *A theft that occurred in Sacramento*, she added to herself. *And change King's investigation of Lindell to our control.*

"Seems like we can call Lindell a suspect or a partner in anything we want," Floyd said. "Doesn't mean squat until we find some evidence to back it up. Or find him."

"And looking at the timeline we have, there's no connection," Brenda said. "Based on Sherman's statement, her husband left days after Farnsworth did. And Vossen confirmed Lindell found out about Farnsworth from him, again days later. Plus, Farnsworth was a loner and a manipulator. Any partner he'd take on would be doomed to be screwed over in the end."

"Extortion, then," Tiner responded. "Lindell forced Farnsworth to make all of the wire transfers into Lindell's account. Once the money was deposited, Lindell killed him, parked Farnsworth's car downtown, and—"

Brenda cut Tiner off. "If what Vossen says is true, no one knew Farnsworth had been milking the accounts. When the bank finally finished looking over the ledgers, there were a number of inconsistencies between work ordered and work done. A lot of stuff went on under Lindell's nose that he never caught."

"What if Lindell figured it out, Bren," Marty proposed, "and decided to collect his fair cut. He gets Farnsworth to make a few bank drafts, then turns greedy and Farnsworth balks. He kills Farnsworth, takes a couple of days to cover his tracks, and make it look like Farnsworth ripped them off and split. Then Lindell pretends to go after Farnsworth. Poof! He's forever gone."

"Then why'd he renew his license?"

Floyd's question stilled the room. The driver's license was a tidbit of forgotten information that was more puzzling to Floyd than the ring because it happened years after Lindell left. And because it did, it became as much an indication to Floyd that the renewal had been done to perpetuate validity about his absence.

"A man goes to all the trouble of helping to steal tens of thousands of dollars," Floyd went on, "all the trouble of killing someone and covering it up well enough to get away without the least bit of suspicion, successfully goes into hiding for a couple of years, and then risks everything by renewing his driver's license?"

"It could be part of the cover up," Tiner offered. "Maybe he thinks by renewing his license it perpetuates the belief that he's still out there looking for Farnsworth."

Floyd started to speak but Keller interrupted him. It turned out her words were his. "Then why didn't he renew it in ninety-nine?"

"You knew?" Floyd asked, surprised.

Keller nodded. "We made the connection between Sherman and Lindell. His DL expired in ninety-nine."

"But we didn't discover that until after—" Brenda choked on her words. She turned to face Tiner, throwing him a menacing glare. "You sonofabitch! You *were* following me!"

"Oh, shit," Marty swore under his breath as he retreated to a corner of the room.

Tiner held up both hands in defense against Brenda's heated blast. "I wasn't following you. I swear."

"So after I left, what? Did you go pump Lisa for info about what I was up to? What bullshit line did you feed her?"

"Take it easy, Brenda," Floyd said, attempting to soothe the growing tensions all around.

"Take it easy? Yeah, that's how I took it, all right."

"All I told Lisa was we were working on a similar case and I didn't get some of the information she gave you." Tiner's explanation only added fuel to Brenda's fire.

"You didn't happen to mention to Lisa you didn't get it because *I didn't give it to you*! That's pretty low, Tiner, working one of my friends because you can't get to me.

Where'd you learn that shit, from her?" Without taking her eyes off Tiner, Brenda leveled her pointed finger at Keller.

"I beg your pardon?" Keller snapped back.

Brenda whipped around and lined up her glare down her finger at Keller. "Isn't that sort of what you did when you sent Tiner out to hit on me after seducing Floyd didn't work for *you?*"

"King, you better back her off," Keller warned sternly.

"Why?" Brenda countered in a rage. "What are you afraid of? That Floyd might find out to what lengths you'll go to manipulate people? Or perhaps Tiner'd find out you convinced him that I'd find him so irresistibly charming that I'd melt and get all chummy with him and then spill my guts?"

"You're way out of line, Detective." Now Keller was the one sighting her comments down a finger aimed at Brenda. "My asking King to dinner was strictly business and had nothing to do with whatever twisted sexual fantasy you conjured up in your mind."

"And, of course, your dinner also had nothing to do with distracting Floyd so Tiner could pay a visit on Collette Farnsworth."

"We're done," Keller announced to Floyd angrily. If the redness on the back of her neck was any indication of just how angry Keller really was, she'd be spitting fire if she stayed. She collected her things and commanded Tiner to her side. "Whatever investigation you have better stop with that ring," she admonished. "You tamper with our case, and I'll cut you down, King. I'll cut *all* of you down at the knees!"

Keller quickly spun on her heels and stormed from the room. Tiner was a step behind her, but stopped at the door and peered back at Brenda over his shoulder. It was not with the same desirous interest of his past glances. This look was pained and contemptuous. He waited until Brenda looked back, until he was sure she recognized how he felt for what she'd done before following Keller's exit.

"Marty."

Marty, expecting Floyd to ask for privacy, had already pulled himself from the wall and began his exit. As he passed Brenda, who was now sitting in a chair absently picking at her thumbnail, he set his meaty hand on her shoulder and gave a light squeeze. It was a touch from him that under any other circumstance would cause Brenda to recoil like a kid fearing cooties. But she sensed the comfort in the light pinch of the fingers he let slide off her neck as he continued by. The comforting touch released the tension that held back the heaviness welling inside.

To Floyd, Marty curled a grin and winked.

As soon as Marty was gone, Floyd sat down next to Brenda and waited for her to speak. As she had moments before, she got right to what was foremost on her mind.

"I fucked that up pretty good."

Floyd smiled at the frankness of her admission and chuckled, "Yeah. Pretty good." Floyd let a quiet minute pass to give Brenda a chance to collect herself before needling her with, "So, Tiner's been hitting on you?"

"I wanted to tell you earlier, Floyd, but I didn't see any reason to overreact and make a big deal out of it."

"That's not your nature," he teased.

"Still, I shouldn't be keeping secrets from you."

"If you had had any feeling for him and not told me, then I'd be upset," Floyd replied. "This? Guys are going to look and flirt and offer to buy you drinks and cars and trips to Europe ... I can't stop that from happening. You're an attractive woman who should be upset if men *don't* take an interest.

"And one more thing. You're not on report with me. I don't need you telling me about every man whose head you turn. It won't do anything but make me feel like I'm not paying you enough attention and damage my fragile male ego."

"What if they throw flowers?" Brenda cracked, attempting to ease into Floyd's humorous outlook.

"Flowers? Yeah. Better tell me."

"Cash?"

"You think highly of yourself, don't you? I'll draw the line at a bidding war. I still have a mortgage to pay off."

"So you don't care how often this happens, to the extent that it's what you can afford."

Floyd chuckled. "My point is I'm not going to spend every waking hour wondering if the next guy might be *the* guy. If he is, then I've misjudged myself and you and us. I don't think I have."

As Floyd said this he rested his hand on Brenda's forearm. Brenda blushed, in part from the warm feeling of his touch and partly in realizing how foolish her outburst had been. It wasn't about Keller's tricks or Tiner's single's bar mentality. It was about feeling secure in not falling to that type of temptation and feeling secure in trusting Floyd not to fall, as well. She set her hand atop his and gently rubbed it. Brenda realized what she new all along. She was sitting with "the next guy".

"I feel so dumb," she sighed.

Floyd nodded, but added nothing, intentionally letting her wallow in her self-pity until she caught on that that was what he was doing.

"What, no more words of sympathy?"

Floyd bit back a grin. "There's a fine line between sympathy and apathy."

Brenda's hand came off Floyd's and flicked him backhanded on the chest. "So what happens now?" she asked.

"We still have some work to do," Floyd told her. "I'm guessing once Keller cools her jets she'll be out to find Lindell. Hopefully we can find him first."

"She sounded like she's going to do whatever it takes to keep us from doing that."

"We'll work around it," Floyd said with a wink. "Like we do."

❧

Keller and Tiner idled at the last controlled intersection out of Santa Ramona waiting for the signal to give permission for them to leave. Although the crimson that painted her neck earlier had faded, Keller's rage was still evident in her tight jaw, flared nostrils, and wild eyes. She was seeing red beyond the glowing light hanging before her, and it wasn't solely because of the tirade thrown at her by Brenda. Though the Santa Ramona detective's accusations were baseless, with the exception of Tiner pulling an end-around to get the Sherman information from her friend, Keller was hardly in a position to put forth a strong denial in light of her own devious plays.

Tiner had never seen his partner so angry, but it didn't surprise him that she could reach such heights of fury. What amazed him more was that she swallowed the urge to fight back and walked away. Swallowed it, hell, Tiner told himself. More like she choked the urge down like a kid with a mouthful of lima beans. Tiner suspected the only reason Keller didn't defend herself against Brenda's charges was due to the whipping he and Keller received from Lt. Burrows the day before for being as active as they had been, which wasn't the half of what their commander didn't know. To engage in a pissing contest would only serve to further expose their activity to their supervisor and lead to stricter discipline.

As Keller's temperament actually eased with every block she put between herself and the Santa Ramona detectives, Tiner wound up cursing the red light for interfering with that progress. He watched Keller's knuckles turn white from wringing her hands tightly around the steering wheel. Her ire, like the traffic she had pushed past in her haste to get back to Sacramento, was catching up to her at every signal. The instant the red light changed they were through the intersection so quickly that Tiner wasn't sure if he ever saw the green light come fully on.

Keller hadn't uttered a word since putting Floyd on notice, and Tiner spent a majority of the silence building up the guts to break it. He would have to talk to her sooner or later, and though he didn't trust that later would be any better than now, he waited until they crossed Highway 50 into the southern fringe of their home town.

"Um, you're not mad at me, are you Grace?" Tiner asked tentatively.

"I'm not mad at you, Curtis," Keller answered in an even tone.

"What now?" Tiner asked.

"What now?" she asked rhetorically. Then with eyes narrowed and nostrils flared she venomously spat, "We find Peter Lindell before they do and shove that ring right up King's ass."

What began as a brisk march around the building's perimeter slowed to an easy gait as Brenda walked the incident out of her mind. She rejoined Floyd and Marty in the squad room, pleasantly surprised that Marty showed continued sensitivity by not taking a verbal shot at her when she approached Floyd's desk and sat down. The two men were sorting through the photos Brenda picked up from Vossen but abruptly stopped when she disclosed the secret Vossen had withheld from the original investigators.

"According to Vossen, Farnsworth and Sherman were lovers."

She related to Floyd and Marty what the architect told her about his partner's past relationship with their contractor's wife, along with his suspicions that it continued until Farnsworth vanished. And while Vossen appeared to have revealed a tenable motive for Peter Lindell to kill Farnsworth, the picture Vossen painted for Brenda lacked the clarity of a master's brushstroke.

"He claims Collette Farnsworth knew it was going on, but I, for one, don't buy it. They went on trips. Shared cabins up in Tahoe and hotels elsewhere. There was too much opportunity for temptation or confrontation," Brenda pushed forward the photograph of the Farnsworths and Lindells that Vossen said he took on the Lake Tahoe boat ride. "This was one of their last outings together. If there's distress in the marriages or between the couples, or even between just the women, I don't see it."

Floyd didn't see it, either. The Lindells looked happy. Peter and Eileen had their arms crossed behind each other's back, each with a hand cupping the other's waist. Eileen appeared to be leaning into her husband, almost resting her head on his shoulder, and Peter wasn't at all repulsed by it. Both were smiling toothy smiles and had crow's feet wrinkling the corners of their eyes. Even the Farnsworths put forth an air of contentment. Their pose, like their marriage, was close enough to present the perception of togetherness without the physical contact as with the other couple. Collette kept her hands clasped at her own waist and Edson held a dignified stance with his right hand clenching just below the lapel of his open suit jacket. Their smiling expressions were likely influenced as much by alcohol as the fact that their marriage, having faltered for some time before Edson left, allowed plenty of practice in public displays of the necessary amiability to disguise their private discord.

At first glance, knowing none of the history between the Farnsworths or the Lindells, one could easily see two couples having an enjoyable time together at a dinner party on a boat in the middle of a lake. But Floyd had met Collette Farnsworth who, judging by the ultimatum she placed on her husband, was not the tolerant type. Certainly not tolerant enough to share a vacation, let alone a Kodak moment, with her husband's girlfriend.

"And another thing," Brenda continued. "I have a hard time believing Collette would know Eileen was fooling around with Edson and Peter wouldn't."

"Lindell knew about his wife and Farnsworth before he married her," Marty said to Brenda. "Vossen told you that. Maybe Lindell took his wife's word that there was nothing between her and Farnsworth even though she was still tramping around with him behind Lindell's back."

Marty introduced the possibility that Sherman was supposed to meet up with Farnsworth once the dust settled and Lindell found out about it as their plan came to fruition.

"Lindell goes ballistic. Not only does he find out about their ongoing affair and her intent to leave him, he finds out how Farnsworth's been screwing over the company to finance their future. Now Lindell's taking it in the shorts personally *and* professionally. He catches up with Farnsworth at the office while he's draining the accounts and ..." Marty made a slicing motion across his neck. "... Lindell can't come home now, so *he's* the one who actually drops off the radar screen, not Farnsworth."

Floyd stared at the photograph while his partner concocted his theory, stared at the one item that stared back at him. With his chin resting lightly on his thumb and his index finger crooked across his upper lip, Floyd slowly shook Marty off. As reasonable as Marty's conclusion sounded, as reasonable as *any* conclusions derived thus far, the latest hypothesis didn't bear out any cleaner than the others. It could have happened that way, but it didn't. And for one reason.

"We still have an unexplained piece of the puzzle," Floyd went on. He pulled his finger from above his lip and dropped it onto the photo, the tip of it landing squarely on Farnsworth's right hand, suspended at his breast and decorated with the ring. "If Peter Lindell is involved in Edson Farnsworth's disappearance—and based on what we have it's still no sure bet he is—assuming he is, though, it's also reasonable to assume he put the ring in the shed."

Marty and Brenda nodded, then Floyd questioned why Lindell would have taken such a risk.

"Remember, during the initial days of the investigation the police, who knew based on Sherman's statement her husband went after Farnsworth, had yet to speak with Lindell. Surely he must have been aware he was on their list, especially having announced to his wife and business associate his intent on hunting Farnsworth down. And he returns while Farnsworth is still missing? Or worse, maybe Farnsworth turns up dead? Why chance the exposure of coming home to hide something he could just as easily toss into any alley dumpster in the state?"

"Because he wasn't afraid of being caught," Marty answered. "Or of being turned in by Sherman."

Brenda followed by adding, "If that's the case, Sherman knew whatever it was her husband did and for some reason was convinced to help to cover it up. And, after ten years, is still helping to cover it up."

"How does the ring come into play?" Floyd asked, encouraging his partners to continue airing their thoughts.

"Lindell hides the ring in the shed without her knowing," Marty said. "It's insurance. He tells her he has something to incriminate her—the ring, only he doesn't tell her what it is—and warns her if she opens her mouth, he makes an anonymous call to the police. Maybe that box that busted open on what's his name—alphabet boy ..."

"C," Floyd answered.

"Yeah. Maybe those were Farnsworth's clothes in that box. Anyway, that would explain why the damn thing sat in the shed for so long. She had no idea the box was there."

"Then, again, she could have," Brenda countered. "It could just have easily been *her* insurance against *him* coming back."

"*If* you can explain how she got possession of the ring—" Floyd replied.

"Yeah, I'm gonna doubt Lindell gave it to her willingly," Marty interrupted.

"—and why she didn't pack it up with all of her other valuables," Floyd continued.

Floyd exhaled heavily as he pushed back from his desk. Every plausible point they formulated had an equally plausible counterpoint that had an equally frustrating omission in its application. Like a row of on-edge dominoes, each line of thought clicked smoothly in succession only to stop abruptly where the gap exceeded the domino's ability to strike the next and continue the chain. Floyd went back to the domino that started their speculating in the first place.

"Sherman's romantic involvement with Farnsworth makes a good motive for Lindell," Floyd concluded, then shook his head. "I just don't see it threatening Sherman to the point of needing a safeguard against him. A little public embarrassment versus accessory to murder? Where's the encouragement for her to keep quiet?"

"She's got a house worth half a million," Marty pointed out. "That's a lot to lose for opening your mouth."

"The house is already in her name," Floyd reminded Marty. "Why would she have to cut a deal to keep it?"

Brenda thought for a second, then asked, "What about the possibility that she was bought off? Following Tiner's theory, Lindell could have been in on the money transfers, or at least knew what was happening, and could have cut whatever his take was with Sherman to buy her silence about ..." Brenda shrugged, "... whatever. We all agree she knows something, and my bet is she's hiding information about her husband."

"Or something incriminating about herself. Some secret about her that protects Lindell as long as he has the ring—" Marty cut himself off, his face screwed in confusion. "But he doesn't have the ring. The ring was in the shed, which makes no sense if Lindell is using it to control Sherman. It makes absolutely no sense for him to put it there."

"It would make more sense that she did. Which brings us back to the question of what Sherman knows."

Marty mimicked a merry-go-round calliope and spun twice in his chair. He stopped, feigned dizziness, and answered with a slur, "Something."

"She knows, she doesn't know ..." Floyd mumbled, returning his attention to the photograph. He stared at each individual, then at the group trying to decipher what exactly was the missing link between them.

"But we don't find out to what extent Sherman's involved without Lindell," Floyd concluded aloud. "Unfortunately, until we have a reason to challenge her, all we can do is sit and wait and root around a little more. Stir the pot a bit."

"You're not worried she'll get spooked from all the recent attention vanish like everyone else?" Brenda asked Floyd.

He shook her off. "She's smart. Smart enough to figure out that if we had any evidence against her she'd be behind bars right now. As long as the attention focuses on her husband, I think she'll continue to portray herself as the poor abandoned wife trying to break free from her heartbroken past. And she still has her house to sell. We'll give her no cause for alarm, that way any anxiety she develops will be strictly her own doing—or undoing. If we're lucky."

17
Thursday evening, August 21st

Coming home regularly for dinner was another of the lifestyle changes Floyd made in order to create a stable environment for Shelby when she left her mother to live with him. It helped greatly that she was old enough to cook, even greater that she was a fairly decent one. Not that Shelby's cooking was responsible for what he described as his slight weight gain. Floyd attributed that to a slowing metabolism and his lack of activity during his recovery period from the leg trauma. His health-conscious daughter added his poor diet to that list and was in the process of making changes that were—as he found fortunate—as flavorful as they were subtle. As Floyd opened the front door it was like taking the lid off a pressure cooker. The aromatic cloud of garlic and herbs he liberated filled his nose and mouth and started a chain reaction of salivation and stomach churning. Shelby just finished setting the table when he walked in.

"Dinner will be ready in a minute," she announced.

Floyd retreated to his room and secured his gun and spare magazine in his lockbox. He put his badge, handcuffs, and holster in his dresser drawer, and set his wallet and keys on his nightstand. He completed his transformation to civilian by shedding his nicer clothes in favor of a pair of jeans and a Sacramento State T-shirt his daughter's boyfriend had given to him the previous Christmas as the wrapping around a nice bottle of single malt Scotch.

Shelby was pouring them both a glass of Chardonnay

when he returned to the kitchen. He greeted her with a kiss on the forehead, and in return she handed him his glass along with a bowl of steamed green beans to carry to the table. He settled into his chair as Shelby brought the remaining food: a bowl of herbed red potatoes and a platter on which rested a small, skinless roasted chicken.

The meal was gone in a fraction of the time it took Shelby to prepare.

While Floyd and Shelby engaged in the normal how-was-your-day conversation during the meal, both were distracted. Floyd had the thus-far elusive Peter Lindell on his mind and the growing concern that the contractor would remain so. All indications now were that if Lindell was going to be found at all it would entail pressing Eileen Sherman, who Floyd was convinced had an idea, at the very least, in which direction to point them.

Like her father, Shelby had her own preoccupation, one that she anxiously waited for the right time to squeeze into the dinner discussion. Twice she almost spoke her mind, only to have the words impeded by a mouthful of food used to hide her shortage of nerves. With the meal finished, Shelby poured her father another glass of wine and topped off her own while contemplating her approach.

"I was thinking of going away for the weekend." Shelby heard her words explode from her mouth, but her father's reaction told her it was merely the rush of finally saying them and not her self-consciousness in doing so that gave the impression of increased pitch and volume.

"Okay." Floyd's indifference wasn't from not caring. Shelby had taken a number of trips with friends and, with one notable exception, her travels had been uneventful. Floyd cared to the extent that he knew where she was going and how to contact her, and that she call when she reached her destination. The rules were not so much rules as they were a courtesy. Shelby was an adult whom Floyd allowed to come and go as she pleased. His concern was that she was safe whether she lived under his roof or not. Trust and maturity and judgment weren't issues. He was still a parent. "Where're you headed?"

"Ken's uncle has a cabin up at Shasta. We were thinking of taking off Saturday after the game and coming back Monday afternoon."

"Family gathering?"

Floyd's only reason for asking was to needle his daughter. He knew before seeing her pained expression to his question that the trip was for two. Years ago, with temperance and a lecture on responsibility more to set his mind at ease than to educate her, Floyd accepted that his daughter had a sex life. He also knew for some time Shelby's relationship with Ken had developed beyond a casual romance. While the two had been alone in Ken's apartment regularly and she had stayed the night more than once, Shelby had never "gone away". She certainly never announced plans to do so. This trip was going to be one of those tests to find out how strong that bond was between the couple, and, in a sense, how strong the bond was between father and daughter. But there was an underlying signal being sent.

"I'm kind of nervous, daddy."

"Good nervous, or bad nervous?"

"Well, both," Shelby replied. "I really love Ken, and I know he loves me. I mean, everything points to a long-term commitment."

"From where I sit, that would be the good."

Shelby smiled at her father's approval of Ken, though it had been a foregone conclusion for some time that he was comfortable with the young man courting his daughter.

"I'm worried about ... I don't want it to fall apart."

When she said it, Floyd felt his heart thump hard in his chest. Shelby was talking about the divorce. It was the first time she had ever expressed openly that her parents' failed marriage was influencing her long-range plans.

Floyd put a lot of effort into absorbing much of Lynn's wrath in the waning years of their crumbling marriage, sheltering his daughter from the fallout. But he couldn't insulate her from the damage to the family. Floyd talked to her during the ordeal and as much as possible afterward, at first to reinforce her emotional durability then, eventually, his own. Shelby the child impressed him with her toughness and maturity and restraint. But what affected her as a child did so differently as an adult in facing the prospect of entering an arena where she had firsthand exposure to good going bad. Even the strongest armor has weak points. Floyd slid out of his chair and sat in the one next to her. He embraced her and she returned the hug, though hers was more of a cling.

"I don't want to end up bitter like mom did. I know you always tell me I didn't do anything wrong—"

"You didn't, Shel," Floyd cut in. He sat her back, still holding her hands in his. "Things could have been done differently, not that it would have changed the ultimate outcome. What your mother and I went through, what the *three* of us went through ... you have to take advantage of it as a learning experience and grow and move on. You didn't run away from it before. There's no reason to run now."

"Is that how you look at it with Brenda?"

"To some extent, yes. But Brenda's not like your mother. I'm not the same either. That doesn't mean a closer relationship between us will work. It just means I'm better prepared to deal with a conflict or two."

"It's still scary."

Floyd smiled and ran a comforting stroke down his daughter's cheek with the backs of his fingers. "I wish I had a pearl or two of wisdom to pass on to make it easier."

"You've given me a triple-strand necklace of wisdom over the years already, daddy." Shelby leaned forward and kissed her father's cheek. "I love you."

"I love you, too. Just go and have a good time," Floyd told her. "You'll do what's right."

Successful in offering relief to Shelby's concerns, he shooed her away from the kitchen so he could start cleaning. Floyd loaded the dishwasher with the silverware, plates, and pots before tackling the congealed grease coating the bottom of the roasting pan. It looked worse than it was and after five minutes of scrubbing with a steel wool pad, that job was done. All that remained was to find containers for the few leftover potatoes and small portion of beans, and figure out how much of the chicken was salvageable.

At first glance the carcass didn't appear to have enough left on it to make much of a meal. His grandmother would have no problem, he recalled fondly. She could make a week's worth of potpies and soups from a ravaged Thanksgiving turkey, a survival skill he attributed to her living through the Depression era and having to make the most from the least. The childhood memory of watching her painstakingly pick and pinch out the crevasses with her gnarled, arthritic fingers was the force behind the guilt that prevented him from tossing the decimated bird before him into the trash. Floyd cut away as much meat as he could, then gave his best grandmotherly effort at picking when the blade of the knife became more of a threat to pare his own flesh rather than the bird's. Fifteen minutes of scavenging left him as surprised as he was proud when his toil was rewarded with a quantity of meat the size of his fist. Scraping away at the bones and cartilage brought to mind his recent visit to Neil Dobbs' lab at the city college and images of him meticulously shaving his road kill down to the bone.

Then Floyd stepped back.

Staring at the bones on the counter and thinking about Dobbs brought something else to mind—the box of bones, *human bones*, in Dobbs' storeroom.

The box with Eileen Sherman's name on it.

Floyd abandoned the chicken remains on the cutting board and set the unclean knife and platter in the half-filled sink. He rinsed his hands and grabbed the dishtowel to dry them as he quick-stepped to his bedroom. He took his wallet from the night stand and, sitting on his bed, sifted through the business cards filed inside until he found the one Grace Keller gave him with her home number on it. Floyd swung his legs over the width of the bed to the other side and was now sitting next to his phone. Three rings later, Keller answered. She was not happy.

"I've got no business with you, King."

"Even if I have a hunch where Farnsworth's body might be?"

Floyd's announcement created dead air on the line. Floyd interpreted the silence as a re-establishing of business ties and told Keller about Sherman's job at the city college, about Dobbs, and about the collection of bones sitting in Dobbs's storeroom, a gift he received from Eileen Sherman.

"At the time we met with Dobbs we were looking for Sherman in order to find Peter Lindell. We had no reason to think Sherman knew anything about Farnsworth's disappearance, let alone that she could have played a role in it."

"You knew she was dirty, King." Keller's tone revealed she never fell for Floyd's seesaw attitude toward the woman. "What closed that gate for you?"

"Brenda found out something about Sherman that somehow never came up."

When Floyd detailed the intimate history between Sherman and Farnsworth, a series of expletives erupted from Keller.

"Why am I not surprised to hear about it?" she mumbled as she calmed herself. "How long have you held on to *that* little piece of trivia?"

"Brenda found out from Vossen when she picked up the photos from him this afternoon. The way things progressed earlier—or regressed—there wasn't much opportunity to put it on the table."

"That should have been the *first thing* put on the table, King. And don't give me any of your bullshit excuses why you didn't. You'd have to be an absolute fucking moron not to see a motive there. What else are you and your partners sitting on?"

"Nothing. And if you hadn't stormed out of our meeting you and Tiner would be sitting there with us. We can talk about this later—"

"Forget it. I've had enough smoke blown up my ass for the week."

Expressing no mood for engaging a dispute, Floyd sighed a conceding "whatever" and told Keller he'd wait for her at the city college until nine tomorrow morning.

There were no "good-byes", just the clicks of telephone receivers being replaced on their bases.

18
Friday morning, August 22nd

The directions Floyd gave Keller led her to the administrators' parking lot that, as Floyd learned on his last trip to the campus, would provide easier access and more available spaces than the student lots. Floyd arrived earlier than the nine o'clock meeting time he set and was leaning back against the trunk of his car. A boyish campus police officer on his morning rounds stopped and questioned Floyd's presence in the staff lot. Floyd identified himself and explained that he was waiting for a colleague for a meeting with a professor. To Floyd's surprise, the officer didn't press the issue, unlike many private security officers Floyd had encountered over the years who felt they had a territorial right to know real police business. He told Floyd to leave his police parking placard on the dash of his car and he'd see that no one bothered it. And when Floyd asked if it was required that he check in somewhere, the officer smiled and told Floyd he already had before respectfully taking his leave.

Floyd spotted Keller's silver Lexus gliding into the lot a few minutes before nine. He pulled himself away from his car and walked to where she parked to pass along the campus officer's parking instructions. As they walked from the lot and across the campus, Floyd told her about the possibility that when Farnsworth disappeared he and Sherman were continuing an affair that began years before either had married. The news didn't sit well with Keller who, despite Floyd's assertion he himself learned of the relationship only the day before, continued to grumble her belief that it was just another essential piece of information he was intentionally withholding.

With classes in session, the campus was less crowded than the morning he, Marty, and Shelby joined the push of students through the main quad toward the science building. Following a short search of classrooms that included interrupting a lecture, Floyd and Keller found Neil Dobbs relaxing in his corner office. His attire had changed from his prior beachcomber style to a canyon explorer outfit consisting of green cotton canvas cargo shorts, a tan Henley shirt, and hiking boots. The tail of hair he usually tied behind his head was loose and held out of his face and behind his ears by a floppy, dingy white, Tilley hat. Floyd knocked on the window and Dobbs gave him a nod of recognition as he stood up to open the door.

"Detective King," he greeted in his pleasant tone with a handshake. Floyd introduced Keller, then Dobbs' upper body swayed side to side as he appeared to be looking around Floyd. "No Shelby this time."

"Afraid not."

"Shame," Dobbs said in a disappointed tone. "Still looking for Eileen?"

"As a matter of fact we ran into her not long after we left your lab."

"No kidding?" Dobbs rocked his rear back onto his desk and casually crossed his arms. "I didn't think I helped you enough to make you feel obligated to come back and thank me."

"We appreciated you sharing your time with us. I was wondering if we could have a little more. For educational purposes."

"Educational purposes," Dobbs repeated with suspicion. "Okay. What would you like to know?"

"I'd like to tap into your skill at preserving skeletons. How hard is it to clean bones?"

Floyd's question pulled Dobbs further from his weighty gaze. Dobbs sat forward and rested his crossed forearms on his desk as he shifted his mind into a teaching mode.

"You mean the process? Removing the flesh and cartilage and connective tissue?" Dobbs pursed his lips as he contemplated his response. "Not too difficult. Like anything else it depends on how prepared you are and how good of a job you want to do, or in my students' case, how high you want your grade."

"What's the easiest way?"

"Easiest or quickest?"

Floyd hadn't thought about a difference. "Both."

"For us, soaking works just fine." Dobbs reached down to the floor at the side of his desk and came up with a stack of four eight-by-eight aluminum baking pans. "We strip as much of the carcass as we can first, then we soak them for a day or two in a water and ammonia mixture. Usually whatever remains can be picked off by hand or scraped gently with a small putty knife. Occasionally I'll have a couple of students needing extra credit who will volunteer to take the tougher bones home and boil them. Once we get down to nothing but bone, we give them a dip in a fifty-fifty solution of water and Elmer's glue as a preservative."

"You could do this to human bones, then?" Keller asked.

"I've never done it with a human bone, but I'd assume it's no harder than with any other animal. Just need a bigger pan. The real problem you run into with size is waste. That's why I set a limit. I'll allow birds or animals up to the size of a skunk. No cats or dogs. We double-bag the remains and take them to the animal control department and they do what they do with any other dead animal."

"So if someone had, say, a human body and didn't want to create a slaughterhouse in their garage, how would they do it?"

"Bury it. Depending on the size and the weather, it will decompose to a skeleton over time, maybe in few months. But even if it isn't completely decomposed, the remaining cleaning shouldn't be any different than what I just described."

"Can you tell by looking at the bones if they were buried or not?" Floyd asked. "Will there be discoloration from the soil?"

"I'm no forensic expert, but bones are porous. I'm sure whatever is in the soil will leach into the bone. Most bones will appear stained, buried or not. The Elmer's treatment will whiten the bone surface, but as far as determining the precise cause of the stain ..." Dobbs shrugged apologetically. "Anything else I can help you with?"

"We do have a favor to ask," Floyd announced.

Dobbs smiled. "Cops only ask for favors when they don't have enough probable cause to get a judge to sign a warrant."

Floyd explained to Keller about Dobbs' background growing up with a police officer for a father, something to which he felt Keller could relate. Though Keller didn't appear to make any correlation between herself and Dobbs and their fathers, Floyd couldn't tell if she didn't recognize it or refused to.

"Betting on a long shot?" Dobbs asked.

"Pretty long," Floyd admitted.

"And long enough that you don't want to cause an unnecessary stir," Dobbs added with an intimate wink.

"We'd like to take a look at your collection of bones," Keller said, getting to the point a bit too abruptly for

Floyd's liking, she noticed. But as Floyd told her, she couldn't dance. Keller saw no point in learning how in the middle of the song.

"I have a lot of bones, Detective Keller."

"We're interested in the box Eileen Sherman gave you."

Dobbs led Floyd and Keller from his office to the back of his lab and the adjoining storeroom. Dobbs entered first, followed by Floyd, who already knew what to expect on the other side of the door. Keller didn't and froze at the door, surveying the storeroom like it was a crime scene. She wasn't squeamish at seeing the numerous trays and carts of the half-assembled animals skeletons in the process of being reconstructed by Dobbs' students, just a bit off guard at the overall macabre décor of the room. Dobbs crossed the room and retrieved the box from under the counter. He hefted it onto an empty cart and rolled the cart to the door.

"Let's take this into the lab. I don't want to disturb the projects."

Floyd grabbed the door Keller had already backed away from and held it for Dobbs as he pushed the cart into the lab. He stopped at the first black bench and flipped the flaps apart. He lifted the cushion cover and spread it on the Formica counter, then removed the first layer of bones and spread them on the cushion. He repeated the process with the second layer, and began the process a third time before Keller stopped him.

"Jesus Christ," Keller grunted in disbelief. "One body had all these bones in it?"

"Just like yours and mine, Detective. There are two hundred-six bones in the adult human body. Fifty-two of them are in the feet."

"Where's the skull?" Keller asked. Of the little she knew

about skeletons, she knew which part of one would be the most important. Dobbs, however, disappointed her.

"I don't have it. I've got everything from the C-3, the third cervical bone"—Dobbs twisted his shoulder and head and pointed to a spot high on the back of his neck—"to almost all of the feet. I'm missing four small bones in the left foot, so subtract those, the two cervical bones and the twenty-nine making up the skull ... that's one hundred and seventy-one."

"How often do bones come up missing?" she asked.

"They don't. When I said missing I meant missing in that they were never part of the collection. I took a full inventory when Eileen gave them to me, and I take an inventory of every bone whenever we break open the box and again before we put them away. Every bone I originally received is still accounted for."

Floyd peered into the box at the next layer. "So these are catalogued?"

Dobbs nodded. "I have a master list with the names of the bones numbered to correspond to the numbers I tattooed on the bones, themselves."

Keller turned to Floyd. "Tough work to put a name to a skeleton without a skull."

"You don't have any medical records on file somewhere, do you?" Floyd asked Keller.

Dobbs overheard the question and his face blanched. "Medical records?" Dobbs murmured in disbelief. He pulled a stool under his rear and dropped on top of it.

"We gave you the whole file, King." In light of their communication problems and cross-accusations of withholding information, Keller took the question as an insult. "And anyway, there was no need for medical records because there was no body to identify."

"Identify?" Dobbs swallowed hard. "You mean you actually know whose body this was?"

"We don't know anything for sure, Mr. Dobbs," Floyd said, trying to calm the professor and break his wide-eyed stare.

"That's why you're looking for her husband, isn't it? You think he killed someone and she—" Dobbs suddenly realized the short course he was giving in skeletal preparation to the detectives was actually part of their investigation. Slack-jawed from shock, Dobbs stood and backed away from the bone-covered bench. His hands rose and came to rest with interlaced fingers atop his hat.

"My God," Dobbs exhaled. "It's not something you think about—" His words caught in his throat before he looked at Floyd and Keller and continued. "*I* never thought about it, about the bones being anything other than ... well, bones."

"If it makes any difference, right now that's all they are." Keller's attempt to lighten Dobbs' panic only seemed to reinforce the repulsion he was feeling.

"Let's go to your office," Floyd suggested, and was promptly followed out of the lab by Dobbs and Keller. Now that the collection of bones Dobbs had been playing with for the last five years had potentially lost their anonymity, Floyd could tell the instructor was uncomfortable just being in the same room with them. As they exited the lab, Floyd watched Dobbs' attention turn to the long, black counter and the several articulated skeletons positioned there, including the cat he called Cheshire. Floyd wondered if Dobbs, having to face the possibility that his human skeleton might be the remains of a murder victim, was now envisioning his collection of strays as lost or abandoned pets.

"You going to be all right, Mr. Dobbs?" Keller asked.

Dobbs felt his way into the chair behind his desk and nodded absently.

"It's important that you understand you didn't do anything wrong," Floyd told him.

"No. Of course I didn't," Dobbs agreed. "It's just ... I mean I can't believe Eileen would—"

"Ms. Sherman's involvement has yet to be determined. It's important that we don't jump to any conclusions," Floyd said, continuing the attempt to ease the man's distress.

"It's also important that you understand we still need your help," Keller added.

"You were right earlier when you said we asked for a favor because we didn't have enough to take to a judge. We still don't."

"But we're close," Keller said. "I'd say pretty damn close."

Floyd nodded, then to Dobbs he asked, "In handling the bones, have you ever noticed any signs of trauma?"

"You mean like blunt force or cut marks?" Dobbs searched his mind for a few seconds. "No, nothing like that. There's one calcified break to the left ulna." As he recalled this he ran his right hand along his left forearm. "It's a complete heal, though. By that I mean it had to have occurred long before death."

"Would you have any objection to us taking the bones and the ledger?"

Dobbs looked at Floyd as if he'd already asked enough of him. His only objection would have been going back into the lab to pack the box, but he nonetheless agreed and seemed almost relieved to see Floyd carrying the burden out the door.

"If they turn out to be inconsequential we'll return them," Floyd called back.

"Hell, keep 'em," Dobbs told him in the open corridor outside the lab. "I'll order a fabricated set through the district office. At least I'll know where *those* came from."

The box's size made it a bit awkward to carry, but in Floyd's favor classes were still in session and the return hike to the parking lot was absent the pedestrian obstacles of students moving from building to building. He rested the edge of the box on the car bumper in order to free a hand to fish the keys from his pocket. He tossed them to Keller so she could open the trunk.

"Dobbs didn't look too terribly hot on handling those bones," Keller noted, referring to his reloading of the box.

Floyd wrangled the box into the trunk, closed it, and got his keys back from Keller. "Kind of different now that he's dealing with a person and not a thing."

"I hope we didn't fuck up his career," Keller said, then without thinking added, "Be like one of us getting sh-" She bit off the word "shot" before it hit the end of her tongue, although she may as well have completed her analogy as she felt Floyd must certainly had. "Sorry."

Floyd gave Keller a no-harm, no-foul wave.

"What now?" Keller asked.

"We need to find out if Farnsworth ever broke his left arm."

"Do you think his wife would know?"

"His ex-wife," Floyd corrected, explaining the importance of the reference when they spoke to the woman. "I would think she'd know. If not, I hope she knows who his doctor was. And I can't see why she wouldn't sign a medical release for Edson's records. My feeling based on my first encounter with her is she wouldn't mind assisting in confirming Edson's death."

"If she does ..."

Keller completed her thought by pulling her cell phone from her jacket and dialing. In an amusing flashback, Floyd looked down at her waist and wondered if her pager would go off. Keller saw the direction of his attention and the twitch of a smirk at the corner of his mouth and turned her body.

"Curtis. It's me ... Maybe, but I don't have time to explain it. I've got a job for you." Keller gave her partner directions to Eileen Sherman's apartment complex, along with a physical description of the woman and a description of her car.

"Call me when you get there. If you don't see her car, wait for it. If it's there, don't lose it or her by letting them go anywhere." Keller's end of the conversation halted with a deflating breath and a roll of the eyes. "You're a cop, Curtis," she snapped into the phone. "Arrest her for something." Keller punched off her phone and stared at the trunk of Floyd's car shaking her head. "Shit."

"I'm sure Curt can handle things. Sherman won't run."

"Huh? No, it's not that. All this time believing Farnsworth simply vanished ..." She let her thought drift to her father, to his report. It was an investigation they wouldn't let him finish, but he'd ultimately be criticized for.

"He may have."

Floyd's encouragement that Farnsworth may still be alive came without the confidence needed to convey reassurance. The strength of his inner desire that Edson Farnsworth was in the trunk of his car couldn't be ignored. Not by him, nor by Keller, who was mindlessly toeing a small rock protruding from the asphalt. The rock was Farnsworth and Floyd and Santa Ramona ... her father's investigation. The mounting frustration. The wanting of Floyd to be wrong, but the dread of knowing he was probably right. The rock, like her thoughts, held fast against her repeated attempts to dislodge it. Keller brought her foot back and extra few inches and caught the rock squarely with her toe.

And still, the thoughts remained.

Giving up on the stone, Keller turned toward her car. "Well? What are you waiting for? We aren't going to find out shit standing around here."

༄

Collette Farnsworth, apparently getting an extremely early jump on happy hour, greeted the detectives at the door with eyes already glassy and breath tinged sweet with alcohol. Floyd introduced Keller, to which Farnsworth, in what must have seemed humorous in her inebriated state, commented that she could make life easier for everyone by visiting both departments rather than meet every officer individually at her front door. Keller, developing an immediate dislike for the woman, wished her to take one step outside so she could arrest her for public intoxication and oblige half that offer. Instead, Keller asked if they could step inside. Farnsworth said she wouldn't have expected anything else and led Floyd and Keller down the short hallway to the front room.

"We may have found your ex-husband," Floyd said, closing the door behind him.

"Yeah?" She asked Floyd over her shoulder without breaking stride before, with a mild cackle in her throat, adding "Dead? Or alive?"

"Dead." That word broke her stride when Floyd said it. "If it's him."

Farnsworth sat herself in front of her drink, started to raise the glass to her mouth, but stopped and set it back on the coffee table. "What do you mean, 'if'?"

"Knowing could be as simple as the answer to one question." Floyd told her.

"Did Mr. Farnsworth ever break his left arm?" Keller asked.

"Break his what?"

"We found a bone—actually several bones—and one shows a healed break."

"Not during the time I was with him. I don't know that I saw Edson ever engaged in any activity strenuous enough to break a sweat much less a bone. Before that?" Farnsworth gave a quick toss of her shoulder.

"Any chance we could get access to his medical records?"

Farnsworth got up and walked to a closed door opposite the front room and pushed it open. She beckoned the detectives to follow her into the darkened room. When Farnsworth hit the wall switch and the lights snapped on, the overall illumination wasn't much better against the darkly furnished interior. Two walls of the room were paneled with sheets of dark cherry. A third wall, essentially a floor-to-ceiling bookcase of the same dark wood, contained a small library of every conceivable genre and, Floyd would correctly assume, a handful of first editions. Interspersed throughout the literary collection were ceramic vases and small bronze busts, perhaps not priceless pieces but well beyond the capacity of his wallet. A tall window, obscured by partially drawn drapes and a veil of beige voile panels, cast a muted glow over the rich cherry desk centered in front of it. A brass desk lamp, a large, round brass ashtray, and a brass pen set pointing upward in V-shape fashion surrounded the green blotter protecting the highly-polished surface. The most curious decoration was the black, nineteen-thirty-style desktop phone that sat next to the dual ringer-topped parlor box.

Farnsworth pointed Floyd and Keller to the two leather chairs fronting the desk while she walked to a roll top desk in the corner of the room. She slid the top back and fiddled through a small drawer. She removed a business card and took a seat behind the desk. The phone, it turned out, was as functional as decorative. Farnsworth lifted the receiver from its cradle and snapped off a series of numbers from the rotary dial. She identified herself then asked for Henry Eddlemen, eschewing the use of title.

"We run in the same circles," she said, explaining the informality of address. "Henry retired two, maybe three years ago, but he still maintains a few patients." She rubbed the meat of her thumb across the pads of her fingers indicating the doctor was being compensated well for the professional courtesy. "I don't think Edson had a doctor other than Henry. He was like a family doctor going back to Edson's father. And Edson retained him for worker's comp claims. Anyway, if there was one thing Edson was consistent about it was his health. Regular physicals. If Edson sustained any damage to his body short of a paper cut, Henry'd know."

Farnsworth returned to the telephone and engaged in an exchange that was more tolerant than amiable. With the pseudo-pleasantries concluded, Farnsworth explained the reason for the call and asked the doctor if he could be of any help. Without a word, Farnsworth held the receiver toward Floyd.

Floyd asked three questions. The answer to the first one was that Dr. Henry Eddlemen had been Edson Farnsworth's doctor from birth. The answer to the second question was that Mr. Farnsworth had never broken a bone or sustained any injury that would have broken his left arm. The final answer, one that Floyd expected but was nonetheless disappointed to hear, was that Edson Farnsworth's medical records would be turned over to the authorities provided proper documentation was submitted first.

"And, no, Collette's permission would not be sufficient to circumvent that process," the doctor added as a pre-emptive measure to what he anticipated to be Floyd's next question. "Until there is verification of Edson's death, I have to respect his expectation of medical confidentiality."

Floyd thanked the doctor and assured him that the proper channels would be followed. He handed the phone back to Farnsworth who, following her exchange of empty promises of getting together with the doctor sometime, hung up.

"Anything else?" Farnsworth asked.

What else could there be? Floyd wondered. Edson Farnsworth had never broken his left arm and, therefore, Sherman's box of bones was precisely that. While there was still a possibility Sherman had knowledge of what, if anything, happened to Farnsworth, he and Keller had nothing to bolster that possibility, no screws to tighten on her, no snags for her to trip over. In the end, the failure to identify the skeleton as Edson Farnsworth put the focus back on Peter Lindell.

"No, ma'am. I suppose not." Then, not wanting to walk away showing signs of defeat, Floyd added, "For now, at least."

Back outside, standing on the curb, Floyd leaned back against his car and stared at Farnsworth's house. He felt like he just played his last nickel in a slot machine and come up empty. The headway he and Keller had made in the last week trying to unravel the mystery of Edson Farnsworth's ring and his disappearance had run its course. For Floyd, it looked like another file to be nestled in his desk drawer with all the other dead-ended cases he collected. For Keller, she could take satisfaction that their failure would stave off any harm that could come to her father's reputation. Hollow satisfaction, because she did nothing to support his efforts over any new doubts that may have been created through their efforts.

"What now?"

Floyd shrugged then slid his hands into his pockets. "Now that we're back to square one?"

"Square one's got only one route, as far as I can see. And we've run it." Keller took her keys and twirled the ring on her finger like a gunslinger, catching the fourth rotation into her palm. "Sometimes those gates are closed before you get to them, you know?"

Floyd chuckled half-heartedly.

"Who knows? Maybe Lindell will turn up one day and ..."

"Maybe," Floyd sighed and headed toward his car. "I'll see ya' around, Grace."

"Yeah, Floyd. I'm sure you will."

19
Friday afternoon, August 22nd

At his desk, Floyd tapped out his synopsis of the investigation of Edson Farnsworth's ring on the keyboard of his laptop. There wasn't much to write, but Floyd always compiled his notes at the conclusion of both successful and failed investigations, reasoning that failed investigations always contained information that provided valuable background material down the road. Just like the report Keller's father submitted helped him, his report may help someone else. Floyd hoped it wouldn't take another ten years.

He inserted his three completed sheets of paper into the manila folder containing his copy of the original Farnsworth file and set it aside. On the corner of his desk, under the two packs of photos Brenda obtained from Len Vossen, was the enlarged photograph of Farnsworth's ring. Floyd reached for it—it, too, belonging in the file—and as he did he knocked the two packets over the end of his desk. He cursed his clumsiness as he got up and walked around his desk to retrieve them. One of the packs split open and fanned two dozen snapshots along the floor. As Floyd squatted over the spill to collect them, something in one of the pictures caught his eye. Floyd hovered motionless over the photo wondering if he was actually seeing what he was seeing. He picked up the photo and, leaving the rest of the pack on the floor, returned to his desk.

The photo was one of the sets taken on the boat at Lake Tahoe. It had three men in it. Floyd recognized two of the men as Farnsworth and Lindell, both of whom flanked another man who Floyd presumed to be Len Vossen. Unlike the other photos of the evening taken at close range, this photo was taken at a distance so the men were shown with all but their feet cut off. What grabbed Floyd's attention in this particular photo was the white discoloration protruding from Lindell's left jacket sleeve. He stared at it trying to convince himself it was anything other than what he believed it to be but failed to do so.

Floyd gathered the remaining pictures off the floor and spread them out on his desk, separating the lake photos from all the others but scrutinizing each one as he did. When he completed his lake pile, he picked through them slowly, paying particular attention to Peter Lindell's left arm. It was easy to see how they missed it. In the half-dozen other photos, Lindell's left arm was either cut off at the elbow or obscured by the body of another person. In the only full body picture, the white showing below Lindell's sleeve was more than likely passed over as nothing but a white shirt cuff. This "cuff", Floyd noted, appeared to extend over the back of Lindell's hand to the knuckles and wrapped into the palm. Floyd dug through his desk for a magnifying glass and focused it over the photo. It was either a cast or a wrap, but there was no doubt in Floyd's mind it was connected to a left arm injury.

Only how could he confirm it? Asking Sherman was definitely out of the question—it'd be like firing the starter's gun for her escape. And asking Vossen or any one else? They might be able to confirm Lindell had an injury, but was it *the* injury? What Floyd wanted was medical proof Lindell suffered a broken arm. Floyd recalled Collette Farnsworth mentioning that Edson's doctor, Henry Eddleman, was also employed by Farnsworth &

Vossen as their workers' comp physician. If Lindell's injury was job related ...

Floyd called Farnsworth and asked for Eddleman's number. Farnsworth gave him Eddleman's office number, the only one she offered as she steadfastly refused to provide the doctor's home number. Floyd checked his watch. It was mid-afternoon. He called Eddleman's office, identified himself, and asked to speak with the doctor. The receptionist put Floyd on hold, forcing him to suffer through most of an emotionless, canned orchestral rendition of Elton John's *Yellow Brick Road* cut every few minutes with taped apologies for the delay, appreciation for the patience, and promises that someone will be available to answer the call momentarily.

Momentarily turned out to be ten minutes later. The receptionist thanked Floyd for waiting and ... nothing. The line clicked over to silence. Thinking he'd been disconnected, Floyd reached for the redial button on his phone. But there was a second click followed by a man's voice.

"Doctor, this is Floyd King. I spoke with you earlier from Collette Farnsworth's home."

"Yes, Detective. And I certainly hope this isn't another attempt to obtain medical information from me about Edson. As I explained previously, I'll be more than happy to cooperate with the authorities provided the proper legal orders are presented to me."

"I understand, sir. In the spirit of getting those orders I'm trying to avoid bothering you and your staff with frivolous wastes of time for documents that may not be necessary."

"All of which means ...?"

Floyd recognized the doctor's get-to-the-point tone as

one Lt. Bern frequently shot at him. Unlike the bandying about with which he strained the lieutenant's patience, Floyd went right to the point.

"You were not only Mr. Farnsworth's doctor, you were also the designated physician for his company, correct?"

"Yes, for workers' compensation claims."

"According to Len Vossen they had a pretty good track record in terms of safety and days lost to injury."

"I don't know the numbers but, no, his contractors didn't have employees streaming into the office. I don't see where—"

"Did you ever treat Peter Lindell for any injuries?"

"I may have, but again, those records are—"

"I'm not asking for any medical records, Doctor. All I want to know is if you ever treated Mr. Lindell. Specifically for a broken left arm. If you didn't, then there will be no need for me to get the court order, and no need for me to bother you again."

"If my memory serves me correctly, yes. I don't recall precisely when—early nineties, sometime late in ninety-one."

"And it completely healed? There were no complications, no rods or plates or extensive surgical repairs?"

"None. To the best of my knowledge the injury healed normally and didn't cause any physical limitations or further complications."

Floyd thanked the doctor and sat back in his chair with the photo in hand. He had found Peter Lindell, and it was a certainty he could prove Eileen Sherman was involved, though to what extent was still up in the air. Floyd stopped short of concluding that Edson Farnsworth killed Lindell, and that Sherman disposed of Lindell's body to aid her lover's getaway. He stopped short because there was still the matter of the ring in the shed, and the ring had broken all of his theories thus far. He still couldn't create a viable scenario for any of the three putting the ring in the shed because it didn't make sense to him why, if Farnsworth, Sherman, or Lindell did so, it remained there all these years.

Floyd was right when he told Keller they were back to square one, and that square had never changed: Finding Peter Lindell was the key to determining what happened to Edson Farnsworth. There was no doubt in his mind that Sherman was involved—*is involved*, he corrected himself, noting the continuance of the ten-year-old charade—only the question as to how deep beyond the apparent murder of her husband.

Floyd recalled the conversation he and Keller had with Neil Dobbs about processing a large body. *Bury it*, Floyd's voice told him.

He picked up the phone and called the on-duty night judge.

It was time to find out just *how* involved Eileen Sherman was.

20
Saturday morning, August 23rd

The timing couldn't have been more perfect had Floyd intentionally set it up.

As the three unmarked vehicles carrying the detectives from Santa Ramona and Sacramento rolled to a stop in front of the house on Mill Creek Road, so did Eric Champs. The realtor turned in his car and spoke to the couple riding with him before getting out to meet the approaching crowd, whom he thought, having never met any of them, to be a party of house hunters. Champs lit up his infectious smile and pressed his tie as he made a bee-line to the man leading the column of bodies up the walk, extending his hand in the guise of a greeting that was actually intended to halt the uninvited party's advance.

"Hi!" he bellowed with exuberance to Floyd while throwing warm nods to the people behind him. Champs gave a prolonged look at one man in particular, the scowling bald man with the cigar clamped in his mouth who appeared to be the most aggravated of the group. But Eric Champs, the true professional he believed he was, would never back down from a crowd. And his showmanship wouldn't allow him to turn away from an audience.

"I'm Eric Champs." Champs produced a high-quality, embossed business card and pressed it into Floyd's hand before he got off the last syllable in his introduction. "I am the agent of record for the seller."

Floyd read Champs' card as the realtor wound up his sales pitch to the detectives, his eyes dragging across the Eric Champs slogan in blue italics on the bottom of the card as Champs uttered them with confidence and enthusiasm.

"Whatever it takes!" Then to Floyd, "I don't know if you're aware, but this is an exclusive listing. Not that I'm not willing to open the place for show. It's just that, well, the commission and all. I'm up for negotiating, you know, a finder's fee, but ... that's the way the business works, right? You have a card? You're an agent with ..."

Floyd's card wasn't as fancy in comparison to Champs', but it was significantly more eye catching under the circumstances. "Santa Ramona Police Department," Floyd answered.

"The police?" Champs looked up from the card and noticed all eyes on him, including his clients, who were peering curiously through the windshield. He recovered his momentarily lost boldness and gave a short, reassuring wave to his prospective buyers that everything was under control, even though it wasn't. He lowered his voice and asked, "You're not, you know, looking for a place to house a sex fiend coming out of prison, are you? That would be—"

"We're here to search the grounds," Floyd told him.

"Search the—?"

A light, pulsing metallic squeak from behind turned Champs around. It was the evidence technicians' van pulling to a stop alongside the realtor's car. If seeing "Santa Ramona Police" in large black letters on the side on the white van wasn't enough to spook the couple in the back of Champs' car, the three men in blue jumpsuits exiting the van and walking toward the house was.

"Now wait just a second," Champs began his protest as he spun back around to face Floyd, who immediately silenced Champs' rant by producing a search warrant and slapping it to the man's chest. "What's this?"

"A warrant. I made sure I pursued more legitimate avenues rather than resort to shortcuts."

Champs looked at the law enforcement contingent one face to the next, their expressions a mix of dark emotions—the impatience of the techs, the irritability in Bern's cigar chewing, Marty's and Brenda's unsympathetic disdain, Keller's stony displeasure—with the exception of Floyd, whose contemptuous glare was enhanced by a victorious smirk that foretold payback.

"You see, *Mr.* Champs," Floyd began, leaning into the realtor to echo the very words Champs brayed over the phone before cutting Floyd off as an annoyance earlier in the week, "I know all the tricks of the trade, and I've mastered a few, myself. See, I'm not like one of those housewives trying to earn an extra buck playing detective between school plays and dinner, or around the kids' soccer games on the weekend."

Recognition struck Champs and he realized, to his embarrassment, Floyd was feeding him the same line with which he dismissed the detective over the phone. When Floyd finished, Champs handed back the warrant unread and made a futile attempt to save face.

"Well, I guess when you have the law on your side you can pretty much do as you please." Champs walked up to the door, unlocked it and shoved it open. "I trust what you're looking for won't involve ripping up the floor boards or cutting holes in the walls."

"Whatever it takes, Mr. Champs," Floyd chirped derisively as Marty walked the agent back to his car. "Whatever it takes."

Champs' unlocking the front door was an unnecessary

act. What Floyd wanted, what he felt, was out back under layers of dirt next to the flattened ground where the shed was once located. The patch of ground where nothing would grow. Floyd led the techs around the side of the house, through the gate, and into the back yard. The techs paused on the concrete patio when Floyd did, and remained there as Floyd walked slowly across the grass toward the fence.

Floyd knew.

The same feeling gripped Floyd just like when he was at D. Lawrence Craig's house, just like when he stepped into the garage and saw the freezer. As soon as his foot landed on the small patch of barren dirt, he knew.

He stepped back and stood for a moment picturing in his mind how the corner of the yard might have looked with the shed erected over the large barren patch in the corner. He turned and faced the house, then took three steps backward and stopped. The seven others formed an irregularly shaped arc in the middle of the lawn and were as intent in studying Floyd's antics as Floyd appeared to be in his visualization. Floyd turned his attention to the three techs and beckoned them forward.

"This area here," he said, motioning at the turned soil. "We're looking for four small bones. Pay extra attention to the dirt closest to either end."

The evidence team leader nodded to Floyd, then to his two partners, who began unwinding twine to mark off their excavation grid. They worked quietly, scraping into the soil inches at a time, then sifting the dirt through a wire mesh and picking among the clods and rocks. They repeated the process again and again, mechanically moving from grid to grid, to the screen and back, periodically stopping to take a measurement and notes before continuing on.

The detectives passed time in relative silence, as well. Brenda sat in the shade on the concrete stoop leading to the back door of the house. To keep Marty occupied, Bern sent him into the house to poke around, with instructions to look specifically in any crawl or attic spaces that Champs and his cleaning crew might have missed. Floyd stood far enough away from the techs to not disrupt them, but close enough to keep a vigil on their progress. Keller, who stayed close to Floyd in the center of the yard to keep an eye on *him*, made intermittent phone calls to Tiner, whom she stationed again outside Sherman's apartment complex in the event Sherman would have to be detained.

Nearing the end of their second hour of work, one of the techs called out from his position at the screen. His voice was hardly loud but carried across the silence of the yard like a dog's bark. The lead technician donned a new pair of latex gloves and lifted the object from the mesh. Floyd stepped forward and the tech held the object out in the palm of his gloved hand. It looked to Floyd like a cross between a small rock and a piece of wood. The tech took a small brush and massaged the object's surface. Little by little the dirt coating fell away and revealed the object's true dingy white color and tiny pores.

"Bone."

Floyd felt a surge in his chest as the tech commented on his find. Floyd turned to Keller. "Call Tiner and tell him not to let Sherman leave the complex under any circumstances." Turning back to the technician, Floyd instructed him to keep looking. "Keep it in the same area. The bones came from one foot, so they should be close together."

The excitement near the dig brought Brenda and the lieutenant forward. Bern gnawed on the end of his cigar as he inspected the recovered bone.

"I better call the chief. Detective Keller, would you call your lieutenant and let him know we'll be coming into town? And if it's okay with him, I'd like to keep you around until we sort this mess out." Then to Floyd, "I'm right in assuming there's a mess to sort out in all of this?"

"It's slowly sorting itself out, Lieutenant," Floyd said. "I'm sure whatever's left will fall into place with a visit to Eileen Sherman."

"Got another," an evidence tech announced. "Maybe two."

"Doenacker!" Bern called toward the house. Back to Keller, "Let him know that I'll touch bases with him later, and that as it stands right now the case is a murder in Santa Ramona and our suspect is living in Sac. I'd like you there when we pick her up and while we question her in case our victim was killed on your side of town when Farnsworth vanished." Then again, louder and impatiently, Bern growled for Marty. "*Doenacker!*"

Within seconds, Marty emerged from the side of the house dusting off the front of his jeans and shirt. "Inside's clean. No cobwebs or dust bunnies. How about you guys?"

"Three bones," Brenda told him. "They're looking for the fourth."

"Doenacker, you stay here with the evidence team," Bern ordered. "As soon as they're finished with the preliminary search for the bones take them and get them authenticated. I'll phone ahead and have a medical examiner on standby. Take the box with rest of the bones with you."

"There's a sheet of paper in the box," Floyd told Marty as he tossed him the car keys. "Sort of like a parts list that identifies all the bones and the missing ones. All we need is for the M.E. to give a tentative match between what we recovered here and what Dobbs didn't have." He called to Brenda, then turned to Keller. "Can we get a lift into town?"

21
Saturday afternoon, August 23rd

"Is she still here?"

Keller's facetious taunt drew a hard stare from her partner as she walked around him to the complex gate. She didn't really desire an answer, and Tiner wasn't going to oblige, anyway. She went straight for the manager's call button and jabbed at it with her finger as if she were poking the man directly in his chest.

"Yes?" the voice crackled over the speaker.

"Sir, this is Detective Keller, Sacramento Po-"

The electronic lock buzzed before Keller finished identifying herself. She gave Floyd a conceited smile of satisfaction over her shoulder as she pushed the gate and held it open for him. Floyd stepped into the courtyard followed by Brenda and Tiner, with Keller bringing up the rear, though not for long as she quick-stepped past Tiner and Brenda to catch Floyd.

Keller took the lead as they neared the door, but it was only for the initial contact with Sherman. Once their presence was established, she'd yield to Floyd. "How you gonna play this?"

"On our side of the fence." Floyd grinned alluding to his and Keller's ongoing "gate" analogies. Their exchange was lost on Brenda, though through her familiarity with Floyd as she watched him work over the years she was able to interpret the reference as the approaching end of something.

As soon as Sherman cracked open the door she expelled

a sigh of annoyance embellished with skyward throw of her eyes. She noticed Brenda standing behind Floyd and Keller and slowly rocked her head.

"Is this a trend that will continue, that you add on more officer every time you come to my door? What's going on?"

"I don't think you'll have to worry about that in the future, Ms. Sherman," Floyd said.

"If this is more about finding Peter, I can't help you. I've already told you all I know."

"No, ma'am. We don't need any more of your help. We found him."

Sherman looked from Floyd to Keller to Brenda, then back to Floyd and emitted a "You—" that came out not as much as a question hung in mid-air by shock as it appeared simply lost for an ending as though there was nothing left to say.

"Ms. Sherman, we're here to arrest you."

"But I—"

"You have the right to remain silent, ma'am." As Floyd began the recitation of the Miranda advisement, Brenda moved around behind Sherman and ratcheted a pair of handcuffs around her wrists. Sherman offered no more than a flinch to the metallic clicks, then a subdued "Yes" when Floyd asked if she understood her rights.

"Do you have any objection to speaking with us?"

"I suppose there's no reason not to. Not at this point. When that first officer came by asking about Peter, I had a feeling something was up. How did you find him?"

"It's a long story, Ms. Sherman," Floyd told her. "I think we both have one. Let's go talk about them."

❧

Interview Room #2 was one of two twin rooms used by the Santa Ramona Police for interrogations. A narrow monitoring booth separated the rooms. Like Room #1, #2 was a square room that had chalk white soundproof walls and ceiling panels. The majority of one wall was made up of a large, mirrored sheet of glass that succeeded in its function of hiding the identity of those doing the watching even if it didn't conceal the concept of being watched. Floyd had frequented Room #2 enough to be familiar with every inch of wall and tile, with every scratch on the table top, and with the rising pitch of the hinges as they tightened against the strain of the hydraulic closer mounted at the top of the door.

Floyd held the door open as Brenda escorted Sherman inside and to one of the plastic chairs at the end of the table. Keller followed but remained back from the activity as Brenda released the cuffs from Sherman and Floyd set up the tape recorder. When everything and everyone was in place, Floyd started the recorder, announced the date, time, and location, and identified the persons present. He verified with Sherman that he had read her her rights before beginning with the interrogation, such as it would be. Floyd reviewed some personal history with Sherman, confirming she had once been married to Peter Lindell, that she had reverted to her maiden name in nineteen ninety-five, and that she held a position teaching at Santa Ramona City College. With the preliminary information gathered, Floyd moved right into the crux of his interview.

"What can you tell me about the circumstances that led to Peter Lindell's death?"

"That day Peter came home early, the day he found out from Len Vossen what Edson had done, he was out of control." Sherman described a near-blind rage she faced in attempting to calm her husband. "It scared me. The anger. Peter'd always been so even tempered. I'd never seen him act out irrationally. Ever."

She cited a number of examples of incidents that she expected would have infuriated her husband, but instead, after a moment or two of soul searching and reasoning, he found alternatives and made adjustments. The one notable example was how he removed his name from the property deed in an effort to protect her from any liability resulting from his business.

"Jay Whiting almost ruined him. It was an eye-opening experience for Peter, and for me, too, being on the verge of having nothing and struggling to keep our heads above water. Peter continually reassured me everything would be okay, that he was working out a way to get us back on our feet."

"Through Edson Farnsworth."

"Yes. Peter didn't tell me at the time, and when I found out ..." Sherman closed her eyes and shook her head. "If things hadn't been so unstable, I'd have objected. But Peter and Edson had been friends before I'd ever met either one of them."

"How good was their friendship?"

"They grew up together, I know that much."

"And what about your past with Mr. Farnsworth?"

"Edson and I had a relationship that ended when I married Peter. Actually, it ended before that, when Edson first left Santa Ramona. I still cared for Edson as a friend, but he had created a place for himself that I couldn't be a part of. We were cordial, but we kept our distance. Collette made sure of that."

"Was your husband insecure about your past?"

"Oh, no. Peter trusted me. We never really discussed

Edson, at least not in the past tense, so to speak. I think Peter was afraid reminiscing would bring up my relationship with Edson. It wasn't like we set a rule on talking about it. It was more of a mutual understanding."

The personal relationships Floyd established between Sherman, Lindell, and Farnsworth were a good foundation to create a motive, but there didn't appear to be a strong enough level of conflict individually or as a whole. He decided it was time to move on to the business dealings between Lindell and Farnsworth.

"So what Farnsworth did with the accounts and the company and the ultimate discovery that he'd been manipulating work orders ... would those have been enough to fuel Peter's anger the way you described?"

"I'd have thought not, but clearly I was wrong. He was even worse the next morning."

"After he met with Vossen."

"Yes. He didn't come home all night."

"No idea where he went?"

"I assumed he was either working on a plan with Len to get out of the hole Edson dug, or he was out looking for Edson. But I didn't know. Peter never said."

Floyd opened his file to Sherman's original statement and took a moment to review it. He wondered if he would have sensed things differently had he been the principle investigator, that maybe he would have asked to see Lindell's things and possibly found the packed bag or an absently misplaced wallet. Perhaps his curiosity would have led him around the house, or outside to the back yard where he would have seen the freshly turned soil of what became Lindell's burial plot. And perhaps standing there he would have known ten years ago what he knew earlier in the day, what he knew from Craig's garage, what he knew that night some six years before while walking toward the crest of the hill in East Pines Park beyond which was located the tree where young Bill Anders was hung. That same knowing feeling he had standing in the dark outside his own home that his hostage daughter needed him. Or maybe, like Detective Mitchell, he would have taken Sherman's words at face value with no cause to suspect her husband of doing anything other than chasing a ghost. Even now there was no reason to discount Sherman's statement as an accurate account of her husband's actions the day he left. She simply ended it where she had to, with Lindell gone.

""What happened when he finally came home?"

"Peter was in a fog. He looked awful. He obviously hadn't slept and was mumbling to himself in between bursts of cursing Edson's existence. I tried calming him, but it was like I wasn't even there. He started packing—more like just stuffing clothes randomly into a duffle bag—spitting obscenities and threats about going after Edson and what he'd do when he found him. I tried to stop him ..."

Sherman's head rocked slowly as she recalled her unsuccessful intervention. Brenda passed her a paper cup of water, which she accepted and downed in two swallows. Sherman set the cup on the table but held it on edge and stared into it. Her face showed no effort of thought; it showed reflection. The vision that played in her mind played similarly for years, a mental video so familiar to her it produced no outward response. It was apparent Sherman hit the transition point that would take them all to Peter Lindell's death. The detectives waited patiently, then Sherman righted the cup and released it, along with the ten-year-old burden she'd been carrying.

Peter hit her, she told them, then clarified that it wasn't

as much a strike as a hard shove, and even then, not really a deliberate assault. More like he walked through her instead of going around her. The contact knocked her back into the doorframe, the edge of which caught her shoulder and head.

"Now *I* was angry. And in pain. As he passed I reached out and grabbed at the back of his shirt. He stopped, dropped the bag, and spun around. I yelled at him. I told him he was crazy, that what he was doing would ruin us. He yelled back that we were already ruined. That's when I found out about the contracts he had leveraged against the business. He was right. There was no way he'd recover; no way he could start fresh. As soon as word spread about how he was duped with the work orders, his reputation in the construction trade was trash."

"Is that when he told you he was going after Farnsworth?"

Sherman nodded. "I begged him to let it go, to let Edson go. We had a house that no one could touch. I was working. We still had each other. None of that mattered to Peter." She paused and sucked in a deep, steeling breath, holding it for a brief moment before letting it escape with the admission to herself, "I didn't matter."

"He picked up his bag. I reached out to stop him and he hit my hand away. This time there was no mistaking it. He *hit* me. I slapped him. Hard. He called me a traitorous slut and accused me of still being in love with Edson, that I was trying to save Edson over him. He said some hurtful things—wanting to know how long I'd been seeing Edson behind his back, if I'd really been thinking of him when we were ..."

In her first show of heartfelt emotion, Sherman began to cry. She wiped a tear streak from her face and asked for a tissue, a box of which Brenda retrieved from the monitoring room and set before her. Floyd allowed Sherman a moment to collect herself, after which Sherman continued with her story.

"I slapped him again. He shoved me to the floor. When I got up, the fireplace poker was in my hand. I don't know how ... I couldn't remember picking it up, but it was there. I don't remember hitting Peter, but he was on the floor bleeding from above the ear. And I was standing over him. It was so quiet. It was ... it just ... happened."

Sherman began crying harder and shaking as her relief valve having finally broken open. Floyd suggested a short break not only for Sherman's benefit, but so he, Brenda and Keller could decide how to proceed. It seemed Sherman's relationship with Farnsworth was indeed a factor behind a murder, though not in the manner they anticipated. While they had most of the admission, legally obtained, for sure, there was the matter of the burial plot in the backyard and the remains getting into Dobbs' possession. But mostly there was the ring. There was still no explanation as to how Edson Farnsworth's ring got into the shed.

Sherman drank another cup of water and dried her eyes, then took a deep breath before answering Floyd's question about what she did with her husband once she realized he was dead.

"I wasn't sure what to do at first. I thought about calling the police, but I had no marks on me to substantiate a self-defense claim. I knew eventually my relationship with Edson would come up and that, along with Edson's disappearance, would make me look pretty good for killing Peter to help Edson. So, I buried him out back of the house. I was afraid that with Edson gone and Peter dead, it would be my word against speculation. I figured my best option was to make it look like Peter went through on his vow to search for Edson."

"And depending on the person who asked, used one of three stories about him being gone or even existing, correct?"

"Yes, and initially there was only a small group I worried about convincing. The police, naturally, which turned out to be easy since Peter wasn't a suspect. There was Collette, but she couldn't care less about Edson so it was no surprise she never showed any interest in what happened to Peter. And the bank. They were ticked off about not being able to recover their losses through me. My assets were protected."

"The reason for changing the title on the house in the first place," Floyd said.

Sherman nodded. "The only person who seemed concerned was Len. He called and stopped by occasionally to check on me, wanting to know how I was holding up or if I'd heard from Peter. Otherwise, it turned out there were no complications."

"And if Mr. Farnsworth returned? You didn't anticipate that as a complication?"

"Not really. Edson wasn't coming back. He couldn't after what he did. And Peter ... well, Peter wasn't coming back. I was prepared to continue the ruse that he was still looking for Edson."

"Did part of being prepared include knowing you would be digging up his remains later?" Floyd asked.

"No. That was something I thought about months afterward. I knew I would have to do something eventually. It disturbed me knowing he was buried back there. I came up with a number of possible remedies to the problem of disposing his body. They all had one drawback or another, usually the risk that someone would catch me in the process.

"About eight months after Peter ... after the incident, there was a seminar at the city college here—the different campuses hosted one every year—and part of that was a tour that took us into Neil Dobbs' lab. That's when I came up with the idea of cleaning his skeleton and giving the bones to him."

"How long did that take?"

"About five weeks," Sherman answered, adding, "That was about three months after I found the courage to do it."

"Where?"

"At the house. A little at a time. I was fortunate in two aspects. First, I had stripped away Peter's clothing before I buried him. Second, I didn't bury him too deep. The amount of time between burying and digging was close to a year, so the body had decomposed enough that I didn't have to worry about disposing a lot of flesh or organs. I boiled the bones, cleaned them, and washed them with a glue solution to make them appear processed. When I finished I packed them all into a box and waited for an opportunity to give them to Neil."

"That opportunity came when you got the job transfer to the Santa Ramona campus," Floyd concluded. "Was that planned, as well?"

"No. The district was making room for more computer science classes, so my department was moved here, to Santa Ramona. That was in ninety-five. I told Neil that I lost a lot of storage space because of the move and asked if he wanted to take some things off my hands."

"The bones," Keller said.

"Neil jumped at the offer. It's hard to get money for

such high-ticket items like a human skeleton. Even for a fabricated one. I told him an old professor gave them to me. He didn't even care that it was missing the skull."

"Or missing four bones from the left foot." Floyd's announcement caused Sherman's jaw to slowly drop. "That's how we connected the skeleton you gave Dobbs to the burial spot in your backyard. But we didn't know we we're looking at your husband at the time."

"We thought it was Edson Farnsworth," Keller added.

Sherman cocked her head like a dog hearing a strange noise. "Edson?"

"Our suspicion is that your husband killed Farnsworth," Keller said, "and that you helped by disposing of the body. We were looking at the bone collection as being Farnsworth."

Floyd explained, "When we studied the bones, however, we found a healed break on the left ulna. We talked to Mr. Farnsworth's doctor, he confirmed that Farnsworth never broke a bone in his life."

"But Peter did, " Sherman whispered.

"We found a picture of Peter and you—"

"On the boat at Tahoe," Sherman correctly interrupted. "He broke his arm earlier that month. Fell at a job site."

"Which was how we were able to confirm the injury. Farnsworth's doctor treated your husband for the workers' comp insurance."

Sherman nodded as Floyd ran down the sequence of discovery, then her understanding waned as her brow creased in confusion. "What led you to look for Peter in the first place? It's been over ten years and everything had been so settled. No one was looking. No one was even curious about Peter."

"What changed was when Farnsworth's ring turned up."

Floyd explained how in tracing the ring's recovery the focus fell on her husband. With Lindell being gone, it seemed logical to them that he had a hand in Farnsworth's disappearance and hid the ring. But when they couldn't find Peter, they went looking for her.

"In doing so I found something that drew my attention toward you: Peter's driver's license renewal. Nobody really thinks about their license expiring. I don't. I always get a notice mailed to me from the DMV and then look at my license and go, 'Oh, yeah'. You pretty much know the date—it's your birthday. But most people need to check the year. Peter's was renewed in the year it was due, in ninety-five. Three years *after* you said he left."

"I got it in the mail," Sherman began, "... the renewal notice. I forged his signature, paid the fee, and mailed it back. At the time I thought it was a good idea, making it appear that Peter was still alive. And it helped a little when I petitioned for the separation, making it look like he abandoned our marriage."

"And it also helped that it would be delivered to you in the mail as opposed to having to go to the DMV to pick it up. Even if your husband was on top of things and went to some office to renew it, it would be mailed to the address on the license. No one ever has any idea when something like a license will be received in the mail. And since he didn't make an address change, for Peter to have received it, assuming *he* renewed it, he would have to have maintained contact with you. But you made it clear you had had no contact with your husband since he left. All I could come up with was that you renewed it for him. And with the inconsistencies in your statements, it gave the impression that not only was Peter involved, but you were covering his tracks."

"It's too bad you didn't know about the ring being in the shed," Keller added.

Sherman angled forward in her chair toward Keller expecting the detective to expand on her revelation. Floyd, reacting to Sherman's posture as a sign she was ready to admit her participation in Farnsworth's disappearance, leaned forward, as well. Sherman broke first, but what she uttered was hardly the sought-after confession.

"In the shed?" Sherman asked.

"I'm sorry?" Floyd responded.

"She said Edson's ring was found in the shed."

"Yes, ma'am. It was."

"How did it get there?"

"Your husband put it there," Keller said in a condescending, "as-if" tone. "Or *you* did."

"I most certainly did not," Sherman defended. "And how could Peter do it if he was dead?"

"He obviously could have done it before you killed him. There are four days unaccounted for between the time Farnsworth made the bank transfers and your husband packed to leave."

"No, he—"

Keller pressed on. "That's plenty of time for your husband to commit a murder. You said yourself your husband was gone the entire night before."

"Peter couldn't have killed Edson."

"You can prove that?" Keller challenged.

"I *know* that! I know my husband."

"You do? Ms. Sherman, just moments ago you described for us behavior you'd never seen from your husband. It's certainly possible that he could have turned as violently against Farnsworth as he did toward you."

"It's not possible. It's not—"

"You told us how livid your husband was over Farnsworth destroying his business. You even said he accused you of protecting Farnsworth, that he suspected you were still seeing him. Those are two pretty strong motives for someone to kill over." Keller took a step forward and pointed an accusing finger at Sherman. "You killed your husband, all right. But you really killed him in retaliation for him killing your lover, Edson Farnsworth!"

"You're wrong!"

"What made your husband so angry, Ms. Sherman? What did you tell your husband that set him off? That you were planning on leaving with your beloved Edson? Is that why Peter killed him? Is that what happened?"

"I already *told* you what happened!" Sherman sobbed.

"You told us what you want us to *believe* happened, just like you did ten years ago! What proof do you have that your husband attacked you? He's the one who's *dead*! Maybe you attacked *him*!" Keller slapped her palm on top of the table; Sherman's body shuddered. "Let's cut the bullshit! What *really* made you break your husband's skull, Ms. Sherman?"

"Stop!" Sherman wailed as tears squeezed from her tightly pinched eyes.

"Why don't you just admit what we already know? Peter killed Farnsworth because he was bleeding Peter financially while you were bleeding him emotionally! And *you* killed Peter not in self-defense but because he ruined your plans to be with Edson!"

"Okay, okay, everybody just settle down a second."

Floyd intervened and attempted to calm what was turning into an unnecessary escalation of emotions. With a reassuring smile to Sherman, Floyd excused himself from the table and motioned for Brenda and Keller to follow him to the corner of the room. He looked back at Sherman, who watched them curiously as she dried her eyes. Sherman's face, her shoulders, her whole body sagged from exhaustion, and Floyd was certain her mind was just as debilitated, a condition whose process was accelerated by Keller's merciless verbal battering. He saw no benefit to subjecting Sherman to more questions—anything further would be suspect, tainted by mental fatigue. And to go back to investigating Lindell's death after Keller basically accused Sherman of partaking in Farnsworth's? Better to start fresh in the morning with a rested suspect and less impassioned interrogation, Floyd reasoned. He knew Keller wouldn't be happy, but then there was no pleasing her to begin with.

"I say we break this off for now. We have a confession—"

"*You* have *yours*," Keller protested, as expected. "What about Farnsworth? Sherman may be good for having a part in that, and I'll bet I can crack her in another minute."

"And what if you can't? What kind of case are you going to present? You don't have a body. No one even knows if Farnsworth is dead."

"Floyd's right."

"Isn't he always?" she asked Brenda smartly. Then to Floyd, "Fine. I'll back off. But as soon as you're done questioning her about killing her husband, I want her for Farnsworth."

The trio returned to the table, though Keller kept her distance from Floyd and Brenda to make a point that she was not in league with the Santa Ramona police. Sherman couldn't hear the words exchanged in the corner, but she could see in the detectives' faces the strain those words caused. As much for Sherman's benefit as their own, Floyd called an end to the question and answer session and told Sherman they would pick up in the morning after a night's rest. He leaned toward the tape recorder and announced the date and time and the end of the interrogation, then shut the machine off. He thanked Sherman for her cooperation and asked that she go with Brenda for final processing en route to the temporary holding area pending her transfer to the county jail.

As soon as Brenda walked Sherman out of the room, Floyd walked over to Keller. He wasn't angry, though he wasn't particularly pleased at her bull rushing Sherman. It was still his case to lead and he had every right to dictate its progress. But he saw no point in lecturing Keller and widening the rift that already existed between them. Floyd offered some advice instead.

"The thing about those gates, Grace, is you want to make sure when you do close them, they stay closed." Then with a wink added, "And you also want to keep your fingers out of the way. I'll see you in the morning."

22
Late Saturday afternoon, August 23rd

Brenda, having deposited Sherman into a holding cell where she could get some rest before ultimately being transferred to the county jail, met up with Floyd in the squad room after he'd parted company with Keller. It was close to four o'clock and they were exhausted, but more than that, hungry. Floyd suggested a quick bite to eat and a pit stop at either her place or his for a short nap. When Brenda picked up her purse from her desk, she saw the double stack of photos—minus the two Tahoe pictures showing Lindell's cast—she planned on returning to Vossen. Floyd said they could do that on the way.

Fortune smiled on Floyd and Brenda. Vossen appeared in the outer office preparing to lock up for the day as the detectives arrived. He smiled warmly at Brenda through the glass front door, clearly pleased to see her yet again, and opened it. Vossen was just as polite in holding the door for Floyd, though he seemed a bit disappointed that Brenda didn't come alone, or maybe that she came with a man.

"Mr. Vossen, this is my partner, Floyd King."

Vossen shook Floyd's hand as a formality. His attention was on Brenda. "You're becoming a regular visitor, Detective."

"I hope my visits aren't too intrusive."

"Oh, not at all. Just the opposite."

"I came to return your photos. We kept two from the party on the boat. I made out a receipt ..." Brenda handed

Vossen the two packets and a slip of paper, Vossen's copy of the receipt. "I'll let you know when we don't need them any more and arrange to send them back."

"So they were helpful?"

"Not in the manner we expected, but, yes, they were of great help." Brenda told Vossen without going into detail how the photos intended to help them track down Peter Lindell as the possible murderer of Edson Farnsworth ended up proving Lindell was killed by his wife as he prepared to hunt down his former friend and business associate.

"So Peter never went after Edson?"

"No. The fact that everyone thought Peter did gave Ms. Sherman a plausible cover up for the murder. The only unresolved issue, the issue we really intended to unravel, was the chain of possession of Mr. Farnsworth's ring."

"Who'd have thought that Eileen could ...?" Vossen sighed, leaving his question hanging. "I certainly would have never suspected she could do something like that. And to Peter. I imagine then it's possible she could have killed Edson, as well."

"That most likely will be something the Sacramento detectives look at down the road."

"Well, I congratulate you on your success thus far. Though with Peter dead and Edson nowhere to be found I expect you'll find it difficult determining how the ring got into the shed."

"Yes, I—" Brenda suddenly froze, her head tilting as her face screwed in puzzlement. She bit thoughtfully on the inside of her lower lip, inhaled deeply through her nose, then slowly shook her head straight as her eyes leveled squarely on Vossen.

"Brenda?" Floyd called. "What's the matter?"

"I never told him we found the ring in the shed, Floyd."

"You, uh ... yes, you did." Vossen chuckled, his voice rising noticeably with nervous tension. "That first day you came to see me ... when you showed me the photo of Edson's ring. Remember? You—"

"I told you we found it in town." Brenda countered. "I never told you where."

"How did you know the ring was in the shed, Mr. Vossen?" Floyd asked.

"She told me," Vossen insisted, pointing at Brenda. "She handed me the ... and she ... she *told* me. Come on, you guys."

Vossen chuckled again, flustered, as he backed around the receptionist's desk. He became even more rattled as the back of his leg bumped into the front corner of the desk. He excused his clumsiness with a meek, embarrassed grunt and continued down the side of the desk dragging his hand along its edge as a guide, unable to take his eyes off the detectives. He sidestepped toward the chair and sat. As hard as Vossen tried to look comfortable and unfazed, his face betrayed his awareness that he made a mistake. A *big* mistake.

"I didn't—"

"You didn't what, Mr. Vossen?" Brenda cut in.

"We never told anyone where the ring was found," Floyd said. "Not Eileen Sherman. Not Collette Farnsworth."

"And I *know* I never told you." Brenda stated emphatically.

"So the only way you could have known ..." Floyd began.

"... was if you put it there," Brenda finished.

"Or knew who did," Floyd added. "Which means ..."

It was over in an instant. Or so it seemed as time

contradicted itself by moving so quickly while passing so slowly. Like being in a car wreck. Like watching a disaster unfold before one's eyes. To be so acutely aware of so many details and sensations that it's hard to believe what seemed an eternity was all over in a blink. But then the last ten years of Len Vossen's life had been just that: a blink in which the details of what happened ten years ago caught up to him much faster than it took to live those same ten years.

"I think it's time we find out what really happened to Edson Farnsworth, don't you, Mr. Vossen?"

Floyd had Marty process Vossen into custody then escort him to Interview Room #2, to the same chair from which Eileen Sherman admitted to killing her husband. It was getting late, close to eight in the evening, a delay in part due to Floyd's request for Grace Keller to be present and in part to Vossen's request to have an attorney with him while he gave his statement.

"I'll cooperate when he gets here," Vossen promised Floyd when the detective finished reading Vossen his rights. "Not that it's going to change anything, mind you. It's just a formality."

Keller barely made it home when she received Floyd's phone call summoning her back to Santa Ramona. Not surprising, an argument ensued over jurisdiction in questioning Vossen. Keller demanded that Vossen be brought to Sacramento and turned over to her as the murder of Edson Farnsworth clearly took place in her city. Floyd staunchly defended his position that until the matter of Vossen's knowledge of the ring in the shed was cleared up, his case took priority. He also warned Keller about being premature in concluding that Vossen having

Farnsworth's ring at one point didn't predetermine Vossen's guilt with respect to Farnsworth's disappearance.

"There's no evidence the man's even dead." Floyd's reminder drew an exasperated sigh from Keller, prompting Floyd to admonish the Sacramento detective. "Don't blow this, Keller. Vossen's willing to talk right now, so we may be able to clear both cases in less than an hour."

As an enticement for her to play ball, Floyd added that getting their supervisors involved would likely get them both removed from their respective investigations. Floyd said he didn't want to call Bern any more than she wanted to call her lieutenant—not that he ever intended to do so any more than Keller would have in making a similar threat—but left the option up to her.

Keller's tone softened slightly on her drive back to Santa Ramona from "This is bullshit" in signing off on Floyd's phone call to "This better not be bullshit" as he walked her down the corridor into the interview room. Upon entering the room, Keller walked directly toward Vossen's attorney and handed him her business card, suggesting he keep his calendar open. "You may be working double-duty for a while."

The attorney turned to Floyd to ask the purpose of having a Sacramento detective present during the interview.

"Santa Ramona's interest in questioning your client is in regard to the ring and his relationship with Peter Lindell," Floyd explained. "Because the ring belonged to Mr. Farnsworth, and because the investigation into Mr. Farnsworth's disappearance is still open, Detective Keller was invited in the event information comes forth which may have a bearing on their case in Sacramento."

As he did with Sherman, Floyd placed a cassette in the

tape recorder and started the machine. Keller, displaying the distrust she'd felt for Floyd and Santa Ramona over the course of the previous week's interaction, opened her handbag, removed her own recorder, and placed it next to his. Once the date, time, and participants were noted, Floyd reminded Vossen of his rights and began the session. It followed a structured fashion by which Floyd established a background on Vossen and his association with Peter Lindell. Then Floyd covered the more recent police visits to Vossen: the two with Brenda by herself and then, again, hours earlier when he was with her returning the photos, when Vossen revealed his knowledge about the location of Farnsworth's ring.

"How did you know the ring was in the shed at the house on Mill Creek Road?" Floyd asked.

"I put it there," Vossen replied. "To set Peter up for killing Edson."

Hearing this caused Keller to bristle with energy. She fought to restrain herself from demanding Floyd step aside so she could question Vossen about the murder of Farnsworth. Floyd, though, had insisted when he signed her in at the front desk that she allow him to clear up everything regarding Vossen's connection to the ring and Lindell's death. Only then would he turn the architect over to her. Keller reluctantly agreed to Floyd's plan, but only after Floyd gave his word he wouldn't stray from his path. And as long as he kept his word, she'd keep hers.

Floyd was in a bind, as well. Having promised not to delve into matters concerning Farnsworth's apparent death, he had to alter his line of questioning and carefully word those questions to avoid leading Vossen into Keller's territory. Thinking for a moment, he chose to work Vossen in the same manner in which he'd worked this case from the start. Backwards.

"When?"

Vossen couldn't recall the exact day, claiming things were going so fast at that time that one day was as much the next as any other. He narrowed it down to within a few days of meeting with Lindell, when he told the contractor about Farnsworth draining the accounts.

"I tried to get the damn thing inside the house," he explained of the ring, "into a cabinet or bureau or into Peter's bedroom, but I never got the chance. I wanted to get rid of it so badly ... Always having that ring in my pocket, in my car ... anywhere near me made me uncomfortable. I parked down the street from the house one afternoon and waited for Eileen to leave. When she did, I didn't even try to get in. I went around to the back yard, to the shed, stuffed it in some box, and got my ass out of there."

The box that broke on C, Floyd concluded. The sudden shift of the contents caused by the bottom of the box failing allowed something small and weighted—the ring—to find its way to the floor along with the shirts that C couldn't grab while he was attempting to close the loose cardboard flaps.

"Did you know Lindell was dead at the time?"

"No. Eileen told me he'd left to find Edson, which turned out to be a fortunate break for me."

"How so?"

"Peter made threats against Edson the night I saw him. Now he was out looking for Edson. All it would take was an anonymous call to the police telling them where to find Edson's body and ring, and my testimony that Peter threatened payback on Edson. All I was waiting for was Peter's return."

"So all this time, after ten years, you were still waiting Lindell out, still planning on framing him for Farnsworth's death, correct?"

Vossen shrugged. "If I had to. The only reason I set Peter up in the first place was because I was never one hundred percent confident in the story about Edson vanishing. Peter was a back up in case the police investigation found some evidence to refute the story of Farnsworth stealing the money and running off. As it turned out, no one ever questioned Edson's disappearance."

"Or Peter Lindell's. For the record, then, you had no knowledge that Lindell was dead, correct?"

"None whatsoever."

"And the last time you saw him alive was when?"

"The day I told him about Edson and the damage to the business."

"How long was he with you?"

Vossen thought for a minute. "Until mid-afternoon, I guess."

"Do you know where he went after he left you?"

"No."

"And nothing in Lindell's threats of finding Farnsworth and killing him gave any indication he had knowledge of where Farnsworth was."

"I can only tell you *why* he left my office. I didn't know where he planned to go, but wherever it was, he wouldn't have found Edson."

"How did you know that?"

"Because Edson was already dead."

As everything related to the ring and Peter Lindell was now clear, Floyd ran out of questions. It was time to pass the baton to Keller. He did it with, "One final question: Where did the killing of Edson Farnsworth take place?"

"In his office. In Sacramento."

Floyd stepped back and Keller eagerly stepped forward in his place. "It's about time we get to some nuts-and-bolts questions here. Not that my colleague's pursuits are without merit, but ..."

Keller squinted into her tape recorder's window to gauge the amount of tape remaining on her cassette, then pushed the machine in front of Floyd's. She stood up straight and rolled her shoulders back like she was preparing for activity more physical than an exchange of words. It was all a show. Keller was stalling, testing the patience of Vossen and his attorney to find out how much control she commanded over them. It was similar to a kids' game of throwing a punch and pulling up short to see who's going to flinch first. Vossen fidgeted in his seat, but his experienced attorney had not moved an inch.

"Okay," Keller began, "you admitted to using the ring to make it look like Lindell was involved in Farnsworth's death. You also told us where the murder took place. What you haven't told us was who killed him and why. So, Mr. Vossen, did you kill Edson Farnsworth?"

Vossen paused, then nodded. Keller pulled a chair out and sat across from the architect. She reached forward and nudged the tape recorder half an inch closer to him.

"Nods don't translate well from audio tapes, sir."

"Sorry, Detective Keller. Yes, I killed Edson."

Without a prompt to begin explaining how he did it, Vossen jumped right into his story about how he suspected his partner of submitting false change orders on construction contracts and hiding over-billings in the company ledgers. There were also a number of monthly withdrawals Vossen claimed to be suspicious of that Farnsworth always explained away to the architect's satisfaction.

"I've said all along I'm as much to blame for what Edson did because I wasn't paying attention to the financial aspects of the business. I was caught up in my passion for doing what I loved, which was designing, and ignored the danger of what Edson was passionate about, which was money."

According to Vossen, the night of the encounter was purely chance. He went to Farnsworth's office to retrieve the ledgers and any receipts that didn't match contracts. He arrived unaware that Farnsworth was in the process of finishing the last of the bank transfers. There was an argument, an exchange of threats, and then, "I grabbed a wooden sculpture that was on a desk and hit him with it."

"How many times?"

"Just the one time was all it took. I only meant to scare him, to swing it *at* him. I never intended to actually hit him. But as he tried to push by me, my arm came forward and ..."

"And where is Mr. Farnsworth now?"

"Up in Rocklin."

Vossen detailed how he initially planned to take Farnsworth's body up into the high Sierras and find a remote location in which to dump it. But as he began up the winding roads through the foothills he became concerned that someone would see him toss Farnsworth's body or that the body would be found and someone would identify him or his car.

"I figured dumping him into an isolated ravine ... hell, no one would find him. But then I got to thinking about the risks and became paranoid. I figured if Edson were ever found, he'd have to be found in a place that pointed the police toward someone else before they started taking aim at me. I came up with the idea of framing Peter on the drive back to town."

"And you stopped in Rocklin?" Keller asked, her

tone and expression indicating her awareness that the architect's selection of Rocklin, a city north of Sacramento in Placer County, was not random and that she expected an explanation without having to ask for one.

Vossen nodded, drawing a sour look from Keller. "Sorry. Yes. Peter was working on a job for us there, a small medical office complex. That contract was one of three that wasn't affected, so the work continued even after Edson and Peter were gone. I buried Edson at the site. He's under a concrete slab, but you can still get to him without breaking up too much of the building."

"Did you take anything else from your partner beside his ring?"

"No, just that." Vossen told Keller that anyone who knew anything about Farnsworth's obsession with his ring knew that it would be a symbol of triumph for someone to take it from him. "The ultimate defeat. But I guess that's what death is, don't you think?"

Keller rolled her eyes at Vossen's poetic analogy. "And after you buried Farnsworth, you went back to his office?"

"No. I had no reason to."

"Where'd you go, then? To a bar? A movie? What does a person do after killing someone?"

The string of questions, especially their crass delivery, didn't appear to rattle Vossen as Keller would have liked them to.

"I didn't do anything, Detective Keller. Nothing. I went home."

"I see. So at what point did you move Mr. Farnsworth's car?"

Vossen stumbled through a pause. "Oh. Right. I moved Edson's car when I returned from Rocklin." Vossen chuckled. "I'm sorry. I thought I mentioned that."

"No. You said you went home."

"Well, I did go home, but—"

"I can play the tape back, Mr. Vossen." Keller reached for the recorder, her hand hovering over the control buttons.

"There's no need—"

"You clearly stated you had no reason to return to Mr. Farnsworth's office."

"And I didn't. I ... I went to the garage. Then I drove his car closer to the bus terminal to make it look like Edson'd taken a bus out of town. *Then* I went home."

"Okay. Suppose you clarify something for me, Mr. Vossen. If you drove Mr. Farnsworth's car, why didn't we find any of your fingerprints anywhere on it?"

"After I parked it, I wiped off the steering wheel and door handles."

"You did? What did you use?"

"My shirt. I untucked my shirt and used the bottom of it as a rag."

As Vossen lifted the front of his shirt and wiped the edge of the tabletop to demonstrate, Keller slid forward to the edge of the chair. The elbows of her crossed arms rested on the table before her, supporting her upper body as she leaned over them. Her eyes, fixed on Vossen, turned dark and cloudy. An approaching storm.

"Mr. Vossen? Who really killed Edson Farnsworth?"

"I, uh, I did."

"You, *uh*, you did not," Keller mocked.

Vossen's attorney, quiet to this point, introduced his objection to Keller's pressing Vossen by clearing his throat. "Detective Keller, I've been rather lenient in the degree of latitude I've allowed you and Detective King in questioning my client. But I'm at a loss to see what point you are trying to establish. His cooperation, his *voluntary* cooperation, is to your benefit. That you persist in badgering him—"

"Badgering him?" Keller feigned offense and clutched her hand to her heart. She stood and with a slight bow softly apologized. "I'm so sorry if my investigation has insulted you, counselor. I guess I got carried away." Then to Vossen, "And you, too, Mr. Vossen. I don't know what came over me. You have been very accommodating and ... please, just one more time for the record. Did you—"

"I told you, I killed—"

"Let me ask it first, *okay?*"

Keller cut Vossen off as he did her, but with a harsher tone. Like the apparition it was, Keller's penitent disposition vanished. Despite Vossen's voluntary cooperation and his attorney's leniency, she wasn't going to allow either of them to dictate the pace or the direction of her investigation. And, as Floyd learned early in their association, she wasn't the least bit shy about stepping up and demonstrating her authority in this arena. Thus, she continued her scolding.

"In an investigation, it's critical that we establish the progression of our conversation on tape so that it can be transcribed accurately onto paper. We don't want to confuse our readers into thinking they missed anything or that something important was omitted. So, for the sake of maintaining order, let's adhere to the *Question* and Answer format, all right? That means we can't have the answer to a question before the question's asked. This ain't *Jeopardy*, Mr. Vossen."

"Detective Keller, please ..." the attorney groaned impatiently.

"Or is it?" Keller stepped to the edge of the table and planted her hands flat, bracing herself over her extended arms as she leaned inches from Vossen's face. Vossen pressed back into the chair and looked up from downcast eyes while absently kneading the hem of his shirt between his thumb and fingers.

"What do you say, Len?" Keller asked in a voice that had lowered to a near growl. "Shall we try fucked up confessions for one-hundred?"

The attorney bolted up from his chair. "Detective!"

Keller ignored him. "You didn't move the car, Mr. Vossen. And you didn't wipe it down, either. You couldn't have wiped the car down without wiping off Mr. and Mrs. Farnsworth's prints, and they were *all over* it." Keller pushed away from the table. "You had no reason to kill Farnsworth, at least not at the time he died because you had no clue what he was about to do. Or what he had been doing, for that matter. But there was someone who knew about your partner's plan. Part of it, at least."

Keller turned away from the table to Floyd and motioned for him. She whispered something in his ear that Floyd, in turn, passed along to Marty and Brenda at the back of the room. The two detectives exited the interview room and Floyd gave Keller a nod.

"We're going to find out, Mr. Vossen. We've gotten this far, and there's no way in hell we're not going to see this all the way through."

Vossen turned from Keller to his attorney. They leaned into one another and exchanged whispers. Keller strained to listen to their comments and failing in her ability to do so. She read their faces. Vossen had the drawn, panicked look of a man treading in deep water and running out of energy to keep afloat. Vossen's attorney, apparently a man who disliked surprises and was facing one every time his client opened his mouth, appeared lost in defining their options. Keller smirked and gave them a nudge in reaching a decision.

"I'm not against you gentlemen taking a private moment to confer, but you should know that in about"—Keller lifted her wrist and calculated the time dramatically from her watch—"thirty or forty minutes, those other two Santa Ramona detectives will be rolling in with Collette Farnsworth. My guess is we'll be a little pressed for time by then."

Vossen's head snapped back toward Keller. His face sagged from the weight of Keller's disclosure, projecting a sign that was just as revealing to her. Keller unclasped and removed her watch from her wrist. Vossen and his attorney watched Keller slide it across the table toward them, watched it until it stopped a mere inch from the edge. When they looked up at the detective, she smiled a wickedly proud smile.

"Tick. Tick. Tick."

23
Saturday evening, August 23rd

Marty and Brenda could hear the click of Collette Farnsworth's heels grow sharper as the woman neared the front door of her home. Marty turned to Brenda, curled a quick grin and shot her a wink. He liked this part of the job, the you're-coming-with-me part.

The door swept back framing Collette Farnsworth in the lacquered oak doorway. She was dressed casually, for her, in a plum cashmere sweater and matching wool slacks. In her right hand she held a long-stemmed glass half-filled with red wine. The only surprise she registered upon seeing the unexpected company of Marty and the woman with him was a single raised brow over a lazy, glassy eye.

"Well, Detective ..."

"Doenacker."

"Yes. And this would be yet *another* detective, I presume."

"Detective Garibaldi," Brenda said, raising her badge.

"A pleasure." She turned back to Marty. "I suppose you'll be wanting to come in?"

Marty nodded and Farnsworth backed away from the door, her invitation for the detectives to enter. Once inside, Marty and Brenda paused and parted to allow Farnsworth to lead them further into the house.

"What wonderful news have you brought with you today?" Farnsworth asked Marty as she passed him.

"It's over, Mrs. Farnsworth," Marty declared.

"It's over," Farnsworth repeated over her shoulder.

She lifted her glass frivolously in a toast and sang out, "Congratulations to whatever ended."

Brenda moved to Farnsworth's side and removed the drink from her hand with hardly a word of protest from the woman.

"If you want your own you can help yourself, my dear. The bar's over there."

"Happy hour's over, too," Brenda announced, adding with a smirk, "For you. You're under arrest, Mrs. Farnsworth."

Farnsworth snorted contemptuously. "Under arrest?" Then to herself, "Huh. That's a new one." Then back to Marty and Brenda, "I've been under a lot of things in my life. Under appreciated. Undermined. Undersexed. Under the influence. Now, under arrest. For what?"

"Murder," Marty told her.

"Really, Detective? Murder? Who'd I kill?"

"Your husband."

Marty's announcement sobered Farnsworth quicker than a cold shower. She turned from Marty to Brenda.

"Len Vossen is sitting in an interrogation room with an attorney at this moment giving a confession," Brenda said.

"Well, if Vossen admitted to killing Edson, why are you bothering me?"

"Mr. Vossen gave a convincing admission to his part in everything. Everything *except* for the part about killing your husband," Brenda continued. "And not that he didn't try. He just couldn't pull it off."

"How did you come to the conclusion it was me?"

"We'll let the attorneys and prosecutors explain the details, but it all started with your husband's ring."

"The ring," she echoed, then muttered to herself, "I always hated that fucking ring."

Collette Farnsworth walked into her living room, followed closely by Marty and Brenda, and sat on her sofa. She crossed her legs, smoothed a few creases from her pants, and rested her clasped hands in her lap.

"I guess I really shouldn't be surprised. I had a feeling that day your friend showed it to me ..." Farnsworth shook her head, dismissing the thought as inconsequential. "All that moron had to do was get rid of the body. That was our deal. Len dumps Edson down some canyon and I'd cover a chunk of his debts with the money Edson had accumulated. When I saw the ring, I knew Len royally fucked things up."

Marty and Brenda were content in allowing Farnsworth to ramble. They knew as long as they didn't ask any questions, everything she said would be admissible in court.

"I was watching Edson, you know. For a long time, too. I knew he was ripping off the company. I had been keeping an eye on his safe, watching it fill. Edson didn't know I had the combination." Farnsworth exhaled a snort. "He thought he was so slick. He was getting away with cheating clients for so long he probably didn't think anyone would catch on. But he didn't count on me. I was a banker's daughter, for crying out loud. I grew up watching my own father screw over his closest friends for an extra buck.

"I went to his office one evening and did my monthly snoop through his desk. It was my way of keeping tabs on the sonofabitch. I found his fake passport, his open-date plane ticket to Florida. Where he was going after that ...?" Collette shrugged. "Since I didn't know when, either, I checked the safe daily after that. One day the money was gone. That's when I went looking for him. And I found him."

"In his office," Marty said.

"Yup. At his computer finalizing his plans. I waited in the outer office, in the dark. Waited for him to come out."

24
Friday, April 16, ten years earlier

Edson Farnsworth sat in front of his laptop computer terminal in the corner of his darkened Sacramento office. It was late afternoon, and while most of the office workers in the city quickly closed shop for the weekend and hastily fled the downtown center to maximize their off time, Farnsworth's focus was still on business.

His intense stare cut through the glow of the monitor as his fingers tap-danced purposefully along the keyboard. Each clicking keystroke moved him closer accomplishing a series of bank transfers that would be the foundation for his new life. His plan, in place for several years, was devised to systematically siphon money from construction projects while waiting for the company's assets to accumulate into a substantial retirement nest egg.

Farnsworth was proud of himself, typing away while thinking about all the little pieces of the plan that fell perfectly into place. There was the education he received courtesy of his father, himself a shrewd businessman who could hide a dollar bill under a penny disguised as a dime. His painfully necessary marriage to Collette, done more to establish credibility than family. And, of course, Len and Peter, carefully selected for the combination of their trade skills and financial ineptness. They were fools who placed unquestioned trust in him, giving him financial autonomy, the freedom to move money as he saw fit. Like precisely machined gear teeth, they unfailingly powered the vehicle he was now driving toward his freedom.

He entered the last account number, then his password and leaned comfortably back into his chair as he gave the "Enter" key a demonstrative stab. Seconds later, confirmation. The series of transfers were complete and by Monday another series would take place so that by the time Len or the bank realized he was gone there would be no trail worth following. In the trunk of his car sat a packed suitcase, fake passport, and plane tickets that would ultimately land him in Brazil.

There was a distant sound, a door closing. Or was it, Farnsworth wondered. He had been riding such a high since booting up the computer that every sense felt heightened. And now the thrill of completing his task ... it had to be his imagination. Always one to err on the side of caution, however, Farnsworth stepped out of his office and into the reception area. It was dark there, too, but having sat in a dimly lighted room for much of the past hour he could pick out the grayed silhouettes of the office furniture and even make out the features of the carpet pattern. There was another noise. A car engine started. Farnsworth concluded the door he heard was someone else leaving the building from another office, someone going home after working late.

Like me, he said to himself facetiously.

Farnsworth turned back into his office to gather his things. He closed his laptop, which would soon settle at the bottom of the Sacramento River, and grabbed his jacket and car keys. He thought back to all he'd accomplished over the years, then realized his only real accomplishment was just now coming to fruition and everything else was just a means to the end. He walked out of his office, locking it like any other day, and headed for the front office door.

Edson Farnsworth reached for the doorknob but halted

when he heard another sound from behind him. It was a word seething with hate that filled his ear a split second before the whipping rush of air that preceded the hollow crack that was the thick shaft of wood impacting his temple.

Bastard!

25
Late Saturday evening, August 23rd

Floyd walked Keller from the building to her car in which Brenda had placed a handcuffed Collette Farnsworth for the drive back to Sacramento. Keller, still on a high from her raking over Len Vossen, had a spring in her step would undoubtedly continue well into the night. Though Farnsworth was agreeable to repeating her story to Keller about what she knew of her husband's plans and how she ultimately altered them, Keller opted to take Farnsworth back to Sacramento where she intended to squeeze from her the remaining details of Edson's demise in the comfort and privacy of her own department.

"It was pretty amazing, you know, how two entirely separate killings ultimately benefited each other. The whole Farnsworth thing couldn't have worked out better if Sherman killing Lindell had been a part of Farnsworth's murder from the start," Keller said.

"Vossen blew it, and not just for the ring." Floyd pointed out an underlying flaw in Vossen's misguided acceptance of Collette Farnsworth's financial assistance. "Collette was clearly just as manipulative as her husband and yet Vossen foolishly trusted her as much if not more than he trusted Edson in order to keep his ass solvent. She said he sold his soul to fend off the banks. Foolishly, he sold it to her. But even that wasn't his complete undoing."

Floyd concluded it was Vossen's determination to point everyone toward Lindell that ultimately tripped him up.

"Too bad he didn't trust her scheme one hundred

percent. We would have never come this far had Vossen stuck to Collette's plan and ditched Edson, ring and all, like he was supposed to."

Keller agreed with a nod. "And Vossen probably wouldn't have fared any worse taking his lumps with the banks. If he'd dropped a dime on Collette instead of letting her drop sixty-five-K on him, he'd have saved both his business *and* his ass. Stupid."

"We have the jobs we have because people do stupid things. Especially when they panic," Floyd reasoned. "I'm glad things worked out for us in the end."

"Did they?" Keller asked, clearly annoyed at what she interpreted as Floyd's carefree conclusion. "How about all the shit I have yet to face when I get back into town? There's going to be more than just a media buzz about Sac P.D. riding Floyd King's coattails again."

"Why? It shouldn't be any big deal beyond you recognizing a similarity between a Santa Ramona investigation and an old Sacramento case and carrying on from the information your father collected. His report and your coming up with the missing piece your father never obtained solved a ten-year-old murder. Sounds like solid police work to me, not to mention a good public interest piece for the news. You know, the father-daughter angle along with the dogged determination of the Sac police. Spin it right and your boss can milk a few good media days out of it."

"Until they trace the story back to Floyd King and how it was really Santa Ramona that broke the case. What happens when the cameras descend upon your quite little village again? What will you tell them?"

"Same thing I told you from the beginning, all I was interested—"

Keller held up her palm to him. "I know, I know. The ring. Right to the end, huh, Floyd."

Floyd gave Keller a reassuring nod as she got into her car, telling her, "Right to the end, Grace." As he closed her door, Keller rolled down her window. "That's my story. That's how I'll write it up. They'll only be able to report it one way."

"I suppose you're right," Keller agreed then added wryly, "But, then, you always are." Keller extended her hand for King to shake. "It's been an experience, King. No doubt we'll cross paths again."

"I'd be disappointed if we didn't."

Keller craned her neck back and tossed her chin toward Brenda, who was standing a few feet behind Floyd. "Thanks for helping out."

Brenda returned a polite nod. "No hard feelings about the other night. Heat of battle, and all."

"No feelings whatsoever, Detective." Keller turned and looked over her headrest to shoot a glance at Collette Farnsworth. "Whaddya say Mrs. Farnsworth? Shall we go talk about ex-husbands for a while?"

Without waiting for a reply, which she wasn't going to get from her prisoner, Keller cackled as she started the engine and put it in gear. She rolled up her window and gave a half-salute wave goodbye as she pulled away.

Floyd walked back into the building with Brenda at his side. There was still unfinished business for them, beginning with the summary reports that needed to be completed for both the department and the District Attorney on Peter Lindell's murder. In the hallway just outside the door to the squad room they ran into Lieutenant Bern, who was going home for the second time that evening.

"Where's Doenacker?" Bern asked upon seeing only Floyd and Brenda.

Floyd flashed a spirited grinned. "Does not seeing him worry you, boss?"

"Not seeing him thrills the shit out of me. Not knowing where he is when you're around worries me."

"He'll be touched by your concern."

"I'm only concerned to the extent that having to keep tabs on the three of you together is easier than any combination of the three of you separated," Bern grumbled, adding, "Not that it's any less work."

"Marty's driving Len Vossen into Sac," Floyd reported, easing his supervisor's mind. "Vossen didn't have anything to do with Peter Lindell's death, so there was no point in keeping him with us. We probably won't even need him in court, which is just as well since Sacramento and Placer Counties will be keeping him occupied for a while."

"Anything else I should know about before I leave?" Bern asked around the three-inch piece of cigar he stuck in the crook of his mouth.

Floyd thought for a moment about the brief synopsis he gave Bern earlier outlining where their case stood with Eileen Sherman, as well as where their case ended with Len Vossen and Collette Farnsworth. "No, Lieutenant. It's all paperwork at this point."

"Which I trust you'll have completed and on my desk first thing in the morning."

"Probably not."

Bern emitted a throaty grunt expressing no surprise at his subordinate's honesty. Leaning into stepping away from the pair, the lieutenant told Floyd, "Just give me a preliminary write-up before eleven, something I can put in the captain's hand to get the chief off his back." Then, three steps past Floyd, Bern stopped and turned. He pulled the stub of tobacco from his lips and shook his head slowly.

"I don't know how you do it, Floyd. Honest to God, I don't. And I've worked with best of 'em. You really have a knack for pulling shit out of thin air."

Floyd shrugged. "It's like hitting a piñata, L.T. Whack it enough times and eventually one good whack in the right place makes all the goodies fall out."

"Yeah, well, I've got marks from some of your swings and misses." Bern jammed the chewed cigar end back into one cheek and smiled from the other. "Good night, you two," he said as he walked away. "And good job."

"He actually looked happy," Brenda said.

"It'll wear off by morning. Come on."

Floyd and Brenda entered the darkened, deserted squad room. Darkened because only half of the room's fluorescent lights were on, which was how Floyd preferred them as the full bank of ceiling lights washed out the room with intense brightness. Deserted because Floyd's favorite pair of detectives to despise, Mark Lomas and Tom Brieger, the two detectives who pulled night duty, had penciled themselves out on the assignment board, meaning they could have been anywhere except on a call. Not that Floyd cared beyond being glad they were anywhere but the squad room. Brenda followed Floyd to his desk and sat in Floyd's chair, rotating it lazily a few inches to either side while he busied himself at his file cabinet. She watched him remove something dark, which he palmed and held close to his side while he grabbed a chair and dropped into it beside her.

"I've got something for you," Floyd said.

The announcement stilled Brenda, and she hovered forward curiously. Floyd lifted his hand and opened it, exposing a folded, black handkerchief. He held it out for Brenda to take. Instead, Brenda fell back into the chair and began her slow side-to-side swivel.

"The hanky?" Then, under a suspicion-cocked eyebrow and with half-hearted appreciation, Brenda said, "Gee, Floyd, that's thoughtful and all, but I'd have a tendency to think the D.A. will be a little pissed off about you keeping souvenirs, especially something you're supposed to submit as evidence."

Floyd smiled but said nothing. He kept his hand out toward Brenda, who relented and took the black cloth from Floyd's palm. She felt a lump inside it and fingered it. Recognizing the shape immediately, she recoiled in shock as she set the handkerchief on the desktop.

"Jesus, Floyd! The ring, too?"

"Open it."

"You're nuts! Are you *looking* to get in trouble?"

"Well, sort of. Go on, open it."

Brenda peeled back the corners and revealed a ring. It wasn't Edson Farnsworth's ring, as she expected. It was solitary diamond set in a narrow, gold band. Brenda's jaw dropped and eyes widened simultaneously. She carefully lifted the ring from the cloth and set it in the palm of her hand, unable to take her gaze from it as she spoke through a knot in her throat.

"Oh, my God, Floyd. It's beautiful."

"You can put it on if you want."

"Are you sure? Floyd, if I've pressured you in any way ..."

"No, I've been thinking about this for a while. Even more so the last few weeks. What's held me back has been the fear that I'll hurt you like I hurt Lynn and Laura. But, then, you aren't them and in many ways I'm not the me who helped screw those relationships up. I just had to be sure."

Brenda slipped the ring down her slender finger and

held the back of her hand in front of her face, rotating her wrist to let the faint light flash across the clear stone's polished faces. "Is Shelby all right with this?"

"She doesn't know. I needed to make this decision on my own, so no one does. Well, except the lieutenant. I got him to give us a couple of days off. Together. I thought we'd take a trip and have that talk you wanted to have. If you still want to have it?"

"Well, yes. Of course. But we have to talk to Shelby first."

"We'll talk to Shelby first," Floyd concurred. "Then Marty."

"Don't ruin the moment, Floyd. We can't do this over again."

Floyd laughed. "Nor do I want to," he said, leaning into Brenda, taking her ring-clad hand in his and kissing her. "Not ever."

From the Author ...

A Box of Bones is my first attempt at a sequel. The manuscript I initially began writing for my Floyd King character, which time-wise takes place before *Shudder*, was still half a draft away from completion when I shifted gears and decided to draft a few chapters from the notes of what was to be the third Floyd King novel, which subsequently became the second because it was completed first. Got it?

As with all my novels, I try to find some element of writing with which to challenge myself. In this case, I wanted to use already established characters to see if I could maintain continuity in their personalities while allowing them to grow. A bigger challenge was identifying the main characters in a way that didn't require reading *Shudder* while giving a little extra to those who had. I also looked for something creative around which to center the premise of the story. I researched the process of body decomposition and the skill of skeletal articulation, making minor alterations and applications to fit the story. It's with the same creative allowance I am able to drop a town in the middle of nowhere, or in between two somewheres, as a backdrop for Floyd King's world. You won't find Santa Ramona on a map in the foothills east of Sacramento, but should you happen to take a drive into the first rolling folds of the Sierra range, you'll be there.

In giving credit where credit is due, I begin where I always begin, and should always begin, with my wife, Denise, for her love and support and for having the computer skills I lack that put the final touches on creating something that can be read.

Thanks to my sister, Cathy Kennedy, for taking the time to read it. To my dear friend, Debbie Siegling, for continually reminding me in a most pleasantly encouraging manner that she needed something to read, and for patiently enduring about six additional months of "almost there" and "this close". A big nod of appreciation to Frank Signorino for the time and effort he put into scrutinizing my draft and finding things that the computer and I weren't sharp enough to catch. To longtime friend, Fred Fernandez, for his enthusiastic encouragement and promotion of my work.

To the real Ray Peña, a tremendous thanks for allowing me to borrow some of the playfulness of his personality in order to create the character I needed to link my opening chapters. I had as much fun developing that character as I had in working alongside the real one. Gracias, Señor Peña, and all the best to you in your retirement.

I also include thanks to the people at Global Book Publishers and BookSurge.com, a belated thanks to Bob Mariani for helping me become more focused, and best wishes to my Number One fan in Tulsa, Bessie Barnett.